THE ROOTS OF EVIL

Quintin Jardine

THE ROOTS OF EVIL

HEADLINE

First published in 2020 by
HEADLINE PUBLISHING GROUP

1

Cataloguing in Publication Data is available from the British Library

978 1 4722 5591 4 (Hardback)
978 1 4722 5593 8 (Trade paperback)

Typeset in Electra by Avon DataSet Ltd, Arden Court, Alcester, Warwickshire

Printed and bound in Great Britain by
Clays Ltd, Elcograf S.p.A.

HEADLINE PUBLISHING GROUP
An Hachette UK Company
Carmelite House
50 Victoria Embankment
London EC4Y 0DZ

www.headline.co.uk
www.hachette.co.uk

This book is for Mia Abernethy Teixidor, *una llum de la meva vida*, and for Rex Masato Jardine, Granddad's Number One Boy, who is the other.

Both men heard the first chimes of midnight . . .
but neither heard the last.

One

'Happy New Decade, my love,' Sir Robert Morgan Skinner murmured to his wife, as the fireworks lit the darkness outside, and he had finished shaking hands with everyone around him, as tradition demanded. 'May it bring you all you wish for.'

'The last one did pretty well in that department,' Professor Sarah Grace replied. 'It brought a few surprises too.' She inclined her head towards a pair who stood a few feet away from them, watching the scene through the bay window of the golf club's first-floor dining room. 'For example, if you'd told me this time last year that those two would be here, let alone as a couple, I'd have sent you for a cognitive test.'

'How many times?' he murmured. 'My daughter and Dominic Jackson are not a couple. They are house-mates, no more than that.'

'So you say.'

'So Dominic assures me.'

'Are you telling me you asked him?' she chuckled.

'I didn't have to. Before Alexis moved in with him full-time, he came to me and asked if I had any objection. He told me something she'd kept from me herself, that she hadn't been able to settle back into her flat after she was attacked there.

More than that, he said that psychologically she was on the edge. He believed she had never had a really close friend outside of family, and that it was telling on her. The more success she had in her career, the more it contrasted with what she perceived as failure in her private life. She felt empty inside.'

'But everybody loves Alex,' Sarah protested.

'Everybody but Alex herself, it seems,' Bob murmured. 'I said what you just said, but Dominic was adamant, that her self-esteem was at a critical point. "She's never failed at work," he told me, "so when she perceives that she's a failure as a person, she has no idea how to cope with it. Let her move in with me, Bob, and I will be the friend she needs so badly . . . but nothing more than that, I promise you." Given that the man has an honours degree, a masters and a doctorate in psychology, I wasn't about to argue with him, so I agreed. And it's worked. Look at her, for Christ's sake! Compared to how she was, she's blooming.'

Sarah looked again at her stepdaughter. 'I'll grant you that,' she admitted. 'Why didn't you share this with me at the time?' she asked.

'You were away at that forensic pathology conference in Paris when it happened. By the time you came back she'd moved in. I told you then what the arrangement was.'

'And I doubted you then. This is Alex, remember.'

'Her mother's daughter? Is that what you're saying?' His voice was low; his smile was not reflected in his eyes.

'No, I didn't mean that at all,' she said, hurriedly. 'But I do know her; we are close.'

'Not so close you can't accept that she's capable of sharing a house with a man but not a bed?'

'And can you? Really?'

2

'I believe her. So should you. End of story.'

'That story, okay.' As the fireworks climaxed, she glanced once more at Alex's huge companion. 'I wonder what this crew here would say if they knew his history, that all those qualifications of his were gained in prison doing a life sentence for murder, under another name?'

'They would say nothing, because he's here as my guest. God knows what they would think,' he conceded, 'but trust me, nobody would utter a word.'

'Not in your presence,' she said, 'but as soon as you left the building, the place would be chattering like a tree full of starlings. This is a golf club, for heaven's sake. Rumour and innuendo spread faster than on Facebook in places like this.'

'Yeah, maybe they do, but nobody is going to find out this secret. Dominic keeps a low profile professionally, and the circles he moves in, nobody's likely to link him with Lennie Plenderleith.'

'Until Alex calls Dominic as an expert defence witness in a High Court trial,' Sarah suggested. 'There are still plenty of advocates and a few judges who were around when he was there last.'

'Yes, but he's changed a lot since then; the beard, the change in body shape since he stopped pumping weights.'

'He's still two metres tall.'

'That's not as exceptional as it used to be.'

'Isn't there a parole officer who knows who he is, or was?' Sarah argued.

'They would be bound by confidentiality,' her husband countered, 'but Dominic doesn't have to check in anymore. Yes, he's still on licence as a life-sentence prisoner, but the terms of that licence are as limited as they can be. He has a passport; he can go anywhere he likes without asking permission or informing anyone.'

'How about the USA? My home country is very choosy about who gets in. He'd be required to declare his personal history, and withholding information from US immigration is never a good idea.'

Bob grinned. 'We let your president into the UK.'

'Our president doesn't have any murder convictions.'

'There are those who would say he doesn't have convictions of any sort.' His attention was caught by the three-piece band shuffling back into position. 'Come on, kid, let's dance the night away.'

'Give my feet a break, Twinkletoes,' his wife groaned. 'They've suffered enough for one night.'

'Are you suggesting I'm not a *Strictly* candidate?'

'I'm not suggesting anything, I'm telling the world out loud: cops can't dance.'

As she stepped away from the window, Alex heard her. 'That's a given,' she agreed. 'I did my level best with him, but my old man has no sense of rhythm, none at all.'

'How about you, Dominic?' Sarah asked.

'I don't think that dance floor's big enough for me,' he laughed as they approached. 'Besides, I think it's time to run the gauntlet and drive home. If I'm not pulled over between here and Edinburgh, at one a.m. on January the first, it'll be a sad reflection on the state of policing in modern Scotland.'

'But don't let us drag you away, Pops,' Alex insisted. 'This shindig still has a while to go, by the looks of things.'

'No, I think we're done.' Bob glanced out of the window. 'All of a sudden it's chucking it down out there. If you are going, maybe you could drop us off at home, and wish your brothers a Happy New Year in the process.'

'Brothers?' she repeated.

He grinned. 'You don't think Jazz is going to be in bed, do you? Mark certainly won't be, and Ignacio doesn't have the clout to make them. Trish would lay down the law if she wasn't spending Christmas with her folks in Barbados, but the boys won't take it from him. Besides, I promised him that we'd be back in time to let Pilar and him catch up with some pals at a party.'

'I haven't met the girlfriend yet,' Alex observed. 'They're on the same uni course, yes?'

'That's right, she's a would-be chemist too. She's from Madrid; her father's a banker, and her mother's Norwegian. The mum did her degree in Edinburgh too; she got a two one in chemical engineering at Heriot Watt.'

'Do you think it's serious between them?'

'Ignacio's in love,' he conceded, 'and the lass seems smitten too, but everybody does when they're twenty. You've heard me talk about my old Uncle Johnny . . . he wasn't really my uncle though; he was my dad's best pal. He was a man of many sayings and one was that you shouldn't look at your girlfriend, you should look at her mother, because that's what she's going to look like in twenty-five years or so.'

'He sounds like a real old sexist pig,' his daughter declared. She glanced towards her stepmother, who was making her way to the toilet. 'Mind you, if that's true, my little sister's boyfriends will be impressed when that time comes. Sarah looks fantastic with the new silver hair. I'm still getting used to it.'

'Yes,' he agreed, 'me too . . . and it's natural!'

'You're kidding me!'

'No, she's been covering grey streaks for a few years now. One day, after we'd been out for dinner with Mario McGuire and Paula, on a whim she copied her and spent a small fortune having all the dye removed. What you see is pretty much how it looked.'

'Maybe I should try it,' Alex mused.

'No way!' her father said. 'You're far too young. Plus, your Grandma Graham didn't start to go grey until after your mother died, and you're very like her. If you did have the tint taken out, you'd be wasting your money.'

'I'm also very like you,' she pointed out, 'and you were grey in your mid-thirties.'

'True,' he conceded, 'but I still say don't do it. One's enough.' He nodded towards the door where Dominic was waiting. 'Let's go . . . once I've said goodnight to the Captain. Got to observe the formalities.'

'When will it be your turn for that job?'

'Never. I was a cop for thirty years, love, and I finished at the top of the tree. I'm an autocrat to my bootstraps, not a committee man. In fact, I rage against those, like Jimmy Proud did, God bless and keep him.'

Skinner said his farewell to the golf club captain and his party, joining his own on the back stairway that led out to the car park. He recovered an umbrella from his locker, sheltering his wife and daughter from the bite of the cold rain as they bustled back to Dominic Jackson's massive SUV.

It was a short distance to the Skinners' home, no more than three minutes' walk, but they were both grateful not to have to make it as the rain grew heavier, battering on the roof of the Mercedes G Class. Their driver pulled up as close to the door as he could, and all four leapt out and into the porch of the modern villa. As Bob had expected, only their two youngest children, Seonaid and Dawn, were in bed; Mark and James Andrew were still awake, but both were flagging. Alex kissed her half-siblings . . . Mark was half her age and Jazz was twenty years younger . . . then she and her escort disappeared into the night, as Bob and Sarah went upstairs to change out of their formal clothing into casual.

'Who are you first-footing?' Skinner asked Ignacio, his oldest son, as he came back down.

The young man stared at him. Clearly, the phrase meant nothing to him.

'Christ,' he lamented. 'Did your mother tell you nothing of your Scots heritage when she was bringing you up in Spain? Traditionally, the first person across your threshold in the new year should be a tall dark handsome man. In an ideal world he'll be carrying a lump of coal and a bottle of whisky.'

Beside Ignacio, his girlfriend Pilar Sanchez Hoverstad laughed. 'I don't think I would let anyone in if he was carrying a bottle of whisky,' she said. 'Vodka, yes, or maybe schnapps.' She pulled a face. 'But not whisky, never. And what is coal?'

'Yes,' Ignacio echoed. 'What is it?'

'Seriously? You mean . . . ? Fuck! I give up. Where are you going?'

'To our friend Ronnie's house. She lives on Goose Green, where you used to live with Alex.'

'Ronnie? She?'

'Veronica, Dad, Veronica Goodlad. She's at uni too, studying English.'

'Well, you'd better get moving,' Bob said, 'or she'll have graduated by the time you get there. Have you got a bottle of anything to take with you?'

7

'Two,' Pilar replied. 'Spanish wines; a Tempranillo and a Verdejo.'

'Very nice,' he murmured. 'Can I come?'

'The hell you can,' Sarah retorted, as she re-joined them.

'Nah. You're right. I'm too old for all-nighters. On you go, you two, but don't forget to be back for the Loony Dook at midday.'

'What's that?' Pilar asked.

'A swim in the sea on New Year's Day, on Gullane beach. It's become a tradition.'

'In the sea?' she gasped. 'Nacho, you never told me that. All you said was to bring my costume, that we were going to swim. I thought you meant in a pool.'

He nodded. 'I know, they're crazy here. You don't have to, really.'

'No, I will,' she insisted. 'If my mother was here, she would. She is very proud of being Norwegian. I have her blood so I must too.' She looked up at Bob. 'Are you doing it?'

'Yup. Jazz too.'

'I don't know about that,' Sarah murmured.

'Try and stop him.'

'I think he's beyond my control,' she admitted.

Bob escorted his oldest son and his partner to the door, returning to the living room with a brandy in one hand and a bottle of Corona in the other. He handed the goblet to his wife and settled down beside her on the sofa. 'Want to watch Jools Holland?' he asked.

'Tomorrow maybe; it has less attraction now that I know it isn't live. Mind you, I'd like to be in the audience when they record it. Could you fix that for next time? You've got contacts everywhere.'

'Not quite,' he corrected her. 'I have contacts in the media, in the security service and in the police. None of those will cut much ice with the producers of the *Hootenanny*.'

'What about your former wife's actor boyfriend? He's got cred with them, surely.'

'Maybe,' he acknowledged, 'but given that I once offered to make Aileen a pair of earrings with his nuts, he might not be too willing to use it. Ask me in six months and I'll see what I can do.'

'Who knows where we'll be in six months? I've been following the press coverage of the new coronavirus in China after I read a piece on a pathology website ten days ago or so. Unless they find a quick and effective treatment, and very fast, that could become global. If it does, the consequences are anyone's guess. Who's to know what'll happen?'

He frowned, and his mood darkened. 'Who was to know a couple of years ago what would happen with Jimmy Proud? Hell no! More recently than that, could I have imagined Alex being attacked in a secure penthouse apartment? Hell no! Could I have foreseen what would have happened to poor Carrie McDaniels?' He shuddered.

'Go back those two years,' she countered. 'Could we have imagined that now we'd have a beautiful second daughter? Not really. Or that you'd be chair of InterMedia UK? I didn't see that coming. Or that you would be back in the police?'

'I'm not back in the police,' he corrected her. 'I'm mentoring rising CID officers. As for InterMedia UK, that's only a division of the parent company, and it's at the pleasure of my friend Xavi.'

She sipped her brandy and smiled. 'Your friend Xavi Aislado: the only man I know who's as big as Dominic Jackson.'

Bob nodded. 'That's why he was a goalkeeper, until his knee packed in on him. Big Iceland, they used to call him at Tynecastle. Strange thing is, I never saw him play. I only knew him as a young journalist.'

'How did you two get close? Did you feed him insider information?'

He raised his eyebrows. 'And put my career in jeopardy? I don't think so. The fact is, Xavi tells people I saved his life. I didn't; I turned up after he'd been shot, and I got him to hospital, but it was never life-threatening.'

'That's not what he means when he says that,' Sarah argued. 'He told me that if you hadn't turned up when you did, he might have put another bullet in his head and you'd have found three bodies instead of two.'

'He may say so, but he wouldn't have done that. Yes, what happened was tragic, but he's too strong a character.' He sighed. 'That's another story, though. Let's look forward today. Have you made a New Year resolution?'

She laughed. 'Yes, I resolve to dissect the next person who calls me "Lady Skinner". I'm an American; we don't do titles.'

'Of course, you do!' Bob declared firmly. 'Half of your compatriots refer to themselves by their job titles. Chief this, Coach that: look at *Blue Bloods* on the telly, everybody round the table has a title; it's a status thing. You do it yourself, Professor Grace.'

'Yes, I do, because I've worked damn hard to attain the status. Lady Skinner makes me out to be an appendage of my husband. It's archaic, it's . . . it's . . . anti-feminist!'

'Enlighten me, do.'

She raised her brandy goblet. 'Certainly, Sir Robert.

Suppose I had been honoured, not you. Suppose I'd been made a dame.'

'You can't be; you're a US citizen.'

'Piss off, Skinner, just suppose, for the sake of argument.'

'I don't want an argument.'

'You asked me to enlighten you; let me. If I'd been made a dame, that's the female equivalent of a knight, right?'

He smiled and eased himself closer on the sofa. 'If you say so. I've never really thought about it.'

'I do say so. So there I am, Professor Dame Sarah Grace. What are you?'

'Bob.'

'What else, idiot?'

'Whatever you'd like me to be. How about Chief Skinner? That's what they called me whenever I visited the States.'

'But what would everyone else call you, instead of Lady? What's the male equivalent?'

'Gent? That's how it works with public toilets.'

'Nothing!' she cried, her nostrils flaring. 'There is no gender equivalent to the courtesy title given to the wife of a knight . . . or to a husband,' she added, with a flourish. 'It's all right for the little wife, but it would be demeaning for a male to walk in his wife's shadow . . . or his husband's? Is that not sexism, is it not a denial of feminism? Go on, tell me.'

He put his head against hers. 'The only thing I will tell you is that when you have a certain amount to drink, and get argumentative, you also get very horny. So what say I display my masculinity . . . ever notice that there's no such word as maleism? . . . by carrying you upstairs, Lady Skinner, and we carry on this discussion in a more intimate setting?'

A few strands of her silver hair fell over her right eye. 'Are you suggesting that we bring in the new year with a bang?'

'Perceptive as always.'

'And you'll concede that I'm right?'

'Whatever it takes.'

She put her arms around his neck. 'In that case, Sir Robert, I'm all . . .'

He was in the act of lifting her from the sofa when they were interrupted by the powerful voice of P!nk, Skinner's ringtone. He paused, looking Sarah in the eye.

'Go on,' she sighed. 'You've never been able to just let it ring, and you never will.'

He laid her back down, took out his mobile, glanced at the screen and took the call. 'Deputy Chief Constable McGuire,' he growled, slowly, 'if you're pished and calling to wish me a Happy New Year, you can stick it up your arse.'

'I'm not drunk but I wish I was, Bob. Happy New Year, of course, but it's off to a lousy start.'

The tension in his normally unshakeable friend's voice snapped him into full wakefulness. As she looked up at him Sarah saw his eyes narrow and his mouth tighten. 'What's up?'

'I don't want to tell you over the phone. How steamin' are you? How heavy a night was it at your golf club do?'

'It was okay, but on the quiet side, as these formal events usually are.' He glanced at his Corona and saw that it remained more than half full. 'I'm okay; not okay to drive, but every other way.'

'Can I send a car for you? There's one in your area.'

'Seriously?' Skinner checked his Rolex. 'At five to two on New Year's Day?'

'Seriously. Could Sarah come too?'

He felt a ripple of apprehension. He realised that McGuire

was asking for her as a pathologist, not as his partner. 'Not a chance of that,' he replied. 'Get someone else if that's necessary. Kids,' he explained. 'Ignacio's gone out and Mark's still too young to be left in charge.'

'How about Alex?'

'She's gone too. Look, Mario, I'll come if you really think it's necessary.'

'Bob, you'd have killed me if I hadn't called you. I'll send the car right now.'

He blinked as the call ended, shaking off the last of his drowsiness. Sarah stood. 'You really have to go out?' she asked. 'Is this a set-up? Have you and your chums planned a stag New Year? Or are you being lured into one?'

'My chums are all too serious for that, plus, if it was a ruse, he wouldn't have asked for you and your little bag of tools. No, it's a mystery, and I have a feeling that when I get to where I'm being taken, I'm not going to like it at all.'

Two

The police car pulled into Skinner's driveway within three minutes of McGuire's call ending; by that time he had donned a padded, hooded rain garment that he had bought one cold October night in Barcelona, but barely used since. He slid awkwardly into the back seat behind the uniformed PC driver and her companion, an older man with sergeant's stripes whom he recognised from his time as chief constable in Edinburgh. He cursed himself inwardly for being unable to put a name to him.

'Been busy?' he asked, making conversation in the hope of prompting a recollection.

'No, sir,' the sergeant replied. *Auld*, Skinner remembered, with a surge of relief, *Bertie Auld, a crazy Rangers supporter even though he had been named after a Celtic legend.* 'It's no' like the old days.' He paused. 'Well mibbe's it is in the town. I'm not used tae East Lothian.'

Eyes met in the rearview mirror. 'Do you know what this is about, Bertie?'

'No, sir. The DCC never said. He just told us tae pick up Sir Robert and bring him into Edinburgh, toot sweet, blue light if we need to.'

'Where in Edinburgh?'

'Haymarket, sir.'

'Eh? Haymarket what? The station?'

'No,' Auld replied. 'He said they'd meet us at the War Memorial, that was all.'

'They?' Skinner repeated.

'Him and the chief.'

He was taken by surprise. 'Maggie too! What the hell? Has there been a military coup?'

The car slowed as they entered Aberlady. As always there were cars parked on either side of the road, but only one other moving vehicle, a Nissan Leaf, travelling slowly and making its way carefully through the space. 'Do you think we should be stopping him, Sarge?' the young driver asked.

'We don't have grounds, PC Gregg,' Auld told her. 'He hasn't hit anyone, he's taking care not to, and it isn't an offence to do fifteen miles an hour.' He had hardly finished speaking when the car clipped the wing mirror of a wide pick-up truck. 'That, on the other hand . . . Show him some blue, Janice, and pull him over.'

The Nissan pulled into the kerb, past the last of the parked cars, the police vehicle stopping in front. Auld stepped out; the PC made to follow until Skinner intervened. 'No, wait here, Constable. I'll go; I know that registration. She's one of us.'

He moved quickly to join the sergeant who stared in surprise as he moved past him leaning over beside the driver's window as it opened. 'Noele,' he said, 'are you okay?'

'Sir? What are . . .' There was a pause as the woman composed herself. 'I'm okay, Bob, just a bit shaken up. That fucking pick-up shouldn't be allowed to have unfolded mirrors that wide.'

'Agreed, but what the hell are you doing here, and who's looking after the wee one?' He paused, turning to Auld. 'Do you know DS Noele McClair?' he asked. 'She works with DCI Pye and DI Haddock on Serious Crimes. Our kids are best mates.'

'Very good, sir,' the veteran sergeant said quietly, 'but has she been drinking? There's lights on in that house over there and people are lookin' at us. Bloody social media, ye ken.'

McClair replied for him. 'I had a glass of Prosecco with my mother at the bells, Sergeant, and I gave myself a breath test before I left the house.'

'Why did you leave the house, exactly, Noele?'

'Duty, sir. I had a call from Sauce. He said I'm needed. He did offer to have me picked up, but I said I'd rather be in control of my own movements.'

'Did he tell you why?'

'No, just to meet him at Haymarket. I imagine he meant the divisional office at Torphichen Place.'

'This gets stranger and stranger,' Skinner murmured. 'That's where I'm heading, at the request of the DCC. Noele, don't worry about getting home, that'll be taken care of. Park up, come with me and let's get there as fast as we can.' He glanced at Auld. 'Use all the blue lights you've got, Bertie.'

Three

The rest of the journey into Edinburgh passed by almost entirely in a silence that was broken only by the chatter of the police transmissions on the patrol car radio. The road traffic was as quiet as Skinner had expected it to be, and the broadcast transmissions were routine, none of them offering any clue to the reason behind the summons to the capital.

As they entered the city, PC Gregg turned left at the Willowbrae traffic lights, then right into Duddingston Village, choosing the road through Holyrood Park, where they saw the first of the revellers, their number growing steadily as they carried on into the Cowgate and beyond through the Grassmarket.

'We're coming this way, sir, because Princes Street's cordoned off for Hogmanay,' the driver explained. As a mere detective sergeant, McClair seemingly did not merit an explanation.

'It takes us nicely down to Haymarket,' she observed, asserting her presence.

Skinner sensed an edginess in her, one that he felt himself. McGuire's call, and its nature, was unlike any he could recall either receiving or making in his career. His unease grew as they turned out of Grove Street into Morrison Street. It was empty, but for a black Range Rover, beside which stood two people recognisable to everyone in the police car, even out of uniform.

Mario McGuire signalled that they should pull in behind his car. Chief Constable Margaret Rose Steele was by his side.

'Where's Sauce?' McClair wondered aloud, as they came to a halt. 'I'm supposed to meet him.'

'Let it play,' Skinner told her, as he opened the door. The rain had become sleet, and the temperature made him thankful for his choice of overcoat. 'He'll be somewhere. Hasn't it occurred to you that you're not the only DS on his team? In fact, you live further away from base than any of them, you're off duty and yet he called you.'

She offered a nervous smile. 'He's always saying I'm the best.' She slid along the back seat and stepped out beside him.

'Thanks for coming,' the chief constable said, as she approached them. 'We didn't expect you both to arrive together.'

'But you knew DS McClair was coming?'

'Yes, she was called in on my instruction.'

'Even though she's a single mother like you? There must be a powerful reason for that.'

'All four of us have got young children,' she retorted. 'We should all be with them, but this . . . Well, it overrides that.'

'Even for me? I'm a civilian, remember.'

'Neither of you are here because you're cops,' McGuire said, beckoning. There was something in his eyes that Skinner could not read, for all the years he had known the man. 'Come on and we'll show you what this is about.'

They fell in behind him as he led them a few yards down Morrison Street, pausing as they reached its junction with Torphichen Place, where the West End Police Office was located. As they turned the corner, Skinner tensed. Beside him Noele McClair gasped.

A crime scene tent had been set up at the entrance to the station. It was large, covering the pavement and half the roadway. At its entrance a ginger-haired man was climbing into a disposable tunic.

'He's here?'

McGuire nodded. 'Aye, Bob; for this one, accept no substitutes.'

Arthur Dorward was head of the Scottish Police Authority's Forensic Services Unit, and he was not a delegator. For major incidents he was usually the first on the scene. He turned as they approached, frowned, then stepped inside the tent.

'He's not happy about a Hogmanay call-out either, it seems,' Skinner murmured.

'Who would be?' the chief constable replied. 'We all need to be suited and booted,' she continued, accepting a package from a crime scene technician.

Skinner shed his overcoat and donned the sterile garb as quickly as he could, only to find that McClair had a problem. She was wearing a skirt. 'Sauce never said,' she protested.

'That's okay, Noele,' McGuire assured her. 'Nip into the station and change in the ladies.'

'Mario,' Skinner barked as she left them, irritation overcoming him. 'What the fuck is this?'

As he spoke a tall young man emerged from the tent, grim and white-faced. His ears had escaped from his sterile cap. He stopped short when he saw his former chief and continuing mentor, his eyes widening. 'Are you going to tell me what this is about, Sauce?'

Detective Inspector Harold Haddock's mouth tightened until it was no more than a slash across his face. He shook his head and looked away, then retraced his steps.

'I've had enough of this,' Skinner growled. He made to follow, until Steele put a hand on his arm.

'Please, Bob, wait for DS McClair. She's going to need you, as a friend.'

Scowling, he obeyed her, biding his time until the DS returned, her change of clothing completed, then stepped through the opening into the covered enclosure, with her following behind.

The area was bathed in cold, bright white light. At its centre was a car, a blue estate; a sheet had been placed over the windscreen and roof, against glare from the floodlights, he supposed. It looked vaguely familiar to Skinner, but he was unable to place it . . . until Noele McClair spoke.

'That's Terry's car,' she cried out. 'It's my ex-husband's car. What's it doing here?'

'That's the thing, Noele,' Sauce Haddock replied. 'It was dumped here at twelve forty-one. The driver jumped out, got into the passenger seat of a car that was following him and it got the hell out of here. He was wearing a black balaclava, so we never got a look at his face.'

'But why?' she asked, her anxiety building. 'What's this about?'

'This is the reason,' the chief constable said. She stepped up to the car and pulled the covering sheet away exposing some of the windscreen.

Reflected light blazed off the glass, blinding them all for a second, until Skinner moved past McClair, up to the vehicle, and looked inside.

The front seats were unoccupied but two male figures were sprawled in the rear. He jerked the nearside door open and leaned inside. He knew Terry Coats, the detective inspector who had lost his career for sailing too close to the wind, the husband who had lost his wife and daughter for going far beyond it. He recognised him at once, even with a third eye in the middle of his forehead from which a single trickle of blood ran down his nose, across the stubble on his upper lip and into his mouth.

He stood, turning to face Steele and McGuire, fury in his eyes. McClair had moved up behind him, but he held his position, blocking her view of what was inside the car. 'What the fuck!' he hissed. 'I thought I'd trained some tact into you two. Obviously you skipped a couple of lessons, to be pulling this stunt.'

'I'm sorry, Bob,' the chief constable replied. 'It was my call, not Mario's. Neither of us have ever experienced anything like this, so I felt your advice was essential.'

'You must have skipped the self-confidence lesson as well, Maggie. Okay,' he continued, calming a little, 'I'll take that as a compliment, but why bring Noele here?'

'What was the alternative? Having a police car call at her house, with her child there? Sauce knew that her mother would be there for New Year, so I thought it was best if she was brought to the scene.'

'You got that fucking wrong!' he yelled at her, in a way that he never had when she had been an officer under his command.

McClair looked up at him. 'The scene of what, Bob?' she asked, quietly.

He sighed. 'Terry's in there, lass, and he's dead. He's been shot.'

The colour fled from her face, in an instant. Her cheeks seemed to collapse into themselves, giving her a skeletal look. She leaned against him, and he put his arms around her. 'What's the silly bugger done now?' she murmured, into his chest.

'That we will find out, Noele,' he promised her. 'I'm sure he'll have left a trail. From what I knew of the man, he didn't do subtle.'

'Can I see him?' she asked, her voice tremulous. 'I mean, we'll need a formal identification, won't we?'

'You can do it at the morgue, before the autopsy. But it's not "we". You can't be involved in the investigation.'

'Why not?' she said, bitterly, disengaging herself and looking back at Steele, McGuire and Haddock. 'We were divorced.' She paused. 'Or do you have to eliminate me as a suspect? Is that it?'

'The thought never crossed our minds,' Haddock replied. 'You're too close; that's all, Noele, you must know that. I will need to talk to you though, about Terry's movements, associates, stuff like that.'

'I won't be able to tell you much, Sauce. I only see Terry,' she gulped, 'only saw, him when he came to pick up our Harry every other Saturday.'

'We may have to go further back than that.'

'But not now,' Skinner declared firmly. Even in her distress, McClair had the impression that he had effectively taken command. 'You've done what you saw as necessary, Maggie. Now do what's decent and have Bertie Auld take her back to Gullane right away.'

'Back to my car,' she corrected him, as the first tears began to fall.

'No, back home. You're not driving tonight. PC Gregg can drop Sergeant Auld off in Aberlady; he can take your motor back.'

'He can't,' she murmured. 'He's not insured.'

'He is, as a police officer. Don't you worry about that; let's just get you home to Harry and your mother. And if you need someone to look after the wee fella in the next few days,' he added, 'you can drop him off at mine. Sauce,' he ordered, 'take her back inside to change, then straight to the car.'

As Haddock obeyed his instruction, Skinner, still bristling with anger glowered at the two senior officers. 'I can see why you wanted me here,' he conceded, 'but bringing her here was miles over the top. You could have told me about Coats, and I could have gone to see Noele at home.'

'I agree, Bob, we could, and in hindsight, we should,' McGuire was grim-faced, as tense as before. 'But there's more. You need to look in the other side of the car.'

Puzzled, he did as the DCC asked; he walked round behind the vehicle, and once again opened the rear passenger door and leaned in. As he did, he noticed for the first time the rank smell of death with which he had become familiar during his police career, a mix of blood, sweat and human waste.

The other occupant was slumped sideways, restrained only by the curve of the back seat. He wore a heavy knitted sweater and faded denim jeans. Skinner recognised his trainers as Air Jordan, James Andrew's choice of Christmas present, and seriously expensive, the top of the Nike basketball range. The man also had been shot, but through the back of the head: that was all too obvious as the bullet had exited through the left eye, taking all of it away, turning the socket into a mess of gore and bone chips.

He stood once again. 'Yeah,' he said with a shudder.

'Look again, Bob,' Maggie Steele told him.

He did so, forcing his gaze away from the awful wound and fixing it on the undamaged section of the slack-jawed head. He stared at the body for several seconds; as he did so, a cold hard fist seemed to grip his stomach and twist.

'Aw my God,' he gasped. 'Is this for real? It can't be. How the fuck . . . this is Griff Montell?'

'Yes,' the chief constable confirmed. 'Inspector Griffin Montell. You recruited him as chief in Edinburgh, and you have a personal connection with him through his friendship with your Alex. We need to know how he wound up dead in the same car as Terry Coats, and we're hoping you can help us find out.'

Skinner's head swam, as he recalled his history with the dead man. It was an exaggeration to say that he had recruited him, but he had approved his transfer from his police force in South Africa and had made the best use of the skills outlined in his service record by putting him straight into CID, without any pointless acclimatisation in uniform. Montell had more or less been driven out of his home country when a failed marriage had left him with court-awarded child support costs that he could not have met on a Rand-based salary. The solution he had chosen had been to move to Scotland where the conversion rate from sterling allowed him to do that easily.

Montell was a colourful character, as well as being a good detective. Skinner's daughter Alex had been attracted to him when they were neighbours in Stockbridge. And there had been a third person in that block, he realised.

'What about Spring?' he asked. 'She's his next of kin. Has she been told?'

Montell's twin sister had emigrated with him. She was gay, and her romance with Superintendent Mary Chambers had caused family and professional friction for a while; indeed it might have cost Montell his job if Skinner had not been there as a moderating influence.

'She doesn't live in Edinburgh full-time any longer,' McGuire told him. 'She moved in with Mary, and after she retired they bought a flat in Pretoria, where she and Griff grew up. That's where they spend the winter. I know this because Mary told me. I have her mobile number, so I'll try that. If it's switched off I'll ask the police there to track her down and get her to contact me, and I'll ask her to break the news.'

'What about his ex-wife and kids? You might have contact details for her on his personal file. She'll have to be told.'

'Again, that's a job for the morning. I might ask Mary to do that too.'

'Meanwhile I've got to tell Alex,' Skinner murmured.

'Were they still . . . ?' Steele ventured. 'We all know that when she was attacked in her home, Griff was there. He was injured protecting her, wasn't he?'

'If you're asking whether they were still sleeping together,' Skinner retorted, 'not so far as I know. It wasn't a steady thing. Griff was a friend, and if she was lonely or low, she could give him a call.'

'She'll need to be interviewed,' the chief constable said.

Something about her manner brought Skinner's temperature to boiling point once again. 'She'll need to be consoled,' he snapped, 'and that's my job, mine and Dominic's.'

'You mean Lennie,' Steele observed.

'No, I don't, Maggie. Lennie's in the past; Dominic Jackson is a different person altogether.'

The chief constable frowned. 'I'm a sceptic when it comes to rehabilitation,' she declared. 'I'm not convinced by people who claim to have reinvented themselves in prison.'

'Across the board, neither am I,' he fired back, 'but I knew the big fella before you did, and I liked him. The fact is you don't really know him at all, and you never did. Many of us are moulded as people by our social circumstances; I'm one of them . . . and so are you. So was the young Lennie Plenderleith, but he didn't have my good fortune. He wasn't born into a middle-class professional family so he was never spotted by the education system. In his case, his father was a brute and he was brought up that way.' He paused, recovering his temper. 'The prison service doesn't do IQ tests on inmates as a matter of course, but I had them run one on Lennie and it was off the fucking scale.'

'You never told me that,' she said.

'No,' he agreed. 'Nor did I tell you that I visited him a couple of times a year when he was inside, in the Governor's office so the other prisoners didn't twig and mark him down as a grass.'

'No, you didn't; not even when I was your executive officer. You didn't trust me?'

'It wasn't a matter of trust, Mags, it was private, between me and Dominic, that's all. However, I do trust him to take care of my kid, and that's all you need to realise now.' He paused. 'No, not quite, you also need to realise that if anyone in the media ever makes a connection between him and Lennie Plenderleith and I find out that it came from the police, I will find the source and I will end their career. Now,' he barked, abruptly, 'can we get indoors, sit down with the SIO . . . Sammy Pye, I assume . . . and work out how this double-murder investigation will proceed.'

To McGuire and Steele, it was as if Bob Skinner had never left the service. Automatically he had slipped into command mode. Automatically, they obeyed. The DCC nodded and led the way into the police station. They removed and discarded their sterile clothing in the reception area, then climbed one floor to the station commander's office, which Steele had occupied herself earlier in her career, before the old Edinburgh force had become part of the unified Scottish police service.

'Mario,' she said, as the door closed behind them, 'text Sauce and ask him to join us. You were wrong about Sammy being SIO, Bob; he's on extended sick leave and Haddock's filling in for him as Serious Crimes commander in Edinburgh.'

'What's his problem?'

She hesitated; he realised that she was considering what she could tell him. 'Within these four walls, he's been diagnosed as having motor neurone disease,' she replied. 'Don't breathe a word, though: not even Sauce knows. He thinks it's a virus.'

'Fuck,' Skinner sighed. 'What a New Year this is turning out to be. Poor Sammy, we've all known him since he was a . . .' He stopped in mid-sentence as there was a knock at the door.

Haddock came into the room without waiting for a reply; he was still wearing his paper suit. 'Chief, sir, gaffer,' he said. 'You wanted me.'

'Yes, Inspector,' McGuire replied, 'we do. We have an investigation to launch, and you're in charge.'

'Me, sir?'

'Who else? It's a serious crime; that's what it says on your office door, and you're in charge of the team.' He hesitated.

'Okay, Sauce; we know you're relatively new in rank and inexperienced, but the chief and I have got faith in you. By the same token, we're not going to leave you exposed to everything. The media will swallow its collective tongue when it learns that a police officer and a former cop have been executed like this. I'll front up all the public statements and briefings, and Allsop's team in the press office will deal with one-off questions, so you won't be in the spotlight at all, until the day that you make an arrest. Then, you can go out front. You can run the inquiry out of this office if you like, with all the personnel you need. If the investigation goes beyond Edinburgh, you'll have the support of Serious Crimes wherever necessary. They'll report to you, regardless of the rank of the senior officer. On top of that, Sir Robert will be there in the background, acting as a mentor, as he's done in the past.'

Skinner started, but McGuire forestalled him. 'I don't need to ask you, Bob, do I? You're as keen to find the person who pulled that trigger as we are.'

'No, you don't need to,' he agreed, 'but you and I won't be seen together, Sauce. When we meet, it won't be here, and we won't be observed. I'll help you every way I can, but if I'm seen to do so, it'll undermine your authority, in the eyes of the press, and possibly of your own team. Now,' he continued, 'what's your first priority?'

'Process the crime scene,' Haddock replied immediately.

'You don't know where the crime scene is,' Skinner pointed out. 'One was shot in the back of the head, the other,' he touched his forehead, 'right there. Coats might have been killed in the car, but Griff wasn't, no way. Even if he'd been leaning forward so that the gunman could get a shot off, if that had happened there would have been debris all over the place, blood, bone fragments, brain tissue. Earlier you described the car being dropped off. I take it you've got CCTV footage.'

'Yes, there are three cameras; one covers Torphichen Place, one's on Dewar Place Lane, and the third looks at the rear of the building and the car park.'

'What about the other vehicle? What do you have on that?'

'We have a registration,' Haddock told him. 'Problem is it belongs to a Vauxhall Insignia, three years old, owned by a leasing company in Bristol. The car on camera is a Renault Megane.'

'You'll be able to narrow that by looking at the style of the vehicle, model details and so on.'

'I'm not holding my breath, gaffer. Before you ask, I've ordered a search of all available street camera footage, for both vehicles. If we get lucky . . .'

'Don't call it luck; call it the result of proper police procedure.'

McGuire grunted. 'We'll be sure to do that at the press briefing. But if we do get lucky,' he continued, 'we'll find footage of the driver and the passenger getting out and they won't have bloody helmets wrapped around their coupons.'

'Which makes that your top priority, Sauce,' Skinner added. 'The next being to process the vehicle and get every trace of DNA from it. You're bound to find traces of wee Harry, Terry and Noele's son, in there, but it'll be so similar to his dad's that you won't need to take a sample from the wee chap. Likewise, Noele, for hers is on the database for elimination purposes. Again, add on the luck factor and you might find someone who's on the system for the wrong reasons.' He paused. 'That's what we're thinking,' he said. 'Now, tell us, as the SIO, what's in your head?'

'Okay,' Haddock replied. 'Once all the by-the-book stuff is done, we're going to be trying to find out how the hell Terry Coats and a uniformed police inspector came to wind up dead in the same car.'

His mentor nodded. 'Yes, you will be,' he agreed, frowning. 'And maybe I can help you. When you were investigating the murder of that bothersome blogger, Austin Brass, you had Terry Coats in the frame as a potential suspect.'

'That's right. We had him under observation and you and I tracked him to a hotel out by Edinburgh Park. We wondered what he was up to; it turned out it was an air stewardess that he was banging on the side. That was when he and Noele went their separate ways.'

'Correct. What you don't know is that, after she kicked him out, Terry turned up at my house full of hell and looking for trouble. I had to,' he paused, 'calm him down. When I'd done that, and he'd come to his senses, he came out with a bizarre story.' He laughed, softly. 'He said he'd been working under cover.'

'Under duvet, more like,' McGuire grunted.

'I knew the first part of that,' Haddock added. 'You told me at the time that you'd had to deck him.'

'I didn't have to,' Skinner admitted, 'but he took a punch at my boy; that's as big a line as you can cross. What you don't know is the tale he spun me. His excuse was that he'd come upon what he said was a money-laundering operation, convert-ing stolen Krugerrands through an airport shop, after they were smuggled in by flight crew on a certain airline. He told me that he'd checked the background with a guy he knew . . . Griff Montell. He said that Griff had mentioned a big gold robbery that had happened during his time on the South African force.

I thought it was bullshit, but I told him he should take the story back to Griff. At the time he was upset about being moved off CID, and I thought that on the off-chance there was anything in it he might see it as a way back in.' He frowned. 'Then I got wrapped up in the Brass investigation, and in the other thing that followed it, and what with Alex being attacked and everything, Coats and his story went right out of my mind until now.'

'Can you remember the details?' the DI asked.

'That's what I'm trying to do, put them together in my head. I didn't make any notes at the time. I was too busy persuading myself not to give him more of a doing for hitting Ignacio. The cabin-crew girlfriend's name was Aisha Karman, he said, and she was one of those laundering the money. She worked on an airline called Wister Air. I remember that because it struck me that I had never heard of it. Yes,' he nodded, 'it's fitting together now. Aisha from Wister Air would make purchases in the store but rather than use cash or card she'd pay in Krugerrands.'

'That was the tale?'

'As much of it as I can remember,' Skinner said.

'Well,' McGuire observed, 'I think we can be fairly certain that if he did go back to Griff, he never took it to CID, otherwise I would have heard about it. And yet they were found dead together.'

'We need to search both their homes,' Haddock said. 'Their phones, their diaries, everything.'

'Agreed. Get on with it.' The DCC turned to Skinner. 'Bob, Griff and his sister lived next door to your Alex, didn't they?'

'That's right; overlooking the Water of Leith. She told me he still lives there.'

'Do you know if he had any female involvement, other than being friendly with Alex?'

'I know he used to have a thing with Alice Cowan, the officer we had to let go, but I haven't heard of anyone since then . . . other than Alex, when the pair of them felt like it.'

'Still.' McGuire frowned. 'Sauce, add Cowan to your interview list. They might have kept in touch.'

'She's on the list already,' the young DI replied, boldly. 'But interviews are the second phase. Before them I need to get SOCOs into Griff's flat, and into Coats' home as well. They're working in Griff's office as we speak. When they're done there, I'll go through his papers myself.'

'Do you know where Coats lived?' Skinner asked.

'No, but I can get that from Noele.'

'I suggest that you try his employer first, rather than troubling her. Coats worked in security at Edinburgh Airport. Anyway, its management is going to want to be told that one of its senior people has been bumped off, rather than reading it in the *Evening News* online. In fact, you might want to do that right now; you'll be putting Arthur Dorward's people in Coats' office too. Before they get there, it needs to be sealed off.'

'You're right, gaffer. We have patrol officers full-time at the airport. I'll tell them to do that and put a guard over the door. That isn't something we can leave to the airport staff. Until we know what Coats was up to, and who else was involved, I suppose they'll all be persons of interest.'

'True,' Skinner agreed, 'but you might find there aren't all that many of them. In effect it's our patrol officers who are the real security people. Have you got a pathologist on site yet?' he asked.

'Yes, she arrived just before I came up here. Her name's

Emily Badger. She's new, which I guess is why she copped the on-call slot on Hogmanay. She brought an assistant; I just hope she's up to it. I wish Sarah could have come.'

'It's as well for you she didn't, without being told what she was walking into, like I wasn't. She knew Griff well and she'd met Terry Coats. That would not have been good and I would not have been pleased,' he shot a sidelong glance at McGuire, who wore a sheepish expression, 'as in very not pleased.'

The chief constable intervened, rapping the desk that once had been hers. 'People,' she exclaimed, 'even as we sit here, this thing is expanding. Sauce, you'll need more personnel than you have, especially with DS McClair not being available to you. Things are quiet in the west just now, so I'm going to take a chance that they don't heat up. I'm going to second Charlotte Mann and Cotter, her DS, to you, with a couple of detective constables as well.'

'Lottie's a DCI, ma'am,' Haddock pointed out.

Steele smiled, faintly. 'In that case you'll need to be very nice to her. As Mr McGuire said earlier on, you will still be the SIO.' She glanced at the DCC. 'Mario, you advise them please, and make sure they understand the chain of command.' She stood. 'Okay, unless anyone has something else they need to ask, let's get on with the job. I'm going home, but I'll be available and I will,' she emphasised the word, 'expect to be updated.'

'Do you want a car home, Bob?' McGuire asked as she closed the door behind her.

'Not yet, Mario, thanks. I'll stick around for a while. When we get into Griff's office another pair of eyes might be helpful. In fact, I'll probably stay here until it's a reasonable time to go and see Alex. But, listen,' he added, 'what are you going to do about the media? Even on the first of January, traffic being diverted away from a large police office won't go unnoticed. Are you going to get Peregrine Allsop here from wherever he fucking nests?'

'Hah! Our Head of Communications is in Australia, would you believe. I called Jane Balfour, our new Edinburgh assistant, as soon as I got word of this. She sounded half cut, even though she was supposed to be on call, so I told her to get her act together and get along here for eight o'clock. Meanwhile all media calls come straight to me. So far there have been none, but you're right, anytime now it has to happen. "Police incident, no threat to life, more details later." That's all I'll say for now.'

'That'll hold them, for a while at least,' Skinner agreed. 'Once you get Ms Balfour in place make sure she knows that I don't exist in the context of this investigation: just in case she sees me around. I don't want my name being leaked to any journo pals.'

He rose. 'We'll leave you to get on with it, Mario, if we may. Sauce, this office has a canteen . . . or it used to. It's probably closed today, but there must be a coffee stock somewhere. I'm in need.'

As he had predicted, no staff were working in the small canteen, but there was a coffee machine. 'Costa,' he muttered. 'Always fucking Costa.' Nevertheless he made himself a latte with two extra shots. Haddock settled for tea. They sat at a table in the empty room.

'You all right, son? You were as white as a sheet when I got here.'

Haddock drew a breath and nodded. 'It was a shock, no question,' he confessed, 'but I'm holding myself together.

I could ask you the same thing. You knew Griff better than I did.'

'I've had thirty years' practice at holding it in, but that,' he jerked his thumb in the general direction of the door, 'that out there, it had me close to losing it.' He glowered at the DI. 'It was bad enough trying to involve Sarah in it, although I can under-stand it, she's the top pathologist in this part of the country. But calling Noele in to look at the father of her kid with a hole in his fucking head . . . not for repetition, but DCC McGuire and I will be having a further conversation about that.'

'That wasn't him,' Haddock said quietly. 'That order came from the chief constable herself. Big Mario wasn't there at the time. I could hardly question her, gaffer, could I?'

'Are you sure about that? Could she and Mario have spoken about it before?'

'No, or I doubt that it would have happened. I heard them discuss calling you; I was in the commander's office while they closed the street off. He said that he needed you there, and that while he didn't think you would both come, he'd ask if Sarah was available. She said that if there was a choice it should be Sarah, but he overruled her. He said no, that he needed you here. Then he went out; she was quiet for a bit and then she told me to call Noele and get her here. I sort of looked at her for a second, but she just said "Now!" as in "Don't say a word, Haddock." This is nothing really new, gaffer. The whisper is that the DCC is taking all the big decisions at HQ, and that she seems to have lost her self-confidence. I hope that's not true. It was the chief who spotted me when I was a plod, and she was in that office along the way. It was her that helped me develop. I've done better than most folk think I should have, and I know it, but it's thanks to her.'

'Don't sell yourself short, son,' his mentor said. 'You deserve to be where you are. I know they called Sammy Pye "Luke Skywalker" because he was such a high-flyer, but you'd have cruised past him on the runway.' He sighed; realising that he had made a mistake by referring to Pye in the past tense. He glanced at his companion, but he gave no sign of having noticed. 'But Maggie,' he continued, 'ah, that's not so good. You're telling me it's just a whisper, but before you know it whispers can turn into shouts.' He paused. 'Mind you, those can often be unfounded too. It might just appear that way; we both know what a forceful character Mario McGuire is.'

'Yes, but he also hears everything,' the DI countered. 'If he knew that sort of talk was in the air and there was nothing in it, he'd have squashed it.'

'True,' Skinner conceded.

'Can you do anything about it?'

'Me? I'm not the chair of the Scottish Police Authority, Sauce.'

'No, but you made her, just as she's made me. You could talk to her.'

'I could, but . . .' He finished his coffee, then returned to the machine and made another. 'This might bear out a theory of mine, Sauce,' he said as he resumed his seat. 'I suspect that the chief's job is so big now that each holder has a shelf life. Even before unification, I think that was true. I was chief in Edinburgh, and then in Strathclyde, even if it was only to shut up the shop and hand over to the national force. One of the reasons why I didn't apply to be its chief constable, apart from disagreeing profoundly with it, as I still do, was that I felt my time was up. I wasn't afraid of it; I looked at the terms, at the length of contract, and I doubted that I had it in me to see it out. Look at what happened to Andy Martin. He was gone inside two years, leaving behind him a trail of enemies who'd once been friends . . . including me, but that had fuck all to do with the job. Maggie's been in post for not much longer. Okay, she hasn't been abrasive, as Sir Andrew was, but she may have gone too far in the other direction. She's always been reserved; her upbringing may have something to do with that, but we do not go there. She's a brilliant police officer and she was the outstanding candidate when the job came up, but it may be that the inevitable limelight's been too much for her. I know for a fact that she turned down the damehood that was offered after she was appointed. On top of all that, she's a widowed mother, who lost her husband and survived cancer while she was carrying her child.' He looked the younger man in the eye. 'You said that I could talk to her. If I did that it might be to persuade her that there would be no shame in resigning and going home to look after wee Stephanie. How would you feel about that?'

Haddock was silent for a few seconds, considering the question. When he replied, he was hesitant. 'Selfishly?' he began. 'It would depend on who took over. It would have to be advertised nationally, and I don't know that I trust the Authority to get it right; I wouldn't like to see somebody parachuted in from England who's never walked a beat north of the border in his life. The DCC? Absolutely. ACC Mackie? Okay.' He glanced at Skinner. 'You, if you applied for it? No reason why not. You're still years short of retirement age.'

His mentor laughed, quietly. 'You can forget that one. I would still have a very short shelf life, plus I've gone in another direction. I have commitments elsewhere with InterMedia, for which incidentally I get paid a serious amount of money, twice the chief constable's salary for a part-time job.' He winked. 'Oh yes, I have an avaricious side. No,' he continued, 'not me. You're right, there would be a danger of the wrong appointment being made, but . . . while I'm not a member of the Police Authority, I do know the chair, and quite a few of the members, and I've got some influence I think. I'm fairly confident that an in-house appointment would be made. Mario is the outstanding home candidate, no question. Brian Mackie? No. Brian's an excellent manager, excellent senior officer, but he's not a leader, not a general. But let me throw another name at you. Neil McIlhenney.'

'I don't know him. That said I know of him; anyone who's moved to the Met from here and has done as well as he has, yes, he has to be in the game. But would he want it? Isn't he a . . . ?'

'Deputy Assistant Commissioner? Yes. Will he go all the way? No. Louise, his wife, has given up stage acting, so he's not constrained by her career. I doubt that he'd go against his best mate, but if Mario didn't want it, you never know.'

'Will you talk to the chief?' Haddock asked.

'I'll have to think that through,' Skinner declared, killing his second coffee and blinking as the caffeine hit. 'Meantime, let's see if you and I can get into Griff's office yet.'

Four

Ignacio Watson Skinner stood in the doorway of the garden room, looking at his stepmother in surprise. He was slightly drunk, but less so than Pilar who clung to his arm as her world swam around her. Sarah was on the sofa, peering at her iPad. An empty goblet, a Corona bottle with a sad piece of lime at the bottom, and a mug with the word '*Profesora*' emblazoned around it, one of his Christmas gifts, were on a small table beside her.

'Is it that late?' he slurred. She looked round, startled, as he spoke. 'Have you been to bed and up already? Has Dad crashed?'

'No to both of those,' she replied. 'I haven't been to bed yet, I was going but I had a New Year message from the international medical examiners' body. It's a bit of a downer, about the new virus that's been identified out in China. It sobered me up; if it's even half true, we could be in for a very nasty year.'

'Where?'

'Everywhere.' She smiled and checked her watch. 'When I was your age, I'd still have been going at New Year's. Come to think of it I suppose I still am.' She checked the goblet; it was empty. 'No, maybe not.'

'If Dad is not upstairs,' Ignacio began, 'where is he?'

'He was called out, by the police. A car came for him and took him up to Edinburgh. I don't know why, but I do know there's a body involved, because they asked for me too.'

'Ohhh,' Pilar murmured. 'Nacho.' Her olive complexion had turned significantly pale.

Sarah recognised impending disaster. She rushed across, peeled the young woman from Ignacio's arm, and half-carried her into the cloakroom toilet. He looked on as the door closed, a soft grin on his face.

He was still smiling when his ringtone sounded. He checked the screen before answering. 'Mum,' he said, 'we spoke already. Are you drunk too?'

'I don't drink anymore,' Mia Watson replied. 'Ignacio, have you heard from your stepfather in the last hour?'

'From Cameron? No, why should I? I spoke to him with you, at midnight. What is wrong?'

'He's vanished,' she exclaimed her voice rising. 'Gone. Disappeared. We were at the Hogmanay celebrations in the hotel. I left around quarter to one; my ears were starting to hurt it was so loud. He said he was going to have a cigar in the garden, then follow me back to the house. When he hadn't shown up an hour and a half later, I went back there to dig him out; the thing was over by that time and all the guests had gone to their rooms or been taken home by the courtesy bus. I couldn't find him, Ignacio; he wasn't there. I sent all the staff out to look for him in the grounds, in case he'd been taken ill, but nobody could find him.'

'Did you call the courtesy-bus driver?' her son suggested. 'Maybe he went on it, to make sure everyone got home. It's the kind of thing Cameron would do.'

'The bus is back. He was never on it.'

'Is his car still there?'

'Yes, both of them. Ignacio, there isn't a trace of him. It's as if he's been abducted by aliens.'

Five

'He was neat,' Haddock observed.

'You haven't spent enough time in uniform,' his companion told him. He had donned another sterile suit, after the DI had asked the crime scene officers to take a break to give them access. 'Neatness is obligatory, with the station commander on the prowl all the time. Unlike your average CID office, which is a fucking shambles.'

'Maybe in your day . . .'

Skinner beamed. 'My day . . . Jeez, slide the Zimmer over will you. Listen, if a CID office is spotless, it means everybody has time to keep it that way and that means you're not doing the job properly. What are we looking for here?' he asked, moving on.

'Anything that links Griff and Coats.'

'I doubt that would be in plain sight.' He looked at the immaculate single-pedestal desk. The only paper on it was a printout of the station's duty rota over the Christmas period. He leaned over and tugged the smaller of the two drawers; it slid open easily, revealing nothing more than a box of tea bags, three pens, a comb, a pair of nail scissors, tweezers, a pack of Kleenex tissues, a tin box which claimed to contain

42

a multipurpose credit-card-sized tool, and a spectacle case bearing the RayBan logo. He opened it and found a pair of glasses; he took them out and held them up. 'I never knew he needed these,' he murmured.

'Reading glasses,' Haddock said. 'He didn't like to be seen wearing them. I called in here one day unannounced. He whipped them off sharpish.'

Skinner examined them, weighing them in his hand. 'He still shelled out for lightweight designer frames though. You won't get much change out of four hundred quid for these. I know this because I looked at them or something similar last year and wound up going for a cheaper option. How old was Griff? I can't remember.'

'Thirty-nine.'

'My reading glasses came with my forty-ninth birthday, when I realised that my arms weren't long enough anymore.' He moved across to a tall metal locker at the back of the room; it was locked, but he took the tweezers from the desk and had it open in less than five seconds.

The DI whistled. 'How often have you done that?'

'Not a lot since I was at your rank. If you don't have that skill, acquire it; you'll save a hell of a lot of time trying to find keys.'

He looked into the locker. It contained two uniforms on hangers, trousers and tunics, one of which bore the epaulettes of an inspector, square silver pips. Alongside them were a casual jacket and a pair of jeans, hung upside down, weight to the bottom. He took them out and examined them.

'Hugo Boss,' he murmured reading the jacket label. 'And going by the logo, these jeans are Armani. I bought a pair of those in Girona; a hundred and seventy euros. Maybe I'm out of touch; an inspector's on just over fifty grand these days, but . . .'

'Griff was single,' Haddock pointed out.

'So are you. Okay, you live with Cheeky, but she's an accountant, a good earner, and I don't see you wearing gear like this. Marks and Spencer, as I recall, last time I saw you without sterile clothing. And you don't have a couple of kids to support, as Griff has in South Africa.'

He replaced the clothing and peered into the locker once again, looking at a shelf above the rail. 'What's here?' He removed several items. 'Photo album.' He flipped it open. 'His kids. Paracetamol. Deodorant. Condoms. Johnnies in a police-office locker?' he exclaimed. 'Was he banging somebody in this building? Better find out, Sauce, as discreetly as you can. And . . . what the . . .' He paused and held up a cardboard square. 'A pay-as-you-go SIM card,' he murmured, curious. 'What the fuck would a uniformed police inspector be doing, Sauce, with this in his private locker?'

The DI exhaled, loudly. 'I don't know, gaffer, but I need to find out. How do you get a warrant on New Year's Day to access somebody's bank account?'

'You waken a sheriff and get him to sign it; or her. Then you hope they don't hold it against you in the future. Justice never sleeps, chum; it never sleeps.'

Six

Skinner checked his watch as he stepped from the police car into the drizzle, outside the block that held Dominic Jackson's duplex home. It showed eight fifty-two. Deeming that to be a reasonable hour to call his wife, he dug his phone, awkwardly, from his padded raincoat and pressed 'Home' on his favourites list.

It was James Andrew Skinner who answered the call, not his mother. 'She's still asleep, Dad,' he said. 'Where are you?' The boy sounded puzzled by his absence. There was no one awake to tell him about his departure, Skinner guessed.

'I had to go out on business,' he explained. 'I'm just about to go to Alex's. What are you doing for breakfast?'

'I've done it,' his son replied. 'Mark and I had cereal and French toast. I had to make it, as usual. He's bloody useless.'

'Language, Jazz.'

'Sorry, Dad, but he is, you know that. The last time he tried to make toast he set off the smoke alarm.'

'You have a point,' he conceded. 'Did you feed the girls too?'

'Of course, although Dawn had porridge, not cereal, and juice. Seonaid cleaned up after her.'

'Good for her. If you want to score some Brownie points you might make your mum some French toast too. And coffee.'

'Why would I want Brownie points, Dad? I'm a Scout.'

'You know what I mean, smartarse.'

'Language, Dad,' James Andrew retorted. 'I'll do it, but I'll get Seonaid to check whether she's awake.'

Skinner smiled as he re-pocketed the mobile, but it left his face quickly as he pressed the videocall button labelled 'Jackson, Consultant psychologist'.

Another male voice answered, but deeper and darker. 'Bob? What's up?'

'I need to see Alex. I'll explain when I get up there.'

'I'm not sure she's awake,' Jackson said. 'Come on in and I'll give her a shout.'

The lift took him to the top floor quickly; it was littered with festive detritus, relics of the city's famous and notoriously com-mercialised Hogmanay celebrations. The door to the duplex penthouse was open as he stepped out, his host waiting within.

'Coffee, I guess?'

'God yes, Dominic. Please.'

'Anything else?'

'No thanks. I won't be hungry for a while.'

'So what's up?' Jackson asked again. 'Something big. I can see it in your eyes. You've got the thousand-yards stare.'

Skinner sighed. 'I'm sure I have. I'd be worried if I didn't.'

'What's the matter, Pops?' his daughter asked, from behind. 'Have you and Sarah had a barney?'

He turned. She was wrapped in a thick dressing gown over cotton pyjamas and wearing white slippers which bore the logo of a Barcelona hotel. As she saw his face, her expression changed, and her mood.

'What is it?' she asked anxiously. 'Is it one of the kids? Is it Aunt Jean? That's your death look,' she said. 'I know it.'

'No family, love, no family,' he replied, softly. 'It's Griff Montell. He was dumped outside the Torphichen Place police station just after midnight, in a car with another man. They'd both been shot in the head.'

In an instant, she went ghostly white; her hands flew to her mouth, pressing inwards, hard. 'No!' It was a muffled hiss. She turned to Jackson, then paused, turning back to her father. Then she stopped, as if unable to choose between them, spun round and half-ran across to the doors that opened on to the deck. She jerked them apart and stepped outside, oblivious to the rain as it grew heavier.

Skinner followed and put his arms around her, drawing her gently back inside. She buried her face in his chest as, for one of very few times in her adult life, she let others see her cry.

'Surely not,' she whispered, when she had regained her self-control.

'I'm afraid so, love.'

'Why?'

'That's always the first question.'

'A serving police officer?'

'I know.'

She looked up at him red-eyed and angry. 'I think I'll accept that offer to go to the Crown Office,' she murmured. 'I want to prosecute the people who did this.'

'The Lord Advocate who'd let you do that hasn't been born yet, Alexis.'

'I'll put coffee on,' Jackson said. He looked as shocked as his housemate.

'Thanks,' Skinner said, 'and maybe a shot of brandy in Alex's if you've got any. Sod the hour.'

'Why are you involved, Pops?' she asked, as he sat her in an armchair. 'Did they send you to break the news?'

'No, that was my choice. Mario called me in; I've been there ever since. Sauce is the SIO, and I've been asked to lurk in the background.'

'Is Sauce going to want to talk to me?'

'I'll do that for the moment,' he replied, 'although he probably will later. We needn't do it now though, if you don't feel ready.'

'No, make it now,' she insisted, 'while my blood's up.'

'Okay, if that's what you want. You should gather yourself together.'

'Yes. I'll throw some clothes on.'

She left him, returning a few minutes later, wearing black, polo neck and trousers. *A subconscious choice?* he wondered.

At the same time Jackson arrived with coffee on a tray, three mugs. He separated one and handed it to Alex. She sipped it and nodded.

'Do you want me to leave you to it?' he asked.

'Hell, no,' she declared. 'I need you here.'

Her father took a slug from his own mug, nodding approval. 'Thanks, Dominic. I like Colombian. When did you last see Griff?' he asked his daughter, continuing without a pause.

'Two weeks ago,' she answered briskly, back in control. 'We met for a pre-Christmas drink at the Dome.'

'How did he seem? What was his mood?'

'It was a bit mixed. He was bright and brash, but not quite full on. A shade distracted. Eventually I asked him what was

48

up. He said, "Ah, nothing really. Fucking uniform; I find it constraining." His exact words.'

'Was that all he said about it?'

'No. I told him he should ask to be reassigned, but that made him turn quite morose. He said there were no vacancies for detective inspectors, not where he wanted them. "Sure, if I wanted to go to Inverness," he said, "I might get back in there, but I don't really fancy investigating sheep rustling in the Orkneys." Then he was quiet for a while. I said, "Come on, what else is bugging you? Out with it." It all came out after that. First he said that his face didn't fit with Mario, or with you . . .'

'Me?' Skinner exclaimed. 'What the hell have I got to do with it?'

'He thought you still pulled Mario's strings, that he was your puppet. "Super-Mario-nette," he called him. And he reckoned that you had a down on him because of me, and the relationship that we had.'

'Well, he was wrong, wasn't he?' he said. 'You're a big girl, you're in the same situation I was when I was your age, single, not really looking for a permanent relationship, but not dead from the waist down either. You and Griff, you were like me and . . . well, Allison Higgins to name one. Didn't you tell him that?'

'As a matter of fact, I did, but he said that no father has the same rules for his daughter that he had for himself. Griff's got, had, a daughter, remember. He thought he was on your shit list. Latterly, Griff thought he was on everybody's shit list.'

'Even after he saved your life when those guys broke into your flat? He still thought I had marked his card?'

Alex nodded. 'Even after,' she confirmed. 'But that wasn't

the only reason why he thought his CID career was over. He said that everything seemed to be moving very fast as the new national police service bedded in. A few people were zooming up the ladder, and all the senior posts were gradually being filled by people who'd be in them for years. He named a few; Lowell Payne, who was a sergeant not so long ago and now runs counter-terrorism in Scotland, Lottie Mann . . . he said she'll be a detective superintendent before her DCI badges have lost their shine . . . Sammy Pye, Sauce Haddock, who he said is being fast-tracked to succeed Mario eventually, and even Noele McClair, Sauce's DS. Then he talked about his time in South Africa, before he relocated; that's something he did very rarely. He said it was different there, that things were much more set, that, okay, corners were cut but that criminal investigation was a settled community . . . one big happy family, he said, even if a bit of interbreeding went on.'

'That sounds pretty racist for Griff,' Skinner said, 'hell, it sounds racist for anybody.'

'No, I don't think he meant it that way; I didn't see it in that way, not at the time and not now. He meant something different, I'm sure, but I don't know what.'

'He probably meant that the in-crowd looked after each other,' her father murmured. 'Maybe I used to do that too,' he admitted. 'That night, did he mention Terry Coats?'

'Who's Terry Coats?' she asked, puzzled.

'Noele McClair's ex.'

'Was he the guy who turned up at your house and punched my brother?' Alex asked. 'I never knew his name; Ignacio told me about it, but he never said who it was, just that it was somebody with a beef against you. I asked him if you barbecued it, and he said that you did, more or less. And no, Griff never mentioned him either. Why should he?' Her mouth fell open, for a second. 'Ahh . . .' she whispered then fell silent. 'I can think of a reason, of sorts. To get Griff out of his mood, I suggested that he get hammered. He wasn't completely averse to that proposition, so he had a few expensive cocktails.'

'Did he splash the cash often, or were you paying?'

'We split it. Griff wasn't tight in any way, he offered, of course, but I always insisted we go Dutch. Anyway, he had a few more than usual, but he had hollow legs so he wasn't falling over or anything like that. I had a couple too, and I got . . . cool, let's say.' She glanced at the floor, momentarily. 'We hadn't been together since the night of the attack. No particular reason on my part, but we just hadn't. Anyway, I suggested that we might go back to his place, to round off the night and maybe extend it into next morning.' She paused. 'Dominic and I have an agreement that I don't bring men back here.' She looked at Jackson.

'That's right, Bob,' he confirmed. 'Alex proposed that from the off, and I agreed that it might be best, for a few reasons.'

'It doesn't cut both ways,' she added, 'but the only woman who's ever come here since I moved in has been the cleaner.'

'Not even as clients?' Skinner asked. 'You consult here; it even says so at the door.'

'No way; if I had a proper office and a female receptionist, yes, I'd have female clients here, but I don't so it wouldn't be wise.'

'I get it. Carry on, Alex. He never mentioned Terry Coats, but he did mention Noele on his list of promotion rivals.'

'Yes. He'd mentioned her before, as someone he knew through the job and then again that night, when he was sounding off. But the funny thing was, or it struck me as funny eventually, was that when he listed her, he just called her "Noele", didn't use her surname.'

'What made it funny?'

'I'll get there, Pops. When I suggested that we go back to his place, he was embarrassed. I'd never seen that from him before, never, so it took me by surprise. Then he said, "No, Alex, better not, it wouldn't be right." I jumped straight to the conclusion that he thought that Dominic and I . . .' She let the sentence tail away unfinished. 'I told him that he'd the wrong idea about us. But he said "No, I haven't, it's more from my point of view." He looked sort of coy and finally I caught on. "You've got somebody else," I said, and he nodded, and said, "Yes, I have. Are you upset?" Of course I said no, that I wasn't and I meant it. And then, half-pissed or not, the Skinner brain clicked into gear, and I thought back to what he'd said earlier and I said out loud . . . although I don't think I meant to . . . "It's Noele, isn't it? Noele McClair." He just smiled and nodded.' She frowned, as she replayed their conversation. 'Is that why you asked me about Terry Coats? Did you know that Griff was sleeping with his ex-wife?'

He stared at her in silence, more surprised than he had been in longer than his memory stretched. 'No,' he told her, 'I hadn't a clue. I asked you about Coats because he was the other man found dead with Griff in that car. And what I am thinking now is that I am so fucking glad I didn't let Noele look inside!'

Seven

'This lock is Fort Knox, pal,' the locksmith said. 'I know; I fitted it. In fact, I fitted the whole security system.'

'He had a security system?' DI Haddock exclaimed. 'I thought the building was secure.'

'It is, but only at the door on the street through the video entry system. Mr Montell had his own. That CCTV camera to the side of the front door, that's his.' He pointed to a corner of the corridor in which they stood. 'So's that one. There's cameras inside too, all monitored through the Cloud. The alarm's state of the art; it's got sensors on this door and all the windows; serviced every year. This front door's new too. Some of them in this building you can practically push open. No' this one. The frame's bolted into the wall so it can't be jemmied out. This lock,' he said, as he opened it, 'they call it a Doormaster. It's as good as you'll get. Between you two and me, I did the security locks on the chief constable's house. This set-up's better than hers. Voila,' he boomed as he opened the door. 'Wait a minute, one more thing to do.' He stepped into the hall and punched a code into a panel set on the wall. 'There you are, it's disarmed; Mr Montell can do that remotely, arm and disarm.' The locksmith smiled as the DI and his colleague followed him inside. 'I don't suppose you're gonnae tell me what he does, this guy, for you to get a warrant on the first of January to search his house. Drugs? Arms dealer? Jeweller?'

'You're right, Mr Francis,' the DI agreed. 'I'm not going to tell you. Now, I'd like you to step outside and wait in the hall, in case we need you again.'

'Oh, you will, trust me. I'll be here. The main room's straight ahead.'

The two detectives slipped on paper overshoes and gloves, then followed his direction into the apartment's spacious reception area.

The Water of Leith meandered under the window, making its way towards the port from which it took its name. Its level was high after the heavy rainfall of the previous days, but it was still well short of being a torrent. Broken twigs, vegetation and the inevitable single-use plastic were carried by on its surface, drawing a grunt of disapproval from Detective Sergeant Tarvil Singh.

'Folk that do that should be in fucking jail,' he growled.

'What?' Haddock asked.

'Chucking milk bottles in the Water of Leith.'

The DI smiled at his righteous indignation. 'The prisons wouldn't be big enough.'

'Maybe we could reintroduce transportation to Australia. There must be enough space, going by the number of Aussies working in pubs around here.'

'Come away from the window, Tarvil,' Haddock said. 'You're like an eclipse of the sun standing there.'

The massive Sikh obeyed. 'What are we looking for here, Sauce?' he asked.

'When we find it, we'll know. Anything that will connect

Griff and Terry Coats. Anything that will tell us where they might have been last night when they were killed. We've been through Griff's work diary, and through his whole office computer. There was nothing on it that wasn't police business.'

'Last night?' Singh repeated. 'How do we know for sure when they were killed?'

'Emily Badger, the pathologist, was confident that they died not long before the bodies were dumped. They were still warm and there was no sign of rigor when she examined them. So far, the forensic team haven't found anything that gives us a clue to where they were shot, but it's early days for them. One question I need to answer is, why was Griff here at all? He was signed off on leave from last Friday night until a week on Monday, and he told Sally McGlashan, the South East area commander, that he was going to South Africa to visit his sister and Mary Chambers, and to catch up with his kids.'

'But did he say when?'

'Yes. He told her he'd a flight booked on Saturday night.'

'It's Wednesday now. Could he have been there and back?'

'In theory yes, but would you go to the southern hemisphere at the end of December for just a couple of days? Jackie Wright's in the office already; I've asked her to check whether he actually had a flight booked. I've decided to run the inquiry out of Fettes rather than Torphichen Place. It's logical; that's our base and we've got more facilities there.' He paused, looking around the room, frowning. 'Wait a minute,' he said softly. 'It's cold in here, Tarvil, isn't it? I've still got my coat on but it's freezing.'

'Now you mention it . . .' the DS agreed.

Haddock stepped back into the hallway, where he had noticed a thermostat. 'This is set to ten centigrade,' he called out. 'It's a holiday setting, just to make sure nothing freezes. That's consistent with what he told Chief Inspector McGlashan. And yet he was still in Edinburgh. How come?' He re-joined Singh. 'Another mystery, but let's get started, see what this place tells us.'

Together they opened each drawer and cupboard in the living area, emptying each one out. They found nothing but table linen, place mats and crockery, everything in order, everything arranged logically. Similarly, the drinks cabinet contained nothing more than a range of liqueurs and glasses, and a cocktail shaker.

'Kitchen?' the DS suggested. 'You can read the book of my life in mine. Everything gets stuck in a clip behind the door.'

Haddock grinned and nodded. 'With us, it's a jar. Let's have a look, but this room's just like his office, im-fucking-peccable. If that's the same . . .'

The kitchen was a galley shape. The sink was below the window, which also overlooked the river; there was a combined washer dryer and a dishwasher plumbed in beneath. The wall above the work surface was fitted with cupboards for the length of the space until they reached a large fridge freezer. Above a chopping block, next to the hobs, an array of knives hung on a magnetic strip. But there was no clip behind the door, no credit card receipts in a jar, no visible evidence of occupation.

'This could be a show flat,' Singh observed, contradicting himself as he opened the fridge to find butter, cheese, an unopened carton of orange juice, half a dozen bottles of Peroni, and on a rack, a bottle of Prosecco and two of a white wine with a distinctive label. 'No milk,' he said.

'Let's see those.' Haddock stepped alongside him and took

one of the wine bottles from the rack. He examined the label. 'Chateau Vartely,' he murmured.

'Aye?'

'Moldovan, Tarvil. It's unusual; I only recognise it because somebody gave me a bottle for Christmas. It was at the Fettes party. I took it home and stuck it under the tree, but the label fell off, so I don't know who it was from.'

They searched the cupboards one by one, finding nothing other than tinned and packaged food, more crockery and utensils. They were about to move on when Haddock glanced at the washer dryer. 'He's forgotten to empty it,' he said, pulling the door open and removing the contents, in a bundle. He selected an item and held it up. 'Tommy Hilfiger shirt.' He tossed it back in the pile and chose another. 'Armani boxers. Wouldn't you . . . Eh?' He spotted two other garments and held them up, peering at the labels. 'Frilly knickers, black. One matching bra, thirty-eight C cup. I doubt that these were Griff's.'

'No, wrong size,' Singh growled.

'That and they're Marks and Spencer.'

'Do you reckon they're Alex Skinner's?'

The DI gazed at him, unsmiling. 'It won't be me that asks her,' he said. 'Come on, let's look in the bedrooms.'

They returned to the hall, where they saw four doors. Closest to the entrance was a cupboard that contained the heating boiler and other standard items, including an iron and board and a Dyson vacuum cleaner. *Top of the range*, Haddock noted mentally. They moved on to the bathroom, finding nothing in it other than two towels on a rail and soap in a dispenser.

The third door was secured by a circular Yale lock. 'I'll get Mr Francis back in,' the DS said.

'Let's check the bedroom first. I guess it must be Griff's.'

It was an en-suite, again with a river view. The wardrobes were fitted to make the most of limited space, and the bed was king size. It had a printed duvet, avoiding the need for a cover; its pattern was a version of the South African flag. Singh opened a pair of double wardrobe doors, looked in, and began to examine the contents. It contained ten shirts by Pink on hangers, four suits, two of them with the labels of a private tailor, three casual jackets, one of them in supple tan leather, four pairs of trousers, hung upside down, a white tuxedo and a heavy winter overcoat. Two further hangers and a trouser clip were unused, side by side on the rail. Beyond them were a pair of denims, ladies' size, and a grey midi dress.

'Our man Griff had a fair clothing budget.'

'That bears out what we found in his office locker,' Haddock confirmed. He took the denims from the rail and held them up. 'M and S again. You can forget them being Alex's. They're too short; she's at least five nine. We have to go over everything again, Tarvil. We need to find this woman, whoever she is.'

'Is there a bar code on those jeans? On the label?'

'Good call,' Haddock muttered, examining the garment. He found what he was looking for beneath the washing instructions, took a photograph and sent it to DC Jackie Wright, with a message. 'Check if we can establish from this where this garment was sold. If possible, see if we can link it to a card payment. I need to know the buyer; it'll be a woman.'

The next wardrobe contained open shelves, stacked with socks, boxers, neatly folded casual shirts, and a few female undergarments including nylon tights, still in their wrapping. 'She wasn't a live-in, whoever his woman was,' the DI murmured. 'Does the bathroom tell us anything?' he called out to Singh, who had moved into the en-suite.

'It tells us what the empty hangers in the wardrobe do,' the sergeant boomed, 'that he had left for a trip. There's no shaving gear, or deodorant, or aftershave. However,' he continued, lowering his voice as he re-joined his colleague, 'there's these.' He held up, between his gloved fingers, a pink toothbrush and a small black cylinder. 'There's no toothpaste, so I'm assuming that Griff took it, and his own toothbrush, and that this is hers. As is the lipstick. We might get prints off them.'

'We'll get prints off the whole fucking flat,' Haddock pointed out, 'and if she's on file we'll trace her, but good thinking nonetheless.'

'Not just a pretty face.'

'Not even. Let's check the last room.'

They summoned the locksmith; he was smiling. 'I told you that you'd need me again.'

'Can you get in?' the DI asked.

'It's my job,' he replied. 'If my customers lose their keys, and it happens, they come to me for replacements. You cannae just walk into a shop and have one done. This looks like any other Yale but it's not.' He stepped up to the door, selected a key from a ring and opened it. 'This is his office,' he announced.

The room was smaller than the others. The window had a Venetian blind but the slats were open far enough for them to see that it faced downriver, rather than overlooking it. There was a wall-mounted TV, a small sofa, and a Cyrus music system that Singh, an enthusiast, knew must have cost at least two thousand pounds, but the space was dominated by a fitted workstation, with the same facing as the bedroom units, that housed a twenty-seven-inch iMac.

Haddock touched the computer. 'We need to get into that.' He glanced at Mr Francis. 'I don't suppose you've got his password as well?'

'Naw, you're on your own there,' he paused, 'but you'll need to get into this too.' He stepped past the detectives and opened a door in the workstation, revealing a safe. 'I don't have the combination for this boy either . . . but you can get in with a key in an emergency, if you know where to find the keyhole.'

He knelt, awkwardly, because he was a bulky man, sorted through his keyring once again, then rolled the maker's name upwards, revealing a slot. 'You find the odd idiot who'll burn out a dozen drill bits trying to get into one of those things,' there was a click and the safe swung open, 'but this is all you have to do.' He pushed himself to his feet. 'I'll leave you to it again. Is that me done?' he asked.

'Yes,' the DI said, 'if you leave us the keys you used.'

'Mmm.' Doubt showed on his face. 'I don't know about that. Mr Montell won't be very pleased when he comes back. Does your warrant mean that I have to?'

'No, it doesn't, but that's irrelevant. Mr Montell won't be coming back, Mr Francis, because he's dead, but not a word of that outside this building, and not a word about what went on here. Understood?'

The locksmith nodded. 'Aye, no worries. I value the work I get from the police. Okay, you can have the keys.'

'That's good. Just one more thing before you go. When did you fit all this stuff?'

'Two years ago; this was a bedroom before. Gimme time and I can give you the date that I done it.'

'It must have cost a bit.'

'Oh yes.' He grinned. 'A fair few grand, with all the bits and installation. I shouldnae tell you this, ken, but I gave him a discount for cash. I'd still love to know what he did, but I don't suppose you're goin' tae tell me.'

'I can't do that, but thanks for your help. Enjoy the rest of your day.'

Mr Francis unwound three keys from his selection and left, closing the front door behind him.

As soon as he was gone, Haddock dropped to his knees in front of the safe and looked inside. It contained a thick brown envelope, a plastic food container, and on a shelf near the top, two watch boxes and a cloth bundle, all of which he removed. Branding on the boxes showed that one was a Rolex and the other a Breitling. The former was empty, but the latter contained a steel and gold timepiece with a jewel-encircled black face that weighed heavily in the DI's hand as he examined it. 'Breitling Galactic,' he read, from a booklet in the box. 'Not much change out of ten thousand for that, if any, I'll bet.'

Singh bent, picked up the bundle, and unwrapped it. 'Holy Moses,' he murmured. 'What the fuck is going on, Sauce?' The pistol looked small in his huge hand, but deadly nonetheless. 'This is a Beretta, fifteen-shot magazine, one of the most popular handguns in the world and one of the best. I know that because I did a firearms course a few years back, and this is what we used. What is a uniformed police officer in the West End doing with one of these?'

'Or this lot.'

The DI looked up at the sergeant from his kneeling position. Before him lay the brown envelope, ripped open to reveal two thick stacks of banknotes, and the food container, its lid removed, displaying stacks of coins, each one around an inch in diameter.

'What are those?' Singh asked.

'These are Krugerrands,' Haddock replied.

'Are they chocolate?'

'Not from the weight of the box; no, these are the real thing. Each one of these is worth around a thousand quid, maybe a shade more.' He sighed. 'You know, I was hoping that we'd be able to lock up here and go home to catch up on some of the sleep we've missed. No such fucking luck. I have to get the DCC down here, and somebody else too, somebody who's going to be kicking himself when he sees these.'

Eight

'Yes?'

The woman who opened the door had to be in her sixties, Skinner guessed, but she could have been his own age from the smoothness of her complexion. However, there was no doubting her hostility as she frowned at him, a frown that turned into a glare as she saw the police car in the courtyard of the converted steading.

'It's all right, Gran,' a much younger voice called out from behind her. 'It's my friend Seonaid's dad, Mr Skinner.'

'Ah.' Noele McClair's mother's posture eased, but only a little. 'Come in,' she said, grudgingly. 'Harry,' she called out to her grandson, 'back to the kitchen. You're not getting off with peeling the potatoes.'

He tried to place her accent; it was Glaswegian, but refined, Kelvinside, or possibly even more up market, Bearsden.

'Is Noele . . . ?' he ventured.

'She's in the living room. I told her to go to bed but she said she couldn't.'

'Has she told you why she was called out?'

Lines of pain appeared around Mrs McClair's eyes. 'Yes, she has. Harry doesn't know yet, so be careful. I'm fair blazing mad that my daughter was put through that; I hope you had nothing to do with it, or that young Haddock.'

'I didn't,' he assured her, 'and Sauce wasn't in a position to prevent it. For what it's worth I agree with you. It was a misjudgement by senior officers, albeit in a very stressful situation.'

'I hope you told them,' she said, firmly.

'I did, make no mistake. Not that I have any influence any longer.'

'That's not what I've heard.' She opened a door at the end of the hall. 'Dear, Mr Skinner's here. I think he just wants to make sure you're all right.'

'More than that,' he whispered. 'I think she's going to need you again after I've gone.' He moved past her quickly, into the living room.

Noele McClair stood as he entered, out of courtesy rather than deference. He waved a hand, signalling her to sit down again and joined her, taking an armchair beside a floor-to-ceiling picture window. 'How are you doing?' he asked. 'Has it sunk in yet?'

'I don't really think so,' she sighed. 'Maybe it will after I've done the formal identification. We'll see. At the moment my main worry is how to tell Harry. He worships his father. He's only seven, Bob, it'll crush him.'

'It won't. My Alex went through the same thing, and she came out all right. You'll need to keep him close for a while, now and when the people who killed Terry are brought to court. If Sarah and I can help in any way, you only have to ask, no notice required.'

She smiled at him, her eyes filled with tears. 'Look at me,' she croaked, with a strange stifled laugh. 'I'd washed my hands of the bugger. We were divorced, and I was over him.

Or I thought I was; now here I am unable to stop crying.'

For a second or two, he found himself wanting to get out of there, to leave her with her grief without piling on even more. But he was held in place by the thought of how she would react if she heard the further news through the media, or even in casual conversation with a CID colleague.

'You don't have to do the formal identification,' he pointed out. 'You're not his next of kin any longer; Harry is, although obviously he's too young. Are Terry's parents still alive? Does he have siblings?'

'His dad died when he was young. His mother remarried and moved to Norway. I have no idea how to contact her. There's a sister though, Beatrix. She lives in Paisley. But she's flaky. She's bipolar and on medication. I don't think she'd be up to doing that. No, Bob. I'll do it. She doesn't have support, but I do, of a kind. I haven't mentioned this to anyone, anyone at all, not even my mum, but I'm in a relationship.'

'I know,' Skinner said softly.

She blinked the tears away and stared at him. 'You do? How would you?'

'My daughter told me.'

'Seonaid? But she could only have heard from Harry, and I haven't let anything slip to him because I'm not sure how he'll take it.'

'You misunderstand me. My oldest daughter: Alex. She had a drink with Griff Montell just before Christmas; he let it slip then. I'm sure he didn't mean to, but Alex is a defence advocate, and she's very good at cross-examination.'

He felt the moment approaching. He was full of trepidation, unsure how to go on, until finally his expression betrayed him.

'There's something else, isn't there,' she said. 'Something I don't know. Something that made you come here rather than phoning me.'

Still he prevaricated. 'Did Terry know about Griff?' he asked her. 'Did you tell him?'

'Hell no!' she exclaimed. 'Why would I do that? He never told me when he was shagging that air hostess. He was out of my life. Look, Bob, between you and me, the first thing I did when the divorce went through was join an online dating site and get it all out of my system. Not for long though; having sex with strangers isn't my thing. Griff's different, though. He's nice, he's funny and I like him. So must you; after all he protected Alex from those intruders, and got himself cut in the process.'

'Yes, he did.'

'I wish he was here now,' she sighed, 'but he's gone to South Africa for a couple of weeks, to visit his sister, and his kids.'

'No.'

She stared at him, finally clear-eyed.

'What do you mean, no? He left at the weekend.'

Skinner stood abruptly. He walked out of the living room, and through to the kitchen. 'Mrs McClair,' he said, 'I need you through here. But not Harry.'

She followed him without a word. When they returned Noele was on her feet. 'Bob, what's up? Why are you really here? And why are you asking about Griff? Are you going to tell me he shot Terry?'

'Please,' he said, 'sit down again. Noele, I'm here because there were two bodies in the car you saw this morning.' He faltered for a second or two, as his own emotions threatened to overcome him, but he carried on, albeit with a slight tremble in his voice. 'The other one was that of Griff Montell.'

For a second or two Noele McClair lost control of her bladder. She fell against her mother who eased her on to the sofa, with the good sense to remain silent. She stared up at Skinner, yet through him as if he was not there.

'That's not true,' she protested, finally. 'You're mistaken. It was somebody else. Griff's in South Africa, I tell you.'

'Believe me,' he told her with utter sincerity, 'I wish that he was. I've known him for longer than you have, and I will never be able to describe to you or anyone else what it felt like to look into that car.'

'No, but I think I can imagine. Bob . . .' She fell silent, words beyond her.

'I'm going to leave you now, Noele. Your mother will look after you, but if you want to talk to me later, I'm only a phone call away. In fact, if you need me to come back I'll do that. For now, if you would like a sedative, or sleeping tablets, I can arrange for a police surgeon to issue a prescription and have them delivered to the door. Say the word.'

'Why not, dear?' her mother said. 'It sounds like a good idea.'

'Thanks,' she replied, 'but no. I need to keep a clear head for Harry. He's got to be told before this becomes public knowledge, and that could be today.' She looked up at Skinner. 'You could do one thing for me, though; take him home with you, tell him he's to have lunch with Seonaid; Mum or I will pick him up this afternoon. I need to get cleaned up and get my act together in general. When he comes back, I'll be ready to tell him about his dad.'

'I'll do that with pleasure,' he told her. 'He can even have a hurl up the road in a police car. Wee boys love that.'

She gave him a watery smile. 'I don't think I want to be in

one, ever again. That's me finished with the job. There's one thing I know for certain; I will never be able again to walk into a violent crime scene without being taken back to this morning.'

'I can understand that,' he agreed. 'But don't be in a rush to hand your warrant card in. You're best out of CID, sure, but I'm sure that the chief can arrange a transfer to a quiet posting in uniform. Let me talk to her, please. We both know she owes you one, and I won't be slow to tell her.'

'Okay, but don't commit me to staying.'

'Fine. Now, Mrs McClair, would you like to round up Harry and meet me outside.'

He was waiting by the police car, on the point of calling Sarah to tell her that there would be one more for lunch, when his ringtone sounded. 'Sauce,' he barked as he took the call, 'what is it now?'

'Gaffer, can you come back into town? There's something I need you to see.'

'Eh? No fucking chance. If it's urgent give me a WhatsApp video call and show me. Quick about it, though. I have a lunch guest to take home.'

Nine

'What did he say when he saw them on his phone?' Mario McGuire asked. He was standing in the kitchen of Griff Montell's home, while crime scene technicians worked in the other rooms.

'It wasn't repeatable, not with the SOCOs here,' Sauce Haddock replied. 'It was along the lines of him cursing himself long and loud for not taking Terry Coats' story about the Krugerrand smuggling seriously, and not following it up with Montell after Coats mentioned his name as the pal who'd told him about the South African bullion robbery. He reckons that if he'd done that, or taken it to you, the whole thing would have been uncovered then and Coats and Griff would still be alive.'

'Maybe so, maybe not,' the DCC growled. 'Has it occurred to him that if he had followed it up with Montell, he might have been the one dumped in the back of a car? No,' he added quickly, 'don't answer that. It's a stupid question; he thinks he's bulletproof, even though he has a scar on his leg as evidence to the contrary.'

'I've never heard about that.'

'You wouldn't. Secret squirrel stuff; I got shot on the same operation myself, worse than him, but not at the same time.'

'And they say this job isn't dangerous.'

'It isn't, for nearly all of us,' the DCC said. 'There's just the odd one that keeps on looking for it, or the unlucky ones like Stevie Steele. Did Bob say anything else, other than the self-recrimination?'

Haddock nodded. 'Yes, he said we should check with the National Lottery. He said it's possible to buy Krugerrands on the bullion market, and he suggested that's the sort of thing a rich South African might do. He told me that I should check all possible sources of Griff's obvious wealth, before assuming he was bent.' He grinned. 'I said I didn't need telling that.'

'How many coins were in the box?'

'I didn't empty it out, but looking at the number in one stack, I reckon there are at least two hundred and fifty.'

'Fuck me! That's a quarter of a million in folding money. How much cash was in the envelope?'

'Eighty-eight thousand and a few hundred; all in used notes.'

'Lottery win, my arse. Go ahead and check it like Bob said, but I can tell you now that Inspector Montell did not win the jackpot. I'm equally certain that he didn't have a rich uncle who snuffed it and left him loaded. We need to set you up with an interview with his twin sister. I'll arrange that through Mary Chambers when I manage to speak to her. Her mobile's going to voice mail. Alex Skinner needs to be interviewed as well,' McGuire added. 'Gently, mind, but we need to ask her to recall everything that he's ever said to her. It might have a relevance that wasn't apparent at the time.'

'Agreed, sir,' the DI acknowledged. 'I'll ask DCI Mann if she'll take that on. They know each other. Alex acted for Lottie in a custody hearing a while back, when her husband tried to take her kid from her.'

'I remember that one; he was another bent cop. Jesus, Sauce, I tell you I'm going to go through this force like an industrial strength laxative. We can't keep having surprises like this.'

I'm going to, Haddock thought, *not the chief constable*. He filed the remark in his memory bank as he continued. 'There's someone else who needs to be interviewed, boss; one that I am definitely going to do myself. Noele McClair.' He explained Skinner's discovery that she and Montell had been in a relationship. 'The clothing Tarvil and I found here, the personal effects: they're hers.'

'Oh my God,' McGuire exclaimed. 'How many fucking worms are in this can? Sauce, sorry but you will not interview her, you're too close. You take Alex, and have Mann and Cotter interview Noele. You know her, they don't. They shouldn't do it at her place either. They need to bring her into Fettes and do it in formal surroundings.'

'If you say so sir, but why? This is Noele, we don't need to play her by the book surely. She's a victim by association.'

'Maybe, but she's also a person of interest, until I decide that she's not. From what you're saying, she's been here, she shared Griff's bed, she hung her dress in his wardrobe beside his designer gear. Has she ever been in his office? Did she know about the stash of gold and the cash? Most of all, did she know about that firearm you found? Take nothing for granted, Inspector, nothing at all.' He stopped abruptly, then grinned, self-consciously. 'Listen to me!' he exclaimed. 'I'm sorry, Sauce. I know you don't make assumptions as a rule, and I can't really fault you for doing that with your DS. I'm as shocked by this thing as everybody else, but it's no excuse for me to patronise one of my best detective officers.'

The DI shrugged. 'No worries, sir; you were right. I can't be blinkered. I'll do what you say.'

'What about the pistol?' the DCC asked.

'I've spoken to Arthur Dorward about that,' Haddock said. 'They'll test fire it and run a comparison through the database to see if it's been used in any crimes. I suppose there's a chance that Griff had a firearms certificate, and I'll check that out, but something tells me I won't get a result. That'll raise another question. Where did he get it? All the weapons in the police armoury are checked in and out; I can't believe it would be one of ours, although from what Tarvil said, I know that we do have that weapon in our stock.'

'It could have been handed in during an amnesty. The last one was only a couple of years ago. It's not impossible for an officer to have trousered a gun when nobody was looking and made the paperwork disappear.'

'Not impossible, sir, but trousering a box of ammunition as well might have been more difficult. I found one in the safe; it wasn't full. Neither was the magazine in the pistol. It holds fifteen rounds but there were only thirteen there. That worries me.'

'Me too, but could it have been target practice?' McGuire suggested.

'I thought about that, but . . . if that's what he was doing would he take only two shots?'

'Good point. Let's see what the database tells us. Meantime, is there anything else you can tell me? We've given the media the holding statement we agreed, but we need to go back to them before the day's out. I'm thinking five o'clock. When I saw "we" I mean me. Assuming that I've contacted Spring Montell by then, I intend to announce the names.'

Haddock nodded. 'Do you want me there?'

'The point of me doing it is to shield you; if you feel strongly you should be there that's up to you, but if you are, you'll have to field questions. It wouldn't look good for the SIO to be hiding behind me. And if you don't have any answers . . . well, that wouldn't look good either.'

'I don't at this moment,' the younger man admitted, 'and unless somebody walks in and confesses, I won't have any this evening either. As you know, I have Jackie Wright looking at all available traffic CCTV. She checked in just before you arrived. So far, she has Coats' car first appearing at the Western Corner at twelve twenty-one, and she can track it all the way from there to the police station. The second car, the Renault Megane, was following close behind; it got caught by a red light at Palmerston Place. The driver actually stopped, believe it or not, and whoever was in Coats' car waited up for him. It was safe enough, for there wasn't a soul on the street, and not another vehicle to be seen. After the drop, the pick-up car went through Haymarket, turned into Coates Gardens and after that went completely off the radar. The driver was either lucky or they'd done a very thorough recce before doing it for real. It could be anywhere now.' The DI sighed. 'You know what? I have a wild theory that right now it's parked in the place its owner left it, with its original plates back on, and he or she is none the wiser. It's the perfect day of the year to do that. Steal a car after ten on Hogmanay in a quiet street, and there's a better-than-even chance it's not going to be noticed, far less reported, until the owner surfaces next lunchtime. I got Jackie to check for any Renault Megane reported stolen this morning in Edinburgh, the Lothians and Fife. So far there hasn't been a single one and I'm betting there won't be. We need to find that car, for the

DNA that'll be inside it; barring a lucky break, the only way we can do that is by finding every Megane in the city and beyond. And that's going to be a fucking nightmare, because that's one of the most popular models in Britain. There'll be hundreds of them that are driven by locals, but are leased, with registration documents that show the name of the legal owner. It's impossible, sir. Yes, it's best if I'm not at the press conference. It's a Ronan Keating situation: best say nothing at all.'

McGuire nodded. 'I agree with that. There's one flaw in your thinking, though, Sauce. If you're going to steal a car for a job, why bother to change the registration plates? I reckon that any time now we'll have a sales rep calling the one-one-one number to complain that his have been nicked. And that means . . .'

'That they used their own car for the job,' Haddock moaned. 'I really am knackered. I should have worked that out by myself.'

'We're all knackered,' the DCC said. 'Don't worry about it. But it does mean that, unless by some miracle you find the theft or the disposal of the plates on a street camera somewhere, you are indeed going to be checking the ownership of every bloody Megane in the country.'

Ten

Sarah and Seonaid were waiting in the doorway when the police car dropped its passengers in the driveway. Skinner had made his warning call, without explaining the reason for Harry's visit. As his daughter took her friend off to the play room, he led his wife into the kitchen and talked her through his stressful night and morning.

'Oh my,' she gasped. 'Poor Noele. That's the whammiest double I've ever heard of. Her ex and her boyfriend in the same hit. She has to be the link; she has to be.'

'I don't see that,' her husband said. 'As far as I can see, nobody knew about her new relationship, other than Alex, not even her mum. Terry didn't, at least not from her. What passed between him and Griff Montell we may never know. How they came to die together, we may never know. Anyone ruthless enough to execute a serving police officer, and an ex-cop, is going to be thorough as well when it comes to covering their tracks.'

'Emily bloody Badger,' Sarah hissed. 'She's the rawest of the raw, only on call because I decided that nothing serious ever happens on Hogmanay in Edinburgh because everybody's too busy having fun or having their pockets picked. She gets pulled in on the most significant double homicide in the city in living memory and it doesn't occur to her to call her boss. I have to get in on this, Bob. I have to take over the autopsies. Emily's fine technically, but she's nowhere near ready to be an expert witness in a High Court trial. It's your turn to look after the kids. I have to get into the city.'

Bob nodded. 'I get that, but are you fit? You had a few drinks last night and very little sleep afterwards. It's more important that these post-mortems are done correctly than that they're done today. Sauce is the SIO, you should talk to him and agree a timetable.'

'Okay,' she agreed. 'I'll do that . . . once I've filleted Dr Badger for not putting me in the picture.'

'Maybe you should pause on that one,' Bob suggested. 'Call the mortuary and instruct them that nothing should be done until you get there. That's all you need to do for now. When you put Badger right it would be better in sorrow than in anger.' He surprised himself by yawning. 'Look at me,' he said. 'I need sleep even more than you do. Let's feed the kids, and ourselves, then we can take turns for a siesta.'

'Sounds like a plan, but first . . . you might want to speak with Ignacio . . . although he and Pilar have crashed as well, in his apartment.'

'What's his problem? He hasn't got her pregnant, has he? I'm not ready to be a grandpa, not with two kids at primary school and one at playgroup.'

'I hope not,' she said, severely, 'given the state she was in when they got back this morning! The problem does involve a grandpa, though. Ignacio's mother called him in a panic while I was holding Pilar's head over the toilet bowl. Her husband did a disappearing act in the middle of the night. But after the time you've had, you don't need to be getting involved with that. I expect he'll have sobered up and come home by now.'

Bob frowned. 'Two things wrong with that picture,' he observed. 'One, Cameron McCullough doesn't drink much. I've seen him in his hotel; there's always a glass in front of him but it's rarely empty. Two, Mia doesn't panic; she's a Watson. It's not in her genes. You look after the kids, get them fed. I'd better call her.' He checked his watch; it showed twelve thirty-five. 'Fuck, I've missed the Loony Dook too!'

'Mark and James Andrew didn't. Jazz insisted on going and shamed his brother into going with him. Don't worry, I made them both wear their wet suits. You go do what you have to do. I'll phone the mortuary, check with Haddock and then get lunch underway.'

Skinner moved into the garden room, phone in hand. As he looked out across the Bents, he saw two black-clad figures running up the slope towards the house. Part of him was guilty about not being with them, but his sensible side admitted to relief. Sea swimming on the first of January was pure bravado, he acknowledged, and nothing else.

He went to Mia McCullough's mobile number in his directory. As his thumb hovered over the screen, his mind went back to the time they had met, he a newly promoted detective superintendent, she a daytime presenter on a popular Edinburgh local radio station, not Mia Watson but Mia Sparkles, with a devoted following of early teenagers, of whom his daughter Alex had been one. She was the last surviving sibling of a trio, born into a brutal criminal family; he had visited her at the radio station while investigating the killing of her brother and there had been unavoidable chemistry. Their relationship had been entirely unprofessional on his part; it had also been brief, one night, but long enough to produce Ignacio. She had been pregnant, unknowingly, when she left town in a hurry, disappearing from the potentially fatal repercussions of an act of treachery, and had brought up their son in Spain without ever considering telling his father of his existence, until it was in her interests to do so, and until the boy was in the kind of trouble from which not even Skinner could extricate him unscathed. Mia had settled back in Scotland and had gone back to her old occupation, radio, landing a job on a Dundee station owned by the city's wealthiest man, Cameron 'Grandpa' McCullough. He had his own colourful story, which included an acquittal on murder and drugs charges after the mysterious disappearance of the principal Crown witness, and the narcotics in question. He had laughed out loud when he had been told of their marriage. There had been an inevitability about the events of Mia's life and so it had been entirely predictable. And yet it had been successful; Cameron and Mia McCullough were an undoubtedly devoted couple and Skinner's misgivings about his son's new stepfather had been overcome.

He hit the WhatsApp call button and waited. She answered within ten seconds, taking him by surprise by switching the call to video. Her hair was wrapped in a towel, and she wore no make-up, but she was as striking as ever. He saw the tension in her eyes, the tightness of her mouth, and knew from those signs that the crisis, whatever it was, had not been resolved.

'Grandpa's gone AWOL, I'm told,' he began.

'Completely off the fucking grid,' she exclaimed. 'His phone's off; the cars are all still there. I've had hotel staff search the whole estate but there's no sign of him, neither hide nor hair. I don't know what to do.'

'Have you called the police?'

'No, not yet. If I reported him missing, I wouldn't trust that lot not to leak it. You know how much they love him,' she added, her voice heavy with irony. 'He's a man in his sixties, fit and well, with no worries. What are they going to do? Laugh up their sleeves, probably, but otherwise nothing.'

'They'd have to take it seriously, Mia,' he assured her. 'Do you want me to make the call?'

'No way. It would leak to the *Sun* for sure. I'm taking a chance that it won't leak to the *Saltire*, by talking to you.'

'I wouldn't do that,' he said. 'Besides, it isn't a news story. How can I help?'

'To be honest I don't know.' The lines around her eyes deepened. For a moment, to his surprise, he thought she would cry. 'Bob, the best I can hope for is that the phone rings and I get a ransom demand. The worst I can hope for . . .'

'No, no, no, Mia. You're getting way ahead of yourself. Kidnapping for ransom is very rare in this country; if that's what this is, it would be even more unusual. If I was looking to extort money from Cameron, I'd be kidnapping you, not him. It would be much easier and much less of a physical risk.' He paused. 'That said, we need to look to your security. What arrangements does the hotel have?'

'It's well protected. There are cameras in all the corridors, the rooms are secure and we have a janitor who used to be in the Parachute Regiment.'

'Right. If Cameron doesn't come walking in later on today smelling of cheap perfume and claiming to have no memory of the previous twelve hours, I want you to move in there. Let's give it twenty-four hours. If I'm wrong and it is a kidnap, you should have had contact by then. If not, I will come up with my apprentice and take a look at the scene.'

'Your apprentice?' she repeated.

'Our son. That's always assuming I can peel him off his girlfriend by then.'

'Girlfriend? What girlfriend? He never told me he has a girlfriend.'

He laughed. 'When a young man begins to have regular sex, the last person he's going to discuss it with is his mother.'

On his screen, he saw her nostrils flare. 'If that's the case,' she exclaimed, 'I hope he's a fucking sight more careful than you were!'

Eleven

'This place is a tip,' Tarvil Singh observed. 'I've seen tidier scrapyards.'

'I doubt that he was expecting visitors,' Sauce Haddock said. 'When I lived on my own, I let things slide from time to time.'

The sergeant picked up an empty food container, held it to his nose and sniffed. 'Lamb Balti,' he guessed. 'Letting things slide is one thing; this is more like an avalanche. I don't know how Noele put up with this guy for as long as she did. Griff must have been a culture shock. Did Coats own the place?'

'Yes, he bought it after the divorce from Noele was finalised. The SOCOs got the address from his employer, and the key from them too. There was a spare in his office at the airport.' Terry Coats' home was a small semi-detached villa in Corstorphine, to the west of the city, convenient for his place of employment. Haddock guessed that it was around a hundred years old.

'The SOCOs are done here already? That must be a record for Dorward's crew. He usually makes them do everything twice. They might have cleaned up for us.'

'All they really had to do was establish that this wasn't the crime scene,' the DI pointed out. 'The place is tiny, and they aren't as fastidious as you.' The living room was no more than fifteen feet square and the furniture was minimal; two armchairs, a gateleg table, a small sideboard and a television on a stand. Haddock looked around the debris. 'There's nothing personal at all, apart from that one photo of his wee boy on the sideboard. This is sad, Tarvil, when you think about it. We're looking at the life of a forty-one-year-old man, and this is all there is?'

'What's even sadder,' Singh retorted, his size compressing the room still further, 'is that he doesn't even have a toilet brush. Have you been in that bathroom? Holy Moses, what a mess. And the bedrooms! One thing's for certain, if he was still shagging that cabin-crew woman you caught him with, he wasn't bringing her here.'

'Nonetheless,' the DI insisted, 'we will still search the place. The SOCOs might have been over it, but they weren't looking for the same things as us. Again, we want to find anything that links him and Montell, or anything else that we don't know about that might point us at whoever killed the two of them. Of course . . .' His voice tailed off, the sentence unfinished, his forehead narrowing.

'What?'

'It's just . . . Tarvil, I'm thinking, we've been assuming that Montell and Coats were acting together in this enterprise, whatever it was. But what if they weren't? Griff's lifestyle showed unexplained wealth, but this is the home of a man with barely a pot to piss in. I assume that the split from Noele left him with hefty child support to pay; he seems to have been struggling, rather than raking it in.'

'Aye, so?'

'Well, we know that Griff was booked on a flight from

Edinburgh to Johannesburg via London on Saturday evening. We know that he checked in for it, but he never boarded the flight. Coats worked at Edinburgh Airport. Could he have intercepted Griff when he arrived there? Might they have been rivals in some way rather than partners? Do something for me, while I go through this place. Get in touch with British Airways and find out whether there's an unclaimed suitcase lying in Jo'burg off that connecting Heathrow flight.'

'Technically a bag isn't meant to fly without its owner,' Singh said.

'Mistakes happen. Do it anyway.'

Haddock began to search the little house, examining everything, looking under cushions, shaking every discarded magazine in case something had been stuck between the pages. He found nothing out of the ordinary other than a Ninjago magazine that he guessed Harry had left on a visit. He moved to the sideboard. It revealed a twenty-four-piece dinner set, a bottle of Famous Grouse, three-quarters empty, a miniature chess set and two crystal glasses. Their weight told him that they were quality pieces. He moved upstairs. The bathroom was untidy, but clean, apart from the toilet. The suite might have been an original fitting; it was a pale green colour that made Haddock wince. There were two bath towels on a rail, and a hand towel on a ring beside the basin. The shower was a hose-type attachment over the bath, contained by a plastic curtain. Coats appeared to have been a blade shaver; a Gillette disposable stood in a glass, on a shelf above the basin with a brush beside it. Haddock touched it and felt residual dampness. He winced at the thought that the man who had used it was in a refrigerated drawer in the City Mortuary. Leaving the bathroom, he went into the second bedroom. It showed no signs of use; indeed, with its smoothed and folded bedspread, it was the neatest room in the house. He wondered if Harry Coats had been allowed to stay overnight with his father on his court-approved visits. The main bedroom was a complete contrast. Discarded clothes were piled in a corner. Rather than look through them he kicked them, then shuffled them apart with his right foot to satisfy himself they were concealing nothing. There were two bedside tables but only one reading lamp, with a USB socket in its base, into which a mobile phone cable was plugged. The place smelled ripe; he pulled the drawn curtains apart and threw open the window, letting in the crisp winter air to flush out the muskiness. He opened the wardrobe and again was struck by the contrast between Coats and Montell. There was one suit . . . he checked the label; 'Slater', he murmured . . . two pairs of trousers, one of jeans, a shiny leather jerkin and a sports jacket. The shirts looked over-laundered, the underwear in two boxes was a mix, some of it with BHS labels. On the floor were a pair of New Balance trainers, three pairs of shoes, and leaning against the back wall, a laptop, a Dell Inspiron that Haddock judged to be the newest and most expensive item in the apartment. He reached in to pick it up, wrinkling his nose against the odour of stale clothing. He was familiar with the keyboard layout, owning a similar model himself.

'What's that?' Singh asked from the doorway as he switched it on.

He turned to face him, displaying it. 'Computer. Did you get through to anyone?'

'All the way. There is an unclaimed case in Johannesburg; it came off last Sunday's Heathrow flight and the barcode says it was routed all the way through from Edinburgh.'

The DI smiled. 'Progress. It needn't mean a hell of a lot, of course. Griff may have checked it in to lay a false trail, but it tells us that he was at the airport, and it gives us a shot at picking him up on camera.'

'Do you want me to check that?'

'Yes, but not right away. Go and knock some neighbours' doors first and see if you can establish when Coats was last here. Even if nobody saw him, find out when his car was seen last. While you do that, I'll check in with the DCC. He'll want to know everything there is to know before he sees the press at five.'

Twelve

Mario McGuire looked out across a space that had been the gym of the Edinburgh police service before it was superseded by unification. He had expected a smaller turnout, during what was a two-day public holiday, but there were a dozen recording devices and four microphones on the desk behind which he sat and at the back of the room five TV cameras on stands. One of the latter belonged to his own media department, an innovation by Peregrine Allsop, the director, that Sir Andrew Martin, the former chief constable, had approved without consulting his senior colleagues. Its purpose, McGuire believed, was to strengthen the control of Allsop's department over police communications by allowing him to highlight officers' failings. The director was in the DCC's sights, but Maggie Steele had been reluctant to face the flak that his removal might provoke. He had no such qualms.

The press officer, a small dark-haired woman seated on McGuire's left, leaned towards him. 'I'll introduce you,' she whispered. She made to rise but he put a hand on her arm.

'It is all right, Ms Balfour,' he told her. 'I know every reporter in this room. I don't think we need that.'

'The Director says . . .' she began, but by that time he was on his feet.

'Good evening, ladies and gentlemen,' he began, projecting his voice as the buzz of conversation died away. 'Thank you for coming. You'll be aware by now, I think, of an incident earlier today in the centre of Edinburgh. It's with regret that I tell you now, that not long after twelve thirty this morning, a car was abandoned outside the West End police station in Torphichen Place, at Haymarket. Its driver was taken from the scene by another car. On examination, the bodies of two men were found in the back seat of the vehicle; each had been shot in the head. They have been identified formally and next of kin have been informed, so I can tell you that the deceased were Mr Terry Coats, aged forty-one, formerly a detective inspector with the now defunct Strathclyde Police, latterly employed in the security department of Edinburgh Airport, and Inspector Griffin Montell, aged thirty-nine, a serving police officer stationed at the West End office. Enquiries into their murders have begun, under the direction of acting Detective Chief Inspector Harold Haddock, the senior investigating officer. He has nothing to report at this stage, which is why he's not here, so any questions you can fire at me. I just want to say that DCI Haddock and I, and many of the investigating team, knew Griff Montell as a friend and colleague and are shocked by his death, but I promise you that our enquiries will be conducted dispassionately and efficiently.' He paused, looking around the room as voices were raised in competition for the first question, then pointed to a man in the front row. 'Jim.'

The chosen reporter leaned forward. 'Jim Finney, Sky News. DCC McGuire, obviously you knew Inspector Montell, but did you also know Mr Coats personally?'

'No, I didn't, because I wasn't Strathclyde myself, so our paths didn't cross, but I can tell you that he was the former husband of one of our serving officers, Detective Sergeant Noele McClair. She's part of the Serious Crimes Unit based in Edinburgh, in this building. Obviously she's been recused from this investigation.'

'Can we talk to her?' a BBC reporter seated close to Finney asked.

'That will be up to her, Lisa. I'll consult with her and see how she feels about that. However, she has a child, yes, Mr Coats' son, and he has to be protected. What I do not want to happen is for her to be door-stepped, mob-handed, or even approached at her home by individuals.' He gazed around the room. 'Should that happen, and I am happy to say this on camera, there will be hell to pay. I want her and her wee boy left alone. What I will do is ask her if she's prepared to issue a statement. If she is, it'll come through Ms Balfour here, our press officer.'

'You said "former husband",' Jim Finney said. 'They were divorced, yes?'

McGuire nodded. 'Yes, last year.'

'Were they on good terms?'

'I have no idea, but I don't regard that as having any relevance to this investigation. Do you hear me, Jim?'

'Loud and clear . . . not that you're saying anything.'

'Can I ask, Mr McGuire,' a sharp voice interrupted, 'what these two men were doing in the same car?'

The deputy chief constable managed to keep his feelings from showing on his face. Jack Darke, the crime correspondent of the *Saltire*, would not have made a list of his hundred favourite journalists. 'That's one of the first questions that DCI

Haddock's team is trying to answer,' he replied. 'When we know that, we might come closer to knowing who put them there.'

'Do you have any lines of enquiry at all?'

'Several, Jack, and as always we're going to keep them to ourselves until it's in the public interest to share them.'

'Did Coats and Montell ever work together? Montell was a detective sergeant before he was promoted into uniform.'

'They never served on the same force,' the DCC said.

'That doesn't answer my question,' Darke shot back.

McGuire shrugged. 'As far as I'm concerned it does.'

'Why did Coats leave the police?'

'He chose to. My understanding is that he was offered a uniformed posting that he didn't like, and that was behind his decision.'

'It had nothing to do with him being bent?'

There was a collective intake of breath. All eyes in the room fastened on the *Saltire* journalist, and then on the DCC, as if expecting a volcanic eruption.

None came. Instead McGuire nodded and said, quietly, 'Mr Darke, I'm not going to respond to that, because I know you're trying to provoke me into throwing you out of this briefing. But I know also that your knowledge of police matters is encyclopaedic, and that there's an underlying reason for your question. So why don't you enlighten us, or are you going to keep it for a front-page exclusive?'

The reporter leaned back in his chair and pocketed his recorder. 'I might just do that, Mario.'

'That's your right,' the Deputy Chief Constable agreed. 'Mind you,' he added, 'it's mine to offer a little background information to everyone here. The dead can't sue but there are things a kid might not want to read about his dad when he grows up.' His gaze swept across his audience. 'It's not correct, ladies and gentlemen, to say or imply that Mr Coats was corrupt. However, he was accused by a website called Brass Rubbings of having protected from prosecution a valuable source of criminal intelligence. He did that, yes, but it's in no way unique. Sometimes good detectives have to compromise when it comes to intelligence-gathering; they might decide to let a small fish stay in the water to catch a big one. In this case, unfortunately, the website named the informant, and he was found dead shortly afterwards. That was the background to Terry Coats being moved out of CID, and to his decision to resign. I tell you all this in clarification. It's a matter of public record, so feel free, all of you. With that, I'm drawing this to a close. You'll be briefed when we have something positive to tell you, until then Ms Balfour here is your contact for questions.'

'You're a big Irish-Italian bastard, McGuire,' Darke hissed after him as he left.

He stopped, turned, and looked back. 'Aye,' he said. 'And don't you forget it.'

Jane Balfour followed him through the door behind the desk. 'That was nicely done, sir,' she said when they were out of earshot of the journalists. 'That was the *Saltire* man, wasn't it? I haven't had much to do with him, but when I have he's always aggressive.'

'If he gets too bad, let me know. His boss is a friend.'

'June Crampsey, the editor?'

'No, her boss. I agree with you about Darke, but there are guys like him in every walk of life. June Crampsey knows him well enough, but she also knows that he's a good reporter with contacts everywhere. He gets more exclusives than anyone else in that room we've just left.'

'Contacts within the force?'

'Of course; the force, the courts, the prison service, the legal profession. I know of a few of them.'

'Couldn't you shut them down?' the press officer asked.

'I could, but I don't want to. It suits me to have a back channel to Jack. If there's information I want to get to him and I do it through you, he'll be suspicious. If I feed it through a trusted source, it's accepted.'

'Does he pay his informants?'

'Not cops. I don't know about the rest but not our people. That I would shut down if I heard about it . . . and I would hear about it.'

Jane Balfour smiled. 'I think I can learn from you, sir.'

'Feel free,' he said. 'But don't call me "sir". You're not a cop. Mr McGuire will do for now; when you get to know me better you can call me Mario, but not in front of the troops.'

'And you can call me Jane, in front of anyone you like.'

'Fine. Is there anything you need to know or want to ask me? I need to brief a couple of people.'

'I didn't know that Mr Haddock was an acting DCI. Do you want me to issue a press release?'

'No need. I've just told the media. Sauce doesn't know himself yet. I did that on the hoof, so to speak. I'm bringing someone of that rank on to the team, and it occurred to me that I should make clear his authority as SIO. He'll be acting in the rank for as long as Sammy Pye is off, but realistically until he's retired on medical grounds. Once that happens, we'll see about permanency. This hasn't been shared with your department, but Sammy's diagnosis precludes recovery.

It's a matter of how quickly the disease progresses and that's uncertain.'

'I don't know Mr Pye, I'm afraid.'

'That's a pity. A lot of us go back all the way with Sammy. He's a big loss.'

'Pardon me for asking,' Balfour ventured, 'but does DCI Haddock's temporary promotion need to be approved by the chief constable?'

'Yes, but I'll tell her. I'm the Head of CID, as well as her designated deputy. You haven't met her yet, have you?'

'No.' She smiled. 'Mr Allsop doesn't encourage other ranks to mix with the higher-ups. I'm only here because he's away.'

'Don't be so sure of that. My view, which I think you'll find carries more weight than Mr Allsop's, is that you're the person on the ground in this part of Scotland. When you speak, it's not on Perry Allsop's behalf, but on the chief constable's, so the two of you should meet. I'll try to make that happen, Jane, as soon as I can. Meanwhile, my door's always open to you.' He frowned. 'Thanks for your help in there. Now I really must go.'

He made his way back into the main building, and through to the Serious Crimes office suite. The room was crowded. He looked around for newcomers. One of them was easy to find. Detective Chief Inspector Charlotte Mann was a large and formidable woman who had made her reputation in the hard school of Glasgow CID. In her early days as an officer she had been entered into a boxing tournament at a police smoker against a male opponent and had despatched him in less than a minute. In contrast her colleague, DS John Cotter, was at least four inches shorter and more lightly built. Tyneside born, he had chosen to serve in Scotland and had been picked out as someone with prospects, placed with Mann after her mentor, the legendary Detective Sergeant Dan Provan had retired to a life of happy domesticity . . . with her.

'Lottie,' McGuire exclaimed. 'Thanks for answering the call. You too, John.'

She gazed back at him, her right eyebrow slightly raised. 'I wasn't aware it was optional, sir. But I'd have been here regardless,' she added. 'I knew Terry Coats in the Strathclyde days. Conceited arsehole, but a good detective. He didn't deserve what happened to him, then or now. Once a cop always a cop as far as I'm concerned.'

'Did you ever meet Montell?'

'No. He transferred into your old force from overseas, didn't he? That made him very much Edinburgh. I did hear about him, though, getting cut defending Sir Bob's daughter. How's she taking it?'

'How would you expect? They were close; never a couple, but close.'

'And Coats's wife? How's she? I met her, after Terry had jumped ship from Strathclyde, not long after she made CID. I thought she might have brought him under control, but apparently not.'

'Controlled him in what way?' Cotter asked.

'Women,' Mann replied. 'Terry would have shagged anything with a pulse; and maybe without, if there was nothing else available. He knocked Noele up when she was a plonk. He did the decent thing, marrying her . . . at least that's what we all thought at first. Well, maybe not all of us,' she reflected. 'Dan reckoned that he only did it because her father, Bert McClair, was a South Lanarkshire councillor, and served on the Strathclyde police committee. Right or not, nothing changed with Terry; it didn't surprise me at all when Sauce and Sir Bob caught him in the act. Speaking of Sauce,' she exclaimed, looking past McGuire towards the door.

Haddock swept into the room, his coat over his shoulder and a laptop computer tucked under his arm. Singh followed, closing the door behind them. 'Sorry I'm late, sir,' the DI said. 'Coats' place took longer than I thought it would.' He waved the laptop. 'There was nothing there of any significance, only this. We'll see what it has on it, but I'll tell you one thing, he and Griff weren't riding the same gravy train.'

'What does that mean?' Mann asked.

'It means that we found signs of unexplained wealth in Griff Montell's office and at his home,' the DCC explained.

'And signs of unexplained poverty in Coats's,' Haddock added. 'Jackie,' he called out, 'have we got into Griff's computer yet?'

'Sorry, Sauce,' DC Jackie Wright replied. Griff Montell's computer was on her desk, taking up much of the available space. 'It's beyond me; I've tried all sorts of passwords based on date of birth, his service number, kids' names, everything obvious. I'm going to have to call in the IT people.'

'Have you tried "Alexis"?'

'No, why should that work?'

'It probably won't; it's Alex Skinner's given name, that's all.'

'Okay.' She turned back to the keyboard and punched in the letters, carefully. 'No luck,' she reported.

'Try it backwards,' McGuire suggested.

She did; as soon as she pressed the 'Enter' key the wallpaper disappeared and a photo of Alex herself filled the outsize screen.

'And here were we all thinking they were just good friends,' McGuire exclaimed. 'Not as far as Griff was concerned, it seems. Sauce, when you speak to Alex, I don't think that's something she needs to know.'

'Are you sure about that, boss?' Haddock asked. 'We don't know how Alex really felt about Griff, but we've had an insight into how he saw her. Isn't she entitled to know, and have we got the right to keep it from her?'

The DCC sighed, long and loudly. 'You know, you are right,' he said. 'I've known Alex since I was a plod, and she was maybe thirteen. The first time I met her was at a crime scene in Infirmary Street Baths. The big fella had brought her along because he'd had no option; he asked me to look after her while he was inside. She didn't really need looking after, even then, but I did, and in a way I've been looking after her ever since. We all have, and that's what I was doing there. You handle it any way you like; the purpose is to extract from her as much information about Montell as she has, that we might not. Have you arranged to see her yet? If not, do so now, and make it first thing tomorrow. We've all been up long enough today.'

'What about John and me, sir?'

He turned to Mann. 'I need you two to interview Detective Sergeant McClair. There's no sentiment in this situation; she and one of the victims had an adversarial relationship, so she needs to be approached on that basis, regardless of who she is. Noele will understand that, I'm sure.'

'What do I do if she asks for a lawyer?'

'You refuse,' he told her. 'She isn't entitled, because she won't have been cautioned; she'll be interviewed as a witness. That said, if she wants a Police Federation rep, I have no problem with that. The objective is simple; find out how much she knew about Terry's life. His associates, his love life, his financial position.'

'For example, why he was living in a dump,' Haddock added.

'That bad?'

'Ask Tarvil. He's pretty fastidious; he was for having the place fumigated.' The big Sikh grunted confirmation.

'Okay, deal with that too, Lottie. Was Coats under pressure, and if so what might he have done to relieve it?'

'What about exploring his relationship with Montell when we talk to her, sir?' Cotter asked.

'Yes,' McGuire agreed, 'but very carefully. It's emerged that Noele was in a relationship with Griff herself. Ultimately you're trying to find out how much she knew about both of them. Did each of them share information with her that was common to them both? Did they both drop the same names, people, places, events?'

'Or did she drop their names to someone else?' Mann said.

The DCC and the Haddock stared at her.

'What?' she exclaimed. 'No stone left unturned. No possibility left unexplored. We want to know everything about the victims; those rules apply to her too.'

'Okay,' McGuire conceded. 'Now, acting DCI Haddock . . .' The young detective stared at him. 'Look, Sauce, you are in practice, so it should be made official . . . can we talk about priorities? You're the SIO, what are they?'

'Interviews with Alex and Noele,' he replied. 'There's an argument that we treat them both the same, i.e., interview both on police premises, but I'm not going to go there, one, because there's no connection at all between Alex and Terry Coats and, two, because I don't fancy the heat it would draw from a certain quarter. Once we have everything we're going to get from them, we look at all the video we can find, from the traffic cameras, street cameras around the homes of both men, and security footage from the airport. We've established that Montell checked a suitcase on to his Saturday flight, routed through to Johannesburg, but that he never boarded the aircraft. Various possibilities occur to me, but do any of you have thoughts? DCI Mann?'

'When did he drop the case off?'

'Don't know yet, that's one of the things we'll look at on the airport CCTV. Why?'

'It could have been several hours in advance of flight time. If so, he could have been meeting someone before he caught the plane, and heard something that made him miss it. There are three hotels close to that airport; Dan, my Jakey and I stayed in the Moxy when we flew out of Edinburgh in October. There would have been plenty of time for him to go there before he went airside.'

'That's true,' Haddock agreed. 'If you and John could check them all that would be good. If you get something, excellent. If not, I would like you to visit airport security. Check if Coats was working on Saturday; if so, ask them whether he put any sort of an alert out for Montell.'

'What about our own people? We have patrol officers there.'

'That's right, Lottie, round the clock . . . which makes it unlikely that he was abducted from there, but chances are some of them might have known Inspector Montell by sight and recognised him on Saturday afternoon.' He nodded. 'While you're doing all that I'm going to be speaking to Sir Robert. He told me about a yarn that Coats spun him about bullion robbery in South Africa and gold coins being smuggled into the country and changed in an airport shop. He thought it was nonsense at the time, but he's changed his mind now. Just as we're doing with Alex and Noele, I need to press him to remember as much of the detail as he can. Once I've done that, I'll have the difficult task of speaking to Griff's twin sister, Spring. The DCC contacted her in South Africa through her partner . . . you two may not know, but she's a retired chief superintendent who used to be Griff's boss. She was serving when the relationship began, and he created a hell of a row when he found out, but he got used to it once he calmed down. Whether that translated into regular social contact, that's something I need to find out. I'm doing it by video link at eight tomorrow before I see Alex; that's been arranged by the DCC. We're an hour behind them, so she'll be awake and as ready for it as she's going to be.'

'Speaking of which,' the deputy chief constable declared, 'let's all go home and get some sleep. This is the most eventful New Year's Day I've ever had, and I can't wait for it to be over.'

'Me too,' Haddock conceded. He reached for the coat that he had thrown over a chair, only to be interrupted by a shout from DC Wright.

'Sauce! I think you should see this on Inspector Montell's iMac.'

'Can it wait?' he asked, then corrected himself, knowing his curiosity meant that it could not. 'Of course not. What is it?' He stepped across to her workstation, with McGuire and the two Glasgow detectives close behind.

'There's a folder on here of recordings from his security system. This one's from last Saturday evening, timed at twenty-two forty-nine. It's from a camera mounted on the outside of the building, and . . . look.'

A hazy image was frozen on the screen; it showed the street outside Montell's apartment, deserted, with no one in sight. Wright's hand was cupped over a computer mouse; she clicked it and the recording began to play, rain lashing down, ripples showing in the puddles by the side of the roadway. As they looked on, a figure appeared, walking into view, its back to the wall-mounted camera. The new arrival was wearing a long, dark, hooded raincoat. 'Male or female?' John Cotter murmured.

'You tell me, Sarge,' Wright replied, freezing the picture once more. 'You can't tell from this. Look there, whoever it is, they're wearing calf-length wellies, and those are pretty much unisex.'

Haddock leaned forward. 'What's that he or she's carrying? I can't make it out.'

'It's a plastic bag, Co-op.'

'So somebody's been shopping?'

'Maybe,' the DC agreed, 'but . . .' She hit the 'Play' icon once more; they watched the subject step up to the door, punch a code into the panel and slip inside.

'Okay, so somebody arrived in the pissing rain. What do the inside cameras show? There are four of them; entrance hallway, kitchen, living room, and bedroom.'

'That's the thing, Sauce. They don't show anything. They were all disabled at the time. They didn't have motion activation, so they had to have been turned off. I can see from this that the system allowed him to do that remotely; but by and large they were never switched off, nor even when Noele was there. I found some footage of her that I will only show you privately, if you think it's necessary, and even then only with an order from the chief constable. They were switched off half an hour before whoever it was arrived, then back on an hour later.'

'If that's so, I wonder why he didn't disable the street camera,' Haddock observed.

'It's possible that he tried, only the weather got in the way of the signal.'

'Maybe so, but evidentially there is nothing to show us that whoever that person was had anything to do with Griff. Is it possible that the weather could have interfered with the storage system of the internal camera footage? Mr Francis said it was stored on the Cloud.'

'As backup, that's right, but it's also stored on the computer; that's where I've got this from, so the weather isn't a factor. Griff seems to have been in the habit of erasing it after three months, and relying on the Cloud for longer term. And you're right, we don't have anything visual that links him with the person we saw. However,' she paused, 'we have this.' She went back to the computer and fast forwarded the street camera recording. The detectives watched as its clock raced, until she slowed it with a move of the mouse. 'About now,' she said. 'Watch.'

They did; the rain was as heavy as before, with no one braving it until the door was opened from the inside and the same figure stepped out, wrapped up against the weather, with the hood pulled down. 'There's no way of telling whether the face is being hidden deliberately,' Wright said, 'but from this angle, and the body shape, I would say that the person is a male. I have two begged questions. The first, could that be Inspector Montell himself? The second, where's the Co-op bag?'

McGuire looked down on her; he shook his head. 'No to the first. I'd say that's too short to be him and not wide enough in the shoulders. As for the bag, who knows?'

'I do,' Tarvil Singh replied, loudly. 'In Montell's office,' he said, 'I remember seeing a placky bag, blue and white. I remember because it was out of place. Everything else in his office was as neat and tidy as the rest of the house, a monument to OCD, yet that thing was just lying there, discarded and never picked up. That's right, Sauce, isn't it?'

'Absolutely,' Haddock confirmed. 'It was empty; I know because I knelt on it when I looked in the safe. It'll still be there, and maybe there's a chance Arthur Dorward's people will be able to tell us what was inside it.'

Thirteen

'I'm knackered,' Sarah whispered, leaning against her husband on the garden room sofa. There was a sitting room in the house itself, but they never used it other than to watch television. 'You knackered?'

'I won't know until I try to sleep,' he confessed. 'I've seen things today that will be with me for a long time.'

'You've seen such things many times before. Too many, I know,' she added.

'Rarely involving people I know, though; when I see those, they never go away. You'll autopsy them both tomorrow, but I suppose it'll be different for you. If you brought things home in your head I'd be peeling you off the ceiling through the night.'

'You want the truth?' she murmured. 'Sometimes I do just that. Children: I'm a mum so I associate with the people who've lost them. Burns victims, they're bad, and there was an acid attack a few years ago that will always be fresh in my memory. We're taught to be dispassionate, but they can't train all of the human reactions out of us. Terry Coats, I'll be okay with him, but honestly, I don't think I'll be able to banish all thoughts of the Griff Montell that I met with Alex.'

'Maybe you should,' Bob said. 'Going by the things in his

locker, and the stuff that I'm told Sauce and big Singh found in his house, there was a hell of a lot about the guy that we didn't know.'

'What things?'

'Designer clothes, a wardrobe full of them. Cash, plenty of it. Gold coins worth six figures. A burner SIM card; I can't think of a legitimate reason for a cop to have one of those. Most worrying of all, there was a gun; a pistol. There's no record of him ever having a permit for it. Yet Sauce told me it was clean. The serial number was intact; most illicit weapons, they've been removed. It looked like a standard police firearm, but it isn't. Not one of ours . . . theirs . . . at any rate.'

'Could he have bought it in South Africa and brought it home with him?'

'Packed in a suitcase that's going to be X-rayed? Somehow I doubt that.'

'Is it that big a deal?' she asked. 'I come from a nation of gun owners, so maybe I look at it from a different angle. There are gun nuts in every walk of life.'

'I know there are, but unlicensed possession is illegal in this country; you can go to jail. A serving police officer found with one almost certainly would. That's a heavy deterrent, yet Griff still had one. It was a hell of a risk; I'm afraid that when Sauce finds out why he had it, we're not going to like it.'

Sarah glanced up at him. 'Don't fly off the handle at this but . . . do you think there is the slightest chance . . .' She hesitated.

'That Alex knew about it? I admit that question crossed my mind; I feel guilty about harbouring it, but I'm certain she didn't. I believe that if she'd found out about it she'd have told him to hand it in. She'd have forced him, in fact, given him an ultimatum. She's an officer of the court and she takes that seriously.'

'Did you ask her about the clothes and the other stuff when you saw her this morning?'

'I only knew about the things in his locker then,' Bob told her. 'I decided that the time wasn't right, so I didn't mention them. Sauce is going to interview her properly tomorrow. I'm sure he'll talk her through everything. One thing I do know. When they did have one of their occasional get-togethers, it was always at her place. As first that was because his sister lived with him. After she moved out, Alex made a point of keeping it that way. She insisted that she saw him only as a friend and an . . .' He stopped short.

'And an occasional shag?' his wife suggested.

'If you want to put it that way, yes. The way she put it to me was that she didn't want to get her feet under his table even once.'

'Noele had no such qualms, from what you said.'

'No,' he agreed, 'and from what Sauce told me half an hour ago, there's video evidence of that, and more.'

'Jesus,' she protested, 'he didn't! Did he?'

'Constant video monitoring, according to Jackie Wright. Nobody's saying he got his rocks off watching it, but it's there, on his computer and apparently up in the Cloud.'

'Oh my God, if someone hacks into it. Can't Sauce delete it?'

'In the circumstances, I suspect that he'd need the permission of the procurator fiscal to do that.'

'Did she know? Was the camera obvious?'

'Apparently not. It was built in to the alarm system's motion sensor.'

'Bloody hell, Bob, does ours have that?'

'No, I was offered that option when it was fitted, but I declined. I even made the installer show me the inside of each sensor before he put them up.' He grinned. 'Maybe I've been hanging around the spooks for too long.'

'You and Sauce were on the phone in the office for quite a long time,' Sarah remarked. 'What were you talking about?'

'He quizzed me about the story that Terry Coats spun me, the day that Noele slung him out and he turned up here looking for trouble. The more I think about it the more significant it becomes and the more I regret not taking it seriously. I think I've recalled all the detail now and given him a proper line of enquiry. Coats claimed that the girl we caught him with was part of a scheme to import stolen Krugerrands into the country. She was cabin crew and, with others, would bring coins from South Africa into Edinburgh among her possessions. They'd then be spent in a shop. To me, it sounded crazy at the time, but in fact it's so fucking simple, it's dazzling. They'd be accepted as currency, at a ridiculously low value, and that would be it, they'd be in the country, seemingly legitimately, to be disposed of on the open market.'

'But why do this? Why not simply sell them in South Africa?'

'Because they were stolen. According to Coats, years ago there was a robbery there, in which a huge quantity of Krugerrands were taken. The haul was so big, possibly twenty, thirty million sterling, possibly even more, that the thieves may have sat on them for years before they started to move them on. The source of the information about the robbery was a South African chum of his . . . Griff Montell. His knowledge of the smuggling operation, he said, came from a contact in the shop.'

'How many smuggled coins are we talking about?' she asked.

'No idea. It depends how many people were involved, as well as the woman Coats mentioned.'

'The shop must have been in on it, surely.'

'Very much so; that and the airline Coats' girlfriend worked for; it was called Wister Air. I'd never heard of it, but I did a quick google this evening and it was there, although it doesn't fly to Edinburgh anymore. He never mentioned the name of the shop but he did say that both were owned by a Russian.'

'How many staff were involved in the smuggling?'

'I have no idea, but if Sauce can find Terry's girlfriend, she might know.'

'And Griff, how did he tie into all of this?'

'And how did he happen to have a stash of Krugerrands in his safe, along with nearly ninety grand in cash? My big worry is that Griff didn't simply know about that gold robbery, but that he was part of it.'

Fourteen

Sauce Haddock rubbed his eyes with both hands; they felt as if half a beach had been washed into them overnight. He blinked hard to clear his vision, then shrugged his shoulders as if to shake off the weight that fate had dumped on them. He and Cheeky, his partner, Cameron Davis by her Sunday names, the latter coming from her stepfather, had been planning to grab a last-minute holiday break in the Canaries. In the wake of the double murder investigation, that had been postponed until Easter, and maybe later if Sammy Pye had not recovered from his mystery illness by then. He suspected that the DCC knew what the problem was, and the fact that it had not been shared with him made him worry about the man who was both his boss and his friend.

'You ready to go?' Tarvil Singh asked him, breaking into his thoughts. 'You're miles away.'

He blinked again. 'Sorry, these early morning starts are worst in the winter. Are we sure they'll be there?'

'The DCC said so, but there's only one way to find out.' The DS opened Zoom on Haddock's computer and placed the call. For around thirty seconds they stared at their own weary faces on the screen, until they shrank to a box on the top right corner and were replaced by two women. The older of the two was familiar to them both; Mary Chambers had been the first woman to make Chief Superintendent rank in the old Edinburgh force. She could have gone on to command rank in its replacement, but she was of the Bob Skinner school and had wanted no part of it. With thirty-seven years' service, she had taken her pension and gone into a happy retirement with her younger partner, helping her run the online graphic design business that she had set up. Neither detective had seen her since then; each was surprised by the change in her. The severe box haircut had gone, replaced by a longer look from which the grey had been banished by a glossy auburn colouring. The stiff white shirt they remembered had been replaced by a sleeveless yellow blouse. A medallion hung around her neck and her interlocked fingers were adorned by several rings. Most surprising of all, she wore eye make-up and a pale pink lipstick.

Spring Montell was her junior by almost twenty years but appeared to be catching her up. She and Griff had been identical twins, facially and, to an extent, in build. She wore a black T-shirt; unlike her partner, she was without make-up, her eyebrows were un-plucked, and her grey-flecked black hair was pulled back in a ponytail. Even in her bereavement her appearance came as a shock to the DI. Having known her only by name, he had read too much into that and had expected a slight, ethereal, womanly figure rather than the version he saw on the screen.

'Good morning, lads.' Chambers' greeting sounded slightly tinny, but her voice came through clearly. 'You look bloody terrible, if you don't mind me saying so. In case you were wondering, I'm going to sit in on this,' she announced; her tone did not invite discussion. 'Spring's still pretty fragile, and if I think at any time she's not up to this, I'm going to pull the plug.'

'That's fair enough, Ms Chambers,' Haddock said.

'Sauce, it's Mary, okay? You've grown up and I've grown older.'

He smiled. 'Fair enough, Mary. Spring,' he continued, 'we haven't met. I'm Detective Inspector Harold . . .'

'I know who you are, Sauce,' she said, cutting him off. 'Griff used to talk about you. He called you the Chosen One, and I don't think he was being kind. And you'll be DC Singh; from the way he described you, there can only be one of you. Or is it DS now?'

He nodded. 'It is. I managed to fool the promotion board.'

Haddock leaned forward. 'Have you told the family, Spring?'

'I told my ex-sister-in-law. She was shocked, but not hysterical. They really did part badly. Apart from her, there's nobody to tell.'

'Hold on,' Chambers exclaimed. 'You told me you had a cousin in Cape Town. What was his name again? I can't remember.'

'Tom,' Spring said, a little irritably. 'Tom DuPlessis. I haven't seen him for years, so I haven't called him, but the story made the front pages this morning, so he'll know. Did you see my brother's body, Sauce?' she asked, sharply.

'Yes, I did, in the car when it was dumped outside the police station.'

'Did he . . . ?' She frowned. 'Was it . . . ?'

'He never knew what hit him, Spring,' Haddock replied. 'He was shot once in the back of the head; at close range, the pathologist said. It would have been instantaneous.'

'Was he killed in the car?'

'No, somewhere else; we don't know where yet. We're working on it.'

'I'm sure you are. Why were they left outside the police station?'

'Our guess is that whoever did it was making a statement, to us, the police, I suppose. They must have known that he was stationed there.'

'And are you thinking it was related to something he was working on?' she asked. 'Because I don't see how that could be. Griff felt that his police career had become a waste of time. When he applied for promotion he assumed it would be to detective inspector, but instead the last chief constable, Martin, stuck him in a uniform and gave him a box of pencils to push. My brother knew why he did that too; he told me so often enough.'

Haddock leaned forward, making his on-screen image bigger. 'What did he believe, Spring?'

'He reckoned that he was being vindictive; he believed that it had to do with him sleeping with Alex Skinner, with her being Martin's woman.'

'Ex at the time, I think you'll find,' Haddock corrected her.

'Not always, I think you'll find yourself,' she countered. 'Griff and I shared everything towards the end. We learned that lesson from the fight we had when I teamed up with Mary. He'd talk to me about his love life all the time. He'd talk to me about everything. There were occasions, he told me, when Martin had really pissed Alex off, that she'd phone him, and he'd go along to her place. She'd fuck his brains out, he said, just to let off steam. His promotion happened after they split; he knew that Martin couldn't block it, but he did him all the damage that he could. Griff was convinced that Martin had known everything that went on in Alex's life, even after they broke up. He was even convinced that he'd had her watched.'

'Did he ever mention this to Alex?' Singh asked.

'He may have done, I'm not sure. But he was sure of it; he believed the guy had it in for him, big time. Where is Martin now?'

The sharpness of her question seemed to take Chambers by surprise. She laid a hand on her arm. 'He's in America, love, lecturing in one of the top universities. He left the country after he quit the job; he said he wanted some space.'

'So what? He has children; he's probably home for Christmas.'

Haddock intervened. 'Spring, I have to tell you that Sir Andrew Martin is not a suspect in your brother's murder. Whatever grievance he might have had against Griff, I doubt that he'd ever heard of Terry Coats, the man who was killed with him. Have you? Did he ever mention him to you?'

'That's who the other man in the car was?' she exclaimed. 'Griff told me that he had a new girlfriend, another police officer. Her name was Noele; he said that she was a single mother, the ex-wife of a guy he knew slightly, and he said that his name was Terry Coats. He'd been a cop, he said, but that was all. What's his history?'

'He served in the Strathclyde force, but never in our lot; when he died he was employed in security at Edinburgh Airport. Noele, his ex, is my sergeant; naturally, she's excluded from the investigation.'

'And they wound up dead together? That's weird.'

'It is,' Mary Chambers agreed. 'Do you have a connection between them, other than the woman?'

'Possibly,' he replied. 'Spring, did Griff ever talk to you about a robbery in South Africa around ten years ago in which a shedload of gold coins was stolen?'

Her eyes widened as she stared at him. 'Did he talk to me about it? He was involved in it. He was a victim. He and his partner were the police escort when it happened. It was on the outskirts of Pretoria; they had picked up a consignment from the Rand refinery in Jo'burg in an armoured van, and they were escorting it to a bullion warehouse when they were ambushed on a quiet stretch of road. Griff was shot in the shoulder and in the head; his partner was killed and so were the van drivers. The money's never been recovered.'

'That's true,' Chambers confirmed. 'There's a chap in my bridge club here who was on the force at the time. He told me all about it; I knew some of it, of course, from Spring.'

'Did they have any leads?' Haddock asked. 'We heard that Russians might have been involved.'

'You know how it is, there were all sorts of conspiracy theories; Russians, the Mafia, there was even one nutter who insisted that the CIA had done it to raise cash to fund covert operations in Africa. I doubt that anyone will ever know for sure.'

'Did your card-playing friend fill you in on the details?'

'As much as they ever found out. Most of it was speculation; Griff was the only survivor and he was out of it for most of the time. He stepped out of the police vehicle; one of them shot him before he could even draw his firearm. Fannie, his partner, tried to pull his own gun as he was being hauled out of the car. The robber shot him in the side, then shot Griff again, in the head . . . or so he thought: the bullet knocked him out but it didn't penetrate his skull. The doctor who treated him said he was the luckiest man he'd ever seen. After he recovered they gave him a medal and promoted him into CID.'

'It left a mark on him, though,' Spring added. 'He was different after it. His behaviour changed at home; Annelise, his wife, got the rough end of his tongue . . . nothing else, mind . . . until finally she looked elsewhere. They got divorced, she got hefty child support . . . even though she married an accountant who earned five times what Griff did . . . and that was when he decided he had to look for an international transfer.'

'And you went with him?' Singh asked.

'I decided it was best,' she replied. 'I never liked Annelise. Left to my own devices, I might have done her some damage for the way she treated my brother.'

'What about your parents? Were they happy with both of you leaving?'

'My father left us when we were children. My mother died when we were twenty.'

Haddock leaned forward once more, looking directly into the camera rather than at the screen. 'Did Griff find it easier to make ends meet in Scotland?'

'Of course. He was paid in sterling and that buys a lot of rand. Annelise, the cow, actually went back to court to try and get more, but she was laughed right out of there.' She smiled, savagely. 'Tough shit on her now,' she said.

'Do you know if Griff left a will? We couldn't find one in his flat.'

'Try our lawyer, Edgar Matthew at Smith and Green. We made wills when we bought the apartment. We had a joint life policy to cover the mortgage, and they underlined that arrangement. I amended mine to leave everything else to Mary. He left his half of the flat to me and any balance to Lisa and

Andre, his children, not that there'll be much left, I guess. Griff had expensive tastes, in clothes . . . and women.'

'Is that so?'

'It always was; he was always after the extra buck when we were young.'

'Mmm,' the young detective murmured. 'Mary,' he said changing tack unexpectedly, 'suppose you wanted to smuggle something out of South Africa, something bulky, but very valuable. How would you go about it?'

'Bulky, but valuable,' she repeated. 'A bit like me? It's not something I've ever considered, but off the top of my head, I'd find someone on a container ship, or an oil tanker, or maybe even a cruise liner and bribe him to help me shift it. It would probably have to be an officer; ordinary seamen would be subject to scrutiny. You think about here, you think about smuggling diamonds, but that's not what you've got in mind is it, Sauce?'

'No, it's not. I'm thinking about gold, coins to be precise. Krugerrands to be even preciser. I'll be frank with you both. Griff's home has state-of-the-art security, installed after you moved out, Spring.'

'Come on,' she exclaimed, 'he has an alarm system. He fitted it because he was living on his own.'

'He fitted it because he had a safe, Spring. Were you never there after you moved out?'

'Of course I was, but only to visit. He made my room into an office, so I didn't go in there. If he had a safe, so what? We do, here and in Edinburgh.'

'Do either of them contain a quarter of a million in gold and eighty-eight thousand in cash? Because that's what we found in Griff's. I'm going to ask you straight out . . . sorry,

Mary, both of you . . . do either of you know anything about it?'

Chambers screwed up her face in sheer astonishment. 'How much?'

'Two hundred and fifty Krugerrands. The cash was in your classic brown envelope. Plus one other item: a handgun. Spring,' he asked again, 'do you know anything about this, anything at all?'

She drew a breath. 'Nothing at all, I swear.'

'How about the cousin you mentioned? Were he and Griff close?'

'Fairly; closer than he is with me. I never hear from him.'

'I'd like contact details for him, if you can let me have them. Also, Mary, can you ask your bridge pal if the police report on the robbery is still readily available or if it's archived?'

'I'll call him as soon as we're finished,' she promised, 'I have his mobile. He was pretty senior; he was a Brigadier, I think. The South African Police Service has military-style ranks,' she explained. 'If it helps, I can ask him for advice on how to go about getting it.'

'Thanks.' He hesitated, then went on. 'This is pure speculation, but can you ask him something for me? What types of weapon do South African police officers carry?'

'Will do. Why do you want to know?'

'Because I read too many detective novels,' he replied. 'Either that or I've been around Bob Skinner too long. If he was sitting here, he'd want to know too. One last thing,' he added. 'When Griff didn't show up, did you try to contact him?'

'Show up?' Spring Montell exclaimed. 'What do you mean by that? Where was he going to show up? When?'

'He was booked on a flight to Johannesburg out of Heathrow, on Sunday. He was signed out for a couple of weeks' holiday and told his station commander that was where he was headed. His suitcase made it, but he didn't.'

'If that's the case, Sauce, he didn't tell us.' She dabbed at her left eye as a tear appeared. 'But that's not unusual. Griff always was a surprising guy.'

Fifteen

'Thank you for agreeing to come in, Detective Sergeant. We've met, but if you don't remember I'm Detective Chief Inspector Charlotte Mann. This is DS John Cotter.'

'You're not easily forgotten, DCI Mann,' Noele McClair said. 'Good to meet you, John. Now, are you going to tell me why I'm here rather than you coming to me?'

'With your child being at home, we thought it might be best,' Mann replied.

'With respect, ma'am, no you didn't. I'm here because someone higher up the chain told you to do it that way. Sauce is the SIO but he would have spelled it out for me; that leaves only two, the DCC and the chief constable herself, but he's the boss in all but name when it comes to criminal investigation. I'm here,' she continued, 'because I'm a person of interest. I had relationships with both victims, one past, one current. I'm your only link between them at the moment; if you weren't interviewing me formally you'd be falling down on the job.'

'Do you want to have a rep present?' Mann asked. 'If so, I can postpone this for a while.'

'Christ, no,' she declared. 'You're going to be asking me about things I'll want to stay within this room. Fire away.'

The DCI nodded. 'Fair enough. I would like to record this, but only with your consent.'

McClair replied by leaning across the desk and switching on the recorder. 'Let's do it.'

It was Cotter who began the questioning. 'DS McClair, for how long were you and Mr Coats married?'

'Ten years. Out of those, a couple were okay; after Harry was born.'

'What were the problems with the marriage?'

She whistled. 'Where do I begin? His ego for a start; he really did think he was the Special One. He was a good cop, no question, but he thought he was better than that. Terry thought that rules were for other people, and that corners were there to be cut. He also thought that a chain of command involved body piercing. That's what did for him in the end. When Brass Rubbings came for him he was up shit creek, because he didn't have the fallback of blaming it on somebody else. If you have an informant you know is an active criminal, you don't let him run without getting the approval of someone higher up. Right, DCI Mann?'

'Spot on.'

'Okay,' Cotter continued. 'His ego, and what else?'

She frowned. 'His cock; now that was a problem, for the second half of our marriage and probably longer. I could never be sure where it had been, then latterly, when things were really bad, it wasn't in me often enough. Sorry if that embarrasses you, John, but you want a full and frank disclosure.' She paused. 'Truth is, I put up with it for longer than I should have; but when Sauce and Bob Skinner caught him with that trolley dolly in a hotel, and it became public, well that really was one too many. I should have done it years earlier. I am so much better off without him. Personally, and financially too.'

Her bitterness took the sergeant by surprise. 'Even without his salary coming into the house?'

Noele McClair laughed out loud. 'I think you mean without his gambling debts taking the shoes off our son's feet, and the food out of his mouth.'

Lottie Mann intervened. 'Terry was a gambler?'

'An addict. It was always in him and it just got worse and worse. I had to hide my credit cards from him. I had to divert my salary into a personal account rather than our joint, and I had to ask the bank to remove the overdraft facility on that, because it was still bleeding me dry. The bank wasn't fucking interested of course; they wouldn't do it without his signature as well. When we got divorced they had to. Under the terms of the settlement we were each liable for half the overdrawn amount. I cleared mine by switching it to my personal account. I have no idea what he did. I'm sure you'll find out, once the banks reopen for business tomorrow.'

'What was he like to live with?' the DCI asked. 'Sauce and Tarvil went through his place. They said it wasn't fit for pigs.'

'Good analogy. If Terry had seen two pigs, he'd have bet on which one was the faster. He was a slob. He'd throw stuff on the floor, leave empty beer cans lying around, and expect me to clear up after him . . . which of course I did, without com-plaining nearly often enough.' Her mouth tightened. 'One time I did go mental, though. Harry had left a toy on the floor, a wee Ninja warrior figure. Terry stamped on it, broke it, and told him that would happen any time he left something lying around. The wee man was crying, and I just ripped into him. I don't think I'd ever been so angry with anybody in my life.'

'Suppose Terry hadn't been caught being unfaithful,' DS

Cotter asked, probing, 'would you have split up, or would we be interviewing you as a widow?'

She looked him in the eye. 'There's a fair chance you'd be interviewing me as a murder suspect . . .' She broke off and grinned. 'Oh silly me,' she chuckled, 'that's what you're doing just now.'

'No,' Mann said, firmly. 'We are not doing that. Nor do I believe we would have been. My ex was as bad as yours, but I never actually thought about caving his head in with the pepper mill.' A flicker of a smile showed in her mouth but did not make it to her eyes. 'Okay, maybe I did once or twice, but I wouldn't have done it, for Jakey's sake, and nor would you for Harry's. DS McClair, we just need to know everything you know about your ex and about Inspector Montell. Is there anything you can tell us about Mr Coats after your separation and divorce? Was he still involved with that woman, Aisha Karman, for example?'

'I have no idea, although I doubt that he could have afforded her with the child-support payments. That's one thing Griff and he had in common, but Griff was up to date with his, unlike Terry. I had little or no contact with him after the divorce, other than when he called to pick up Harry every other Saturday. When he did, we never spoke for any length of time. I really did loathe him.'

'When did your relationship with Inspector Montell begin?' Cotter asked, taking back control of the interview.

'At the end of August, beginning of September,' McClair replied. 'I had to go to Torphichen Place to interview a suspect. Sauce had been called away, so he took the other chair. We'd never met before. He was out of CID by the time I transferred to Edinburgh and moved to Gullane. Once the business was done we went for a coffee in the canteen. He mentioned that he knew my ex, sort of; that their paths had crossed before police unification, and that he'd heard Terry had quit rather than be booted from CID and posted to a desk job in the back of beyond. He said that he sympathised with him, that he'd fallen foul of a chief constable too.'

'Did he explain that?'

'Not at the time. I asked him what he meant but he just smiled and said, "Conflict of interests". Later on, he told me about him and Alex Skinner, and how he was injured in her flat, defending her. He said that she'd moved in with somebody, and that their thing was over . . . not that it had ever really been a thing in the first place.'

'Apart from that first occasion,' Cotter continued, 'did he ever mention Terry? Did he give you any indication that he had met him recently?'

'No, none at all. If you're going to ask me how they came to be in the same car after they were killed, I can assure you that it's a complete mystery to me.'

'I was,' the DS confirmed, 'but before that, can we talk more about your relationship with Inspector Montell. How serious was it?'

'I can only speak for me,' she told him, 'but on a scale from one to ten, I would say seven with a real possibility of upward movement. Immediately post-divorce, I had no intention of taking another marital risk, but the more time I spent with Griff the more that started to soften. He was the complete opposite of Terry in every way, kind, thoughtful and generous.' She winked at Mann. 'He was also spectacularly good in bed. I never knew what an orgasm was with Terry; he was one of those guys who didn't realise that women are entitled to come too, or maybe he just didn't know we can.' She leaned back. 'I have this theory . . . fuck no, this profound belief . . . that every young man should be given a copy of *The Joy of Sex*, or something similar, on his sixteenth birthday. I'm pretty sure that Griff was.'

'Who knew about the two of you?'

'I don't think anybody did, until he had to tell Alex Skinner. We were very careful; we were both cops, and we knew that if one colleague found out, so would everyone else in a very short time.'

'Officers found female garments in his home. Can we assume that they're yours?'

'Yes, I kept a couple of things there. I stayed over a few times; my mother would look after Harry, and I'd spin her a yarn. If we were going somewhere after work, dinner, theatre and the like, I needed things I could change into.'

'Were you happy with him?'

She looked at her hands, steepled on the table. 'Happier than I'd ever been.' Her eyes moistened. 'Now it's all been ripped away. Bastards!' she hissed.

Mann edged forward, and Cotter withdrew, slightly, as she took over. 'Did you ever have any thoughts about Inspector Montell's lifestyle?' she began.

'Not really; it was modest. We didn't go to any flash places, no weekend at Gleneagles, or anything like that. If I read you right you're talking about his dress sense, the designer clothes that he liked. I teased him about that; we had a laugh when he confessed that he shopped in an outlet place in Livingston, where they do seconds and the like much cheaper that the real thing.'

'Did you ever go into his office? You must have noticed

there was a lock on the door. In fact, you must have noticed the security in general.'

'The alarm system? Of course; the monitor sensors were just about everywhere. I asked him about it; he said it was just part of being a cop, and I got that. As for the office, no, I never went in there. I had no reason to, and I had no reason to ask him about it.'

'No, of course not,' the DCI conceded. 'In all your time together, did Griff, Inspector Montell, ever mention your ex-husband?'

'No,' McClair said, firmly, 'and neither did I. I didn't want Terry near my new relationship in any way.'

'He didn't give you any hint that they might have been in touch?' Mann persisted.

'No, never. Griff and Terry had absolutely nothing in common. One was a gentleman, the other was an arsehole.' She paused, anticipating the next question. 'I know, and yet they both wound up dead in the same car. I hope you do find out how, but it won't be through me. I have no idea.'

'We will, eventually.'

'Do you have any lines of investigation?'

'We do, but I'm not going to divulge that just yet. Instead . . . look, the two of you were intimate. Apart from the injury that he sustained during the incident in Alex Skinner's flat, did Inspector Montell have any other scars?'

'Yes, he had one big one, on his right shoulder, front and back. It was from a gunshot wound he sustained when he was a police officer in South Africa.'

'Did he tell you how it happened? I'm assuming that you asked him.'

'Sure, but he wasn't wounded in action; it was a stupid

accident and he was embarrassed by it. We did a scar comparison one night; my caesarean, my appendix, his shoulder. I said that mine were boring, but that his must have a story behind it. "Oh yes," he said. He told me that he went out hunting one evening with his patrol partner. His name was Fannie, I think. He said they were after deer and separated to flank a herd. But the light wasn't too good; he made a sudden move and Fannie mistook him for an antelope. I told him I didn't believe him but he swore blind that it was true.' She peered at Mann. 'It was . . . wasn't it?'

'Not according to our information. Did he ever tell you about a robbery in South Africa, when a consignment of gold coins were stolen from a hijacked van?'

'No, ma'am,' she insisted, 'he didn't. That's not something I would have forgotten.' She paused and gasped, her mouth falling open slightly. 'But Terry said something that comes right back to mind. When I found out about his affair with the airline woman, and told him he was gone for good, he tried to talk me round. He said it was all connected to stolen Krugerrands. I told him he could spend the rest of his life thinking up crazy excuses, I wasn't buying any of them and he could fuck right off. He protested, swore it was true, but I yelled at him that he and the truth were total strangers and he should get out of my life. Could it actually have been true? And suppose it was, how would it connect to Griff?'

'If his story was true,' Mann replied, 'it's just possible that the coins he spoke about came from the robbery I just mentioned. How would it connect to Inspector Montell? I have no idea. But I do know that he was part of the escort of the consignment, that he was the only survivor, and that's how the wound from the so-called hunting accident really happened.'

Sixteen

'And here I was thinking it had been a quiet Hogmanay,' PC Andrea Newman sighed, as she drew the car to a halt. 'Where did she say he was?'

'Just before the thirty sign, the ops room,' PC Ronnie Hamilton, her partner, replied.

She looked along the narrow highway. 'What did the informant say? That she saw a bloke sleeping it off in a field?'

'Aye. She said she saw him from her kitchen window.' He pointed across a field to a group of houses that backed on to it. 'She had to have been over there, for there's no other buildings with a view of this stretch of road. That's at least three hundred yards away. She's either got great eyesight or great binoculars. I don't see anybody? Do you, Andrea?'

'Not on this side of the fence, that's for sure. If she did see someone, he's probably woke up and gone home . . . although,' she wondered, 'how would he get here in the first place. If he was walking towards Howgate, he's come from a fair way off. If he was walking away . . . he was a candidate for hypothermia.'

'Maybe a patrol car gave him a lift part way and left him to walk the rest, to sober him up,' Hamilton suggested.

'Strictly against the rules, Ronnie; you know that, after that man froze to death years ago.'

'Some of the folk we've had transferred in don't know that story; they might be a bit lax with those rules. Whatever, he's clearly not by the roadside, as we were told, he's not playing Worzel Gummidge in the middle of the field . . .'

'But he could be lying behind that wee row of trees on the other side of the fence,' Newman pointed out, peering in that direction. 'Come to think of it, I'm sure I can see a shoe; let's find if there's anything in it.'

The copse was only a few yards short of the speed limit sign. She led the way towards it and climbed nimbly over the wire fence. Her bulkier colleague made no move to join her. 'Is it muddy over there?' he called out.

'No, it's okay. Ronnie, there's somebody here right enough.' She moved towards the figure, stretched out at the base of the trees. He was well dressed, in a thick camel coat. The shoes that had caught her eye were patent leather, reflecting the weak late-morning sunshine. 'Come on, sir,' she called up, 'the party's over, it's time to call it a day. Your pretty balloon is well burst . . .'

The man was lying face down; leaning over, she turned him on to his side . . . then recoiled. 'Oh shit,' she muttered.

The fence wire sang as Hamilton put his weight on it. 'You need to stay on that side, Ronnie. This fella's not waking up any time soon. Move the car along to the other side of the trees,' she tossed him the keys, 'and bring some tape if we've got it. We're going to need CID here, medical examiner, the works. This man's been shot.'

Seventeen

'He was always well dressed, Sauce,' Alex Skinner said. 'You know that. You worked with him when he was in CID.'

'That was a couple of years ago,' Haddock pointed out. 'I remember him being smart, but I don't remember ever noticing a designer label on his shirt. There was barely anything else to be seen when we went through his house. But your father told me you made a point of never going there, so you won't have seen it.'

'That's what I let my dad believe, but the fact is, Griff never invited me. The last time I saw him, I suggested it, but he put me off. He told me he was involved with someone else; I accepted that, and I was happy for him. I was in and out of the place often enough when we were next-door neigh-bours, but Spring was there then so I never stayed overnight. If we were having, let's call it a sleepover, he'd come into my place; then my life got complicated for a while and I moved. After Spring left, when we were both single again, I thought that might change, but no, he never once asked me there. The opposite; he would suggest that he come to mine. Mind you I was with Andy Martin for some of that two-year period, so it didn't arise for a while. When that ended, I turned to him for comfort and a little joy.' She smiled.

'Are you sure about that?' he asked, quietly.

'About what?'

'When you were with Andy, didn't it arise?'

She gazed at him for a while, then sighed. 'Maybe, once or twice. It got frustrating at times; in hindsight I could sense Andy drifting away from the relationship. He'd say it was just work, but finally, after being stood up a couple of nights on the trot, I called Griff and asked him if he could come over. He was hesitant at first. He knew I wasn't asking him over for a coffee, and I guess he was worried that screwing the chief constable's girlfriend might not be a great career move. Lust overcame logic, though . . . it always did with us.' Her voice faltered for a second.

'Just the once?'

She shook her head, quickly. 'No, more than that,' she admitted; then she grinned. 'You've been talking to his sister, haven't you? You and she probably think I'm a right slapper, but I'm not, I promise. There isn't a man had breakfast in my apartment, or anything else, other than those two.'

'You're right,' he confirmed. 'I did talk to her. She said that Griff blamed those times for him being moved out of CID. He was sure that Andy Martin had found out and was getting even with him. He even thought that Andy had been having you watched. Do you believe that?'

'Not all of it. I could accept that Andy was jealous of him and that, yes, he might have bumped him into uniform out of sheer personal spite. But having me watched? No, absolutely not. If I'd suspected that . . . and I'm not stupid, I'm a cop's daughter plus you have to be aware of what's happening around you in my line of work . . . I'd have done one of two things. I'd either have squared him up myself, or if I'd been feeling evil enough, I'd have set my dad on him. He knows a couple of things about Andy that he wouldn't want being leaked.'

'And yet those two used to be best friends,' Haddock observed.

'Used to be, Sauce, until Andy's incredible ambition got in the way.' She took a breath, frowning. 'People think he's gone for good, you know, but I don't. My guess is he's just on sabbatical. Aileen de Marco, my former stepmother, used to be a big fan of his. Now that she's taken her political bandwagon down to Westminster, she has influence with the Mayor of London, and he has a big say in Metropolitan Police appointments, so watch this space.' She paused. 'Are you warm enough, by the way?'

They were seated on two Adirondack chairs on Dominic Jackson's deck, taking advantage of a break in the rain and the unexpected morning sunshine. The DI gave an almost imperceptible nod, burying himself deep in a heavy leather jacket. 'I'm good,' he said. 'How long are you going to stay in this place?' he asked.

'That's open-ended,' she replied. 'I realised that I was damaged when I came here; I was as much a patient as I was a lodger. I'm good now. The tenant in my place by Holyrood Park is moving out in three months, when his contract in the Scottish Parliament ends. I could move back then, but Dominic says he likes having me around, that I keep him from getting morose. He shared accommodation with several hundred men for several years, remember. He'd tell you himself that he has trouble adjusting to living completely on his own.' She grinned. 'We'll see how it goes. Do you think Griff had trouble adjusting,' she asked, 'after Spring moved in with Mary Chambers?'

The question took him by surprise, but the answer came easily to him. 'The opposite,' he said. 'The first thing he did was fortify the place.' He described the security system that he and Singh had discovered.

'He never mentioned any of that to me,' she assured him. 'A little over the top, surely. What the hell was he protecting, apart from those designer clothes you were asking about?'

'Lots,' Haddock replied, moving on before she could press him. 'Alex, did you and he ever talk about anything other than work?'

'I never talked about mine. Him cop, me criminal defence lawyer; it wouldn't have been appropriate. He didn't either, but come to think of it, he didn't really talk about anything. We'd discuss current affairs, the latest movies, who'd been slagging who off on social media . . . I remember us trying to work out what exactly the fuck an Instagram influencer is and not coming up with an answer . . . but, beyond that, nothing much. Our relationship was physical, not philosophical.'

'He had a scar on his shoulder. Did he ever tell you about that?'

'He said that Spring shot him accidentally with a crossbow when they were both kids.'

'And you believed that?'

'Why shouldn't I?'

'No reason,' he conceded, 'but the truth is he was shot while he was a police officer in Pretoria. There was an armed hijack, and he was wounded. He never mentioned that?'

'Never.' She smiled, lightly. 'Sounds like we weren't as close as I thought.'

'How did he seem when you were with him? Was he happy, sad, up, down?'

'Same old, same old. Mind you, the last time we were together, the night I had the break-in and he got hurt, he'd been a bit unsettled before it happened. His mind wasn't on the job, so to speak; he wasn't really with me. I got a bit annoyed about that, I asked him what the matter was. The way he reacted, it really pissed me off. That's when I got out of bed and went into the kitchen for some juice, and was surprised by the two intruders.'

'The way he reacted,' Haddock repeated. 'How was it, what did he say that annoyed you so much?'

'It was dismissive for a start; it was as if he wasn't for sharing, at least not with me. As for what he said, I have no idea what that was, because he said it in Afrikaans!'

Eighteen

'I notice you didn't tell her about t' gold in Montell's safe,' DS Cotter remarked. 'Or the gun.'

'I didn't think she needed to know that,' DCI Mann replied. 'That information stays within the investigating team, and Noele McClair isn't part of it. More than that . . .'

'Are you saying she's a suspect?' he asked.

'No, but she's still a person of interest. The two men in her life died together, John, and she remains a possibility as the link that brought them there, even if she isn't aware of it. It's evident that she hated Coats's guts, but we don't really know anything about the true nature of her relationship with Montell, other than what she's told us.'

'We do, surely. DI Haddock told us that he brushed off Ms Skinner because he was in a relationship with DS McClair. I've never met the woman, but I saw her on telly once, after she got one of her clients acquitted in the High Court. In Montell's shoes I wouldn't have been doing that lightly . . . and I'm bloody married!'

Mann treated him to a rare smile. 'If that ever found its way back to Mrs Cotter . . .'

He tapped the side of his head. 'Don't worry, boss, it's all in here. I've always been more cautious than brave.'

'That makes you an exception then, Sergeant. In my experience men don't consult their brains at all when making decisions like that.' She rose from the comfortable chair that she had commandeered and walked across the CID room. 'DC Wright,' she said, 'any joy accessing those bank accounts?'

'Surprisingly, ma'am, yes,' she replied. 'I thought I might have to wait until tomorrow, but no. I have Coats' and Inspector Montell's, and I've been promised Noele's once my TSB contact clears it with the right level of management.'

'What do they show?'

'Terry Coats's Bank of Scotland account is very much what I expected. He was chunkily overdrawn; a little over one third of his net salary went out again in child support and pretty much all of the rest goes in mortgage, credit-card and interest payments. He had two credit cards with the bank, both nearly maxed out and an Amex card that isn't, but a lot of retailers don't take them. I don't know how the guy survived.'

'No other in-goings other than his pay? DS McClair said he was a gambler, but they don't lose all the time. Are we sure he doesn't have any other accounts? He wouldn't have been the first guy who tried to hide assets from his ex-wife. I can tell you that from experience.'

'I can't be certain of that,' Wright admitted. 'I started my search based on the information I had from his employer; same with Inspector Montell and Noele. Once I've got through that first phase I can widen the trawl.'

'My ex had help from his parents in trying to stitch me up, until Alex Skinner threatened them with a court-enforced audit of their assets, and with HMRC as well. That's not her usual line of work, I know,' she added, 'but her father asked her to do me a favour. Have you checked tax records too?'

'No, ma'am, but they're all on PAYE so I wouldn't expect them to be self-assessed. I'll have a look, though.'

'Do that, but don't prioritise it. Now, what did you learn from Montell's banking?'

'About as much as I learned from Coats's. He was paying much less in child support, and he seemed to manage it better. He made the payments using a banking app called Revolut. It lets you do currency exchanges at market rate and transfers funds instantly. He was never overdrawn, used credit cards to manage cash flow rather than borrow, and was able to transfer small sums regularly from his current account to a savings account. He had fourteen and a half thousand in that.'

'That sounds too good to be true,' Mann observed.

'He didn't own a car,' Wright countered. 'Think about it; a car is a big liability, unless you run a banger and don't use it very much. Even then you're going to be hit by bills for maintenance, MOT, insurance, all the things you need to do just to keep it legally parked on the public highway. If you're free of that, and a lot of single people who live in cities are, you have a hell of a lot more disposable income.'

'True. More to spend on designer clothes, maybe, but DS McClair said he told her he shopped for them in a cut-price place in Livingston. Take a look at his credit-card spend and see if it bears that out.'

'I have done already, ma'am. I looked specifically for clothing-store purchases but I didn't find any. Wherever he bought them he must have used cash.'

'He had plenty of that, going by what DI, sorry, acting DCI Haddock,' Wright thought that she detected a faint trace of irony in her tone, 'found in his safe. What about . . .'

'Anything to explain it?'

'Stop reading my mind, Jackie, but yes.'

Wright shifted in her seat. 'I've given it some thought,' she admitted. 'We know that Griff, Inspector Montell, possessed a significant holding in Krugerrands; let's assume that it was legitimate, there being no firm evidence that it wasn't. It could have been a legacy, it could have been a lottery win that he kept quiet about and invested in gold. They found two hundred and fifty; the cash in the safe might have come from the sale of others. If it did, you'd think there would be a record of their disposal, but I can't find any in his banking records. That would suggest, supposing that's what happened, that every one of them was sold privately, for cash. Who would buy them?'

'Jewellers?'

'They might, but more likely he'd have gone to a bullion dealer. There are a few of them around Edinburgh, and I will speak to them all. I've called a couple already but they're closed for the holiday. Tomorrow's Friday, so they might not open until Monday.'

'That's good work, DC Wright,' Mann said. 'Have you ever fancied transferring to Glasgow?'

Nineteen

'Who's the SIO?'

The question reached the detective from the other side of the small copse. He took two long steps to his right so that he could see the source. His exceptional height made his sterile coverall a tight fit; 'One-size' it said on the packet but he was close to being an exception. 'I am,' he said. 'DI Jack McGurk. Who's asking?'

'Dr Emily Badger, duty pathologist,' a sharp-featured, dark-haired woman replied. She gestured to her companion. 'This is my assistant, Denzil Douglas.'

McGurk thought that he caught a flash of resentment in the man's eyes. Douglas was a forensic examiner attached to the pathology department, and the two had met before. 'Hi, Denzil,' he called out. 'I thought you'd have escaped New Year duty, given your seniority.'

'There is only me, Jack,' he grumbled. 'Cuts.' He nodded towards the man who stood beside the DI. 'Hi, Lance. Happy New Year, guys, by the way. We'll maybe forego the handshake, though.'

'Has life been pronounced extinct?' Badger asked briskly as, suited for action, she slid between the wires of the fence.

'Technically not,' Detective Sergeant Lance Anderson told her. 'That said, the worm that's just crawled out of his ear makes it better than even money that he's dead.'

'Leave her alone, Lance,' McGurk murmured. 'She's a bairn. I take it Professor Grace is otherwise engaged,' he said, raising his voice to address the young pathologist.

'Yes, she is,' Badger replied. 'She pulled rank on me, she's doing the post-mortems on the two men who were found dead yesterday outside the police station. I'd expected to be asked to assist but instead I was diverted here.' She moved towards the body on the ground. 'He hasn't been moved?'

'No,' the DI confirmed.

'Not at all? What about the people who found him?'

'They were police officers, brought here by a call from that house over there.' He pointed across the field. 'They knew better than to disturb the body any more than they had to. The informant, she assumed he was a New Year drunk.'

'If so, he's had his last drink. Are we thinking suspicious death? Nobody said when I was called to the scene.'

'Take a look, Doctor.'

She crouched beside the body. As McGurk looked down at her he saw her frown. 'Have you seen this?' she asked.

'Us? Not close up. We've played it by the book and waited for you.'

'Then take a look now.'

He lowered himself down with surprising ease, turned the dead face towards him and peered at it through his varifocals. 'Very efficient,' he whispered. 'Double tap; two shots in the middle of the forehead. Very special forces.'

'So I'm told,' she said, 'and quite a coincidence. One of the men I examined yesterday was killed in almost exactly the same way.' She reached to the back of the head, running her gloved hands over it. 'No exit wound; nor was there with the other one. That means the bullets are still in there, as they were with him; no sorry, as it was, the Torphichen Place man having been killed by a single shot. You should be able to run a comparison.'

'Oh bugger,' the DI sighed. 'It means more than that. It means this just moved above our pay grade.'

'Divisional commander?' Anderson suggested.

'No,' McGurk said, 'above his too. This one goes straight to the deputy chief.'

Twenty

'Ten more minutes and I would have started without you,' Sarah Grace said, as Haddock and Singh came into the examination room of the mortuary, wearing gowns, hats and rubber boots.

'Sorry, Prof,' the DI replied. 'My last meeting went on for longer than I expected.'

She nodded. 'I know who you met. She called me after you left. Was it fruitful?'

'Yes, in that it left me with another question. No, in that I've no idea how to answer it.'

'The answers here are pretty obvious,' she took a breath, 'but my job has to look at all present factors, and determine what is and what isn't relevant.' She turned to the mortuary assistant. 'Mary, let's begin with Drawer Six.'

The detectives waited as the woman left the room; two minutes later she was back, wheeling a height-adjustable trolley bearing a stretcher laden with a white body bag; as she unzipped it, they saw it contained the remains of Griff Montell. Between them, she and the pathologist eased the burden on to the middle of the three steel examination tables.

Professor Grace switched on an overhead microphone. 'The

subject is an adult white male,' she began, 'aged thirty-nine, found dead in Torphichen Place, Edinburgh, in the early hours of the first of January. Rigor has passed, and the scene of crime examiner's report indicates that death occurred very shortly before the remains were discovered. I am now making the Y incision.'

As she went to work with a scalpel a smell seemed to explode into the examination room. Tarvil Singh had witnessed more than one examination in his police career, but unknown to Haddock, he had never made it beyond that point. 'Sorry, Sauce,' he muttered, as he turned and headed for the door.

'It's better that he keels over outside than in here,' the pathologist said. 'I doubt if the three of us could get that one off the floor.'

Haddock's reply was forestalled by the sound of his phone. He looked at the screen. 'Sorry, Sarah,' he muttered as he accepted the call, 'it's the DCC. Sir?'

'Sauce.' Even in addressing him, McGuire's tone was urgent. 'There's an incident out at Howgate. Know it? Village near Penicuik. Uniform called it in, and Midlothian CID responded; big McGurk. A body; male, middle-aged, well-dressed and very dead, dumped behind some trees on the edge of a field. The new pathologist, Badger, attended; when she saw two bullet holes in the middle of the forehead she told Jack it reminded her of Terry Coats and he called me straight off. It's possibly, maybe probably, unrelated to yours but it needs to be assessed by you until we know for sure.'

'Either way, boss, it's a serious crime. That's what we do, isn't it?'

'Yes, but at this moment your team is focused completely on

Montell and Coats. If you decide they're not linked, leave it with Jack. Where are you just now?'

'That's the thing, sir. I'm at the mortuary witnessing the post-mortems. Tarvil's here, but he's outside throwing up his last three curries. So I can barely leave him.'

'Not again!' McGuire laughed. 'He's a legend for that; I should have warned you. Leave it with me; I'll send Mann and Cotter, and tell Lottie to report to you from the scene. One thing you can do for me though. Ask Sarah to make space in her schedule to do another, tomorrow morning. I'll arrange for the victim to be taken into Edinburgh.'

Twenty-One

Few men made Lottie Mann feel small, but Jack McGurk did. She had heard of him from Bob Skinner, who had described him as 'a very good detective officer, but probably lacking command potential'. He looked commanding enough to her as she and Cotter arrived at the crime scene. There were so many vehicles lined up on the narrow Bonnyrigg road that they had to park on the other side of the roundabout that formed the junction with Penicuik, Auchendinny and the village of Howgate itself. Their way was briefly blocked by an officious uniformed constable but a flash of the DCI's warrant card, and a glare, prompted him to stand aside.

'DI Haddock might have told us to bring wellies,' Cotter complained as they surveyed the crime scene.

'You're from fucking Tyneside, John,' she laughed. 'You don't have any wellies. Me neither, but I do wear sensible shoes, and I do carry these.' She produced two pairs of disposable overshoes from her bag and handed one to the DS. Donning them, she climbed the fence and approached the tall figure in the field.

'DCI Mann,' he called out, 'I'm . . .'

'I know who you are, Inspector, the DCC briefed me. This is my DS, John Cotter.'

McGurk nodded a greeting, downwards; Cotter was a foot shorter than he was. 'This is my sergeant, Lance Anderson,' he said, introducing the bearded man by his side. 'That over there is the pathologist, Dr Badger. She's the reason I called in Special Forces. She thinks it might be related to the Griff Montell murder.' He winced. 'That's a bastard. I knew Griff well. We went out on a couple of double dates, him and Alex, me and my wife, before Martin binned his wife and kids and weaselled his way back into Alex's life. How's she taking it? She's a good act, Alex. She and Griff were never altar-bound, but I always thought that was a shame, for they made a nice couple. I've rarely seen two people more comfortable together.'

'In that case you'll know how she's taking it better than I will,' Mann told him. 'I haven't seen her since I've been through here. Sauce has been handling that; he's the SIO in DCI Pye's absence on sick leave. I do know Alex though. She did me a favour once in a domestic matter.'

'Domestic?' McGurk repeated. 'That's not her line, is it?'

'Her old man asked her to help me, and she did. She rammed it so far up my ex and his bully of a father that they've been speaking in high-pitched voices ever since. Down to business though, what have we got here?' She glanced at Badger. 'A young pathologist with a vivid imagination, or should I take this seriously?'

'No and yes, I would say. She came from Torphichen Place to here in successive days. Maybe that scene was too fresh in her mind, but my gut says it's a stone that needs turning.'

'Let's talk to her. Dr Badger!' she called out.

The pathologist looked towards her, then turned as the four

detectives approached. 'Who's next?' she asked cheerfully. 'The chief constable with his shiny hat?'

'The chief constable's a woman, and she's not given to wearing the official headgear. DCI Mann and DS Cotter, Serious Crimes. What can you tell us?'

Badger winked. 'I can tell you that he's dead; that's for sure.'

'If he wasn't, you might be,' Mann growled. 'I had an early start this morning, plus I'm never at my best when standing a few feet away from a cadaver. I'm told you're new to field work; don't assume it's like what you see on telly. There's no room for comedians in situations like this.'

The young pathologist flushed, glanced away and bit her lip.

The man beside her intervened. 'Leave her alone, Lottie. You're right, she's new, and she's had a pretty rough baptism, three gunshot victims in two days. We can all get a bit flippant when we're nervous. Don't worry, I'll break her in. She's learning all the time; for a start she knows now that a crime scene technician isn't a pathologist's assistant. Isn't that right, Emily?'

Dr Badger sniffed, but smiled weakly. 'Yes.'

'So, Denzil,' the DCI continued. 'You're the wise old head around here. What have you got from the scene so far?'

'I can tell you one thing. The Torphichen Place drop-off was a day and a half ago, right? The post-mortem examination will confirm it, but this man's been here for longer than that, a day more, maybe two. I'm going by the animal and insect depredation that's evident on the body. It's been cold, not sub-zero but enough to keep maggot infestation to a minimum, but plenty of other species will have been tucking in. It's evident to me that he wasn't just dumped here, chucked over the fence.

The position of the body makes it obvious that he was placed here carefully. You're the detectives, but you'll be supposing that it was done so that he wouldn't be seen from a passing car.'

'Agreed,' Jack McGurk said. 'Nor by farm workers either; this field's used for potatoes just now. It hasn't been touched since the last ploughing in the autumn and it won't be until the next crop gets planted. You were going through his pockets, Denzil, just before our colleagues got here. Did you find anything to identify him?'

The technician shook his head. 'No, and I wasn't meant to either. There's nothing in his pockets, no wallet, no phone, no coins. He's well dressed, though. That camel coat he's wearing, it could be a Crombie, but the label's been ripped off. It's the same with the suit, but that's expensive too. The shoes? Patent leather, thick leather sole, steel-reinforced heels. He's had a manicure too, fairly recently.'

'How about his underwear?' Cotter asked.

'I'll leave that to you. He shat himself when he was killed.'

Twenty-Two

'How was your day?' Sarah asked, as she came into the kitchen where her husband was in the midst of preparing evening meals for the four children. 'Quiet, I guess.'

'In the context of my normal days, yes,' Bob replied. 'I had one call from Jack Darke, the crime reporter on the *Saltire* trying to complain about Mario McGuire stitching him up at the media briefing last night. Other than that and one Happy New Year call from Xavi Aislado in Girona, all I've had to cope with is Seonaid having a screaming fight with her younger brother, Dawn having a dose of the squitters, and having to send Mark down to the Co-op because the milk was off. Sure; quiet.'

She laughed. 'Nothing you haven't handled before, though.'

'No, but concentrated into a short time-frame. It's fucking Pimm's o'clock, I'll tell you that.'

'What did you say to the man Darke?'

'I told him that I know what happened at the briefing, and that he was lucky Mario took it easy with him. His beef was that he thought he had an exclusive angle on Terry Coats, and that Mario spilled it to the entire room. I told him cheerfully that in my day I'd have nailed his balls to the wall for shooting

146

his mouth off like that. Then I pointed out to him that in a way it's still my day, in that the position I hold with InterMedia makes me his two-up boss, and that it's my signature on his contract of employment, not June Crampsey's. I reminded him that his value to the *Saltire* is linked entirely to the quality of the stories he produces, and that in turn is tied to his maintaining good relationships with the police service at all levels. Then I suggested that the fact he's generally regarded as being an arse-wipe kind of works against that. Finally, I told him that if hear of him being anything other than courteous while representing the paper I'd terminate the aforementioned contract. Then I hung up.'

'Will he take that?' Sarah asked. 'Can he complain to his trade union?'

'Till he's blue in the face, but it won't do him any good. He has no friends there either from what I hear. I emailed June afterwards and told her to give him a written warning, to make it official.'

'You enjoyed that, didn't you,' she challenged him. 'You took the InterMedia job on partly as a favour for a friend, but you've grown into it and it's grown with you. You like the authority it gives you, it's part of you, you can't help it.'

'Maybe so,' Bob conceded, then he smiled. 'Maybe I will take that job.'

'What job?'

'One I was offered ten days ago. You know I have friends in Westminster after that thing McIlhenney and I sorted out a wee while back?'

She nodded. 'Friends who just won the election.'

'That's right. I had a call from one of them, offering me a job. Home Office minister, with a seat in the House of Lords.'

'What!' Sarah exploded. 'And this is the first time you tell me?'

'Sorry,' he said, contritely. 'I promised I'd take time to consider it; discussing it with you is the next part of that process.'

'And?'

'What do you think?'

'I don't know. If it's what you want . . .'

'I don't,' he told her. 'Leaving aside the fact that it would cost us at least three hundred grand a year, because I couldn't combine it with the InterMedia job, leaving aside the fact that I voted Yes at the Indy referendum and will do so again given the chance, it would mean reporting to the current Home Secretary, and if that isn't my worst fucking nightmare, it's definitely high in the charts. I won't put it that way when I turn it down but turn it down I will. Happy with that?'

'Utterly.' She stepped up to him and hugged him. As she did so she noticed a large corner of the kitchen work surface. 'What's that?'

'It's a new year present from Xavi. All the directors get one. Take a look.'

She had to stand on tiptoe to open the lid and peer inside. She gasped, then jumped back. 'Jesus! What is it?'

Bob reached past her and lifted the gift from its container. 'Jamon Iberico,' he announced. 'Spanish ham, complete with stand and knife. A hundred and fifty quid's worth there. You can carve, Professor Grace.'

'No chance,' she snorted. 'I don't do delicate. I'm a butcher not a surgeon.'

'Speaking of which,' he said, 'how was your day? Pretty grim, I guess.'

'Very. And I have another booked in for tomorrow, another

gunshot victim found in Midlothian somewhere: I forget the name of the place. They don't know whether it's connected or not, and I won't be able to tell them unless the bullets I recover match the one I took from Terry Coats.'

'Nothing at all from Griff?'

'Not as much as a fragment. The one thing I do know is that they weren't shot with the same gun. The bullet I took from Drawer Five . . . it helps me to think of them by mortuary numbers rather than by name . . . was a standard nine milli-metre. Whatever killed Drawer Six was much bigger than that; something the size of Dirty Harry's weapon. Remember?'

He nodded. 'A forty-four Magnum, the most powerful handgun in the world.'

'Don't quote me the rest of that, please. It's almost true. You saw the mess it made; it took a big chunk of his brain with it. I didn't spend too much time on either of them, just enough to establish that Drawer Six was exceptionally fit for a man of his age, whereas Drawer Five had the beginnings of an oesophageal tumour that might well have finished him in a couple of years.'

'Do you think he knew?'

'At that stage, maybe not. He might have experienced general discomfort, but not enough for him to seek urgent treatment. Enough of that, though. You know I don't like bringing the likes of that home with me.' She eased him to one side, along the work surface. 'Here; let me take over or these kids are never gonna eat. What about Ignacio and Pilar?'

'They're going to eat with us; I asked them. I thought it would be nice for us to get to know the girl a bit better, given that she's Spanish and everything.'

'Everything including shacking up with your son.'

'Out here maybe, but . . .'

'No,' she insisted, 'up town as well. In theory there are three of them sharing the flat, but in practice the third party, a girl, lives with her boyfriend. Her parents don't know, of course. They're from Horsham, in Sussex.'

'How do you know all this?'

'Alex told me. Ignacio talks to her a lot. Go on, Bob, get out of here, get yourself a beer.'

He was in the process of obeying that instruction when his phone sounded. He accepted the call while uncapping his Corona and headed for the garden room. 'Mia,' he said, a little wearily. 'How goes? Is your old man home smelling of cheap Chanel Five, with his tail between his legs and a brilliant cover story? Myra, Alex's mother, used to come home smelling of Aramis or Paco Rabanne, and I, the great detective, never worked it out.'

'No, he's not!' she shouted in his ear. 'Skinner, will you take this seriously! My husband has disappeared. He's missing. I'd hoped you'd help me, but you're just like all those other cops, you couldn't care less.'

Contrition was not one of his more common reactions, but the anxiety in her voice got to him. 'I'm sorry,' he said, at once. 'We've been dealing with something serious here too. If you've seen the papers today you might guess what it is.'

'I've seen nothing today, no news at all. I haven't even listened to my own radio station. What is it?'

'Two guys have been murdered in Edinburgh. One's a police officer, the other used to be; I knew them both. One of them was friendly with Alex.'

'Oh.' Her voice softened. 'I'm sorry about that. How friendly?'

'Friendly enough for her to be pretty distraught. Did Ignacio ever tell you about the attack in her apartment?'

150

'Yes, he did. Was this the guy who protected her?' she asked.

'That's him.'

'In that case I can understand Cameron not being at the top of your list. But I really am worried about him, Bob. If you think about the life I led and the family I grew up in, that should tell you something.'

'It does,' he conceded. 'You've got my full attention, and concern. Has anything happened, since yesterday?'

'Yes,' she replied. 'We have this guy. His name is Vito Tremacoldi; officially he's on the security staff of the hotel, unofficially he's Cameron's minder. He's been with him for a few weeks. He's never obvious but when Cameron wants him to be around, he is. If Cameron ever needs a driver, like if we're ever going to a party, or even out for dinner, he's the man who takes us.'

'Did you vet him? Is he clean, or does he have a history?'

'He has a security background, Bob. That's all Cameron told me. He's a real Italian, not one of the Scots kind like your friend McGuire.'

'Only half of him,' Skinner reminded her. 'I thought Cameron only employed local heavies.'

'Vito isn't a heavy, he's a professional,' Mia assured him. 'You're doing what everyone always does, you're tarring him with his dead sister's awful past. You know as well as I do that she was the real criminal in the McCullough family, not him. She had some mental people around her, and she was a purebred psychopath.'

'In other words, she could have been a Watson,' he murmured.

'You'll never let me forget that!' she snapped, then surprised him by chuckling. 'Although I must admit that when I was told about her, my mother did come to mind. No, I promise you, Vito is very much on the up and up. He even has a couple of medals from his days in the Italian army.'

'Okay, that's Vito,' Skinner said. 'Go on.'

'He's disappeared too.'

'Why are you only telling me now? That makes a difference.'

'I'm telling you because I've only just found out. Vito has a room in the hotel that he uses when he's here, but he has a place across the river where he stays usually, a show home on one of Cameron's house-building developments.'

'Does he have a family?'

'He's only just joined us, so I don't really know, but he didn't bring anybody with him. He wasn't at the Hogmanay celebration in the hotel,' she said. 'Cameron said he didn't need him and that he should take a few days off, so when he vanished after the party, I never thought to contact him, not until today. I rang him, landline and mobile, and got no reply to either. I'm really worried, Bob. I want him found, sure, but I want it done discreetly. Cameron is who he is; he's wealthy, he's as low profile as he can manage, but he owns the fucking radio station, so all the media will be on to this if it leaks. Some of Cameron's business interests are sensitive; there could be commercial damage if this gets out. Help me, Bob, please.'

He drew a deep breath, and exhaled slowly, thinking. 'Okay, Mia,' he replied. 'I'll do what I can but be aware that if I have to involve the police I will. If that happens, it may go public.'

'Understood.'

'Right. Tell me everything you know, more than that, everything you suspect, anything he's ever done that you might not be sure about. My gut is still saying that he's done a runner for entirely personal reasons and that when you find out, you might not like them.'

'If that's so,' she said, 'God help him. You're right. I am still a Watson.'

Twenty-Three

'Who stole your scone?' Tarvil Singh asked, seeing the frown on the DI's face as he walked into the office.

'Don't ask,' he replied. 'Family business.' He was still focused on a call he had received earlier that morning from his mentor.

'Sauce,' Skinner had said. 'I need a favour. Make a note of this registration.' Later, Haddock realised that it had not even occurred to him to question the request. 'It's a Jag F-Pace; the registered keeper is Black Shield Lodge PLC, but the driver is a man called Vito Tremacoldi. It's gone missing and so has he. Does the name mean anything to you?'

'I can't say it does, gaffer. Should it?'

'Not necessarily, but it might mean something to your partner. He works for Cheeky's grandpa, and the two of them have gone off the radar at the same time. Mia's asked me to find him, without any big public fuss if possible. If that car shows up anywhere, I want to know about it. I could get this information from my friends in Millbank, but I'd rather not go to that level. Will you do this for me? I'll understand if you don't.'

'No, I won't do it for you, Sir Bob . . . but I will do it for Cheeky. Should I tell her?'

'That's your call, son. But in your shoes I'd be trying to imagine the fallout from not doing that.'

'That might not be pretty,' he had conceded. 'Leave it with me.'

Of course he had told Cheeky, as much as he knew, and of course she had phoned her stepmother to ask what was going on. She and Mia McCullough lived in a state of fragile truce not unlike that between the two Koreas, and the fact that she had been kept out of the loop for twenty-four hours did not sit well with her. Once he had brokered a tentative cease-fire, he had made the call through the central traffic control, telling the duty officer that the vehicle was wanted in connection with a potential abduction, all responses directly to him. With his fingers crossed that word of his enquiry would not find its way upstairs, he had headed for the office.

'It's like a ghost town out there, isn't it?' the DS continued. 'Officially this is the first working day of the year, but there's hardly any bugger about. They're up and at it in South Africa though. Jackie had a call from police headquarters in Pretoria five minutes ago; a guy was looking for you. His name's Major Pollock and she put his number on your desk.'

Haddock grunted his thanks and headed towards his office, stopping on the way at DC Wright's desk. 'Jackie,' he said, 'I want you to know that I appreciate the work you're doing for us. I need someone here in the office that I can rely on to do the boring stuff. With Noele being off, it's all the more difficult for you. You're covering a lot of the slack. Please, please, please, pass those sergeant's exams!'

She grinned. 'That's my blind spot, boss, but I'm trying.'

'Did Major Pollock say what he had for us?'

'Not in detail, but he sounded keen. When I called last

night with your request for information, on the contact number Mary Chambers gave you, they put me on to a sergeant. She sounded fairly disinterested, just said, "Okay, I'll get back to you." I was expecting just that, her to call me; instead I got a senior officer. I offered to pass on a message to you but he said no, that he needed to talk to you, preferably by Zoom or Skype.'

'What the hell's Zoom?'

'It's a video-conferencing tool. It's the future, Sauce.'

'I'll sooner stick to the present,' he chuckled. 'I can just about work Skype but I suppose I should keep up with the times. Did Mary have anything else for me?'

'Yes, sorry. She said she put your question to her friend, and he said that police sidearms would generally be a nine millimetre, but the make could be one of several. Helpful?'

'Slightly. Anything else? How about Griff's cousin? Any joy with him?'

A quick frown creased her forehead. 'None,' she answered. She glanced up at him. 'He's very hard to catch, but I may be getting closer. I left messages on his landline and mobile numbers yesterday, and I sent him an email, but nothing's been acknowledged. However, I did a search for him on social media and came up with a Tom DuPlessis who lives in Cape Town, and according to his 'About' info, works for a shipping company. Griff and Spring Montell are listed among his Facebook friends, so I guess that's him.'

'What sort of shipping company?'

'Cruise liners; I googled it. It's called Oceanic Magic.'

'Call them,' Haddock instructed. 'I want to find this bugger.' She reached for her computer mouse as he headed for his office.

The note that Wright had left on his desk gave him detailed instructions on how to contact the South African policeman by Zoom. He followed them step by step and waited, gazing at his own image on the computer screen until it was replaced by that of a square-headed, crew-cut man in his mid-forties, wearing a uniform shirt, with epaulettes of rank on display.

'Detective Inspector Haddock?' he began, quizzically.

'That's me,' he said.

'Sorry, I was expecting someone older.'

'You should see the portrait in my attic,' Sauce quipped, then moved on as the other man's face showed blank bewilderment. 'Thanks for responding to our request,' he said. 'I didn't expect a call, just an email.'

'It's better this way,' Pollock retorted. 'Better to make eye contact; it reduces the risk of misunderstanding. I have to tell you that when your message came across my desk, I had a hell of a shock. I knew Griffin very well; I was his supervisor when he was a cadet, and later he worked under me in the detective division here in Pretoria; I was his lieutenant. I was sorry when he decided to emigrate, but I understood the reason for it. He had little or no option but to leave, and I was more than happy to give him a reference when I was asked for it. The family court gave him a hard time after his marriage breakdown, it really did.'

'So I gather, from his sister and others. I knew him, but not that well. Why did the breakdown happen?'

'He didn't talk about it much,' the major replied. 'I don't believe there was a third party involved. Griffin changed after the incident; he became darker, not quite the open, cheerful guy he had been before. These days you might call it

PTSD, but back then we were all too butch to talk about that. Part of my job now involves officers' mental health; it's a serious issue.'

'You mentioned the incident,' Haddock said. 'I take it you mean the gold robbery. I knew nothing about that until it came out in the discussion I had with his sister and her partner. I doubt that anyone in our force was aware of it, not even Bob Skinner, who approved his transfer.'

'Skinner,' Pollock repeated, 'I remember that name. He was the guy who asked for the reference.' He frowned. 'I suppose I might have mentioned the robbery, but Griffin had put it behind him by then and so I decided just to let it lie. It wouldn't have disqualified him. Plus, of course, it was in his service record. How could I forget that?'

'What can you tell me about the robbery? How was it pulled off?'

'We never did know for sure, not all of it, but we found a tracker on the bullion van afterwards. The route from the Mint was changed every time; there were several they could use, never the most direct way, all on roads that were rarely used. The choice was at the discretion of the escorting officers, but that day, with the tracker on the van, that was irrelevant. How it got there, we never did find out. Our suspicion was that it was put there by either the driver or his mate before they left the Mint, but they were both shot dead so it couldn't be confirmed. If one of them was involved, he never collected his share. Griffin was lucky; he was shot twice but survived. I visited him in hospital.' He touched the side of his head, drawing a finger across it. 'The second gunshot ploughed a furrow, right along there. It was at close range, too.'

'The gold was never traced, I'm told,' Haddock said.

'Fucking untraceable, wasn't it? As soon as it was off the scene and out of its boxes.'

'How much was stolen? I've heard a couple of figures.'

The major raised his eyebrows. 'That doesn't surprise me. The Mint claimed that ten thousand coins had been lost. They said that they were never moved in quantities larger than that, but actually an audit revealed that to be bullshit. In fact, there were thirty-five thousand Krugerrands in the van. It was one of the biggest gold robberies ever.'

'You're telling me that upwards of thirty-five million sterling, current value, was taken?'

'That's right. The financial crash happened just after the theft, so the haul was worth a hell of a lot more than that for a couple of years.'

'What happened to it?'

'The belief was that nothing did, that the thieves put it away somewhere. It was too much to fence; if they had tried, even in small parcels, we have underworld sources that would have let us know if important quantities of Krugerrands suddenly appeared. Again,' Pollock admitted, 'we have nothing more than theory, and that is that most of it is still out there.' He paused. 'Look, Detective Inspector, I'm puzzled. Why are you so interested in this, and why are you asking for a copy of the police file? Be honest with me, please.'

'I will,' Haddock said. 'I'll be completely frank. The fact is, we've got no obvious suspects for these murders. We know that Griff and Terry Coats had encountered each other when Coats was still a cop, although they were in different forces. We've discovered also that Griff was in a developing relationship with one of my officers, who happened to be Coats' ex-wife. Other than that we have nothing that puts them together . . .

except . . . Coats worked in airport security and claimed to have uncovered a smuggling operation there, with gold coins being brought in by flight crew of a specific airline and routed through a certain airside shop. That's how we first heard about the robbery, from Coats; he claimed that he had been told about it by Griff Montell. Yet Griff never mentioned it to any of his colleagues.'

'I can understand that,' the South African said. 'It was a painful memory for him.'

'Given what Coats said about the smuggling operation, can I ask, was there ever any suggestion of Russian involvement in the hold-up?'

'None at all; we didn't have any fucking clue who might have been involved, and that remains true, we still don't. If your investigation uncovers anything, please, please let us know. That robbery is still a big stain on our reputation.'

'Of course we will,' Haddock said. 'Are you okay with giving me a copy of the investigation file?'

'Sure. It's all digital, so no problem. It includes investigator reports, the text of a statement by Griff, crime-scene photographs and all the forensics.'

'Thanks. Can you remember, where were the van driver and his mate killed?'

'They were inside the cab, but they'd opened the door. The assumption was that they'd decided to give up and save their skins, only the robbers didn't intend to leave any witnesses. They hadn't a chance. Somebody emptied an Uzi magazine into them.'

'The same weapon as wounded Griff and killed his partner?'

'No,' Pollock said. 'All the bullets were nine millimetre, but the one that was taken out of Fannie DeWalt came from a different firearm than the one that shot the van crew. We never did find the cartridges that hit Griffin. The shoulder wound was through and through; the head shot we guessed hit the roadway and fragmented. You got an email for me?' he asked.

Haddock spelled out his online address letter by letter. As he finished, the door of his tiny office opened and Wright entered. 'I called Oceanic Magic,' she whispered. 'Tom DuPlessis is their baggage controller. He didn't turn up for work yesterday morning or today. The company can't find him either.'

'Maybe I can get them some help,' he murmured in reply. 'Meantime, get on to them and find out their cruise schedules over the last few years, where they sailed from, where they docked, everything you can.'

He turned back to the computer, to see Major Pollock's concentrated frown as he clicked his mouse. 'There,' he declared, 'that's the report off to you.' He had barely finished speaking when an incoming email notification popped up on Haddock's screen.

'Great,' he replied. 'Thanks for that. I'll study it, and if I have any more questions I'll get back to you. Meanwhile, Major, there's one more thing I wonder if you can do for me. I need to speak to Griff's cousin. His name is Tom DuPlessis, he lives in Cape Town, and he works for a cruise line called Oceanic Magic. My problem is that he's not responding to any messages, and he's missing from work.'

'Are you thinking this might be connected to Griffin's murder?'

'I have no reason to, but you and I both know what we detectives think of coincidences.'

'Absolutely. Until they're proven, we don't believe in them.

Email me the contact details you have for him, and I will order a search for him, country-wide. It's been good to meet you, Detective Inspector Haddock, even if you haven't come out and told me exactly what's in your mind. Level with me: you suspect that Griffin was involved in the robbery in some way, do you not?'

Sauce sighed. 'I wish I didn't, but yes, you're right.'

Twenty-Four

'When will the pathologist be here?' Lottie Mann asked, impatiently.

'The post-mortem's down for twelve noon,' Denzil Douglas reminded her. 'Professor Grace will be here by eleven forty-five, I'd guess, but not much earlier. If you've got time on your hands, Chief Inspector, there's a coffee place in the bookshop round the corner.'

'I'll get by,' she said. 'You can spend some of the time filling me in on what you got from the body.'

'The shitty drawers were Levi's. They'd left the label on those; no surprise, all things considered. As I established at the scene there was no identification on the coat, suit and shirt. However, the shoes he was wearing came from a company called Crick and Son, of Jermyn Street in London, and from the look of them they're hand made. I've sent them to the company by courier and with a touch of luck they'll be able to match them to a last and tell us whose it was.'

'Last?' John Cotter said.

'It's the mould of the customer's feet, that all his shoes are made from. Very expensive.'

'You might say he was well-heeled.'

Douglas stared at the detective.

'Well-heeled?' Cotter ventured. 'Wealthy?'

'Whether he was or not, he's been soled down the river by somebody,' Mann drawled, as Sarah Grace came into the room.

Twenty-Five

'I wish my office was like this,' Sauce Haddock remarked, looking around the spacious glass-walled room.

'I still wish, sometimes, that my office was like yours,' Bob Skinner countered. 'Then reality bites, and I hear the goose-steps of the march of time. Do you want a coffee?'

'Thanks, gaffer, I need one.'

'For fuck's sake, Sauce, as I keep telling you, call me Bob.'

The DI smiled. 'I will when I feel comfortable with it.'

'You didn't just come here for a view of a miserable rain-sodden January Edinburgh,' Skinner said, as he handed his visitor a mug.

'No,' he conceded. 'I'd rather we talked about Grandpa away from the office. I've had no reported sightings of Tremacoldi's car, and nobody's heard from him. Mia's been calling him and so has Cheeky. His phone's going straight to voicemail, and they've been leaving messages, but neither's had any joy. The thing that worries me most is him not getting back to Cheeky. If he's had a strop with Mia that she's not telling us about and gone away for a while to cool down, that I would understand, but him not calling his grand-daughter, that is something else.' He glanced up at Skinner.

'Do you think I should be making this official?'

'That depends how much heat you want to risk. If it was leaked and the *Courier* in Dundee picked it up, the *Saltire* would have to follow. That fucker Jack Darke would be on it like a flash. If he found out there's a connection between Cameron and me through Ignacio and Mia . . . that's if he doesn't know already . . . he'd be all over it. If I tried to shut him down, I wouldn't put it past him to leak that to the rest. It's been a little over two days since Grandpa left the reservation, he's a middle-aged man and with his minder Tremacoldi being gone too there's no reason to fear for his safety. Hold off, I'd say, and let's see how it falls.' He took a mouthful from his own mug. 'How's the investigation going?' he asked.

'In a direction I never expected,' Haddock admitted. 'It's clear that Griff was seriously up to something. He told Chief Inspector McGlashan, and he told Noele, that he was going to South Africa last Saturday, and he even checked in for his evening flight and dropped his bag, but he never got on board. We've got him on camera in the airport, landside, three and a half hours before flight time, then we lose him . . . until about half twelve on New Year's Day, when he and Coats turned up dead.' He sighed. 'The stuff we found in the safe, that really threw me, and now I know about his involvement in the robbery . . .'

'What do you mean by that?'

The young detective updated his mentor on his discovery, from Spring Montell and later from Major Pollock, of the dead man's part in the drama of the unsolved bullion hijacking. 'I've read the report. There was only one thing in it that I wasn't told by Pollock. The route they took from the gold refinery to the depository was decided on the day by the officer in charge of the escort vehicle. That was Griff, as he had seniority. There were six options; the one he chose went over a stretch that was off highway. You can see the entrance and exit on Google Earth street view, but not the track itself. That runs for maybe a mile until it re-joins the roadway. That's where the robbery happened. I've logged the file and attachments on to the investigation database, but I can email it to you if you want.'

'A bit fucking late for that, since this is the first I'm hearing about it,' Skinner exclaimed. 'Why was it left off his application when he came to Edinburgh? Be sure it was, Sauce; I would not have seen that and forgotten about it. Why did Pollock not tell me in the covering letter that came with it? Why was there no mention of it in his service record?'

'Pollock told me that he didn't think it would affect the transfer,' Haddock explained. 'He said it was such a traumatic experience for Griff that he wanted to help him to put it behind him, to leave it in South Africa. He was shot twice and left for dead.'

'But he wasn't fucking dead, was he? And if you're right and he did want to forget it all, why would he tell Terry Coats about it? That's where we first heard about it, from Terry when he was caught shagging the air hostess. Have you found her yet?' he asked, suddenly.

'She's still on our to-do list. I've asked Jackie to trace her, through the airline.' He grimaced. 'The DCC's been good, giving me extra manpower, but I could sure do with having Noele back. Fuck me, I could do with Sammy Pye getting over his bug, and taking the load off me.'

'Neither of those things will ever happen, Sauce,' Skinner said, quietly. 'It'll take a real effort to keep Noele in the job at all, and as for Sammy,' his face darkened, 'it's no bug, I'm afraid. Don't press me about it, but you can take my word for it, he's not coming back.'

The DI stared at him. 'Seriously?' he whispered.

He nodded.

'The place is falling apart, gaffer.'

'Then it's up to the likes of you to hold it together. Who's handling the Howgate murder?' he asked. 'I saw a *Saltire* news feed just before you arrived, but of course I knew about it from Sarah. Who took the media briefing? All it said was that it was a police spokesperson.'

'The new press officer, on the DCC's orders. Pending the autopsy, we're still calling it a suspicious death, but only for the media. Two shots in the forehead.'

'The second one usually rules out suicide,' Skinner observed, grimly. 'Do you think it links to Griff and Coats?'

'I'm not thinking anything. I don't have the luxury of speculation. I can only deal with what I can prove.' He glanced at his mentor. 'What do you reckon?'

'Given the time-frame, I'd be assuming it does until I knew different. Have they identified the victim?'

'Not yet. From what I've heard from Lottie and Jack McGurk, someone wanted to make it hard for us. But we'll . . .' He broke off as his mobile sounded. 'Jackie,' he said as he took the call, then fell silent, listening. 'Thanks,' he said eventually. 'I don't know where that takes us, forward or back.' He turned back to Skinner. 'The count rises. Jackie's just off the phone to the Wister Air HR department. Coats' bird, Aisha Karman, went missing last November. She flew into John Lennon Airport in Liverpool, coming from Amsterdam. She was supposed to join a flight from Manchester to Cape Town next day but never showed up. She was booked into a hotel called the Grange, at Manchester Airport, but didn't turn up there. The airline waited for three days and then reported her missing to the police in Liverpool and they've heard nothing since.'

'When did we catch her with Terry Coats?'

'A few months before that.'

'I reckon you should get in touch with your Scouser colleagues,' Skinner suggested, but in a way that made it sound like an order, 'and request that they get the finger out.'

Twenty-Six

'There you are, Mr Douglas,' Sarah Grace said, as she handed two small containers to the technicians. 'Two bullets retrieved from the brain of Drawer Three. They're the same calibre as the one I took from Drawer Five yesterday. It's up to you to determine whether they were fired from the same gun.'

'Thanks, Prof,' he replied. 'Do you have anything else for me? I've taken fibre samples from all of his clothing, and the shoes are off to London. If that's all there is, I'll head off to the lab.'

She turned to Mann and Cotter. The DCI was paler than she had been an hour before, but her colleague seemed unperturbed. 'Drawer Three was a healthy male, aged somewhere between fifty and sixty, or possibly a year or two older. He was physically fit, a non-smoker and his liver shows no sign of excessive alcohol consumption. His last meal was battered haggis and chips, consumed very shortly before death, with Irn Bru on the side. His bladder evacuated itself when he died, as did his bowels, but Scotland's national drink hadn't made it that far. Wherever he died, I'd say it wasn't far from a fish and chip shop.'

'Vinegar or sauce?' Mann asked.

The pathologist smiled at Cotter's puzzled expression. 'She's asking me, Sergeant, whether he was from Edinburgh, and liked brown sauce on his supper, or from the west of Scotland and took vinegar. Tribal customs that you obviously haven't caught up with. The answer, DCI Mann, is vinegar, but don't read too much into that. Now what may be good news,' she continued. 'I had the body X-rayed and that revealed that the man had a plate in his right femur, put there to repair a bad fracture, around five years ago. I've removed it; it was made in England, but that's not definitive, for these things are exported all around the world. However, it had a serial number, and I'm hopeful that the manufacturer will be able to tell me where it was implanted, and into whom. His killer tried to remove all identification; he was careless when he left the shoes behind, but there's no way he could have known about the plate.'

'Killers,' Mann said, quietly. 'We saw the victim in situ. There's no way that he was put there by one person alone unless he was the size of Drew McIntyre.'

'Who's he?' Cotter enquired. 'One of your Glasgow villains?'

'National hero, more like,' his boss replied scornfully. 'He's a wrestler. How about time of death, Professor,' she continued. 'We know he was there for a while, but how specific can you be?'

Sarah frowned. 'Looking at the physical and other factors, rate of decomposition, and the beginnings of saponification in the area of the body that was resting on a very wet surface, my estimate is that he died some time on Saturday. Looking at insect invasion, and animal depredation, I believe that the body was dumped not long after he was killed. On the assumption that it wasn't done in the daylight hours, you're looking at Saturday night or Sunday morning.' She paused, looking Mann in the eye. 'There's one thing about the body that I haven't mentioned, and it could be important. Three fingers on the left hand were broken, fresh fractures, untreated. That suggests there was a struggle before he died; either that, or the man was tortured.'

Twenty-Seven

'I don't know why they reported it to us, mate.' Haddock was sure he could hear the officer on the other end of the line stifle a yawn. 'If she was booked into a hotel in Manchester, like you say, they should have reported it to the Mancs, shouldn't they?'

'That's a debate for another day, Constable,' the Scot said, failing to keep his irritation from his voice. 'What I'm asking is if she's still on your books as a missing person.'

'Let me look, then. Kaufman, F, no, that's a bloke. Yeah, here she is; Karman, A, female. The file's still open, so she's still missin', as far as we know. Happens from time to time, mate, especially with cabin crew on the smaller airlines. The pay's crap, they line up a better job in one of the countries on their routes and next time they're there, like, they just bail out. Where's this girl from? South Africa? Yeah, I could see that havin' happened.'

'Maybe you could, Constable Lynch, and maybe you're even right, but has your force actually done anything to locate this woman? Even something as basic as circulating her photo?'

'We don't have one, mate.'

'Fuck me!' Haddock gasped. 'Even I've got one and I've only started looking for her today. I'll email it to you. I need

173

this woman; she's a potential witness in a double-murder investigation.'

'Then you better talk to my boss, mate.'

'That would be Detective Chief Inspector Mate, and yes, that would be an idea.'

'Very good, sir,' the Liverpudlian said stiffly. 'If you'll hold on for a minute, I'll see if she's available.'

The minute stretched into a second, and then a third. He was on the point of hanging up when a female voice came on the line. 'DCI Haddock? I'm Inspector Jamie Ellis. You need our co-operation, I'm told.'

'Acting DCI; DI really. I only used it to light a fire under your doorkeeper.'

'Bert Lynch?' she chuckled. 'Sorry about that. He's a year and a half off retirement and he doesn't give one.'

'If you think about having a whip round to send him off early, let me know. I might contribute.'

'He gave me the bones of the story, would you care to flesh them out?'

'Sure. I'm the SIO on a double murder in Edinburgh; one of the victims was a serving police officer, the other an ex-cop. I'm trying to trace a South African woman, Aisha Karman, age twenty-eight, last seen in Liverpool in July. She worked for an airline called Wister Air, but dropped out of sight somewhere between John Lennon Airport and the Grange Hotel, Manchester. Her employer reported her missing, and from the little that PC Lynch could tell me, she still is.'

'She's a potential witness in a cop murder, you say.'

'Yes.'

'Okay,' Inspector Ellis said, decisively. 'I'll dig out the file and put a team on it. Don't worry, PC Lynch will not be on it.

If she's anywhere in the North West we'll find her. Is she likely to co-operate?'

'Maybe not,' Haddock admitted. 'She's suspected of smuggling stolen gold into Scotland, so she might not be too keen to talk to us.'

'Can you give me grounds to hold her?'

'I'm pretty sure I can find a sheriff who'll give me a warrant that lets me bring her back to Scotland, but that'll hold for as long as it takes her to brief a half-decent solicitor. The source of my information was one of our murder victims, so he won't make a very reliable witness.'

Twenty-Eight

'How much progress have they made, Mario?' the chief constable asked, as her deputy came into the room. Outside, the street lights lit the evening, as she finished tidying her desk, and readying herself to go home.

'On tracing the perpetrators?' he replied. 'Frankly, none. On uncovering stuff that we never knew or suspected about Inspector Montell, remarkably well.' He briefed her on the discoveries made in his apartment, on the security that had been installed, and on the facts about his South African service that Haddock had uncovered.

'Jeez,' she sighed. 'You think you know people. Although,' she continued, 'I can't say that I ever really knew Montell. He was a fixture, always there with a smile when one was needed and a word, and yet, now I think back, it was all superficial. He was like a mirror; when you looked at him you never really saw anything of him, just a reflection of yourself.' She shuddered. 'How many people do I really know, I wonder?'

'How many can you know, Maggie? You have going on for eighteen thousand officers under your command, and on top of that about five thousand civilian staff. If you knew any more than three or four per cent of them on a personal level it would be a miracle. Even remembering that many names would be an achievement.'

'I wasn't talking about my officers,' she retorted. 'I meant people in general. Mario, you know me better than any man alive; we were married, but I never let you get close. In the end, I drove you away and you were happy to go. That's how I am. I have a barrier built into my personality and it's impenetrable. Yes, Stevie got inside my wall. Stevie made me happy, Stevie gave me a child. And then Stevie opened that booby-trapped fucking door in that fucking house and Stevie died.' Her face contorted with the pain of the memory. 'I know now I should have had counselling after it happened, but instead I had cancer, then I had Stephanie and I rebuilt my wall around us both. Since my sister went back to Australia to pick up her career again, and I put Steph into day care, we've been completely alone. When you called me to the crime scene in Torphichen Place, I could only go because you sent an officer to stay with her. How many friends do you think I have? People to call up for a chat, people to meet for a drink. None. I'm not kidding, none. I am completely absorbed in myself and my daughter, and that's how I feel most comfortable. At work, I'm exactly the same, introspective, and I can feel myself shrinking. When I took over this job, I hoped I would expand into it. Before, when I was climbing the ladder, it was okay, because I had my little box of things to do and that was manageable. When I became Andy Martin's deputy, it still was, because Andy never delegated anything to me. Then I became chief, and overnight the box was enormous. I've managed for a while, but gradually it's begun to eat me. I've been pushing more and more in your direction and Brian Mackie's and Doreen Irons'. You're running the fucking force now, Mario; I know it, you know it and so does anyone who operates at our level. Yes, occasionally I will try to assert myself; for example on Wednesday morning, when I summoned DS McClair . . . fuck, I'm sitting here trying to remember her first name . . . to the crime scene to identify we had the body of the father of her child. That was an awful thing to do but something inside me said, "It happened to me, so you can face up to it too." Inevitably, I'm taking it home. When I got back on Wednesday morning I shouted at Steph. I don't remember ever doing that, ever. She cried, and so did I and that's when I knew, Mario, that I can't do this anymore. I'm resigning. I'm all my kid's got and she deserves far more of me. Fuck it, so do I!' She looked up at him from her chair, as the tears began to stream down her face.

He stepped across, sat on the edge of her desk, and took her hand. 'I'm sorry, love,' he said, gently. 'I should have realised how bad it was and helped you before now. You do have friends, you know; you've got Paula and me for a start, and big Bob and Sarah, and Brian, and Sauce, and everybody who's been alongside you all these years.' He frowned. 'This is my fault, Mags. You talk about driving me away, and maybe you did, but I didn't go that far. When Stevie died, I should have been there for you far more than I was, but just like you, I was too wrapped up in myself.' He pulled a tissue from a box on the desk and handed it to her. 'Dry them, go on, and tidy yourself up, while I tell you what's going to happen. You're not resigning, you are going on sick leave. You've got mental-health issues and, like any other officer, you'll be assessed by a police-service doctor, and we'll go by the findings. Agreed?'

She nodded and gave him a watery smile. 'If you say so, big guy.'

Twenty-Nine

'Aw no,' Cheeky Davis moaned, as her partner's phone sounded by the side of their bed. 'With this thing going on I wasn't expecting you to have a Saturday morning off, but it's ten past eight.'

'Not for this guy,' Sauce replied, drowsily. 'He's in Pretoria, and they're an hour ahead of us.' He accepted the call. 'Good morning, Major Pollock.'

'I'm calling from home, Inspector,' the South African said. 'I thought you'd want to know this right away. We've found Griffin's cousin. He was stopped late last night by a patrol car about fifty kilometres from the Namibian border. He said he was going on holiday, but the officers didn't believe him, since he had virtually no luggage beyond an overnight bag. He's being brought straight to Pretoria by car but it's a long way, well over a thousand kilometres. As soon as I have him here, I'll arrange for you to talk to him, maybe tomorrow morning if that suits.'

'Thanks,' Haddock replied. 'I'd prefer it if you let him sweat for a few hours.'

'Sure, would you like us to tell him what you're going to be talking about?'

'Yes, please. I want to interview him about certain matters that have arisen from his cousin's murder, including an allegation of gold-smuggling, money-laundering and abduction.'

'Abduction?'

'That's possible. We're looking for a potential witness. Her name is Aisha Karman; she worked for an airline called Wister Air, until she left them six months ago, without notice.'

'What's her nationality?'

'She has a British passport, but she was educated in Port Elizabeth, South Africa.'

'Then she could have come home. I'll do what I can to help you find her. Plus, give me everything you have on DuPlessis or suspect about him and I'll look into that as well. Anything else?'

Yes,' Haddock said, 'one more thing. Why was there no mention of the gold robbery on Griff's service record when he applied to join the Edinburgh police?'

'What are you talking about? I told you, there was.'

'Not according to Sir Robert Skinner, our former chief constable; he vetted him and approved his appointment. He wouldn't have forgotten something like that.'

'Then Griffin must have doctored it himself. That's all I can suggest. After the robbery, he had a lot of "Hero cop" coverage. He didn't like attention like that.'

'Obviously,' the DI agreed, 'and maybe there was a reason for it. Thanks, Major. We'll speak tomorrow.'

He returned the phone to his charging stand, and rolled over . . . only to find himself alone. Cheeky was standing by the side of the bed tying the cord of her pyjama bottoms.

'Come on, babe,' he pleaded. 'Get back in, I don't have to get up for another fifteen minutes.'

She looked down on him, imperiously. 'Make that half an hour and I might be interested.'

He reached out for her pyjama cord.

Thirty

'You'd think that road from Glasgow would be quiet on a Saturday morning, John,' Lottie Mann complained, as they strode into the area of the Serious Crimes office that they had commandeered.

'It's much the same on Tyneside,' her DS pointed out. 'Down there, every bugger seems to head for the Metrocentre at weekends.' He looked around the room. Jackie Wright was at her desk, but otherwise it was empty. 'Fucking typical, we've come the furthest and yet we're almost the first in. Remind me, why are we here?'

'We're trying to find the killer of a police officer,' she reminded him, as she lowered herself into an unyielding chair. 'And there's always something to do. For example, there's the phone records for both our victims.' She reached out a hand. 'Let's have a look at them.'

Cotter shrugged. 'I've been through them, boss; both Montell's and Coats's. There's nothing on either that ties them together, other than obliquely.'

'What do you mean by obliquely?'

'I found an exchange of WhatsApp messages between Montell and DS McClair in which Coats's name comes up.

Specifically, she refers to, quote, that cunt of an ex of mine, unquote, in the context of him failing to pick up her son and making her miss a date with Montell. Yes, we've been told by DI Haddock that Coats told him and Sir Robert that he knew Montell from previous police service, but there's nothing in the messages to indicate that McClair was aware of them being acquainted, far less in regular contact. However, there is plenty of evidence of Coats's gambling habit. There's loads of phone calls to bookies, and his emails show an online history of bets being placed, and even notification of winning bets, albeit very rarely.'

'Aye, fine, John,' Mann said, 'but we're no closer to putting those two men in each other's company. And until we can do that, we're no closer to whoever did them in, so we're contributing nothing to the main investigation. That's what you're telling me really.'

The DS agreed. 'That's what I'm telling you, ma'am.' Then he smiled. 'But that was the bad news. Do you want the good?'

'Please,' she sighed, unimpressed. 'Anything to brighten my day.'

'I've got an email here from Denzil Douglas, the pathology forensic technician. He's had a lightning fast response from Crick, that shoemaker in Jermyn Street he was on about. He says they've identified the customer; his name is, or rather it was, Anatoly Rogozin.'

'Say that again?' the DCI snapped.

'Anatoly Rogozin,' he repeated.

'Fuck! It couldn't be.' She stared at him, then snatched her phone from her pocket, scrolled through her contacts and called a number.

'Lottie,' Bob Skinner answered. 'What can I do for you?'

Thirty-One

'Are you good, Lexie?' Dominic Jackson asked his house-mate.

'I've been better,' Alex Skinner admitted. 'But I was a lot worse before I moved in with you. Do you know,' she said, 'that you are the only person who's ever called me "Lexie"? Not even my dad ever called me that. I like it, but why do you?'

'One,' he replied, 'it suits you, two, it gets you out of yourself. You had a faint touch of locked-in syndrome when you came here, in that you were obsessed with Alex and all the issues she had. Lexie's a different woman; you like it, and I think you like her a bit more than you were liking yourself.' He winked. 'But you're both the same really.' He paused. 'Can I ask you something serious now? How did you really feel about Griff Montell?'

'Honestly? I don't know anymore. He should have been the man of my dreams. He was kind, considerate, brave, funny, attentive, hung like a donkey, and very good in bed . . . two things that rarely go together in my limited experience. I heard a joke the other day: "What's the difference between a clitoris and a golf ball? A man's prepared to spend ten minutes looking for a golf ball." Griff? All I can say is he wasn't a golfer. I've

184

never had a shopping list when it comes to men, but any who don't live up to my basic expectations don't last long. If I'd had one, he would have ticked all the boxes and added a couple more. I can't imagine why his wife left him.' She frowned. 'Why didn't I fall in love with him? Maybe I did at the beginning, but it didn't develop; it settled into something that I can only describe as comfortable. Looking back on it now, it occurs to me that . . . this is going to sound vain . . . I was irked with him because I realised that he didn't mind me not falling head over heels for him. He was all the things I said, made me feel good in many ways, but he never once used the "L" word. He never showed any signs of falling in love with me. I told myself "That's fine, it's cool, it's uncomplicated," but inside, I was hurt, suffering from a bruised ego, but unable to do anything about it. Maybe I did love him, Dominic,' she exclaimed, 'but the one thing I do know is that he didn't fucking love me!'

He looked at her and saw her eyes mist over. 'He didn't love anyone,' he told her. 'He couldn't, literally. What you are describing to me is a man with what psychologists tend to diagnose as an antisocial personality disorder. Everything you've told me, and what I've been told by the deputy chief about his personal tastes, the things Sauce found in his home, and the way he protected it, they all bear that out.'

'Mario spoke to you about him?' she asked, surprised.

'Yes. He's given me a commission; he wants me to draw up a psychological profile of Griff.' He glanced at her with a shy smile. 'It's the first one I've had from that level in the police service.'

'I thought you were wary of accepting those.'

'I am, but there's no possibility of me being called as a witness with this one, as the subject's dead. There can't be a trial.'

'You're going to say he had a personality disorder? Griff?'

'That's what I'm seeing. He reminds me of a man I met in prison. He was utterly charming, the most popular man on the wing in a place where that sort of behaviour can have you marked down as a grass or a . . . you know. He was good company; I spent quite a bit of time talking to him in the gym. He was clever, articulate and highly intelligent. In society he'd been a senior university lecturer in mathematics. And he'd killed four women by the time he made the one mistake that had led him there. I made him a case study in one of my degree dissertations. He was a very high-functioning psychopath. The Inspector Montell you're showing me is exactly the same.'

'Griff? Really?' Her tone was sceptical.

He smiled again. 'Are you thinking that it takes one to know one?'

'No,' she protested, but in truth the thought had crossed her mind.

'You were,' he insisted, 'but don't be embarrassed for I've considered that very question. The first profile I ever did was on myself, and I got an A for it. My conclusion was that I am neither a sociopath nor a psychopath. I did hurt people, yes. Eventually I did worse. But I did it because I'd been hurt myself as a kid. It was the world I'd grown up in and it was what I'd been shown as a norm, but I felt empathy for the people I was hurting, with only a couple of exceptions. When I was convicted, I was called a psycho by one of the tabloids, but I never was. I knew the difference between right and wrong, and crucially I actually did care about it.'

'Are you saying that Griff didn't?'

'Precisely. And more; I read Griff Montell as someone who might have been a very dangerous man.'

Thirty-Two

'Sir, are you up to speed with the murder investigations that we're all working on?' Lottie Mann began.

'Reasonably so,' Skinner replied. He was slightly out of breath and the wind noise in the background made her suspect that she had caught him in the middle of a run. 'Sauce is talking to me,' he continued, more evenly, 'with the deputy chief's approval, and of course I'm getting feedback at home, given that my wife did the autopsies on them both.'

'She also did one yesterday morning.'

'That's right. Are you going to tell me they're connected?'

'No, I'm not, but we've identified the Howgate victim and the name I've had thrown at me got my attention big time and it will yours too, I guess. Rogozin. Remember him?'

'Dimitri Rogozin? Yes, of course I do,' Skinner exclaimed, 'and the thing I remember most about him is that he's dead!'

'That makes two of them. We've managed to identify the man who was found shot dead and dumped out of the city, in Midlothian. Your wife's third new year autopsy. His shoemaker put a name to him, and that's what it is: Anatoly Rogozin. We're just at the beginning of trying to find everything we can about him, but Crick of Jermyn Street has just told us in an

187

email that his shoes are delivered to an address in Chelsea, and payment comes from a platinum Amex card.' She paused, but Skinner sensed that she was simply building up to the headline announcement. 'That card,' she announced, with something akin to triumph, 'is billed to Merrytown Football Club, of our very own Scottish Premier League. Its principal shareholder, as we both know, is your friend, Cameron McCullough. We're going to need to talk to him, sir. Do you know where I can find him?'

He stayed silent for a few seconds, digesting what she had told him before replying. 'My acquaintance, Lottie,' he corrected her, 'but it's a hell of a good question. I'd like to know the answer myself.'

'What do you mean?'

'Grandpa McCullough went missing around the same time as the bodies were dumped in Torphichen Place. He hasn't been officially reported as a misper . . . shit, I've always hated that term and here I am using it . . . but there's a location request out for his minder's car.'

'What?' she gasped. 'Does that make him a suspect?'

'On the face of it, no, because he was in his hotel in Perthshire immediately before he vanished. But what you've told me about the dead guy in Howgate makes me a hell of a lot more keen to find him. It's time I dug out that Special Constable warrant card that Maggie Steele gave me. You and Cotter and I need to head up to Tayside.'

Thirty-Three

Tarvil Singh was never at his most sociable in the morning, and he knew it. In his earliest days as a police officer there had been those who said he was never at his most sociable in the afternoon either. That had been an advantage on Saturday afternoon duty at Edinburgh's football grounds, but after surprising himself by securing a transfer to CID, he had worked on his social and communication skills His preference was still to speak to no one until ten o'clock had gone, but as a detective officer that was difficult to manage.

When the office door opened and Sauce Haddock stepped into the room it was five minutes past his silent zone. He glanced at his watch, a gesture that some senior officers might have seen as insubordinate.

'I know,' the DI said. 'I had domestic matters to take care of before I came in. Let's just leave it at that.'

'Aye, sure,' Singh chuckled. 'You had to make her breakfast; and it'll probably be an expensive dinner the night as well? Where'll it be? Ondine? The Honours? The Ivy?'

'Oh no; they're for when Cheeky's paying. She makes more than I do, Tarvil. Tonight, it'll be lemon chicken at the Loon Fung.'

The sergeant felt himself salivate. 'Ohhh! Lucky bastard.'

'I hope so. The table's booked for seven o'clock. Whether we make it, that'll depend on how today goes.' He glanced around the room, nodding greetings to Wright and the two other officers on duty. 'What about Mann and Cotter?' he asked. 'Are they not here today?'

'Been and gone,' Singh told him. 'They're following up some info on the Howgate incident. I heard her talking to someone, then a few minutes ago they headed for the door. They never said where they were going, and I . . .'

'Let me guess. It being short of ten o'clock you never asked them?'

'Something like that,' he grunted, as Haddock stepped past him and into his little office.

The DI sighed as he sat at his desk. His lateness was attributable, in part, to the need to reassure Cheeky that her grandfather was surely okay, having taken his new minder with him to wherever he was going. 'Right now, love, he's probably standing on the first tee of a country club in Malaga, or maybe even Miami, with three other guys. You know he's taken up golf.'

'I know,' she had admitted, 'because you played with him and you told me how bad he was. Grandpa doesn't like being second best at anything.'

'He's a lot worse than second best. Give a kangaroo a golf club and it would have a better swing than him.'

'Which is exactly why he wouldn't swan off on a golf tour. Sauce, the truth is he only took up the game in the hope that it would make him closer to you, because you're going to be the father of his great-grandson . . . some day!' she had added quickly.

'Some day?'

'Sauce!'

The smile left his face as his mobile sounded and he saw the name on the screen. Arthur Dorward was famously phlegmatic on his better days; at weekends, he was notoriously dour.

'Mr Haddock,' he growled, 'I'm calling you from the crime campus at Gartcosh. I can only hope you're somewhere equally grim.'

'I'm at Fettes,' he replied. 'Does that qualify?'

'Fuck, yes. The ugliest building in Edinburgh, even worse than the mortuary,' he hesitated for a second, 'which, in a way, brings me to why I'm calling you. That gun you sent us for test-firing and comparison purposes, the Beretta. You said it was just for elimination, right?'

'Yes. It came from Griff Montell's safe. He was a naughty lad to have it, but that hardly matters now.'

'You might say that, and I can confirm that it was not the weapon that killed Mr Coats.'

'No,' the DI said. 'I knew from the start that it couldn't have been, given the timeline. Sorry, Arthur, I suppose that was a waste of resources.'

'I'll accept an apology any time, son; even when it's not warranted. The Beretta might not have done for Coats, but it did account for the man we now know as Anatoly Rogozin.'

'What man, Arthur?' Haddock exclaimed, puzzled.

'Jesus,' Dorward chuckled, 'and you're the SIO. Do you not read your own investigation files, or speak to your own officers? He's the guy they found behind the trees in Howgate. Denzil Douglas emailed it to big Lottie's new gofer last night.'

'It's the first I've heard of it. The pair of them are out of the office, but maybe they've left me a note. Who is he, this Rogozin?' he mused.

'That may be what they've gone to find out. But,' he continued, 'leave him to one side for a moment. As I told you, he was killed by Montell's gun; it's up to you lot to find out who pulled the trigger, but given that you found it in his safe, it only points one way. To back that up, remember that Co-op bag you sent me?'

'Yes. We saw it being taken into the building on Saturday night on Griff's monitor camera, although we don't know who was carrying it.'

'Whoever it was, the gun was in it. We found significant quantities of the same lubricant that was used on the pistol inside the bag. Are you sure it wasn't Montell himself that was carrying it?'

'I haven't ruled that out a hundred per cent,' Haddock admitted, 'but the build is wrong. Griff was bulkier than the person on the video recording. But in the light of what you're telling me, maybe we should test all of Coats' clothing for traces of that oil.'

'Test the body too. That stuff's pervasive; if he got it, say, on his hair it could still be there.'

'I'll do that. I'll ask Sarah to have one of her people take another look. Thanks, Arthur. I'll be in touch.'

'Fine, but hold on, we're not done yet. We're thorough here at Gartcosh. We cover everything, including the South African crime report that you added to the investigation file yesterday, the one about the bullion robbery where a police officer was killed and Montell survived. You might find this hard to believe, Sauce, but that cop was killed by the same weapon that took out Howgate Man.'

Haddock sighed, deep and long. 'You know, Arthur,' he said, 'given what's happened this week I'm not surprised at all.'

Thirty-Four

'I was expecting something bigger,' Lottie Mann remarked, as Skinner drew his car to a halt outside a modest cottage-style dwelling on the Black Shield Lodge estate. 'McCullough's a squillionaire, as we all know.'

'It's all they need,' he replied. 'They've got all the facilities of a five-star hotel just up the road.'

John Cotter looked around as he stepped out of the car. 'This is a big property,' he said. 'Are we sure he's not hiding out in the woods, sir?'

'If he was, his wife would have rooted him out by now, with a fucking machete. Cameron's a formidable bloke, but they're well matched.'

As he spoke the cottage door opened, framing Mia McCullough. She had aged well, Skinner reflected. The memory of their brief liaison twenty-odd years before had never faded, nor had his instinctive attraction to her. He was a man who had always admitted to his weaknesses, and she had been one of them. Sarah, on the other hand was his strength and as he looked at his one-time fling he felt a surge of love, paradoxically, for his wife.

'Three of you?' she exclaimed as they approached, with an

accusatory glare. 'From your text I thought it was just you, Bob. I take it these are not social workers come to give me emotional support.' She looked directly at Mann, ignoring Cotter entirely.

The DCI returned her gaze, unsmiling. She knew that Dan Provan, her former CID, and now lifetime, partner would have fired back an instant response, but that was a skill he had been unable to pass on, so she restricted herself to a slightly raised eyebrow as she introduced herself and her sergeant.

'Lottie and John are part of the team investigating the Edinburgh New Year murders,' Skinner explained as she escorted them indoors. 'They're not investigating Cameron's disappearance . . . which has now been given semi-official status, by the way; they're looking for the car . . . but something else has come up. If he was here they'd be asking him about it, but he's not, so . . .'

'So you're settling for second best.'

'Put it any way you like, Mia.' He smiled, trying to ease the tension. 'Coffee would go well.'

'You think this is fucking Starbuck's?' she retorted, then relaxed slightly herself. 'There's a pot on the hob, but it's the servants' day off, so we'll have to help ourselves.'

'Does she really have servants?' Cotter whispered as they followed her into the kitchen.

'Only one, John, and he's missing,' Skinner hissed.

To their surprise, Mia McCullough was not alone. 'This is Cameron's daughter, Inez Davis,' she said, introducing an unnaturally blonde middle-aged woman with narrow, furtive eyes and painted but well-chewed fingernails. 'Cheeky's mum,' she added. Skinner recognised her; on the occasion of their first meeting she had been in police custody. She glanced at him briefly without holding eye contact. 'She doesn't like me calling her my stepdaughter, since I'm only two months older than her.'

'Where's my dad?' Inez asked the officers, abruptly. 'I've asked my daughter's polisman boyfriend, but he was no use.'

'He's occupied elsewhere at the moment,' Mann told her, 'as are we. Your stepmother,' she looked her in the eye as she used the term, 'has probably told you that the circumstances of your father's disappearance don't justify the excessive use of police time.'

'If it was anybody else it would,' she complained. 'You lot have always had it in for my father.'

'Shut the fuck up, Inez!' Mia sighed. 'You've never given a damn for him before, so don't start now.'

She turned to the visitors, handing each a mug, leaving them to add milk if they chose. 'Right,' she said, as the sergeant stirred his sugar, an addition which drew a look of contempt from Skinner, 'what's the emergency, and,' she added, 'what are you doing here, Bob? I know they never did cut the umbilical between you and the police, but it is Saturday and you don't deal with the small stuff.'

'I'll let DCI Mann explain,' he replied.

'As Sir Robert said,' Lottie began, 'we're part of the Serious Crimes squad investigating the killings of Terry Coats and Inspector Griffin Montell.'

'Neither of whom I know, or had even heard of until a couple of days ago.'

'I appreciate that, Mrs McCullough, but a couple of days ago a third man was found dead. He'd been shot and his body was dumped too, but outside Edinburgh. It was partially hidden and attempts had been made to hide his identity, but one item was left behind. From that we were able to establish that he was a man named Anatoly Rogozin.'

The faintest flicker of surprise broke through Mia McCullough's mask of impassivity. 'Go on,' she murmured.

'We're seconded to Edinburgh,' Mann continued, 'but normally we're based in Glasgow. A while back, before John joined me, I investigated the murder of a man pulled out of the River Clyde, near the Squinty Bridge. He was identified as the chairman of Merrytown Football Club, of which your husband is the majority shareholder, and his name was Dimitri Rogozin. I hope you'll understand, Mrs McCullough, that when a second Rogozin turned up dead in Scotland, where members of that clan are not exactly thick on the ground, it got my atten—'

'His brother,' Mia snapped, cutting her off abruptly. 'Anatoly was Dimitri's brother. You'd find out soon enough so I'll save you the trouble of chasing it down. But don't ask me why he was in Scotland because I can't help you there.'

'Was he involved with the football club?' Skinner asked. 'I did some googling earlier on and, as far as I can see, the bulk of the shareholding is still shared between Cameron and Rogotron, the investment company that he and Dimitri jointly owned. When I was involved, Dimitri was chairman but Cameron was the principal owner, with fifty per cent of the shares personally, and twenty five per cent through Rogotron.'

'That's true,' she conceded. 'But . . .' She stopped, frowning.

'Come on Mia,' he said, 'we'll find out. It won't be easy since Rogotron is foreign-registered, but we'll get there in the end.'

She nodded. 'I suppose. No, he wasn't involved with the club; when Dimitri died, Anatoly expected to inherit his share in the club, and he told Cameron that he intended to buy him out. You'll remember that Dimitri was a pompous little arsehole, nothing to him at all behind the bluster and the bodyguard. Anatoly, though, he was a different animal altogether and not one that Cameron wanted anything to do with. So . . . let me get this right . . . yes; Rogotron was constituted in an unusual way; Cameron and Dimitri were fifty-fifty owners, and there was a clause in the articles that said that in the event of the death of either one, the survivor had the right to buy his shareholding, at a figure set by the auditors. So instead of Anatoly taking over Merrytown, Cameron did, completely.'

'How did Anatoly react to that?'

'Badly. Threats were made, but you probably know, Bob, maybe all of you do, that my husband isn't a man you can threaten. In the end, Anatoly thought better of it and went back to running his other interests.'

'He had an Amex card in the football club's name,' Skinner said.

She nodded. 'I know. Cameron gave him that. He called it a fuck-off present. It has a spending limit and it's valid for three years.'

'And yet he did come back to Scotland,' Mann said. 'And when he did, he wound up dead. And just after he was killed your husband decided to go away for a few days, without telling anyone, even you.'

Mia sighed. 'I know what you're going to say, but no, I won't let you. Cameron didn't kill him.'

Skinner laughed. 'That's the thing. We know he didn't, which makes me wonder even more. Why the hell has he done a runner?'

Thirty-Five

Although the image on the computer screen was shaky, it was recognisable as Major Pollock. However, the background had changed, from a drab office wall enhanced by a framed photograph of Nelson Mandela to bright sunshine and a verdant landscape. The sound was different also; snatches of conversation in a language that Haddock did not understand, but assumed was Afrikaans.

'Inspector,' the South African exclaimed, 'I wasn't expecting to hear from you again; not today anyway. I'm at my golf club; we tee off in ten minutes.'

'Sorry,' he replied. 'Zoom invitations seem to go everywhere. I can call you back. I'm a golfer myself; the last thing I'd want would be some bugger interrupting my practice routine by calling me about work.'

Pollock laughed. 'I don't practise. I just go out and try to hit the damn thing straight. I play off nineteen. You?'

'Single figures,' the Scot replied, modestly.

'It would be good to play sometime. You'll be welcome here if you ever visit Pretoria.' He glanced away from the camera. 'From what I can see here,' he said, 'that ten minutes is stretching into fifteen at least. Two guys in a four-ball in front have just found the water off the tee. Go ahead and ask me what you want.'

'Tell, not ask,' Haddock said. 'Are you sure? It might put you off your game.'

'My game's past praying for, Inspector. Go ahead.'

'Okay, if you insist. Some of this is theory but it's based on fact. Can I ask you something? What are your storage and recording arrangements for patrol officers' sidearms?'

'The officer is responsible for his or her firearm.'

'When it's issued is the serial number logged?'

'Yes.'

'When someone leaves the service or changes job what happens to it?'

'It would be reissued, and the serial number would be logged out to the new carrier.'

'Sure, but would the number be checked when the gun is surrendered?'

Major Pollock frowned. 'No, probably not,' he admitted. 'What are you getting at?'

'If I sent you the serial number of the Beretta we found in Griff's safe, could you check it against your records?'

'Yes, and I will do. Now tell me why.'

Sensing his impatience, Haddock replied, bluntly. 'Griffin Montell killed his partner, Officer DeWalt. The image in your robbery file matches the gun we have. Naturally enough, nobody ever thought to check Griff's weapon during your investigation, but even if they had, I don't believe it would have told them anything, unless they had also checked the serial number against that of the weapon issued to him. I believe that Griff helped stage the robbery. He told his accomplices where to wait, in the quietest stretch of track he could find. When they got there, he shot DeWalt straight away. The gun that he used was replaced by an identical firearm . . . not difficult, it's the choice of international police services . . . and taken from the scene, but returned to him later, for his own security.'

'What do you mean by that?'

'My belief is that as long as he had the gun, he felt he was safe. He didn't trust anyone else to dispose of it, because he didn't want it turning up anywhere by accident, and he didn't want to take the chance of being blackmailed.'

'What about his own wounds?'

Haddock stared into the computer camera rather than at the screen, knowing that he was looking Pollock directly in the eye. 'One of his co-conspirators did that; a flesh wound in the shoulder, then he aligned the weapon against the side of his head and fired the grazing shot. Griff was a tough guy, remember.' He paused. 'His medical records here in Scotland show something interesting: a slight deafness in his right ear. Not enough to incapacitate him or make him unfit for service, but noticeable.'

'Okay,' the major conceded. 'But what about the tracker that was found on the armoured van?'

'Easy. It was put there at the scene. It was never in the Mint.'

'You realise you're making my colleagues look sloppy for missing all this in their investigation?' Pollock said.

'I don't think so,' the DI replied. 'I would have made the same assumptions they did. I'd never have thought to check the serial number of Griff's service weapon, or to give him a gunshot residue test. They found an officer dead and another one down at the scene, and they acted accordingly. After the event he did nothing wrong either. He didn't draw attention to himself; he took his reward, a transfer to CID, and sat on his money until he was able to leave the country legitimately, on a job transfer. Once he was clear of South Africa, he was able to move his Krugerrands to Britain.'

'Mmm,' the South African murmured. 'What you're saying, it's a terrible accusation, but it makes sense to me. Maybe the man DuPlessis can shine some light on it.'

'Maybe he can,' Haddock said. 'Like I said, much of it's conjecture, but at the centre of it, Griff's gun killed Officer DeWalt. Everything flows from that. It killed a man in Scotland too. His name was Anatoly Rogozin, but I have no idea how he fits into the story, or even if he does.'

'I'll check it out for you, if you text me the spelling and everything you know about him.' He glanced off camera. 'We're up next, Inspector. My partner isn't going to be very pleased with my game today, but that's nothing new . . . she's my wife.'

Haddock grinned. 'No way would I play golf with my partner,' he chuckled.

'I don't have the choice,' Major Pollock sighed. 'You know,' he said, as he began to move and his image became shaky once more, 'one thing I don't understand. Why didn't they shoot Griffin between the eyes rather than upside the head? That would have been the obvious thing to do.'

'I agree,' the DI concurred. 'I can't work that one out either. If I ever do, I'll let you know. Good luck out there. By the way,' he added, 'missing the water off the first tee sounds like a good plan.'

Thirty-Six

'Sod it,' Jackie Wright murmured, as she studied the Civil Aviation Authority website. 'If you were registered in the European Union, you'd show up here but you don't, so where the hell are you?' Frustrated, she closed the window. 'Marlon,' she called to a detective constable who had been seconded to the team from Glasgow with Mann and Cotter, 'I'm struggling here. I'm trying to find the ownership of an airline called Wister Air. It's got a foreign permit to fly into the UK, but that doesn't tell me its base.'

'What about its own website?' he suggested. His accent was heavily Glaswegian but with West Indian undertones.

'I've tried that. It tells me everywhere it flies to, what I can eat on board and what the special offers are on its duty free, but nothing else.'

'Does it have a corporate section? Most companies do, for investor relations.'

'Not that I could see.'

'That suggests it's privately owned.'

'If you wanted to protect your privacy,' Wright asked, 'where would you register a business?'

Big eyes stared at her. 'I'm Marlon Honeyman, a boy fae

Castlemilk. How the hell would Ah know that?' Then he smiled. 'But if I was a clever bastard who'd done a degree in business studies before I joined the polis, I would probably look at somewhere offshore.'

'If your business had South African links, which haven might you choose?'

'It wouldn't be African, but otherwise pretty much anywhere. It would depend on how much privacy I wanted. Jackie, leave it with me. I'll have a look and see what I can find.'

Thirty-Seven

'Inspector Haddock? Jamie Ellis, Liverpool. I think I've traced Aisha Karman.'

Sauce beamed at her image on the computer screen; her message asking for a Skype meeting had taken him by surprise. 'That's excellent. Do you have a location for her, and can I speak to her?'

'Yes and no,' the officer replied. 'She's in cold storage at Manchester City Mortuary, so I don't think you'll get a word out of her.'

'Shit,' Haddock hissed, as an unspoken fear became reality. 'Are you certain that it's her? How long has she been there?'

'We're absolutely certain. She's been there two months, but she looks brand new. The photo you sent puts it beyond doubt. Her body was dumped on a quiet road just north of Bolton and found by a dog-walker within twelve hours of her death. She'd been shot once in the head at close range, but there wasn't a scrap of personal identification on her, which stymied the CID investigation from the beginning. DCS Jones on the Manchester force is dead chuffed with you, by the way,' she added, 'for taking a big black smudge off her record, just by telling us who she was. I've been seconded to work with her on the investigation. Before you say anything, they might have identified her from the missing-person report in Liverpool, but,' she shrugged, 'they didn't.'

'There was no potential identification at all?' Haddock asked. 'Not even clothing?'

'She was naked; her prints weren't on any database, nor was her DNA.' Inspector Ellis raised an eyebrow. 'However, we do have someone else's. She had sex shortly before she died. My Manc colleagues believe that he stripped her, shagged her and shot her . . .' she paused '. . . hopefully in that order.'

'The donor DNA. No match, I guess?'

'None, anywhere. Our investigators have searched databases internationally. Are you going to make DCS Jones even happier by telling us who he is?'

'I'm not going to promise that, but I do know of a man who was in a relationship with Aisha Karman, here in Scotland.'

Her eyes widened. 'Could you get a DNA sample from him? Do you have grounds for doing that? Do you even need grounds in Scotland?'

'We have the same rules as you do. Once a suspect has been arrested, we can take it with or without consent. In this case, that's not going to be an issue. The man I'm talking about is as dead as Ms Karman, and currently occupying similar accommodation in the Edinburgh morgue. We need to work together on this, Jamie. I'm going to send you a photo of my suspect. If I'm right the DNA puts him together, obviously, but I'd like to paint a complete picture of what happened. Quid pro quo, I'm also going to need to see your investigation file, including all the forensics. Most important of all, you said Aisha was shot so: did you recover the bullet?'

Thirty-Eight

'This gets worse, Sauce,' Tarvil Singh remarked, as Haddock finished briefing him on his calls with Major Pollock and Inspector Ellis. 'We started off with two dead men in Edinburgh, and now we've got five victims in three countries. D'you fancy giving DCI Pye a call and telling him how fucking lucky he is to be missing this?'

'That would be cruel,' the DI told him. 'Sammy would love this. He'd see it as a path to glory and switch into full Luke Skywalker mode, the last of the Jedi.'

'You do know we used to call you R2D2, don't you?'

'No,' he admitted, 'but I prefer that to being half of our official nickname, The Menu.'

'How long's he going to be off?' the big DS asked.

'How should I know?'

'Because you always do. And,' he added, heavily, 'the fact that you're not saying makes me think this is not man flu that he's got.'

'I prefer it when you don't think, Tarvil.'

'I get it. You're telling me not to ask.'

Haddock nodded, then drew two fingers across his mouth in a zipper gesture.

'Boss!' Jackie Wright's call forestalled any comeback. 'Can Marlon and I have a word?' The Glaswegian DC stood behind the desk, with a blue folder pressed to his chest.

'If it's relevant,' the DI replied.

'Your office?'

'Hell no, it's barely big enough for me. We'll use the meeting room. Tarvil, you come too.' He led the way through a door at the far end of the suite into an area that was dominated by the view through its picture window of Fettes College, the great grey Victorian faux-chateau that seemed to have been imposed on Edinburgh, its grandeur emphasising the awful drabness of the police building.

'Every time I look at that thing,' Singh remarked, 'it makes me think of Mervyn Peake.'

'Who?' Wright asked.

'Gormenghast,' Honeyman said.

'Fuck me!' Haddock whispered, as they took seats. 'Right Jackie,' he said, 'what do you and Marlon have for us?'

'It's him, not me,' she replied. 'Marlon, you did it, you tell him.'

He nodded his shaven head, almost dislodging the glasses that were perched on the bridge of his nose. 'I've been chasing Wister Air,' he began, 'the airline name that's mentioned by Sir Robert Skinner in the statement he gave us. He alleges that Coats claimed to him—' He halted in midsentence as Haddock held up a hand. 'Sir?'

'Bob Skinner doesn't allege things, DC Honeyman,' the DI said. 'He tells you things, and you take them on board. You don't question them or doubt them in any way; you act on them. Besides, I was there at the time, more or less, so I know what Wister Air is and how it fits into the story. Go on.'

The detective's mouth tensed at the reproof; he continued, stiffly. 'I've been investigating the company, sir, and I've established that its head office is in Cape Town, South Africa. It flies mostly tourist routes, and that's the market it chases. In Britain it operates out of Edinburgh, Manchester, Liverpool and Stansted, and in Europe it flies from Schiphol, in Amsterdam. It appears to have very little interest in business travel. It makes its money flying British and Dutch holiday-makers to Cape Town, where their pounds and their euros go a hell of a long way.'

'That's interesting,' Singh observed, drily, 'but who owns it?'

'That was harder to pin down,' Honeyman admitted. 'I looked at company registration in South Africa, in the UK and in Holland, but no joy. I looked at some other popular places, including Liechtenstein and the Cayman Islands: nothing. Then I looked at North Cyprus.'

'Is that really a country? I thought it was an occupied territory.'

'To most of the world it is,' the DC agreed, 'but it's recog-nised as a state by one country, Turkey, and to them, it's the Turkish Republic of North Cyprus. It's got all sorts of inter-national embargoes on it, but it is possible to use it as a corporate base. Wister Air was registered there, by an outfit called TCOC, as an offshore company in 2010; it has two shareholders, Anatoly Rogozin Enterprises, based in Monaco, and Lente, spelled like the six weeks before Easter but with a final e.'

'What's that?'

'Nothing that I can discover. It's just a name. I can't get anywhere with that. There are two directors of Wister Air, Rogozin himself, and a Northern Cypriot nominee. That's a common device to get round local requirements.'

'What about Lente's assets?' Haddock asked.

'Shielded,' Honeyman replied. 'Whoever set this up with Rogozin didn't want to be known, and they've made a bloody good job of it.'

Thirty-Nine

'Just occasionally, Mario, there are times when I'm really glad I'm retired,' Skinner declared.

'I hear what you're saying, Bob,' the deputy chief constable replied. 'But they don't last long, fortunately. What you're doing as a mentor for Sauce and other young people, that's invaluable, and I like to think it's a unique resource for our force.'

'Bollocks! You could do that yourself; you've got the experience and you have the skills.'

'No, I couldn't,' McGuire insisted, 'because I'm too fucking busy. You were dead right to walk away from the unified police service. It has fundamental flaws. We all grew up as cops. Those of us who made it to command level had to become managers. At local or regional level, most of us got by even without specialist training, but that's not the case now.'

'You're doing fine,' Skinner said, but his voice lacked conviction and he knew it.

'For now, maybe, but that won't last. The job eats you. It devoured Andy Martin . . .'

'He was swallowed by his own ego!' his friend protested.

'You know that's not true. Andy was one of the best police

officers you and I ever met, but he was a fucking detective. He was used to focusing on specific issues, mostly one at a time. He couldn't handle the breadth of the responsibility. It affected him in every way. He became remote from people he'd worked with all his career and he became dictatorial. He turned from a pleasant guy into a grade-A shit, and when he finally packed it in his former friends had a farewell party, only he wasn't invited. Now I'm sitting here in the senior command office which might as well be in fucking Stromness, and I'm . . .' He stopped, in mid-sentence.

'What?'

'Ach, nothing. Forget it, Bob.'

'Like hell I will,' he said. 'Let me take a stab at what you were going to say: you're sitting there and you're seeing the same thing happening to Maggie.'

'You know me too well. Yes, you're right. She's taking some time off, Bob, at my suggestion . . . actually, my insistence . . . after having a chat with our senior medical officer. Nothing will be announced, but she won't be around for a while.'

'And if she doesn't come back?'

'I don't like to think about that, but one thing I know for certain: I don't want the bloody job. Nobody in their right mind would, not if they wanted to stay that way.'

'Can I help?' Skinner asked.

'There's one thing you could do,' McGuire replied. 'I've spent some time with the NYPD, as you know, and I'm convinced that we need to adopt the New York system, a Police Commissioner who isn't a cop necessarily, but who has oversight of the whole system, with hire and fire powers. He or she would be appointed by Clive Graham, the First Minister, and would appoint their own advisory team on management matters; operationally we'd go back to the old set-up, with ten or a dozen areas each with a chief, responsible to the commissioner. It would spread the load, the public would like it and I think we'd all do a better job.'

'I agree with all of that,' he replied. 'But what can I do?'

'Use your media clout. Run the proposition on the *Saltire*.'

'Hold on a minute. I'm not the editor; June Crampsey is. That would be her shout.'

'So ask her if she'll do it,' McGuire persisted. 'I bet she will; her dad's a retired cop. I'm sure he'd persuade her if it was needed.'

'Let me think about it,' Skinner said, 'but I'm not putting the paper up to be shot down. I won't do it without sounding Clive out first. It might be seen as a climb-down by government, and you know how much politicians hate that.' He took a deep breath and continued. 'Now, what you told me earlier. Run it past me again, but at normal speed this time.'

'The Torphichen Place investigation; it's like that virus, spreading everywhere. Sauce has just finished briefing me. The latest is that the woman Coats told you about has been found in the mortuary in Manchester, with a Jane Doe label on her toe. Their CID have been able to trace her movements from John Lennon Airport to a hotel near the airport in Manchester.'

'That's progress. How did she die?' He paused, with a quick intake of breath. 'Let me guess, she was shot in the head.'

'Got it in one. The bullet's being couriered up to Gartcosh right now. They thought they had a DNA sample too, but that's been corrupted.' McGuire hesitated. 'But that's not all,' he added. 'Sauce has established that the gun in Montell's safe didn't only shoot Anatoly Rogozin, it also killed his partner in the Pretoria gold robbery. I've just been given a profile by Dominic Jackson which suggests that Griff might have been a high-functioning psychopath. It looks as if that's no longer in doubt.'

Forty

'If there is any news about Grandpa, you will tell me, won't you?' Cheeky asked, as Sauce handed her a bacon sandwich. 'I had my mother on the phone yesterday afternoon,' she added. 'He barely speaks to her but somehow she found out that he's missing.'

'She found out from me,' he confessed. 'I called Inez yesterday, on the off-chance that he had been in touch with her. She said he hadn't, and I didn't tell her anything, but . . .'

She grimaced. 'But . . . she seized on it as an excuse to phone me. The last thing I want to do is let that woman into our lives, Sauce. She's a disaster, just like my Aunt Daphne was . . .'

'Nah,' Sauce countered. 'From what I've been told by Bob Skinner and others, including your grandpa, she's not in the same class as Goldie was. She was flat-out dangerous. Inez is just an idiot, or so they all reckon. The puzzle is how she had a daughter like you. Your brains must come from your dad.'

'My dad,' she repeated. 'I'm in my late twenties and all I know about him is that he had the brains to disappear off the face of the earth when Grandpa found out that he'd knocked up his fifteen-year-old daughter. He brought me up, you know, Grandpa did, him and Granny Abby.'

'I know, you've told me, and so has he. He tolerated your mother, but since that time when she and Goldie got you involved in one of their scams, she's been banished into the outer darkness, or to put it another way, managing the radio-station canteen.'

'In that case why did you bother phoning her?'

'Because despite it all, she is his daughter, and she might occasionally speak to him. And she's your mum, so I can't pretend she doesn't exist any more than you can.'

She sighed. 'I know. That doesn't mean she'll get anywhere near her . . .'

He gazed at her, caught by her hesitation. 'Near her what?'

'Oh nothing. Go on, get to work, since you say you have to.'

'Not until you tell me what you thought better of saying.' He grinned. 'You might as well; I'm a professional interrogator, love.'

She frowned, then looked up at him. 'You do love me, don't you, Harold?' she asked, earnestly.

'With all my heart,' he promised, 'even when you call me Harold. Why?'

'I'm late.'

His mouth opened then closed again, then opened and closed once more. 'How late?' he was able to ask, finally.

'Two weeks, and that's not Tom Jones disease: it is unusual, I promise you.'

'Bloody hell, I thought you were on the . . .'

'So did I, but I asked a doctor and she said that every month you take it, even without missing one, there's about a half of one per cent chance of you falling pregnant.' She smiled nervously. 'Do you really have to go to work?'

'Yes, I do, there's a guy in a cell in Pretoria waiting to talk to me. I can't do it from here because there have to be two officers on the call.'

'In that case,' she instructed, 'find a chemist once you're finished, and bring back a test kit.'

First things first, Haddock decided as soon as he fastened his seatbelt. He sent a message to Major Pollock, delaying his video meeting by half an hour, then headed straight for the Gyle Shopping Centre, where he was confident that he would find a pharmacy, even on the first Sunday of the year. Having no idea which of the tests on offer was the most reliable, he chose the most expensive. The checkout lady smiled at him. 'Good luck,' she whispered.

He was about to counter, 'What makes you think it would be?' when he realised that he might never have been happier in his life.

His mind was still full of domesticity when he arrived at his office, and his imagination was out of control. It took a fleeting vision of enrolling his twins at Fettes College to force him back to the day's business.

Jackie Wright had more than earned a day off, although it had needed an order to make her take it, but Marlon Honeyman was on duty, gazing fixedly at a computer screen, oblivious to Haddock's nod of greeting. Tarvil Singh, on the other hand was deep in a copy of the *Observer*.

'Are we in that?' the DI asked.

'What?' he looked around, momentarily startled. 'Us, no, we don't rate the English Sundays. No, I was reading about the new flu they're having in China. It's not too clever.' He looked more closely at his colleague. 'What are you so happy about? It's bloody Sunday. Are you so wrapped up in this that you've forgotten that?'

'It's your cheery face, Tarv. It does it every time. Have you got the South African on stand-by like I asked?'

'Yes,' the DS replied. 'I sent an invitation to the address that Pollock gave us. The custody officers wanted to know how long they should hold the guy. I told them to ask their boss. That was right, wasn't it?'

'Spot on. We don't have jurisdiction and I don't see us wanting him as a witness. Go on, call them back.'

As Haddock pulled up a chair beside his, Singh went to his keyboard and reactivated the Zoom meeting that he had set up. To their surprise the face that appeared on screen was familiar, that of Major Pollock, and he was in uniform.

'Good morning, guys,' he began. 'You probably weren't expecting to see me, but things have changed here. I've had a team of officers investigating movements on cruise vessels operated by Mr DuPlessis' company, and it's proved very interesting. It seems that he and a couple of colleagues have been providing what I'll describe as discreet transport services for sensitive consignments.' He grinned, but grimly. 'In other words, the buggers have been smuggling. You asked me speci- fically about a consignment that Griffin might have received a couple of years ago, but in fact we've uncovered more than that, for people other than him with nothing to do with your investigation. So today, we're both going to be interviewing him. After that I'll decide whether he'll be kept in custody. As yet, he doesn't know what I know, so be ready for me to jump in when the moment's right.'

His hand covered the camera, the source computer was swung around and the two Scots found themselves looking as a middle-aged man was brought into the room. He had a black V-shaped hairline, a sharp nose and a loose, nervous mouth.

'Mr DuPlessis?' Haddock began. As he spoke, a flashback from the morning found its way into his mind, and he had to push it back.

'That's me,' the man on screen replied.

'I'm Detective Inspector Harold Haddock, in charge of the Serious Crimes team in Edinburgh, Scotland, and this is my colleague, Detective Sergeant Singh. We're investigating the murder of our colleagues, Inspector Griffin Montell, and another man. I believe Inspector Montell was your cousin.'

'Yes, he was. Our mothers were sisters, but we weren't close.'

'I believe that his mother is no longer alive.'

'That's correct,' DuPlessis confirmed. 'Mine is, but she lives in Buenos Aires with her second husband. He's a rugby coach,' he added.

'When did you last hear from your cousin?'

'I can't remember. We never communicated much.'

'Try, Mr DuPlessis,' Singh growled.

The sight of the massive Sikh leaning forward to fill the screen seemed to alarm the South African, but not enough to shake his claim to forgetfulness. 'I can't, okay.'

'When we searched your cousin's apartment after his death,' the DI continued, 'we were surprised by some of the things we found. Specifically, there was a significant amount of South African gold coins, far more than you'd reasonably expect to find in the home of a working cop. There was a lot of cash, more than a year's salary for his rank. And there was a firearm, a Beretta handgun, a type regularly carried by police officers around the world.'

DuPlessis shrugged. 'Why are you telling me? Like I said, I hardly knew the bloke.'

'Is that really true?' Major Pollock asked, breaking into the investigation. 'You see, Tom, my people in Cape Town have been making enquiries at your workplace, Oceanic Magic. They have interviewed a woman called Dee Gosford: she's a chief engineer and under questioning she told them . . . confessed would be a better term . . . that a couple of years ago you asked her to take charge of an item for you, and take it to Southampton where it would be offloaded at night, when the rest of the world was asleep. She was paid five Krugerrands for her trouble. She couldn't identify the man who collected the consignment, not unnaturally, because it was dark, but her physical description is a fair match for Griffin Montell.'

'It had nothing to do with me,' DuPlessis snapped, gaining confidence. 'It's her word against mine, and you don't sound like you can prove a damn thing.'

'Give me forty-eight hours,' Haddock retorted, 'and I will.'

'You better believe that,' Pollock added. 'When he does, and when we can tie you to that box, you will be in deep trouble. We, the three of us, have established that the firearm we know to have been in that box was used to kill a serving South African Police officer. The fact that you handled it makes you an accessory to his murder. Twenty-five years without parole, buddy, is not something I would be taking as lightly as you seem to be.'

'Fuck!' DuPlessis shouted. 'What are you trying to pull here?'

'I am telling you like it is. There isn't a single officer in the South African Police Service who has forgotten about Constable Fannie DeWalt, and every one of us is righteously angry that nobody has ever been convicted for his murder. You will help us put that right, Tom DuPlessis.'

'I never knew about the fucking gun! Or anything else!

Okay, yes, a couple of years ago Griff contacted me when he was over here on holiday, and told me he had something he wanted to get out of the country and over to Britain before his ex-wife got wind of it. He asked me to get it across on one of the liners. He knew we did that; quite a few people do, but what we take on board is harmless. We don't move drugs or anything like that.'

'Did Griff tell you what was in the box?'

'He told me it was money, and I didn't ask any more. He paid me in gold coins, fifteen of them. I gave Dee five.'

'How did you get the box?' Haddock asked.

'He brought it to me. I think he had it in safe storage, long term. That's all, I swear. You need me to give evidence to anybody, I will.' He looked away from the camera, across at Pollock. 'Is that it? Are you happy now? Can I get out of here? I got to get back to work, man.'

The major laughed. 'I tell you what. You give me a record of everything you've ever moved out of the country, and the people you've moved it for, and I might think about releasing you. As for going back to work, I think you'll find that after what they've found out about you, Oceanic Magic don't want to see you again.' He looked off to his right. 'Officers, take Mr DuPlessis back to his detention cell, and give him a pen and paper, so that he can write as if his life depends upon it, because that might very well be the case.' As he was being removed, Pollock turned back to Haddock and Singh. 'Can you guys really prove that Griffin collected that box?'

'I hope so,' the DI replied. 'I can promise you we'll have a bloody good try.'

Forty-One

Sauce Haddock wanted nothing more than to step into his car and drive home, his purchase in his pocket and ready for use. He was elated and nervous at the same time, and yet he knew that professionally his day was not over.

As soon as he had ended the Pretoria video conference, he had called the DCC's home number from his landline to update him. As he hung up, on impulse he phoned his mentor.

Skinner's mood brought him back down to earth. 'I can't believe I got it so wrong about a man. I recruited him, I advanced him in the service, and all the time he was a thief and a killer.'

'Me neither, gaffer,' Haddock admitted. 'I don't know whether to feel pleased that we've helped the South Africans solve a twelve-year-old crime or gutted that we've been betrayed by one of our own. I do know that in terms of the purpose of the investigation, I know fuck all. I can't tie Coats and Griff together and until I do that I'm not one step closer to finding out who killed them. Now I've got the Rogozin murder, and Griff's apparent involvement, muddying the waters, and on top of that . . .' He paused as an idea, not previously considered, crossed his mind. 'As you and Lottie found out yesterday,

221

Grandpa McCullough knew Anatoly Rogozin; he turns up in Scotland, he's killed and a couple of days later Grandpa disappears. I'm asking myself, did Grandpa know Griff? Is it possible that after their clash over the Rogotron shares Grandpa saw Anatoly as a threat and had Griff take him out?'

'No,' Skinner said, firmly. 'I don't see that for a second. If Cameron had done that he'd have established an unshakeable alibi, and he wouldn't have drawn attention to himself by disappearing afterwards. To cover that base, though, you might ask Mia where he was on Saturday night.'

'Shit!' Haddock whispered. 'I don't need to. He did set up the perfect alibi; it's me. On Saturday night he and Mia took Cheeky and me to the restaurant in the Caley Hotel. Vito Tremacoldi drove them down from Perthshire; he had a bistro meal in a place across Rutland Street.'

'Do you know when Rogozin arrived in Scotland?'

'Yes, I do now. Rogozin had an address in London. DC Honeyman, our secondee from Glasgow, has him coming into Edinburgh on a flight from London City that afternoon, Saturday, around the same time that Griff was dropping his bag for his trip to South Africa.'

'A trip he never made,' Skinner pointed out. 'I take it you've . . .'

'Gaffer, we've been crawling all over the airport CCTV for Saturday afternoon. Apart from one sighting of Griff at the bag drop there's nothing.'

'And Coats?'

'A man of fucking mystery; we know where he lived but that's it.' As he spoke, his attention was grabbed by Marlon Honeyman's waving left hand. 'I have to go,' he said. 'I think I'm wanted.'

He replaced the handset and stepped out of his room, walking across to the DC's desk. 'What's got your attention?' he asked. 'What the hell are you doing here anyway?' he added. 'There's no overtime allocated and even Lottie's taking the day off.'

'I want to get into Inspector Montell's personal records, sir, and I got sidetracked yesterday.'

The DI nodded. 'Thanks. It's appreciated, and it won't go unacknowledged. From that hand signal, you've found something.'

'I may have. Montell booked a trip to South Africa for last weekend, as we know. That was paid for with a credit card. I got that information from British Airways at the same time as I traced Rogozin, because it's generally quicker doing it that way than accessing it through the bank. The thing that's interesting me is that he was booked on the last shuttle, yet he dropped his bag in the afternoon. As it turned out, he missed the flight, but why would he do that, drop his bag so early?'

'Because he knew that Rogozin was coming and he intended to be waiting for him?' Haddock suggested.

'That's what I'm thinking.'

'In which case, how did he know, and what was the connection between them?'

Honeyman smiled. 'That's above my pay grade, sir, I'm just a computer nerd. However, leaving that aside, the reason I wanted to talk to you, I found something interesting on his debit card. We have Montell checking in his case at nine minutes past three, we have Rogozin disembarking from his domestic flight at twenty-four minutes past. Then, at three forty-seven Montell makes a payment on his debit card to Lothian Buses. Do you know how much a single ticket costs on the airport bus?'

'Four and a half quid. My partner and I caught it last October.'

'In that case he bought two tickets.'

Haddock patted the DC on the shoulder. 'Progress, at last,' he declared. 'There are security cameras on all Lothian vehicles. If we can find out where they got off, we may be in business.'

'Very good, sir, but how does it help us find out who killed Montell and Coats?'

'I've got no idea, Marlon, but there's a story unfolding before us. All we can do is read it and hope that in the end it tells us. Now get yourself back to Glasgow. Accessing the bus camera's a job for tomorrow. You've done enough for today, and I've got another detecting job to do.'

Forty-Two

Edinburgh was back to work on the first Monday of the new year, after the extended break that invariably follows a Tuesday Hogmanay, but Sauce Haddock was almost oblivious of the traffic as he waited for the lights to change. Cheeky's pregnancy test had been positive; to be even more certain they had done a second, with the same result.

They had agreed they would tell nobody until she could make plans at work. She was a senior audit manager with her firm, and her schedule was set out for the full year, with each client having a reporting deadline. He wanted nothing more than to go off on holiday at the first opportunity. The August trip to Madeira that they had booked would have to be cancelled as Cheeky's pregnancy would be too far advanced to allow air travel. And then there was the housing question. They had been considering moving for a while; they were agreed it should be out of the city, but not about the direction. Thousands of new homes were under construction or planned for East Lothian, but Sauce had a hankering for Fife.

'You could leave the police,' she had suggested, deadpan over dinner, 'go and work for Grandpa.'

He had dropped his fork. 'Are you serious?'

She had flashed him the happiest smile he had ever seen, then laughed out loud. 'No. I'd sooner you became a monk.'

'We're a bit late for that.'

His grin became a frown as a horn blast came from the car behind, for a second too long to be acceptable. He drove off slowly; on the other side of the crossing he flashed a concealed blue light but decided to do no more than that. 'Your lucky morning, pal,' he murmured as he beamed once more, into the rearview mirror.

He was still smiling as he walked into the CID suite, until he saw that the deputy chief constable was waiting for him in his office. He had not been expecting a visit from McGuire and hoped that it did not signal a problem, but he relaxed when he stepped out to join him. 'You lot,' he announced in a voice loud enough to carry round the crowded room, 'are moving out of here for a while. The DCI's office is a joke and the rest of you are all crammed in. DI Haddock, you're moving into that virtually redundant meeting room, until DCI Pye comes back. The cubicle's getting knocked down and the layout re-planned. The joiners will be in as soon as this investigation winds down. Sauce, come with me please.'

He led Haddock into what was to become his new accommodation. 'Close the door, will you? What I said there about Sammy coming back, that was for their benefit. I think we both know the truth. I should tell you also that you'll be seeing less of me, for a while at least. The chief's going to be taking a period of sick leave and I'll be standing in for her. That means I won't be getting involved on the ground, and certainly not at the ridiculous level of micro-management that you've just seen. ACC Lowell Payne will be taking on more tasks in addition to the counter-terrorism and organised crime briefs. He'll be your go-to boss from now on, well, for a while at least. Do you know him?'

'No, we've never met.'

'You'll get on,' McGuire assured him. 'He's not one of those ramrod-straight guys. You won't be snapping to attention all the time. He's also from the west: it concerns me that this force has been a bit Edinburgh-centric in its early years; that's something that both Mrs Steele and I are looking to correct. As an aside, he's Alex Skinner's uncle, married to her mum's sister; I doubt he would be if the big man didn't rate him. You can expect to see him within a couple of days, but he won't sit on your shoulder.'

'Is this thing starting to fall apart, sir?' Haddock ventured. 'First Sammy, Griff and what we're finding out about him, and now the chief?'

The DCC frowned and for a moment Haddock thought he had gone too far. He was relieved when he sighed. 'There is the potential for it, Sauce, that I will admit; but I'm damned if I'll let it happen. Sammy's problem, that has nothing to do with the job. Mrs Steele's, well, maybe that has; she's been diagnosed with stress and depression although that's for senior officers' ears only. It won't be made public; the media department won't be told the detail, only that it's medical and she's entitled to the same privacy as anyone else. But aside from all that,' he continued, 'I only really came in here before heading for the Chateau d'If, as I like to call our headquarters, to tell you that Dorward rang me last night to advise me that his guys put in an extra shift yesterday. A bullet was couriered up to Gartcosh from Manchester; Arthur's senior ballistic man examined it microscopically and compared it with the one dug out of the Howgate victim. It's a match. What exactly does that mean? I didn't like to sour Dorward's triumph by telling him I didn't fucking know.'

'It means I should have spoken to you myself over the weekend, sir,' Haddock confessed. 'Remember Bob Skinner and I catching Terry Coats with an air hostess, and the story he spun?'

'Yes. I even remember her name. Aisha, wasn't it?'

'That's right, Aisha Karman. We went looking for her, only to find that she went missing a couple of months back, somewhere between the Mersey and Manchester. She turned up as soon as I sent her picture down there, unidentified in a mortuary drawer. You've just confirmed my hunch, that she was killed by Griff Montell's gun.'

'But how would he . . . ? If she was Coats's bird . . .'

'That's what I'm hoping to find out. I still haven't put Coats and Montell together; I haven't proved a physical link between them, but this gets me right on the edge of it.'

'Then crack on, Acting Chief Inspector. It would be good if you could tie that up by the time ACC Payne makes contact. I'll be seeing you.'

Haddock looked at the door for several seconds after it closed behind the deputy chief. He felt his earlier elation drain from him, as he was seized by a disturbing feeling that an era was coming to an end. Maggie Steele had been a considerable early influence on his career; she had been his mentor just as much as had Bob Skinner in more recent times, and he was deeply concerned by her situation. His gut feeling was that she would not be back, and that another command regime had hit the wall, leaving an uncertain future for everyone in the police service. Bringing himself back to the present, he looked around the room that McGuire had decreed would become the Serious

Crimes commander's office, and took an executive decision.

'Tarvil,' he called out, stepping back into the suite, 'I'm not waiting for the joiners, I'm moving in there now. Help me move my kit.'

'Okay,' the DS replied. He looked across the suite at two detective constables who were trying to appear as inconspicuous as they could. 'Joe, Tyson. Move the DI's desk, his computer and his other stuff from the chicken coop into the big room. You call that delegation, Sauce,' he said. 'You'll never be as good at it as me.' He picked up his phone and hit the zero button. 'DS Singh, Serious Crimes East, Fettes. From now on all calls to the DCI's extension should go to the one in the squad conference room. That's right, from now until further notice. Got that? Good.' He turned back to Haddock. 'Can I move into yours in the meantime, until they knock it down?' he asked.

'No chance. You'd suffocate in there. Jackie,' he called to Wright, 'do you want it for as long as it's there? You'd benefit most from the quiet.'

The DC stared at him. 'Seriously? Yes, please.'

'Get moving, then. Tarvil, I'll be in there; they can move around me. Since you'll have time on your hands, I need you to follow up on the dates we got from the guy DuPlessis yesterday.'

'What are you going to be doing?'

'Being the boss, big fella, being the boss. I think you call it delegating.' He smiled. 'I might never be as good as you, but you're going to lose about ten kilos watching me try.' He heard laughter behind him as he returned to his new office.

'Where do you want the desk, sir?' one of the DCs asked him from the doorway.

'Beside the phone point, back to the window. I don't want to be looking at fucking Gormenghast all day.'

He took a seat at the far end of the table and called Cheeky on his mobile. 'Hi, how are you doing?' he asked.

'Fine.'

'You're not sick or anything?'

He heard her laugh. 'I don't think I'm at that stage yet.'

'Have you told your boss yet?'

'Sauce,' she said, 'in terms of the whole process, we've barely wiped the sweat off our foreheads. I'll tell her when I think the moment's right, but I'll decide when that is. You're not going to phone me every morning, are you?'

'I'll try not to. Will we go looking at houses at the weekend?'

'Do you expect your investigation to be finished by then?'

The question brought him back to reality. 'That's a point. It's going all right just now though; I ticked another box this morning. I'll let you go, but just one more thing. When your grandpa resurfaces, do you want to tell him yourself or do you want me there?'

She laughed. 'I'll tell you what. Let's hold off on that until I'm wide enough for you to hide behind me.'

'I'm expecting him to be hiding behind me from Mia. See you later, love.'

As he ended the call his mind turned to another matter. He and Cheeky had discussed marriage a few weeks before. They had decided that while it was definitely in their future, there was no rush, as they had no plans to start a family for a couple of years. 'Maybe Grandpa will have a view on that too,' he whispered to the empty room.

Forcing himself back to the business of the day, he retrieved the number of Inspector Jamie Ellis from his phone memory and called her. 'DI Haddock,' she answered in a cheery accent that reminded him of *Coronation Street*. 'Did my package arrive?'

'Yes, and it's been acted upon. The gun that killed Ms Karman has been around. It's linked to two murders; the first was about twelve years ago, in Pretoria, South Africa and the other one was last week in Howgate, Scotland . . . that's to say,' he added, correcting himself, 'the body was found there, but we believe he was killed somewhere else.'

'Can you match the firearm to anyone, or is it one of those that can be rented?'

'I wish it was,' Haddock sighed. 'It was found among the possessions of a former colleague of ours, Griffin Montell, who was murdered on New Year's Day, along with another man, Terry Coats. That's my investigation.'

'How did it get from South Africa?' the inspector asked.

'It was smuggled across to him as part of a consignment.'

'That was risky, was it not?'

'Not the way he did it.'

'Mmm,' Ellis murmured. 'Could you forward an image of this man? My colleagues in Liverpool have struck it lucky. They've traced a private-hire driver who's used by Wister Air, her airline. He remembers picking Ms Karman up at John Lennon on what we believe was the day she disappeared, and taking her to the Grange Hotel near Manchester airport. But,' she added, 'he also remembers that as she got out of his car, she was hailed by a man, and instead of going into the hotel, she went across to talk to him. He said that she was animated, excited, as if she was pleased to see him.'

'Poor woman,' Haddock said. 'The excitement didn't last long. I am guessing that the man she met was Terry Coats, one of my murder victims. They were in a relationship in Edinburgh last year, a few months ago, whenever she flew there. I'll send you down an image for you to show to your taxi driver, but I'll send you Montell's as well, just in case I'm wrong.'

'Thanks. Is there anything else we can do?'

'Yes, there is. You might talk to the manager at Wister Air's Manchester office and ask him what, if anything, he knows about Karman. I need to understand why she wound up dead. On the basis of what I know so far, I don't quite get it.'

Forty-Three

'Where's DI Haddock?' Lottie Mann asked, noting Jackie Wright's new location as she took off her coat and slung it over the back of a chair.

'Moved office,' Marlon Honeyman replied. 'The DCC was in earlier and had a fit of reorganisation. He's moved into the meeting room; he said you're welcome to join him in there.'

'Decent of him,' she said, 'but I'll stay with my guys. That said, what are you doing here, Marlon? You worked yesterday; you're entitled to be off today. Haddock didn't ask you to come in, did he?'

The DC shook his head. 'No, it's my choice. I started something yesterday and I want to be the one that finishes it.'

'That's commendable, Marlon, but I've got to tell you, you don't need to prove yourself to me. You've impressed me from day one.'

'I know that, boss, and I appreciate it but . . . I'm a black boy frae Castlemilk; I have to prove myself to everybody else. Not everybody's moved into the twenty-first century; fact is, I've come across one or two that are still living in the nineteenth.'

'Come on,' Mann protested, 'it's not that bad. Look at me, I'm walking proof that things have changed.'

'Sure, boss, you are. You're also a six-feet-tall female and you're scary, so nobody's going to take the slightest chance that you might hear any of the things that are said behind your back. I'm a detective constable, and I'm a bloke, so folk tend not to be as cautious around me. I'm not talking about the senior ranks. I'm not saying that my colour or my social origins affect my promotion prospects. But if you think racism's been eradicated from a force this size, or even that it can be, you go and ask DS Singh. Okay, you might say that's true of society as a whole, and you'd be right, but this is the part that I function in, and I need to go the extra mile because of it.' He smiled. 'Also, I like Edinburgh,' he added.

She gazed down at him, then glanced at Cotter, a silent witness to the conversation. 'Is that right, John? Do they talk behind my back?'

'I'm new here, ma'am,' he said, 'and I'm English.'

'You're also male. Do they?'

'One or two maybe. Nothing to do with the job though.'

'Hah!' she laughed. 'So the fact that I've moved in with a man twenty years older than me who used to be my DS makes me the talk of the steamie? That's not exactly a surprise. I take it as a compliment to Dan, not a slur against me. But I know, Marlon, you're talking about something different. You might think nothing can be done about it, but there is. Any time you believe you've been the subject of a racist remark, report it to me, and I will take it straight to the bosses for investigation. That's not a suggestion, by the way, or an offer: it's an order. Maybe we can't beat it completely, but if we don't try we're all complicit, you included. Now, what's this task you have in hand?'

'I'm in the process of reviewing all the camera footage from the Edinburgh Airport bus from a week last Saturday.'

'Who are you hoping to find?' she asked, switching her attention to his computer screen.

'Inspector Montell, ma'am, and Anatoly Rogozin, the third victim.' He updated her on his discoveries of the day before.

'Actually, he's the fifth victim, chronologically.' All three detectives turned towards Haddock, who had moved silently behind them. 'Rogozin's linked by the gun that killed him to the death of a police officer in South Africa, and to that of a woman in Manchester; the weapon itself is linked directly to Inspector Griffin Montell.'

'Jeez,' Lottie Mann whispered. 'One of our own.'

'Two of our own,' the DI countered. 'Terry Coats was a cop too, and he wasn't an innocent bystander in all of this. We can't prove that yet, but we're close. Sorry, Marlon, I'm interrupting, keep doing what you're doing. Lottie, come on and I'll fill you and John in on the detail.'

The trio headed for Haddock's new office, leaving Honeyman to his video review. He carried on methodically; the bus service ran every ten minutes regardless of how full or empty each vehicle might be. On the Saturday before Christmas they were busy throughout the afternoon. The footage lacked an on-screen time clock, forcing the DC to examine every clip from the arrival of each bus on the stand to its departure.

'Do you want a coffee?' Tarvil Singh called to him. 'I can do that for ten minutes.'

Honeyman almost accepted the sergeant's offer, but sheer stubbornness made him persevere. He ran through two more excerpts. His bladder was on the point of forcing him to take a break when . . . 'What? Is it? Yes.'

Two men boarded the bus, showing their tickets to the

driver. The first was in his thirties, broad built, wearing a black knitted jacket; it appeared to be woollen and was certainly expensive, a designer label, the DC guessed. The second man was older, dragging a small suitcase and wearing a heavy overcoat. They walked towards the camera until they had passed out of its field of vision.

Honeyman paused the recording, went to the toilet and relieved himself. On the way back, he collected the coffee that he had declined earlier, and settled back into his chair, resuming his study as the bus pulled away.

Ten minutes later he knocked on the door of Haddock's office, stepping inside without waiting for a summons. 'Got them,' he announced, 'Montell and Rogozin, together on the bus. I followed them too until they got off. They weren't on board long. They only went to the first stop in fact, Drumbrae, I think it was called.'

'Drumbrae?' the DI repeated. 'Terry Coats' place is five minutes' walk from there. Finally, we've tied them together, Griff and Terry. Marlon, you are a star. Tell me, what was Montell wearing? I'm assuming Rogozin had on the coat he was killed in.'

'A black woollen jacket with a zipper.'

Haddock picked up his phone, found a number and called it. 'Arthur,' he said as it was answered, 'I need your team back into Terry Coats' place. Yes, I know they've been there before, but this time they'll know what they're looking for. We know who was there, we know what they were wearing, we just need to be able to prove it.'

Forty-Four

'This is the strangest investigation I have ever been on, gaffer,' Sauce said, his voice low as he glanced around Bar Italia; no more than half the tables were occupied but he had no wish to be overheard. 'It began with a double murder, but now I find that the victims were perpetrators themselves. It's an inquiry within an inquiry. We're making great progress at one level, but none at all at the other. What am I doing wrong?'

'Nothing,' Bob Skinner replied, as he wiped up the last traces of his lasagne with a piece of garlic bread. 'Are there any questions you haven't asked?'

'Not that I can think of.'

'Is there any part of any crime scene that the SOCOs haven't been over?'

'None that we know of.'

'In your search for the second car in Torphichen Place, have you been over all the available street camera footage?'

'Yes.'

'Have you interviewed all the friends and family members of the victims?'

'All that we can find, yes. Lottie and Cotter traced Terry Coats' mother last Thursday; she couldn't offer anything.

Likewise with his work colleagues; I had a team of DCs interview them. They knew him in the office; the men said he was capable, a couple of the women thought he was old school sexist.'

'What about the story he spun us when we caught him with Aisha? What about the shop he claimed she used to launder the gold coinage?'

'According to her, or so Coats said, the shop was owned by the same company as Wister Air. I've asked the airport's commercial management to give me a list of possibles from among their tenants, but they've still to come back to me.'

'What about the burner SIM card you found at Griff's?'

'One call made to another unregistered UK SIM.'

'Did anything in his papers, on his computer, on any device, give you a clue to who he might have called?'

'Not a scrap.'

'That all being the case, Sauce,' Skinner declared, 'the central part of your investigation can't be faulted. As for all the other stuff, where has it taken you?'

'We know now that Montell and Coats were acting in concert. I had a call from Inspector Ellis in Manchester; she has a taxi-driver witness who's identified Terry as the man who was waiting for Aisha Karman outside the Grange Hotel. She was killed with Griff's gun, which is absolute proof that they're a team.'

'Are you telling me that Coats shot her?'

'That's how it looks, gaffer,' Haddock replied. 'Do you doubt it?'

He shrugged. 'I don't see him as a killer, that's all. Did the taxi-driver witness say there was only one person waiting for her at the hotel?'

'Maybe Griff was in the car.'

'Would she have got in if he had been? I tend to doubt that.' He paused. 'Didn't you tell me she had sex just before she died?'

'Yes, but . . . Well . . . Okay, I get it. The English autopsy report did say that the body showed no signs of a struggle.'

Skinner leaned closer as another diner passed by their table on the way to the toilet. 'Then either I'm wrong, and Coats did have it in him to kill, or he took her to the place where he knew Griff would be waiting.' Unexpectedly, he shuddered and gazed out of the restaurant window, at the pedestrians and the traffic flow.

'What's up, gaffer?' his companion asked.

'I'm thinking about that man, and all the times he was alone with my daughter. It makes my blood run cold, Sauce. It makes me wish he was still alive, so I could kill him myself.' His eyes came back to Haddock. 'You've never had to fire a gun in the line of duty, have you? No, nor have ninety-nine out of a hundred police officers. I have, and even on the basis of a very brief acquaintanceship, that's what makes me confident that Coats didn't shoot the woman. He wasn't capable of it. Mind you,' he added with a twisted grin, 'I'd have said the same about Griff Montell, so don't listen to a bloody word I say.'

He leaned back as the waiter arrived to clear their table. 'Dessert, gentlemen? Or coffee?'

'Double espresso,' Skinner replied. 'Sauce?'

'Cappuccino, thanks.'

'So, what else have you established?'

'We know for sure how Griff got his gold and his gun into the country. His cousin DuPlessis told us he sent it to him on one of his company's cruise liners. He was vague about the dates but Tarvil did some checking and found that two and a half years ago Griff hired a car from Hertz, a big hatchback. When he brought it back two days later, the recorded mileage was consistent with a round trip to Southampton. The date coincided with the docking there of the Oceanic Aladdin, the ship DuPlessis named.'

'Do you know how many coins he collected?'

'Not for sure, no,' Haddock said. 'But apart from that we have established that on his first three years here, each time he went to South Africa to visit his kids, when he came back he disposed of forty Krugerrands to a licensed gold dealer in Glasgow. Do the sums, and that's around a hundred and twenty grand.'

'Yeah,' Skinner chuckled. 'Lucky for some, eh.'

Forty-Five

'Good lunch?' Singh asked.

'Always is in the Bar Italia,' Haddock replied. 'It's become big Bob's local when he's at the *Saltire* office. He was paying, which made it even better.'

'Mmm. My corned beef sandwiches went down really well. I made them myself, too. Washed down by a really nice Cotes du Pepsi. You've just missed your mate from Pretoria. He Zoomed you; I said you'd Zoom him back. Remember the days when you just phoned somebody?'

'Just about. The thing I remember most about them was that it was much easier to lie to someone.'

Haddock returned to his office; although he was still luxuriating in the space, he reflected on the reason he was enjoying it, and told himself that he would give it up in a second to Sammy Pye, if he could be brought back to health. Whether he would cede it so willingly to someone else, that was a different matter.

Settling into his chair, he switched on his computer and sent a Zoom meeting invitation to his South African colleague. Pollock responded within a minute, his face replacing Haddock's own on the screen. The Major seemed to be looking at him wide-eyed. 'What the hell is that building behind you?' he exclaimed. 'Since when did you have fucking Disneyland in Edinburgh?'

'The governors of that place wouldn't appreciate being compared to Mickey Mouse. You called me earlier?'

'Yes, sorry; I forgot the time difference. I have news for you. You were right about Griffin's gun. The one you have was indeed his service weapon on the day of the robbery. The serial number is still on our records, so I guess when we check them all, we'll find one that isn't. Obviously the inventory hasn't been reviewed for twelve years, an omission that we'll correct annually from now on.' He paused. 'In addition to that I have updates for you on both Anatoly Rogozin and Aisha Karman; they'll interest you, I think. How much do you know about Anatoly?'

'More than you might think,' Haddock confessed. 'He had a brother called Dimitri who was co-owner of a football club in Scotland. The other owner was a man named Cameron McCullough. As an aside, that's my partner's name too. She's his granddaughter and she was named after him. The Rogozin brothers have a remarkable distinction given that they were Russians. They were both murdered in Scotland.'

'Wow!' Pollock gasped. 'You have a knack for upstaging me, young man. You're not going to tell me that your wife's grandfather was involved in Dimitri's death, are you?'

He was about to correct the major's use of the word 'wife', but stopped himself; it sounded right. 'No, his killer was arrested fairly quickly. He was a guy with a grievance, no more.'

'What about Anatoly? Did he have a tie-up with him?'

'No. Cameron bought out his brother's share in the club.'

'How did Anatoly take that?' the major asked.

'I don't think he was best pleased, but nothing was made of it.'

'Still, has Mr McCullough been interviewed about the killing? Not by you, obviously.'

'Not by anyone.' Haddock saw his eyebrows rise in the small box in the corner of the screen. 'He disappeared, around the time of Griff's murder, and hasn't been seen since. He and his minder got into a car and drove off into the night.'

'Are you telling me he's a suspect?'

'Not directly. He was miles away when the killings happened.'

'Christ, he couldn't be dead too, could he?'

'In theory, he could,' Sauce admitted, 'but Grandpa McCullough's not your average man. Given his past connection to the Rogozins, sure he needs to be interviewed, but I don't believe he's involved.'

'Or you don't want to believe?' the major suggested.

'Oh no, I could, trust me; but I don't, that's all. Everybody in the game was already dead when he went away, so why would he bother?'

'How's your wife feeling about this?'

'Worried, but she feels the same about me. Cameron might be up to something but I don't believe it has anything to do with this. Now, what about your updates?'

'Yes, those. Anatoly had a place in Cape Town, owned by his airline, another in London, owned by a telecommunications company that he and his brother had part of, and another in Moscow that he inherited from Dimitri. His main South African business was Wister Air, which he bought ten years ago.'

'He bought it?'

'Yes,' the South African confirmed. 'He set up the company in North Cyprus, and used it to buy a small budget airline whose founder was doing okay until he made the mistake of cheating on his wife. Her father was the company's banker, and he didn't take it well. The airline went on the block and Anatoly's company bought it.'

'Not just Anatoly's company,' Haddock pointed out. 'There's another shareholder, an entity called Lente.'

'Mm, I didn't know that, but whoever it is, they're very much a sleeping partner. Anatoly ran Wister Air; Anatoly and nobody else.'

'What about Aisha Karman? What have you got on her?'

'She was Anatoly's girlfriend.'

'She was? But she was screwing Terry Coats whenever she landed in Edinburgh. It was Terry Coats she met on the day she disappeared.'

'Are you shocked?' Pollock chuckled. 'Being cabin crew gives you these opportunities. Not just cabin crew either. My ex-brother-in-law had offices in Durban and Bloemfontein, and a family in each. He still has the offices and the job, but hardly a rand to his name with two sets of kid support to pay. Anyway, the thing about Aisha: we got access to Anatoly's internet and his computer, and we found an email from her to him, sent two weeks ago, saying that she was in Edinburgh, and she needed to see him, urgently. He replied, saying he'd be there. He asked her to book them a suite in the Balmoral Hotel.'

'That would have been fucking clever on her part,' Haddock remarked, 'considering that at that time she was in a fridge in Manchester.'

Forty-Six

'Do you not find the air in Edinburgh too thin for your blood?' Dorward asked.

'Fuck off, Arthur,' Lottie Mann replied cheerfully. 'I'm a regular visitor to the capital city.'

'You don't strike me as the Festival type.'

'I'm not, but I'm a regular prosecution witness in the High Court.' From her position in the doorway she looked around the shambles that had been Terry Coats' living room. 'How are your people getting on here?'

'A hell of a lot better now we know what we're looking for. We're picking up quite a few fibre samples in the sitting room, and even more in the kitchen. The garden dustbin's interesting too. We didn't look at it on our first visit, because I didn't think it was relevant. I wish we had because it's a right bloody mess. Somebody's lit a fire in there.'

'Burning what?'

'I don't know for sure, because a lot of it's melted, but there's been a towel among it. Part of it survived, maybe because it was wet, and it looks like there are blood traces on it.'

'Rogozin's?'

'Lottie, please. Gimme time, okay?'

'Sorry. But at least we know his blood type,' she added, 'so it won't be a problem determining if it is.'

'That's if Sauce is right and he was here.'

'We can't be any more certain than we are. John Cotter went into the chippy round the corner. The guy behind the counter told him that Terry Coats was a regular. Good memory; he remembered that he was in on the evening Rogozin was killed, about five o'clock. He bought a fish supper, a haggis supper, and a single fish. Haggis supper; the Russian's last meal.'

'Single fish?'

'You know how it is, Arthur. There's always too many chips. The fish supper must have been Coats's. He had vinegar on it.'

'But no walnuts?'

The DCI frowned. 'Why the fuck would he have walnuts on a fish supper?'

'Who knows?' he retorted. 'To each her own, but I found a nutcracker on the kitchen table. Not that I really think it was used for cracking walnuts. I'm pretty sure I can see slivers of skin on it. Rogozin's fingers were broken, weren't they?'

'Yes,' Mann confirmed. 'Three of them, on his left hand.'

'Why that one rather than the right?'

'Tell me,' she challenged, patiently. 'The bus footage shows him handing over his ticket, with his right hand. I'm guessing that Montell and Coats wanted it to be usable when they had finished persuading him to do whatever they wanted.'

'For example, sign a document?'

'Arthur, we'll make a detective out of you yet.' She glanced around the room once again. 'When you're done here, we're going to need you to look again at Coats' car. I know the perpetrators are dead, but Rogozin is a murder victim and

Sauce and I need to make a report to the procurator fiscal, for the record. Even if he wasn't killed here, and I'm certain he was, he was dumped from a car. I'm guessing it was that one, but I need to be able to prove it.'

Forty-Seven

Skinner smiled at the camera that he knew was part of the doorbell as he pressed the button. Within, he heard a chain being unfastened, and then a creak as the heavy oak door swung open. 'You want to put a drop of oil on that hinge,' he said. 'I remember saying that last time I was here.'

'Your memory's better than mine, Bob,' Maggie Rose Steele said as she stood aside to admit him. 'I can't recall the last time you were here.' She sounded exhausted and her eyes lacked any sparkle.

'Is the wee one about?' Skinner asked, producing a parcel from a canvas bag. 'I brought her a present.'

'She's napping. She has playgroup until four, and she's usually tired when she gets back. What did you bring her?'

'Lego. Seonaid was getting into that at her age.'

'Lovely,' she said, with a hint of a smile. 'Dolls are out of fashion with Stephanie just now.'

He reached into the bag once again. 'I brought something for you too. They wrapped it in Toppings; I'm not that neat.'

She tore off the paper. 'What's this? *"The Invisible Spirit"* by Kenneth Roy,' she read. 'It's a tome,' she said, weighing it in her hand. 'Just what I need though, something that has nothing to do with the job. Thanks. Come into the kitchen. Intuition must have told me you were coming; I've just made a pot of coffee. Therapeutic,' she explained. 'I'm on medication and it's knocking me out.'

He followed her, taking a seat at a breakfast booth which was set with child's crockery. 'Thomas the Tank Engine gets everywhere,' he chuckled. 'We have something similar.'

'How are your brood?' Steele asked. 'We haven't really talked about personal stuff for ages. Remind me, what's your new one called?'

'Dawn. She'll be the sunset of our breeding programme, I promise. I never thought we'd have another, I admit, but she's a wee beauty, the most like Sarah of any of her three.' He took a sip from his coffee, then a mouthful, albeit with a wry expression. 'That's shit, Maggie.'

She sampled her own, wincing as it reached her taste buds. 'God, you're right. That packet's been in the cupboard for ages. Why did I give it to you, of all people?'

'Because you're on meds; your brain's switched off. Get yourself across the road to Sainsbury's tomorrow and do a decent shop.'

'I'd feel guilty, Bob,' she said. 'I'm on sick leave. It's not right to go out.'

'That's old-school thinking. You're not contagious, you're suffering from stress and depression. You won't cure that by sitting in the house. Get yourself back into the real world. Go shopping, go for walks in Holyrood park, take Stephanie to a matinee at the cinema. You need to get your life back.'

'I don't think I've had a life since Stevie died,' she admitted. 'We weren't together for long, he and I, and before that . . . I really fucked it up with Mario, Bob. You know, I don't think I've ever been a happy person.'

'If that's true, it's time you were.'

'How do I make that happen?' she asked him.

'You go looking for it. Mags, you've never dealt with Stevie's death. It's time you did. First, you need to move house. This place is like a mausoleum. It's dull, it's depressing, it's on a main road and it has hardly any garden. Stephanie needs a change and so do you.'

'I'm done with the job, Bob,' she murmured. 'You know that, don't you?'

'I think I do, and I blame myself.'

'Why, in God's name?'

'For not preparing you better for one thing. For not taking it myself, for another. I went off in the huff because I lost the political argument against unification. If I had taken it, maybe I could have set it up right, and made the fucking thing manageable. But I didn't, it isn't, and it's done this to you, for which, my dear, I am so, so, sorry.'

'What am I going to do, Bob? I'm forty-three, I'm a single mum, and I've been in the police all my adult life.'

'What would you like to do? You'll get early retirement on health grounds, no problem. If you take my advice, you'll finally take the damehood that goes with the job. That on its own will bring you lots of offers, and your CV will bring you even more. You might even find that one of them's from InterMedia.'

'Who'll take over from me? It's a poisoned chalice.'

He winked. 'Do not mistake me for someone who gives a fuck about that. I know who it won't be, but that's all. Before you go, though, there's one thing I would like you to do. The service is in danger of losing another very capable woman, and I don't want that to happen. We both know that last week, when your head was messed up, you made an error of judgement that put someone in an awful position. I want you to reach out to Noele McClair. I want you to visit her and I want you to keep her in the game. Whatever job she wants, give it to her. Don't ask her to step into Griff Montell's shoes at Torphichen Place, otherwise do the best you can. I should have done that for you when Stevie died, I should have taken you right out of the firing line and given you a nice comfy desk to drive, a nine-to-five sinecure that would have given you the opportunity of seeing out your career in a stress-free place.'

She looked at him for what seemed like a long time; her eyes offered a hint of a smile. 'Bob,' she said, when she was ready to reply, 'you wouldn't know a stress-free place suppose you were reincarnated as the Dalai Lama. But I'll find one, and I'll persuade Noele McClair that she's the only person in the service that could fill it. You're right; I do owe her one.'

Forty-Eight

Instinctively, Haddock stood and assumed a stance that approximated to attention, although the man who had stepped into his office was wearing civilian clothes.

'Detective Inspector,' the grey-haired newcomer began, extending a hand, 'or Sauce, as I hear they call you. Good morning, I'm ACC Lowell Payne. The DCC's told you about me, I think. With the chief being off, and him standing in for her, he's made me something akin to his vicar on Earth. I'm not trying to catch you out by turning up unannounced, I promise you. I was going to give you advance warning, but my phone was out of battery, and my car doesn't seem to be recharging it.'

'Welcome, sir,' Sauce replied as they shook. 'Can I see your warrant card, please?'

The assistant chief constable gasped, stared back at him, and then smiled as he drew his identification from within his shirt and displayed it. 'You're taking a chance,' he said. 'Bob Skinner told me you had balls, and that's not a compliment he hands out too often. But you're right, we've never met, so I should have worn uniform.'

'Sorry sir, I was just covering my arse, with you being in

charge of counter-terrorism and everything. Please, have a seat. What do you want to know?'

'Tell me how close you are to an arrest,' Payne responded.

'My team? Nowhere near it, I have to admit. In mitigation, we've cleared up two open investigations in England and in South Africa. We've established that Griffin Montell was responsible for three killings, the first personally and the others possibly acting in concert with former Detective Inspector Terry Coats. We've established that while in the South African Police Service Montell was a principal actor in a massive gold robbery, and that later he smuggled into this country an unknown but significant quantity of Krugerrands and a firearm, the gun that was used in all three homicides.'

'And he was my niece's occasional boyfriend,' the ACC murmured. 'You found that gun in a safe in his flat, I believe. I have been briefed by the DCC, Sauce; I just wanted to hear it from you.'

'We did,' Haddock confirmed, 'and we can prove that it was put back there after the murder of Anatoly Rogozin. We don't know for sure who did that, but we believe it was Coats. Montell was booked on the last shuttle to Heathrow, to catch the Johannesburg flight on the Sunday morning. In theory, that allowed time to meet Rogozin in the afternoon, take him to Coats' place, kill him, dispose of the body, and catch his plane. Tarvil Singh, my DS, has established that it was delayed by half an hour, but he still missed it. Tarvil spoke to a ground-crew employee who remembered him arriving at the gate as the flight was being pushed off the stand. He identified himself as a police officer, but there was nothing she could do.'

'What made him late?'

'Traffic. Apparently there was a pile-up on the city bypass, west-bound, at nine-forty on Saturday evening, just past the Lothianburn junction. Coming from Howgate, where the body was dumped, they'd have joined the by-pass at Straiton and been stuck there with no option but to wait for it to clear, which it did at five past ten. The operator of the drop-off zone at the airport has snooper cameras there to catch punters picking-up, contrary to the by-laws. We're hoping to get some footage of Coats dropping Montell off there. That might, just might, let us track Coats to somewhere near Griff's at the time the gun was dropped off. It's all fucking academic, of course, but it would be good to prove it.'

'Where did Montell go after he missed his flight?' Payne asked.

'This is only a guess, but I reckon that he laid low at Coats' place. He was supposed to be in South Africa, and he needed to appear to be there.'

'That makes sense,' the ACC conceded. 'So, the Rogozin killing. Can we consider that cleared up?'

'It's the fiscal's decision sir, you know that, but that's what my report will say. I've just had the latest feedback from Mr Dorward at Gartcosh. His forensics team can place the victim in Terry Coats' house on the night he was killed, they can prove that he was tortured there and we have his blood on an undamaged section of a towel that they tried to burn in an old steel dustbin. Also, we have fibres from Rogozin's Crombie coat in the boot of Terry Coats' car.'

'What about motive, Sauce? You're telling me the guy was tortured before he was killed. Have you got any idea what that was about?'

'Not much. I do know there was a link between him and Aisha Karman, the Manchester victim, and that her email was used to lure . . .' He grinned. '. . . one of my favourite words that, and I've never got to use it before . . . to lure him to Scotland. Why they wanted him here, that I don't know. However,' he continued, 'it's irrelevant. We can prove who killed him, miles beyond a reasonable doubt. If this was going to a jury, there would be no need to show a motive.'

'It won't go to a jury,' Payne accepted, 'but the Lord Advocate might decide that there needs to be a formal Fatal Accident Inquiry before a sheriff. Indeed I'd be surprised if there isn't, with a police officer involved. Does Rogozin have any family?'

'He has a nephew in Russia, his late brother Dimitri's son and heir, but he's eleven years old: an eleven-year-old who now owns part of an airline, I guess. Yes, the kid has a right to a form of justice for his uncle, and the Russian Embassy will have an interest too. It doesn't worry me though; I'll be happy giving evidence before any kind of a court.'

'But not about the murders of Montell and Coats?'

Haddock shook his head. 'No, sir, not yet, and that's a bugger. We're still in the dark there.'

Forty-Nine

'Is that us finished in Edinburgh?' John Cotter asked his boss. The day was grey, as he gazed out of her office window across open ground, towards the cantilevers of the main stand at Ibrox Stadium.

'Unless we're needed, but it's unlikely. ACC Payne called me half an hour ago. Marlon's staying there as he's in the middle of an internet search, but we're stood down. Worse luck maybe. Did you see what we've had reported from Airdrie by the North Lanarkshire division CID? A man's been found in a builder's merchant's warehouse there, crucified, dead as mutton.'

'Crucified?' Cotter repeated, aghast.

'He was nailed to a wall; hands, arms and ankles. Professor Scott's doing the post-mortem along the road at two and we are invited to attend. Very kind of him.'

The DS pointed to his computer screen. 'Does that mean we're no longer interested in this? I've had a message from Sauce Haddock; he's been told by traffic central control that Vito Tremacoldi's car's been found, in the multi-storey at Glasgow Airport.'

The DCI scratched her chin. 'At the airport? Rich man goes

missing with his minder. It's not exactly a serious crime, is it? It's not even in our area since he disappeared from Perthshire. If it's anyone's it's Sauce's, but,' she paused 'the boy's got enough on his plate, so, I'll tell you what, we'll take a run along there since it's handy, check it out and then head for the Queen Elizabeth Hospital for Graham Scott's autopsy.'

'Unless the victim's risen again by that time?'

'Shut the fuck up, John,' Mann said, but with a grin on her face.

With Cotter at the wheel, they joined the motorway; the traffic was light and no more than five minutes had elapsed when they reached the airport turn-off and saw their destination before them. The DS pushed the communication button at the car park entrance. 'Police,' he said, displaying his identification for the camera.

'You're looking for Level Four,' a disembodied voice advised as the barrier rose.

The access road to the car park was wide but it tested their car's turning circle as they rose from floor to floor. Mann breathed a sigh of relief as they turned off and into a long alley with cars parked tight on either side. 'You wouldn't expect this to be as busy,' Cotter remarked.

'Glasgow's a bigger city than Edinburgh by quite a way,' the DCI reminded him, 'even though the airport's smaller.'

As they turned into the second aisle, they saw two uniformed officers at the far end, standing beside a blue car. Cotter drew up just short of them. 'This is a big bastard,' he said, surveying the Jaguar. 'Do we know when it got here? The number plate should have been photographed on entry.'

'We weren't asked to find that out,' the older of the two constables replied.

'How was it found?' Mann asked her. 'Did the airport alert us?'

'No chance, ma'am. We did it the hard way, just cruising round. It was more by luck than judgement, for they only gave us the number. If we'd been told to look for a big blue Jag it would have made life a hell of a lot easier.'

'I'll feed that back,' the DCI promised. 'Thanks for the ma'am, by the way. I could be a plain DC, for all you know.'

The PC smiled. 'You're kidding. The whole of the Govan police office knows who you are. You're a legend.'

'Less of that,' Mann retorted. 'I'm too young to be a legend.'

'Now we're here, boss,' Cotter said, 'what do we do about it?'

'There's nothing we can do, John.' She peered through the front passenger window. 'It hasn't been reported stolen and we've got no reason to believe it's been involved in a crime. I can't see anything inside that would justify us breaking into it, and unless it's parked here illegitimately, which is bloody near impossible, we've got no grounds for having it towed. McCullough's wife may have her tights in a twist, but it's Tremacoldi's car and there is no Mrs Vito to report him missing.'

'Do you want to ask DI Haddock?'

'No, and I doubt very much that Sauce wants me to ask him either.'

'Sir Robert?'

'He's got no locus, and even if he did, I know what he'd say. Establish the time of arrival with the car park management, and instruct them to advise DI Haddock when the owner turns up to collect it, unless it was pre-booked and they already know when he's due back.' She checked her watch. 'PC . . .'

'Wood, ma'am; Victoria Wood.'

'Right, PC Wood, we've got to be somewhere soon, so I'd like you to do that for me. Find out whether the Jag is pre-booked. If it is, advise acting DCI Haddock of Serious Crimes in Edinburgh. If it isn't, ask the car park operator to do the same, without delay, when the system shows that the car's being collected.'

'Very good, ma'am. What if they don't come back?'

'We'll worry about that in a week . . . or rather, Sauce Haddock and Bob Skinner will.'

Fifty

'It's a terrible line,' the detective constable said. 'Let me call you back mobile to mobile.' He hung up and copied the number displayed on the website of TCOC into his handphone.

'That's much better; I can 'ear you now,' a male voice told him as his call was accepted. He had been expecting a thick accent, Turkish probably, and so the Cockney twang took him by surprise. 'My name's Ronnie Riley. Remind me, please sir, who you are. I didn't quite catch it earlier.'

'DC Marlon Honeyman, attached to Serious Crimes in Edinburgh. I'm involved in a major investigation . . .'

'That's in Scotland, is it?'

'It still was when I got up this morning, yes.'

'So how can I help the Scotch?'

The use of the term made Honeyman's hackles rise, but he forced them back into place. 'I'm trying to find out as much as I can,' he replied calmly, 'about a North Cyprus offshore company called Wister Air. It's the holding company for an airline of that name.'

'Yeah, that's one of ours. We set it up ten years ago for our client Mr Rogozin. A routine run-of-the-mill offshore company, nothing exceptional or dodgy about it. He could have done it

260

anywhere but . . .' He stopped in mid-sentence and began another. 'Why are you asking about it now?'

'Because Mr Rogozin was murdered about a week and a half ago, here in Scotland.'

'Bloody 'ell!'

'We know who did it,' the DC continued, 'that's not in doubt, but we don't know why. My job is to find out as much as I can about him and his business dealings.'

'I'm not sure how much help I can give you,' Riley admitted. 'We help set these companies up, but very often that's the last we see of them. That's how it was with Wister Air.'

'What are the benefits?'

'Of an International Business Company? Massive. An IBC's only subject to one per cent income tax and corporation tax. It's exempt from VAT. The shareholders are exempt from any inheritance or income tax if they sell their shareholding. Even dividends are exempt from tax. Instead of taxes, an IBC only pays a fixed annual licensing fee of five thousand euros directly to the government. Plus, there's no restrictions on them taking money in and out of the country. And confidentiality's guaranteed.'

'I'm sold,' Honeyman chuckled. 'I understand there were two shareholders. Is that right?'

'Yeah, it is. Rogozin Enterprises, and a trust the name of which I can't bloody remember now.'

'Lente.'

'That's it! Spelt wiff a final "e". I remember asking what it meant and Rogozin telling me it means "slowly" in Latin. "Festina Lente", means don't be in a fuckin' rush or something like that. I've no idea where it were based, or even what its legal standing was. They were using a nominee so I didn't care as long as they paid the fee. Rogozin's company was based in Monaco.'

'Yes, I noticed that,' Honeyman said. 'It made me wonder why he bothered to go to Cyprus to set up Wister Air. Now you've explained the advantages, I understand it a hell of a lot better.'

'Sure, there's that, but also the company that Rogozin planned to buy was based there, so it made it easier all round.'

'The airline?'

'That's right. It was a nice little business and probably cheap at the price. The South African guy who ran it, 'is father-in-law sold it out from under him. He was a Russian too, as I remember.'

'Did that sale go through you?'

'No, that sort of transaction,' Riley explained, 'would go through lawyers licensed to practise here in North Cyprus, and would be lodged with the register of companies. I did hear about it though, through a mate of mine who was involved. The purchase price was fifty million euros. Not bad for an airline that was in profit already. But the really odd thing was, it was paid in gold.'

Fifty-One

Looking through the glass wall of what had become Jackie Wright's office, Tarvil Singh saw a smile spread across her normally impassive face as she gazed at her terminal. She looked across at him and started to rise, but he waved her back into her chair and headed for her instead. He stood in the doorway, unwilling to squeeze his bulk into the cramped little room. 'What's making your afternoon?' he asked.

'A result,' she replied, emphatically. 'You know I've been trying to identify which of the airport shops Terry Coats's girlfriend was fencing her Krugerrands through, if we're to believe the story he told Sir Robert.'

'Sure. He said it was owned by the same group who own Wister Air, didn't he?'

'That's right,' the DC agreed, 'and I've spent hours, days, trawling through every outlet at the airport, airside and groundside, trying to find it on that basis, with no success at all. Finally, I gave up on that and looked again, right across the board, with no preconceptions. Look what I found,' she turned her monitor towards him. 'It's a leather-goods shop, airside, showing on the current layout as being tucked in next to Wetherspoons. It's called MK Flight Accessories, an independent business, and the owner is a Mr Morris Karman.'

Her smile infected the DS. 'There's a coincidence,' he chuckled. 'Go on.'

She swung the screen to face her once more. 'Okay, we know that while Aisha was educated in South Africa, she actually had a British passport. Through that I got her place of birth which took me to her birth certificate. She was born in Portsmouth, father's name Steveland Karman, mother Serena Dixon. From there I went to Steveland and found that he has a brother named Morris, who's the same age as the one who shows up in Companies House as the owner of MK Flight Accessories. As well as the Edinburgh shop, the business has airport outlets in Manchester and Newcastle.'

'Crackin' good, Jackie,' Singh boomed. 'Did you find an address for Uncle Morris?'

'Only the one that's listed in Companies House; that needn't be his principal residence, but in this case I think it is. It's in Biggar, in South Lanarkshire, and conveniently in our territory. That means we can invite him to assist us with our enquiries without going through an English force.'

'Yes, we can lift him if we want,' the DS agreed, 'but we're only going on garbled hearsay from a dead man, so we should be gentler than that. Do you know where we can find him? Did you get that far?'

'I called the manager of the Edinburgh shop. She told me he's usually there on a Tuesday, but he called her this morning to say he has a heavy cold and he's having a day at home.'

'Captive audience,' the DS murmured. 'Get your coat, Jackie, I think you've earned a trip out of the office.'

Fifty-Two

'Do you agree with me, Sauce?' Lottie Mann asked. 'Tremacoldi's car should stay where it is?'

'Absolutely. It's there perfectly legally. My partner's step-granny might argue that it's relevant to a missing person investigation, but she'll need to get a lawyer to tell us, and that ain't going to happen. I'll tell her about it, but only as a family courtesy. The car park people are sure it wasn't pre-booked?'

'Yes, and they would know. Do you think that's significant?'

'Not for a minute,' Haddock said. 'Cameron's not the sort of guy who'd book a cheap deal. He'd just roll up and pay.'

'It's at the airport, so the assumption is they've flown somewhere. The ticket was issued at five fifty-eight; so they must have been on one of the first flights.'

'Can you fly out of Glasgow on New Year's Day?'

'Of course,' Mann said. 'Do you think this is the backwoods? There's Amsterdam, for a start. That's a very popular destination with middle-aged men out on the razzle.'

'Maybe so, but I don't see Grandpa slipping off for a few days in the canal-side brothels.'

'When he's got better at home?' she laughed. 'Is that what you're saying? I can tell you from bitter experience, that counts

265

for eff all. Sauce, if you're under personal pressure over this with Cheeky, I can have a couple of guys go over all the passenger manifests from that day.'

'I'm not,' Haddock replied, instantly. 'And even if I was, I wouldn't use police manpower on a personal matter.'

'Bob Skinner would.'

'If I have to, I'll ask him, but I'm not there yet. Changing the subject, how about you? You happy to be home?'

'I was until a couple of hours ago,' the DCI said. 'John and I are just back from a post-mortem. The deceased was found in a warehouse in Airdrie when it opened up yesterday morning. What a mess! He'd been fixed to a wall with a nail gun, had his eyes and his genitals incinerated with a flame-thrower, and left hanging there.'

'Jesus, Mary and Joseph! Who did he upset, I wonder? What was the cause of death after all that?'

'Graham Scott decided that exsanguination was the likeliest, although he also said that it could have been shock. The femoral artery was cut after they had finished with him, so chances are he did bleed out. I only saw photos of the crime scene because I was with you on Monday, but it was a right bloody mess, literally.'

'Rather you than me with that one,' Haddock conceded. 'Have you got a name for him?'

'Walter Thomson, age thirty-seven, mixed race; he had a couple of convictions for violence, but he was suspected of a lot more, cases where the victims were too scared to speak. With the facial damage, he had to be identified by his fingerprints. He was muscle for hire in the East End of Glasgow, where we've never quite stamped out the old protection racket.'

'A gang killing?' Haddock suggested.

'Could be,' Mann agreed, 'but we've got nothing to point us in a specific direction. We don't even have an accurate time of death. A twelve-hour window stretching from about eight on old year's night into Wednesday morning.'

'The same time as Montell and Coats.'

'Possibly, but a completely different methodology. They were executed, this guy was tortured to death.' She sighed. 'Best get on with it, Sauce, I'm told that ACC Payne's coming in to see me tomorrow,'

'Is that right? You're getting more notice than I did. Let me know if there's any news about Tremacoldi's car.'

Fifty-Three

'As far as I know, Detective Sergeant Singh,' Morris Karman said, stiffly, 'what I did was not against the law. My poor niece told me that she was being given gold coins by her lover, Anatoly, the Russian man who owns the airline she worked for. Practically, they were no use to her in that form. She couldn't spend them and she lacked the knowledge to trade them on the gold market. She asked me to help and so I did. I was very fond of Aisha; I'm still in shock about what's happened to her. That's why I'm not at work today; I don't have a cold, as you can see. Tomorrow I'm driving down to Manchester; the police have asked me to identify her body formally. That's not something I'd ever imagine doing. I don't know how I'll handle it, I confess.'

'It won't take long,' the DS told him. 'DC Wright and I, we've both had to help people do that; I'm sure our English colleagues will make it as easy as they can for you.'

'You know who killed her? Have they caught him yet?'

'All I can say is that they're not looking for anyone in connection with Aisha's death. That might sound like police-speak, but it's the literal truth.' He paused as the little man nodded, pursing his lips. 'We need to ask you about the way you helped Aisha dispose of her . . . gifts.'

For the first time, Karman seemed hesitant; he turned his eyes towards the bay window of his sitting room, looking out across ploughed fields. 'I said I didn't believe I was doing anything illegal, Mr Singh. But if you have a different view, maybe I should consult a lawyer before we have this discussion.'

'You don't need to, we assure you. Look, we're Serious Crimes detectives; that means something. If you have sailed close to the wind, it's going to be minor at worst, and not within our remit. We're trying to build up a broad picture of what Aisha was doing and who she was doing it with. We're interested in the circumstances of her death, as part of a broader investigation. Our English colleagues are investigating her murder.'

'In that case, I'll trust you,' he said. 'I agreed to handle the coins for Aisha, but I didn't want to run the risk of being nailed for capital gains tax. To avoid that I came up with a formula that involved her tendering them at one of my shops as payment for an item, any item. A small amount of change would be given for the sake of appearances, then the staff would pass the coin to me. Effectively it became invisible, but legitimately, as a transaction had taken place and it had been accepted as payment. I would trade it in the normal way and give the money to Aisha.'

'Did this happen exclusively in Edinburgh?' Jackie Wright asked. 'Aisha flew into other airports, didn't she?'

'Yes, she did, but it was only done in Edinburgh. I'm there most frequently.'

'How many times was this done? How many coins did you trade for her?'

'Good question.' He frowned, searching his memory. 'Ten or eleven, I think. I can dig out the paperwork if you need it.'

'Not at this stage,' Singh said. 'Mr Karman, did the system stay confidential, or did anybody ever find out about it?'

'Once, it was mentioned to me by someone on the airport staff. I took it up with the shop manager and she investigated. The checkout girl had been talking out of turn. She was fired, but not for that, for helping herself to stock.'

'How close were your niece and the man Anatoly?'

Karman threw him a lazy smile. 'Do you mean was marriage in the offing? Not a chance. Aisha didn't even like the man all that much, but he was the boss, and he was generous with the K-rands.'

'They were a genuine gift? Are you sure about that? She wasn't giving him the money back?'

'That was the very first question I asked her, Sergeant. Was this money-laundering? She promised me that it was not, that they were hers to keep. She told me once that when he was drunk, he called them his "*slegte winste*"; that's Afrikaans for "ill-gotten gains" she explained.' He stopped; as the detectives watched, his face went pale. 'Are you going to tell me that she was stealing the coins from Anatoly and that's why she was killed?'

'No, we're not,' Singh assured him. 'I can't tell you too much, but he didn't know she was dead. We're satisfied that he had no part in it.'

'Are you sure?'

'Certain. Mr Karman, did Aisha ever mention to you a man named Terry Coats?'

'Ah,' he exclaimed, 'the stockbroker. Yes, she talked about him. She and Anatoly weren't . . . how can I put it? . . . exclusive.

I'm not saying she was promiscuous, God bless her, but she had more than one attachment. She met the man Coats by chance in Edinburgh Airport and they had, a fling, I suppose you'd say. More often than not when she had a lay-over in Edinburgh, she'd come and stay with me, but when Coats came on the scene, she started to stop in hotels with him.'

'Did she tell him about the coins?' the DS asked.

'Yes, she did. I know this because she told me she had it in mind to ask him to invest her money when she had enough piled up.'

'Was she still seeing him when she died?'

'Yes, I believe so. Not so frequently, for her schedule was changed in the summer, but occasionally she still came through Edinburgh and they would meet up. Why do you ask about Coats? Is he a suspect?'

'You didn't happen to read a newspaper on the second of January, did you?'

'No,' Karman replied. 'The financial markets were closed and that's all I ever look at. Why? What would I have seen?'

'You'd have seen reports of Terry Coats being found shot dead on Wednesday morning, in Edinburgh, together with another man. Coats wasn't a stockbroker, Mr Karman, he was employed by Edinburgh Airport security, and before that he'd been a police officer in the west of Scotland. He was stalking your niece because he thought she was money-laundering.'

'But she wasn't, I tell you!' he exclaimed. 'I promise you, she wasn't . . . or if she was she didn't know it.'

Singh nodded. 'I believe you, Mr Karman,' he said. 'I accept that your niece was an innocent victim in this business; probably the only one. One last thing: the other man found dead with Coats, was named Griffin Montell, a serving police inspector. Did Aisha ever mention him?'

'No, she didn't, of that I'm also certain. I've never heard of him. If he was a police officer, damn it, he should have prevented her being killed!'

Fifty-Four

'There is nothing irregular about Wister Air,' the woman insisted. 'The European media like to portray the Turkish Republic of North Cyprus as a haven for criminals and gangsters, but I can assure you, sir, it is not. To be registered as an offshore company here, very strict conditions must be met. These are observed because the Register of Companies is directly overseen by government. Wister Air complies with the law.'

'That law, Ms Ecevit,' Marlon Honeyman said, 'doesn't seem to object to one of the owners hiding behind nominee directors.'

'If that owner is a registered company. But ultimately the owners of that company must be revealed; if it was set up in the TRNC they would be required to submit good character certificates from the police in their home country.'

'Okay, I get that, but where was Lente registered: the co-owner of Wister Air?'

'In the TRNC, of course,' Ms Ecevit replied. 'And now it is the sole owner of Wister Air.'

'It is?' Honeyman exclaimed. 'When did that come about?'

'On Monday of last week, when we received by email a

document transferring the holdings of Rogozin Enterprises to Lente. The document was signed by Anatoly Rogozin, as the law requires, and it was registered that same day. That's how it is now. Lente is now the sole owner of Wister Air.'

'What would the law say if it knew his signature had been obtained by torture?'

'That would need to be proved.'

'The first step to doing that is by finding who owns Lente. Can you tell me that?'

'I don't know,' Ms Ecevit admitted. 'You are a policeman from a foreign jurisdiction. I will need to consult the Ministry.'

'Then please do so. I'll call you back tomorrow.'

Fifty-Five

'You are sure about this, Inspector?' Pollock asked.

'It's what our man was told by someone on the ground,' Haddock said. 'If it's true, what are the chances of anyone else being involved?'

'I was planning to let him go this evening,' the major admitted, 'but if he was involved as you suggest, it moves him into another league. Listen, I know this happened in my jurisdiction, but would you like to take the lead in the interview? He doesn't know you, and he may not even know that you have no legal standing as far as he's concerned.'

The Scot smiled. 'If it helps you get a conviction and close a twelve-year-old case, then it'll be my pleasure.'

'Let's go for it. Constable,' he called to someone off camera, 'go get the man.'

While he waited for the prisoner to be brought to the inter-view room, Haddock moved around his office, closing the venetian blinds. He had barely resumed his seat when Tom DuPlessis appeared, handcuffed and looking more haggard than ever.

'What the fuck is this?' he protested. 'You guys, you are unbelievable. My lawyer said you can't hold me any longer.

Release me or I'll sue you; I will, I warn you.'

'I've already advised your lawyer that we have a new matter to discuss with you,' Pollock retorted. 'It relates to a murder investigation that my Scottish colleague is leading, and it's him you'll be talking to. Before we begin, I should tell you that extradition arrangements exist between the United Kingdom and South Africa and that, should he make such a request, I will be raising no objections. Be very careful what you say, sir, for if you are less than frank and honest with him, the consequences could be serious. Detective Inspector Haddock, it's all yours.'

'Thanks, Major.' He paused, looking, unsmiling and un-blinking, directly into the pinpoint of the camera, rather than at the face displayed on his screen. He thought of it as his best Bob Skinner stare, holding the pose as he counted silently to ten. 'Mr DuPlessis,' he began, his voice as cold as his eyes, 'a week ago, your cousin Griffin Montell was murdered, here in my city. I knew Griff as a colleague and, I thought, as a friend. We always insist that we treat every homicide victim with the same respect and that we investigate every crime with the same intensity, but the truth is . . . internationally, I'm sure . . . that when the victim's a police officer we pull out stops that sometimes we didn't even know existed. That's how it's been with Griff. Unfortunately, it's led us to discover things about him that we couldn't have suspected in our wildest fantasies, or even our drunkest, us being Scots. Your murdered cousin, my murdered friend, was a killer himself . . . a high-functioning psychopath, in the opinion of an eminent forensic psychologist. Before he ever came to Scotland, he killed a fellow SAPS officer in the course of a bullion robbery twelve years ago, one that's been unsolved until now. You've already admitted to us that you helped him smuggle to the UK both the weapon he used and an unknown number of gold coins, the proceeds of that robbery . . .'

'I told you already,' DuPlessis shouted, 'I didn't know what was in that box.'

'And we told you already, ignorance isn't absolution. The point is you did it, knowing that it was illegal, and you didn't bother to ask. You were right in what you said before; you were going to walk out of there tonight, because Major Pollock will need your testimony in closing the open file on the bullion robbery and in tying Griff to that crime. But what we've discovered since then in the course of our investigations here, puts you right back in the deepest of deep shit. The day after your cousin was murdered, the body of a man named Anatoly Rogozin was found in Scotland. He was an associate of Griff . . . indeed, Griff met him at the airport . . . and he'd been shot with the gun you smuggled into Scotland. So, you see, you're an accessory to murder both here and in your own country.'

'No!' DuPlessis shouted, panicking.

'Let me finish,' Haddock exclaimed. 'I'm not done yet. Rogozin's main business interest in South Africa was an airline called Wister Air. He purchased that ten years ago, through a company that he had established in North Cyprus, with another corporate entity called Lente. We didn't know for sure who owned that until earlier on today, when we discovered that on Monday of last week, the North Cyprus company registrar received a document, signed by Rogozin, transferring his stake in the company to Lente. That signature was obtained by torture. Rogozin must have been a tough guy, Griff had to break three of the fingers on his left hand before he signed.'

'I know nothing of this,' the prisoner screamed. 'You can't tie me to it.'

'Of course I can, if I want to,' Haddock laughed, 'but I still haven't got to the big finish. For that we have to go back ten years, to the day when Rogozin and Lente purchased the airline they rebranded as Wister Air, again in North Cyprus. It's still remembered there, even in that very unusual business environment, because the Russian owner . . . who was, incidentally, found dead himself in a snowdrift in Moscow six years ago . . . agreed to be paid in gold coinage, valued at fifty million euros.' He stopped and drew a deep breath and looked straight into the camera once again. 'So this is where you have a choice, Mr DuPlessis. This is where you can tell Major Pollock and me how that gold got to the port of Famagusta, via Istanbul, as undoubtedly it did, or he can go all the way through the movements of your ex-employer's liners to find out which one of them was there at the time in question. If he has to do that you'll have no deal with him, and you'll find yourself on a flight to Scotland with no prospect of going home inside ten years, minimum. Your choice, but you don't have a lot of time to make it. My partner's booked us seats for *Star Wars* and Major Pollock's due on the first tee for an evening round.'

DuPlessis threw up his cuffed hands. 'Okay, okay, okay! I'll tell you. I met Rogozin, with Griff, ten years ago. Griff introduced him as a friend and he did all the talking, or most of it. He told me that he needed to move a significant cargo to North Cyprus and that Griff had suggested I could help him. He paid me a hundred thousand US dollars, and fifty thousand for my contact on board ship. But again, I didn't ask what I was moving, because I didn't want to fucking know!'

'Well, now you do, buddy,' Major Pollock said, off camera.

'What Mr Haddock said is right. You have five minutes to put your signature on that, in return for which I will treat you as a witness rather than an accused.'

'What about him?' the prisoner asked. 'What about Scotland?'

'Pal,' Haddock sighed, 'you're not worth the air fare.'

'Done,' DuPlessis sighed. 'Where do I sign?'

'I'll get a clerk and we can do that now,' the major replied. 'Hey, Sauce,' he added, 'you know what "Lente" means in Afrikaans?'

Fifty-Six

'Detective Constable Honeyman,' Ms Ecevit said, in clipped tones. 'The Minister himself has advised that I may give you the information you seek without any further formality.'

'Pleased to hear it,' the DC replied.

'Yes, the register is public. If you walked in from the street you could inspect it. However,' she continued, 'the Minister did make one stipulation, that I should do so in a video call, so that you may display your credentials as a police officer.'

If it's a public document, what's the point? he thought, but instead, recognising the universal practice of a tail being covered, he turned the WhatsApp call from audio to video. When Ms Ecevit appeared on screen, he was glad that he had. He has been expecting a sharp-nosed middle-aged spinster; instead he saw a high-cheekboned woman, possibly in her late twenties, with almond eyes and full lips, who reminded him of the photos of Sophia Loren that his grandfather had shown him when he was a boy. Obediently, he displayed his warrant card, holding it close enough to the camera for her to read the text, and the name.

'Thank you, Marlon,' she said. He could have sworn that

she fluttered her eyelashes. 'You're not what I was expecting. I thought you Scots all had big beards.'

'Only some of us. You're a surprise to me too.'

'Why?' she smiled. 'Did you think the same of Turkish women?'

'Absolutely not,' he insisted.

'Pinocchio, your nose is growing,' she laughed.

He knew that he had to move matters on, or he might fall in love. 'What's your first name?' he asked.

'Zehra.'

He sighed. 'Well, Zehra, I suppose we'd better get on with it.'

'I suppose,' she agreed, with as little enthusiasm as him. 'Did you use a personal mobile to make this call?'

'Yes,' he said, smiling as he understood the question, 'as a matter of fact I did.'

'In that case, I can tell you that the company known as Lente has two shareholders, both South African and both sharing the same birthday. Mr Griffin Montell, and Ms Spring Montell. I have no record of Mr Montell ever having been on North Cyprus, but ten years ago, when the company Wister Air acquired the airline business, Ms Montell was here. Her signature is on the document, alongside that of Mr Rogozin. I have a cousin who is Dutch,' she added. 'She told me that in Afrikaans, Lente means Spring.'

Fifty-Seven

'You realise this has nothing to do with us, Sauce?' ACC Lowell Payne said. 'Isn't it a waste of your time to be sitting in on this interview?'

'Sorry, sir, I don't think so,' Haddock countered. 'Griff Montell's lying in a drawer in the Cowgate, and I'm tasked with finding out who put him there and why. If there's any possibility that his death is related to something that happened in South Africa twelve years ago, I have a duty to explore it.'

Payne turned towards the man who sat at the far end of the conference table. 'Bob?'

Skinner shrugged. 'Why are you asking me, Lowell? I just called in for a nostalgic coffee in my old office, like Mario said I should do from time to time.'

'Piss off. I know why you're here; he told me. I know Sauce is right. I'd value your thoughts as his mentor, that's all.'

'Then I agree, he should accept Major Pollock's offer to let him sit in on the interview. Jesus, it's the least the guy could do; it's thanks to Sauce and his team that he's able to take the robbery off his open investigations list, so it's only right that he lets him bask in the glory. I want to hang around for it too,' he added, 'although Pollock needn't know I'm here. Mary

Chambers is a good friend as well as a valued colleague. She's gutted by what's happened. She had no more idea about Spring than we had about her brother.'

Haddock stared at him. 'You've spoken to her?'

'Of course, I've fucking spoken to her, Sauce,' Skinner retorted. 'She isn't under arrest and I just . . .'

'. . . wanted to satisfy yourself that she couldn't have known anything about it.'

'Yes, okay,' he conceded. 'And I did. The place they have in Pretoria was bought by Mary out of her retirement lump sum. If Spring had bought it, that might have worried me.'

'Did she splash the cash at all?' Payne asked.

'Let Sauce ask her about that. You ready to go?'

Haddock nodded. 'I've just received the Zoom invite.' He went to his mouse and clicked to join the meeting, as the ACC moved in behind him. A few seconds later, his screen changed, showing Pollock, full face. 'Good morning, Major,' the DI said. 'My Assistant Chief Constable, Mr Payne, is joining us; he's my reporting officer.'

'He's welcome,' the South African said. 'Sauce, Ms Montell and I have had a full and frank discussion, and she accepts that it is in her best interests to admit her role in the robbery, given that we can now link her directly to seven hundred million rand that was paid by her company and that of Mr Anatoly Rogozin, in gold, for the business now known as Wister Air. We believe that to have been most of the proceeds of the robbery in which her brother Griffin participated, and she has confirmed this. Ms Montell has given a statement which she wishes to read after which she will be prepared to answer questions, on the understanding that they will not lead to her extradition to the United Kingdom. Mr Payne, as senior officer present do you agree to that?'

'Provided that she doesn't incriminate herself in any crime in my jurisdiction, yes.'

'I won't,' a female voice called out. 'Let's get on with it.' The camera swung round, and its position was adjusted until she was in mid-screen. The woman was dressed in a yellow jump-suit. Her face was a mask, her expression impassive. It occurred to Skinner, who was watching from the side, well out of the field of view of the camera, that she was in a mixture of shock and denial.

'My name is Spring Montell,' she began. 'My twin brother was Griffin Montell, who was murdered in Scotland last week. Although I have been in a relationship with a woman for some time, I am in fact bisexual. Twelve years ago, I had a relationship with a man named Anatoly Rogozin, a Russian national, whom I met through my cousin Tom DuPlessis. Tom was involved in smuggling narcotics into South Africa for Anatoly.' As she paused, Haddock and Skinner had identical thoughts: *She just threw him right under the bus.*

'Through me,' she continued, 'Anatoly met my brother; Griff knew what he did, but had no interest in chasing drug-dealers, not then. He was a street cop and wide with it. One night, the three of us were together, a little drunk, when Anatoly asked Griff if it was true that he sometimes escorted shipments from the Mint to the gold depository. Griff said yes, and not only that, he was the guy who decided the route that the van would take. But he never knew, he said, whether it was actually carrying coinage; that was how the system worked. Then Anatoly said, "What if I could tell you?" He said he had a contact inside the Mint who knew when the real shipments were going out. Griff said that would be interesting. That was how the robbery was planned, and it was how it was executed. The contact gave Anatoly the word that coins would be carried that day, Griff chose the quietest route and the getaway van was waiting for him. Obviously, Fannie DeWalt had to be a casualty; there was no other way. Anatoly sourced a pistol, identical to Griff's service weapon, and that was swapped at the scene for the gun that killed Fannie. Griff kept the original afterwards. It was the only way he could be certain that no trace of it would ever be found. The crew of the van tried to surrender but they were killed. Once the gold had been offloaded into the other van, Griff was shot, in the upper arm, a flesh wound, and then, very carefully along the side of the head. It was only when the gold reached Anatoly's safe house that they realised how much they had, three times what we expected. It was agreed that they would sit on it until they had worked out how they could dispose of it. They waited for two years; by then the police investigation had cooled, and also the financial crash had made the haul all the more valuable by making gold more of a haven. Then the Wister Air deal became possible. Anatoly's Russian friend, who was as crooked as he was, offered to sell him the business in Northern Cyprus, and he was happy to be paid in gold rather than currency. Griff set up Lente as discreetly as he could, with me as a co-owner, and together with Anatoly we went through with the sale. The rest of the coins were split three ways, and when we agreed that it was safe, with Tom's help, Griff and I moved our shares to Scotland. With him a cop and me living with one, we agreed it could never be safer. What I did not know was that Griff had brought the gun, or that it would be used in two more killings. That's all.'

Haddock reclined in his chair. 'Did you have a continuing relationship with Anatoly Rogozin?' he asked.

'Only through our shared ownership of Wister Air,' Spring replied. 'Physically, that ended immediately after the robbery. For several years after that, I had no personal involvements. I didn't want anybody getting close to me.' She surprised the Scots by smiling. 'Then I met Mary and discovered that I preferred batting for the other team.'

'Did Ms Chambers know anything of this? Ever?'

'Nothing. Ever. I swear.'

'What happened to the Krugerrands you moved two years ago?'

'Most of them are still in my safe deposit box in Edinburgh. Over the last couple of years I laundered some of them through my design business. I invented clients and sent them invoices which they settled. Those were the accounts that Mary saw, but not the tax man, ever.'

'Did you know that your brother was planning to kill Anatoly Rogozin and steal his share in the business?' Payne asked.

She gazed into the camera with a grin of open mockery on her face. 'No, I did not, sir. And if I did, I wouldn't be so fucking stupid that I'd tell you and put myself in handcuffs on the next Wister Air flight to Edinburgh.'

Haddock intervened. 'Did you ever meet Terry Coats, the man who was killed with your brother?'

'I never heard his name until you mentioned it.'

'What about Aisha Karman?'

'Who's she?'

'Miss Montell, she was your employee.'

Fifty-Eight

'Did she take an active part in the robbery?' June Crampsey asked.

'I don't know, but by her own admission she benefited from it,' Bob Skinner replied, 'so she's done. Major Pollock will hold a press conference in Pretoria tomorrow, announcing that the bullion robbery investigation has been closed, twelve years after it began. He'll announce Spring Montell's arrest and hopefully he'll incriminate her brother and Anatoly Rogozin.'

'Why isn't he doing it today? He has her confession.'

'He thinks he knows who the contact in the Mint was. He's arresting her now. Rogozin put himself about with the ladies, it seems.'

'What can we report?'

'I'm giving you a heads-up about Pollock's announcement. Nobody else has that, so you can alert our South African correspondent, and be ready to run the story on our online edition as soon as it's broken. But not before. Understand? Not before.' He read her thoughts in her eyes. 'I know, June, in theory we could run it now, but that would compromise my friends and me. Our rivals might make us the story if we did that; they'd accuse us of having insider information and they'd

287

be bloody right. As it is, you'll be ready as soon as Pollock has finished speaking tomorrow; I'm pretty sure you can watch him on a streamed South African news service. The fact is, if any journalist had followed up Montell's murder and asked the right people the right questions, here and in Pretoria, they'd be where you are now, more or less. If the guy Darke was as good as he thinks he is and didn't spend so much time pissing off senior police officers, he could have got there.'

The *Saltire* editor's expressive eyes narrowed. 'The same thought occurred to me,' she admitted. 'Where can we go with it tomorrow, after the South African's made his statement?'

'You can incriminate Griffin Montell, for starters. You can also tie him to Rogozin's murder by saying that the police aren't looking for anybody else in that context.'

'What about the woman in Manchester?' she asked. 'Can we mention that?'

'That's less straightforward. Pollock won't mention her in his statement because it isn't connected to his investigation. When the story breaks, ACC Payne will be available to comment, either directly or attributably through the press office.'

'Not Sauce?'

'No. Lowell's fronting up. You know the score, he won't be able to tell you anything that hasn't been reported to the Crown Office, but by that time the Rogozin case should have gone there. If he chooses to volunteer that police in England have evidence that links his death to an open homicide, that will open the door.'

'Will he do that?'

Skinner raised his eyebrows. 'That'll be his decision, June. If he asks my advice, I'll say do it, because it'll deflect the media's attention away from the big issue.'

'What's that?'

'The fact that Sauce and his team still don't have a fucking clue who killed Griff and Terry Coats.'

'Then the *Saltire* must ask that question,' she insisted. 'Darke's got to put it to Payne.'

He looked at her. 'You know that I don't like Darke,' he admitted. 'Your choice, but I don't think his tone is right for the *Saltire*. However, he is where he is and you're right, if anybody is going to ask that question it should be him, but . . .'

'You'd like him to work that out for himself?'

'Got it in one.'

'Okay, this is how we'll play it. I'll pull Lennox Webster, Darke's predecessor, back on to the crime team and brief her to do the story around the Pollock press conference. If it is available streamed, she can watch it. Then they can both handle the follow-up with Payne. If he doesn't ask the big question, she will.'

Skinner grinned. 'Sounds like a plan. Can I make another suggestion?'

Crampsey smiled back. 'Make it and I'll tell you.'

'Have Lennox do an in-depth interview with Mary Chambers. Once her relationship with Spring Montell becomes public knowledge, and it will, the red-tops will be after her, big time. This is one time I don't mind using my insider position, not in the slightest. I'll speak to Mary first, then if she's okay with it, put the two of them together. Agree?'

'Very much so. It's even worth a plane fare for Lennox if Ms Chambers chooses to stay in Pretoria. Sir, you're starting to think like a journalist.'

'I always did,' he replied. 'That's why I was usually one step ahead of them when I was in the job.'

He stepped back into his office, checking his watch and thinking of calling Sarah to see whether she was free for lunch. His phone was in his hand when it sounded; he looked at the screen wondering whether she had beaten him to the punch but saw that the caller was not his wife, but his oldest son.

'Dad,' Ignacio said. 'There's a package here for you; it's just been dropped off by a courier. It's marked for your immediate attention. I had to sign for it on a screen, and I saw the sender's name, Deacon and Green. I looked it up; it's a law firm.'

'Yes, I know it. Nacho, are you doing anything just now?'

'Pilar and I are studying, but . . .'

'Aye sure,' he chuckled.

'Seriously!'

'Sure, I'll believe you. Look, get dressed, get in your car, the pair of you, put it in the boot and bring it to me, here, to the *Saltire* office. Don't open it. Get that? Don't. There'll be a couple of pizzas in it for you.'

Fifty-Nine

'Chief!' Noele McClair exclaimed. It had taken a few seconds for recognition to dawn; the woman on her doorstep was wearing jeans and a Barbour jacket, over a thick roll-necked sweater and her red-grey hair was ruffled by the wind. 'Come in, for God's sake. It's blowing a hoolie out there.'

Margaret Steele stepped inside, relieved that she had been welcomed, that the door had not been slammed in her face. 'Thanks, Noele,' she said, softly, as she handed over her jacket and stepped into a warm sitting room. 'I've come to apologise. I put you in a terrible position last week by asking you to come to Torphichen Place. I should never have done it; I wasn't thinking clearly. The deputy chief went bananas when he found out. We had a similar experience the two of us, just as we were getting together. We used to be married,' she explained. 'You probably don't know that. Mario was shot and I was there; I was quietly hysterical. I know you and Terry were at the other end of your relationship, but I should have been much more sensitive.'

'We were beyond the other end,' McClair replied. 'It was completely in the past. Terry had become pathetic; he was a loser, and I never actually wanted to see him again. Now I learn from Sauce that he might actually have been a murderer as

291

well, because he was the last person seen with his bit on the side before she died.' She paused, her hand moving to her lips as if she was making a belated attempt to stop her words. 'God,' she whispered, 'listen to me, calling her that. The poor girl, she didn't deserve that. Why was she killed, do you know? Does anybody?'

'Not for certain, no. But I don't know the detail of the case anymore. I've benched myself, Noele. I'm taking time off for a period of reflection, and re-bonding with my daughter.'

'Much the same as I'm doing with Harry.'

'How's he taking it?'

'Not great. He's struggling to get used to not seeing his dad again. We think kids are durable, but they're not.'

Steele nodded. 'I know. Stephanie came home crying from nursery one day. She'd been asked by a well-meaning helper to tell the other kids what she remembered about Stevie. She remembers nothing, because he died before she was born. All I can do is show her photos, and I don't even have many of them, because we weren't together long.' She paused, looking at the floor for a few seconds before re-engaging. 'I've got a second motive for coming here today. Bob Skinner told me something that's disturbing me.'

'That I'm chucking the job?' McClair ventured.

'Yeah, that. I'm sorry if you feel he broke a confidence, but . . .'

'I don't. At the time I'd have shouted it to the street, if it had been awake.'

'Did you mean it?'

'I don't know. I really don't know,' she admitted.

'Well, while you're deciding . . .' Steele smiled. It occurred to McClair that she had never seen her do so. 'I'm on sick leave; it will probably turn out to be permanent, but I can still do stuff, or tell Mario to do it. I'm going to transfer the station inspector from Haddington into Griff Montell's old job in Torphichen Place, and I would like to move you there, on promotion of course. While you're considering your future, it might help you to do so in less stressful surroundings than CID. It's an office job, and it's just over the hill.'

'Maybe I'm over the hill too.'

'I don't believe that,' she said. 'This experience, and my thoughtlessness, hasn't killed you, so it can only make you stronger. The job and its location, are ideal for a single mother.'

'Can I ask you one thing, chief?' McClair ventured. 'Are you suggesting this to clear your conscience?'

Steele nodded. 'In part, yes; I'll admit there is that, but most of all, it makes eminent sense. You're eligible for promotion, your appraisals are all first class, and you can be spared from CID.'

McClair's face twisted into something that might have been a grin, but then again might have been an expression of anguish. 'In that case, yes, thank you,' she murmured. 'I really thought I was back in the lifeboat with Griff, having been tipped over the side by Terry. Now I'm paddling as hard as I can to stay afloat. You're right, chief. If I have a reason to get up in the morning in addition to my son, it can only do me good, so if you can make that opportunity happen, I'll be very pleased and grateful. Now, my mother left me one of her speciality quiches. It's not great, but would you like a chunk?'

'I'd love it, on condition that you stop calling me "chief". I'm trying to distance myself from that. Call me Margaret; everyone else, apart from my sister, calls me Maggie or Mags, when I really do prefer my name as it was given.'

Sixty

He gazed at the brown envelope that lay on his desk, labelled, as Ignacio had said, 'Sir Robert Skinner. For immediate attention'. It was secured by a metal clasp, and whatever it contained was bulging its sides. He picked it up and shook it, for a second time, then felt it, gently. Laying it back down, he called the young intern from Girona whose services he shared with June Crampsey. 'Can you get me John Deacon, please, Artic? He's a partner in Deacon and Green, the law firm. You might remember, they annoyed me with a vexatious defamation claim last year, just after you joined us.' He replaced the phone and he waited, gazing at the two messengers. 'A mystery,' he murmured. 'I don't like mysteries.'

'I thought that solving mysteries was what you did,' Pilar ventured.

He grinned. 'That doesn't mean to say I have to like them. Some of them turned out to be very messy. I'm glad they're behind me . . . at least I thought they were.'

As he spoke the phone rang. He snatched it up. 'Mr Deacon for you,' Paco announced.

'Thanks.' He waited as the call was connected. 'Mr Deacon, Bob Skinner here. I gather you're the source of a package that was delivered to my home an hour ago.'

'That's correct,' the lawyer confirmed.

'And you can vouch for its contents?'

'I can.'

'It might have been helpful to call me before it was dispatched; that way it would have come to the right place, important if it's as urgent as the label implies. What is it? Who's trying to make a quick buck out of the *Saltire* this time?'

'That has never been the motive of any of my clients, Sir Robert, and certainly not this one.'

'Who is that?' Skinner asked. 'I need to know before I open the package. I don't have a scanner in the office. Why have they sent whatever it is through you anyway?'

'That was my client's choice.'

'What's in the envelope?'

'I don't know. I'm simply obeying my client's instructions.'

'You don't fucking know?' he roared. Facing him, Pilar gasped, alarmed. Ignacio winced. 'You've just told me you could vouch for it!'

'Do I detect a touch of paranoia, Sir Robert?' The solicitor's voice carried more than a hint of a sneer.

'You detect experience, Mr Deacon,' he snarled, 'the effect of a lifetime of dealing with people whose every move had malice aforethought . . . and quite a few of them were lawyers. Listen chum, you'd better pray that there's nothing harmful in this package. If there is, and you had it delivered to my home . . . Do you have the faintest idea of how angry I will be, when I descend on your office?'

'You're not a police officer any longer,' Deacon blustered.

'That won't fucking stop me, although I will have a couple of them with me just to keep you safe. Now, before I decide to bypass you altogether and go straight to the Law Society with a complaint about your irresponsibility, tell me, who is your client?'

'Was, Sir Robert. Who was my client,' the lawyer replied, his attitude adjusted. 'He was Mr Terry Coats. I'm sure the name means something to you. On Monday morning of last week, he called at my office. He was unannounced, but I agreed to see him. He gave me that package and instructed me that in the event of his death, whatever the circumstances, I should have it delivered to you. I would have done it sooner, but my wife and I brought in the New Year in New York. We flew last Monday afternoon and this is my first day back in the office, which is why you haven't received it before now. It was only when I got back to Edinburgh yesterday afternoon and caught up with the newspapers that I found out that he really had died. Look, if you had issues with Mr Coats, I'm sorry.'

'I've had a couple in the past, but they're history. Okay, Mr Deacon, I'm about to open the package. I'm intrigued now; if I need to speak to you again, I'll call you back.' He replaced the telephone in its cradle. 'Kids,' he said, 'just step out into the corridor for a second, just to be safe. I don't really think this is anything nasty. I felt like tearing that bastard a new one, that was all.'

'Dad,' Ignacio exclaimed. 'Are you sure?'

He smiled. 'Yes, I'm sure, on you go. From the feel of it I'm pretty sure I know what it is.'

The pair stepped outside. In spite of his certainty, he ignored the metal clasps that closed the envelope and slit it at the other end. He shook out the contents; two items fell on to the desk. A voice recorder, which he had anticipated, and a key, which he had not. 'Well, well, well,' he murmured. 'Terry Coats speaks from beyond the grave. Okay,' he called out. 'You can come back in now.'

'What do you think will be on it?' Ignacio asked, as he saw the recorder.

'I've no idea,' his father replied, 'but I don't want you two here when I play it.' He took his wallet from his jacket, extracted five twenty-pound notes and handed them across the desk. 'There's a table in the Bar Italia; that'll cover anything you'll fancy. Nacho, no drink, you're driving. Pilar? You barely look old enough, so if you want a glass of anything alcoholic, you'd better have ID. Thanks, both of you.'

She gazed at him. 'Can't we listen to it?' she entreated.

He laughed. 'Rolling those eyes might work on my son . . . it worked with me for his mother, which is why he's here . . . but I'm an old dog now; I know all the tricks. Go on, the pair of you, enjoy your lunch.'

He waited until he heard the sound of the lift doors opening before picking up the recorder. It was a Philips model, low-end with few special features; he guessed that it might have been bought with one purpose in mind. Having used similar models on which the sound quality on replay had not been reliable, he found a cable in a desk drawer and connected the small machine to his computer. He pressed the 'play' button.

'Bob, my instruction to Deacon was to destroy this if I was arrested and charged. If you, or anyone else, is listening to it he's either broken his word or Griff Montell's decided I'm too much of a risk, and I'm dead.'

Terry Coats' voice had a metallic echo, but it was clear and loud, so audible that he turned down the computer volume to avoid it being heard through the wall by Paco.

'My intention was that if I had been arrested I would take

my chances with the court, and give evidence against Griff. He must have worked that out for himself, so this is my confession, made to you, because I know that you'll use it in a way that will protect Harry as far as you can. Just don't let Noele hear it, that's all I ask. She hates me already and she'll use it to poison my son against me.'

Skinner paused the recording and whistled. 'That's a big ask, Terry,' he murmured, as if he was in the room. 'If I have to give this to the police it'll be their call who hears it.' He pushed 'play' once again.

'I'm entrusting this to you because in a way what's happened to me is your fault,' the dead man's voice continued. 'When you and young Haddock caught me with Aisha, and I told you how it had come about, it was you who sent me to talk to Montell. You suggested that it might get me back into the police and that he might be interested in helping me as it would give him a way back into CID. Then, you cunt, you went and shopped me to Noele. You really do owe me one, Skinner. I thought I could talk to you bloke to bloke, but obviously not.'

He paused the recording again. He had told Coats that it had been a police decision to let Coats' wife in on his liaison; she was a serving officer in Serious Crimes and it would have been difficult, if not impossible, to keep the story from her. 'I owe you fuck all, Terry,' he hissed at the ghost in the room. 'If you hadn't been dipping your wick in that woman none of this would have happened, and you might still be living quietly in Fenton Barns.' He was still seething as he restarted the player.

'Things got messy after that for a while. It was a few weeks before I took my story to Griff,' the tinny narrative continued, 'not in his office obviously, but in a quiet corner of Ryrie's

298

Bar in Haymarket. He heard me out, without saying any-thing. Finally, he said that he needed to get back to the office, that he'd think about it and that I should come to his place that night to talk tactics. I was seeing Aisha that afternoon, so I said it would have to be the next day, but he said no, to put her off, to tell her that a meeting had come up. I did that. I put her off until her next layover, and I went to Griff's. He sat me down, he gave me a drink and he left the room. When he came back, he was carrying a metal box. He put it down on the coffee table and he told me to open it. When I picked it up it was fucking heavy. That's because it was full of gold coins, fifty of them. He told me they were Krugerrands, that each one was worth over a grand. Then, Bob, he switched on the telly, turned up the sound and produced a fucking pistol from his pocket, and he told me that I was either going to walk out of there carrying those coins, or I wasn't going to walk out at all. I caught on straight away. I said to him, "That robbery you told me about in South Africa, that was fucking you!" He didn't deny it, he didn't have to. He was as calm as you like. It was like he'd turned into Michael fucking Corleone. I said to him, "You realise I could take these straight to Bob Skinner." He said, calm as you like, "Then I'd have to kill him too." That's when I knew for sure he was deadly fucking serious. I took the money, but not before he told me there were strings attached. He was interested in Wister Air and the fact that Aisha worked for it. He said she had made up the story about the money-laundering, and the bit about the airline owning the shop as well. He told me to find out the truth. I saw Aisha a couple of times after that, and I quizzed her gently. Finally, she admitted that she was being given the coins by another boyfriend, by her boss in fact, the Russian who owned the airline. I told Griff; he didn't say anything, or ask me anything about the guy. I know now that was because he knew him already.'

Skinner paused the recording for the third time, considering what he had heard and guessing ahead. He stepped across his office, fixed himself a coffee and then resumed.

'When he had thought about it, Griff said he wanted to meet Aisha. He said there were a couple of things he wanted to ask her. The problem was, she and I were in a sort of a hiatus. Her routes had been changed, and she wasn't flying into Edinburgh for a while. She did tell me, though, that she'd be coming into Liverpool in a week or so, then flying out of Manchester next day, and suggested that we meet up in her hotel when she was there. By that time it was the beginning of November. I drove down there, with Griff, but he said he didn't want to be seen talking to her. He had a look at the map and found a remote spot. He said I should drop him here, pick Aisha up and bring her to him. I did that, but I didn't tell her about him; all I said was I wanted to go for a drive first. She was fine with that. We drove there but when we arrived, there was no sign of Griff. We were on our own, and she was horny, so we had sex. We were barely done when he appeared, opened the rear door and put a bullet in her head, without a word. I screamed, man. I was going to go for him, Bob, I really was, but he put the gun against my head and said if I wanted it to look like a murder suicide that could be arranged. Bob, you have no idea what that man was really like. He even smiled and thanked me for having left my DNA in her. He told me I was tied in for good now and he was right. I hadn't known, but I'd set her up to be killed. I was fucked, man, and I knew it. We left her body there, took her clothes and everything else with us and put them in a bin in a motorway service area south of Carlisle, apart from her airline ID, her passport and her jewellery. Griff gave me another twenty coins after that. Most of the first lot had gone, on the deposit on my house and to pay off bookies. The key I've left you is for my locker at Harcourt Golf Club, in West Lothian. You'll find Aisha's stuff there, with the coins that are left and with a letter for Harry. I want you to keep that for him, until he's old enough to have it. Not that I've finished my story yet. At the beginning . . .'

He paused the recorder as he heard a sound in the corridor. 'Fuck me, Terry,' he whispered, falling silent as his door opened and Alex stepped into the room.

Sixty-One

'He wouldn't let me hear it, Dominic,' she said. 'All he said was that it was Terry Coats' confession, to his involvement with Griff and his complicity in two murders. His complicity,' she repeated. 'I take that to mean that, according to Coats, Griff pulled the trigger on both of them. I'm still struggling to believe it, despite what's emerged since he was killed. He couldn't really have been that evil, could he?'

'He could, Alex,' Jackson replied, 'and he was. I never met the man, but on the basis of what I've been told and read, I see him as a classic case of a predator without a conscience. As I told you, I knew someone like him when I was inside,' he added. 'He made me feel better about myself.'

'How come? What do you mean?'

'He helped me come to terms with what I had done in my youth. Meeting him and talking with him led me to look at myself and confront my own excruciating guilt. I realised that he was irredeemable, but that I wasn't. I wasn't rehabilitated in prison, Alex. I was purged.'

'Can you purge me?' she asked.

'You don't need it.'

'I feel as if I do. I let that man into my life, whenever I

chose. Worse, I let him into me. I indulged myself with him, I used him as it suited me . . .'

'Just as he did with you,' Jackson pointed out.

'That makes us both the same,' she countered.

'No, it doesn't, not in any way.'

'It does in my eyes,' she insisted. 'I suppose I suspected there was something different about Griff, but it suited me not to explore it, to leave it under the surface. It suited me because I am a spoiled, self-indulgent cow. I always have been. When Andy Martin and I got together the first time, he was my dad's right-hand man . . . and he was ten years older than me. In most walks of life, fucking the boss's daughter can be seriously damaging to your career prospects, but I didn't care about that. I wanted him and I took him. When he and I were engaged, I saw someone else and I had a piece of him too, only he got caught up in one of my dad's investigations and I got found out. Then I got pregnant by Andy and I had a termination without ever telling him.' She paused, her eyes glistening, then carried on, the words tumbling out. 'I'll never have a child, Dominic, I can sense that now, and I don't deserve to. That split us up, Andy and me, but at the first opportunity I took him back. I took him away from his wife and two kids. He couldn't stand the guilt in the end, but you know what? It never bothered me, at least it hasn't until right now, because I have never really cared about anyone or anything other than myself. Tell me I'm wrong,' she challenged him.

'No,' he said, quietly. 'I won't, because you make a very good case against yourself, and someone who's more objective than I am might well agree with you. But as I said earlier, you don't need me to purge you, because you're in the process of doing that right now. The time you've spent with me has been all about that. You came here because you were lost and bewildered but you didn't know why. I did; I could see that you were filled with self-loathing, but I couldn't help. You had to work it out for yourself, like I did in prison.'

'Is there any of it left in you?'

'No,' he replied. 'Not anymore. I still hate what I was, but to tell you the truth, I quite like what I've become.'

'And I need to start to earn my own respect,' she murmured, 'which is why, I think, it's time for me to go back to my own place. I've got one more confession, Dominic. There was one night, one sleepless night, when I stood naked on the other side of your bedroom door, ready to open it and step through. But, thank Christ, I realised that if I did I'd be betraying your trust and my dad's, and I'd be destroying my self-respect for ever.'

He smiled. 'Yes, thank Christ you did, for I might have closed the door behind you. Do you think I'm perfect?'

Sixty-Two

'At the beginning of last week, last Tuesday, Griff told me to meet him at his place, at lunchtime. While I was there, he used his laptop to access police missing-persons reports in the Manchester area. He found a photograph of Aisha, dead, and a "Do you know this woman?" post. He'd already accessed her email account on her phone . . . it had her date of birth as her password. How stupid was that? . . . and used it to send Anatoly Rogozin a message saying that she needed to see him in Scotland, urgently, because she believed that he had been compromised, over certain events twelve years ago. Those were the words he used. Rogozin replied right away, almost instantly. He said he would be on the Wister Air flight on Saturday afternoon, and that she should meet him. Then Griff booked himself a flight to South Africa, British Airways. I asked him why; all he said was that he owed his sister a visit, and his kids. On the Saturday, he told me to be at my place in the afternoon. He didn't tell me why, just to be there. I was watching the racing on Sky, and watching myself lose on the second leg of a four-horse accumulator, when he arrived with a bloke in a Crombie overcoat. It was Rogozin. The guy looked slightly bewildered. Griff introduced me and said I was the cousin of

Aisha who'd sent him, Griff, to pick him, Anatoly, up, and that she'd be there any minute. I went along with it; I even went to the chippy for three suppers when he told me to. When I got back, everything was still kosher. We ate the suppers in the kitchen. Rogozin liked his haggis, and he even had some Irn Bru, after Griff made a joke of it. Then in an instant, it all changed. Griff said, "Anatoly, bad news. Aisha's not coming. She's dead. Dead because you compromised us, yourself, everything, by handing out K-rands like chocolate money when you were pissed. Your *slegte winste*, for fuck's sake! She could have been a SAPS undercover officer for all you knew! So here's what's going to happen," he said, and he produced a piece of paper. "You're going to sign over your share of the airline to Spring and me, right here, right now. Do it and you might just catch your flight home." Rogozin tried to stand up but Griff knocked him back down. Then he turned on the radio loud, picked up a nutcracker, grabbed the guy's left hand and broke his middle finger. Rogozin screamed like a bastard, but he wouldn't sign, so Griff broke another finger. I wanted to stop him, but I knew he wouldn't just be breaking my fingers, so I just stood and watched. He signed after the third one, on the dotted fucking line. I thought, okay, that it was over and we could all have a drink, that's how panicky I was. But no, while Rogozin was nursing his hand, Griff picked up a cushion, pulled his gun from the back of his belt and shot him in the fucking head, twice. Poor bastard barely knew what hit him. Maybe that was as well. Rogozin had crapped himself while his fingers were being broken, and I nearly did too, because I thought it was me next, but he just said, "Sorry about that, Terry, but it had to be done. We need to get him out of here, then you need to take me to the airport. I've got a plane to catch." There was a wee bit of blood. He mopped that up with a kitchen towel. He gave it to me and told me to burn it and the cushion in the dustbin later on, then we carried the body into the garage and put it in the boot of my car. I drove us out of the city, south past Straiton and Ikea, and through Auchendinny. It was quiet out there; no cars about. We were just short of a village when he told me to take a left turn and stop there a couple of hundred yards along. We waited for a minute just to be sure, and then we got Rogozin out and hid his body in a field behind a stand of trees. We'd removed anything we thought might identify him before we left the house. When we were back in the car I just drove straight on, but he told me to turn right around and head for the fucking airport, pronto. It had taken us longer than he'd thought. Then his grand plan really went tits up. We went back on to the by-pass at Straiton, right into a fucking tail-back from an accident. We could see blue light in the distance and we knew we were going nowhere until it was clear. I reckoned then that he'd blown his flight, but he stayed calm and eventually we got through. While we waited, he told me I had to put the gun back in his safe. He wrote down the combination, gave me his keys and said he could switch off the security from his phone. We got to the airport, into the drop-off, he gave me the gun, and he jumped out. I could have shot him then, and taken my chances, but I was too fucking scared to think straight. He missed the flight, of course. He turned up at my place back of midnight. I was drunk by then. He said he couldn't be seen at home, so he'd have to stay there for all the time he was supposed to be in South Africa. On the Monday, he said he needed to use my computer to send the document Rogozin had signed to Cyprus. I said okay, and I persuaded him that I needed to do a food shop. While I was out, I bought this recorder. I used it to make this statement. I'm about to put it in the package that you'll have received by now, Bob, and give it to John Deacon, my lawyer. I'm quite convinced that Griff will kill me, sooner or later, or that at least he'll try. There's always the possibility that the police will actually do their job and trace Rogozin's murder to us, but I doubt that. We're both pros and we haven't made any mistakes.' The voice stopped, as if the confession was over, until there was a long sigh, and Coats resumed.

'So, Bob, that's the story, and since you've heard it, I'm dead. I'm handing it all to you because I can't think of anyone who's better equipped to ensure that psycho Montell gets what's coming to him, preferably heavy calibre in the back of the head. When you get a chance, tell Harry his dad will always love him,' Terry Coats' voice faltered; he had been on the verge of tears, 'but that he should always look up to his mum,' he continued, 'and do what she says.'

Skinner switched off the recorder and laid it on Haddock's desk, beside Aisha Karman's possessions and a sealed envelope with 'Harry' scrawled across it in a shaky ballpoint script. 'It's all yours,' he said, 'apart from this.' He picked up Coats' letter to his son and put it in his pocket.

'I should really look at that,' the DI said.

'Maybe, but you're not going to. It's going into my safe for the next ten years, or until I decide that the boy's ready for it.'

Sixty-Three

'What will Sauce do with the recording?' Sarah asked. Bob's call had taken her by surprise; his excitement was obvious, but normally he would have contained it until they were both at home. She had listened, silently, as he had told her about the package that Terry Coats had sent him from the dark vale of death.

'If he takes my advice,' her husband said, 'he'll give it to Lowell Payne and let him deal with it. Obviously, a report on the death of Anatoly Rogozin will have to go to the Crown Office. In common parlance there is a thing known as the buck, and my guess is that the fiscal will pass it as fast as he can to his boss, the Crown Agent, and so on, until it winds up on the desk of our new Lord Advocate. On the face of it, there are two options. Will she hold the simple line that nobody else is being sought in connection with the death and close the case with no further action? That will lead the media to assume that it was a suicide; most of them won't even report it, or they'll give it page five treatment at best. Alternatively, will she order a full-scale Fatal Accident Inquiry with evidence led in public before a jury?'

'Which do you think she'll choose?'

'I could argue that she doesn't have a choice. The statute says that she has the discretion not to hold an FAI when, if I remember the wording right, the circumstances have been adequately established in criminal proceedings: repeat, proceedings, not just by an investigation. Obviously, she isn't going to fancy a public hearing that reveals that the police service had within its ranks a ruthless, cold-blooded killer. She won't want it, the Justice Secretary won't want it and the First Minister sure as hell won't want it with an election coming up in a year's time. The shit will spray over everybody, me included, because I was the guy who recruited him, and advanced him within the service. I was taken in as completely as everyone else. If you can see yellowy stuff on my face, it's egg.'

'You can prevent that, can't you?' she said. 'You're on good terms with the First Minister.'

Bob grinned. 'Yes,' he conceded, 'I could, but I'm not going to. The *Saltire* will run a piece tomorrow demanding that an FAI into Rogozin's death takes place. We'll run the piece and then we'll report on the South African Pollock's press briefing where he's expected to out the Montells and Rogozin as the people behind the unsolved bullion heist. After that, the Lord Advocate will announce a formal inquiry before the Sheriff, of that I'm certain.'

'What makes you that sure?'

'She'll do it because I'll tell her that if she tries to hush it up, the paper will publish the text of Terry Coats' confession in full and embarrass her right out of her brand-new office.'

Sarah frowned. 'But you said you gave the recording to Sauce.'

He nodded. 'And so I did, but I made a copy. It was addressed to me, not the police, and it isn't *sub judice* since there won't be a prosecution, the principals all being dead. I'll be a witness to the authenticity of the tape and after the hearing, we will indeed publish it, both in text and audio form online.'

'What will Mario say?'

'He's already said it, a resounding "Go for it". He'll say the same to the Lord Advocate.'

'So, case closed?'

'Hell, no,' he laughed. 'The purpose of Sauce's investigation is to solve the murders of Griff Montell and Terry Coats. In that respect he hasn't taken a single step forward. This whole business has been a diversion.'

'What does he do now?' she asked. 'Bob, the poor lad's been hung out there to dry.'

'Not exactly. The question hasn't changed that much. Apart from each of them having a vested interest in killing the other one, who else wanted them dead?'

'Do you have any ideas?'

'One,' he admitted, 'but for now I'm keeping it to myself. I'm sure Sauce will get there without my help.'

Sixty-Four

'Sauce,' Arthur Dorward sighed. 'My team's been there twice already. We've gone over the house centimetre by centimetre; we've found everything there is to find. What's changed that you want me to do it all again?'

'What's different is,' Haddock replied, 'I know now that Griff Montell was effectively hiding out there after missing his flight to South Africa. He couldn't take the chance of being seen in Edinburgh, and he certainly could not take the chance of hiding out in his own place, in a block of flats in the middle of Stockbridge. I don't think he'd have gone out; in fact, I'm sure he wouldn't. That tells me that he was probably killed there, and if not, abducted from there. But it wasn't his home; it was Terry Coats' place, and no bugger knew he was there. So, whoever killed them both went there looking for Terry.'

'How would they know where Terry lived?' Dorward asked.

'Research document number one, Arthur. He had a landline phone, and he wasn't ex-directory. The internet tells you all the T. Coats entries in Edinburgh and they can be cross-checked against the electoral register and the valuation roll. I've just done the first part myself. I need you to go back in now, and look for identifiable traces of anyone who shouldn't have been there.'

'The house had previous owners, Sauce. He hadn't lived there very long.'

'In that case, we'll eliminate them.'

Dorward sighed again. 'Okay, I'll do it; first thing tomorrow the team'll go back in there. While we're at that, what will you be doing, Clouseau?'

'I'll be talking to Noele,' he replied. 'I should have given her a call before now.'

Sixty-Five

Skinner was halfway up the Aberlady straight, behind the winking light of a lone cyclist, when his phone sounded and his screen told him that Lottie Mann was calling. He considered rejecting her call; unusually he found that he was tired of business that should no longer have been his, but he knew that the DCI was self-reliant and would not be calling on a whim.

'What can I do for you?' he asked, trying to keep the tiredness from his voice.

'Nothing,' she replied cheerily. 'I thought I should let you know that Cameron McCullough is back. Tremacoldi's car checked out of the Glasgow Airport car park two hours ago, but the buggers only just got round to telling us.'

'How many passengers?'

'I don't know. I suppose I could access video if it was necessary, but the ticket was paid with Cameron's credit card so at least we can assume he was in it.'

'Thanks for letting me know. Two hours, you said?'

'Yes.'

'In that case he should be home by now, and Mia will be attaching electrodes to his nuts.'

'Unless she knew where he was all along and the whole thing was just a charade.'

'Why would they do that, Lottie?' Skinner asked.

'Maybe he was up to something they both wanted to keep from the rest of the family,' she suggested. 'Especially Sauce's partner, given her connection to him.'

'No,' he said. 'I don't see that. If it was a charade, Mia would have called the police and made a noise. But she didn't, she called Ignacio asking if he'd heard from him. She's cunning and devious, but not that much. He'll have a story, Lottie, and I'm sure I'll hear it soon enough, but right now, I don't give one.'

'I could find out what flight they were on.'

'So could I with one phone call to my friends in Thames House, but I really can't be arsed. Let it lie. Thanks again.'

He ended the call, overtook the cyclist, and drove carefully through Aberlady's overcrowded main street. He had reached the nature reserve car park when curiosity crept up on him. 'Call Cameron McCullough mobile,' he commanded. He was unsure if the call would be connected, but after half a minute it was.

'Where the fuck have you been, and do you need paramedics?' he asked.

'We were at Big Bozo's stag, in the Ice Hotel, in Norway, up near the Russian border,' McCullough replied. 'We took a private jet out of Glasgow with a couple of other guys. It was the easiest way of getting there. I didn't tell Mia I was going. I couldn't have or she'd have wanted to come. The Ice Hotel's on her bucket list.' His voice was a hoarse whisper. 'I'll need to take her now for sure, and I'll hate every fucking minute of it. It's fucking freezing up there.'

Skinner laughed, out of sheer surprise. 'It would be, you stupid . . . That's why they call it the Ice Hotel. I like Stacey Kent and I like the song, but it's never made me want to go there. Who the fuck is Big Bozo anyway?'

'A footballer Merrytown sold to Everton just after I joined the board. He retired at the end of last season, and now he works for us part-time, as a scout. It was quite a turn-out, I'll tell you.'

'And quite a fucking alibi too,' Skinner chuckled.

'What do you mean? Why would I need an alibi, man?'

'You haven't spoken to Mia yet?'

'No, we're only just back at the Lodge. We had trouble getting through Glasgow. The Kingston Bridge was choc-a-bloc.'

'Then I'll leave it to her to explain, once she's cleaned up the blood. Good luck with that one, Cameron.'

He was still grinning when he stepped indoors.

Sixty-Six

'Sauce,' Noele McClair declared, 'the fact that Terry died with me hating him isn't relevant. It doesn't affect my thinking in any way. I'm a serving police officer and it's my job to assist you in every way I can. You're asking me to name people who might have wanted to see him dead, but I can't. Bob Skinner phoned me last night and told me what's going to be in the press over the next few days and weeks, but even knowing that I can't help you. I wish I could, because I'd like to put in a plea in mitigation for the guy that shot them. No,' she said, correcting herself quickly, 'I shouldn't say that. I never wanted to see Terry dead. I said I hated him, but to be honest I didn't really. I was angry with him, and I'd never have taken him back, but really he was a victim of his own weaknesses, for slow horses and fast women. He was a walking cliché. You know, he was best man at another cop's wedding, before we were together, when he was a plod, and he felt it his duty to shag the bridesmaid. So he did. I heard the story from the bridegroom, not him. She was the bride's sister, their father was a superintendent in East Kilbride, where both lads worked, and he caught them at it, round the back of the Stuart Hotel, trousers round ankles, dress up round waist.' In spite of herself, Noele smiled, glancing away from her phone's camera. 'The man didn't know what to do. If he'd filled in a PC at his own daughter's wedding the story would have come out. In the end, he turned and walked away, then made sure that he and Terry never worked within miles of each other again.' She laughed, sadly. 'That was the thing about him; he got away with all sorts of stuff because he had this natural charm about him, with other people. Not at home, though. There he was the opposite, depressed and depressing. Griff, on the other hand, he was completely different. Reserved around others, outgoing and sharing with me.' In an instant her humour vanished. 'Do you know what I'm wondering now, Sauce? Can you guess?'

'I think so,' Haddock replied. 'You're wondering whether he came on to you because you were Terry's ex, to increase his hold over him.'

'Exactly. Silly me, he had me believing I was a desirable woman, while he saw a sad sex-starved single mum with stretch marks and saggy tits.' Haddock shuffled in his chair. 'Sorry,' she said, 'I'm embarrassing you.' She grinned again, briefly. 'Actually, they're not bad . . . and I put cream on the stretch marks. I will survive, Sauce,' she promised. 'I'm still standing, and I have a future. Those two are history, and I'm over them.'

Sixty-Seven

'He said less than I'd expected,' June Crampsey complained, as the streamed press briefing ended, six thousand miles away from Edinburgh. 'He didn't name Griff or Rogozin as participants in the robbery. Without that statement, I'm stuck with a story that says, "Edinburgh woman charged with gold robbery". I want more than that. Fuck it, Bob, we're in the exclusives business here.'

'I guess,' Skinner said, 'that whatever the South African equivalent of the Crown Office is has told him not to say anything that could be prejudicial to a trial. Spring might have confessed yesterday, but this morning she'll have every sharp defence brief in the country offering his services. We have our story, June, regardless of what Pollock did or didn't say. Nobody is going to sue us if we run it, because it's undeniably true. The only question is whether we could find ourselves in contempt of a South African court by using the story on our internet edition. We should take legal advice on that, but while we're doing it, Lennox Webster can be writing her story, based on what Pollock said and what I've told her, identifying me only as a source outside the police service.'

'What about ACC Payne?' Crampsey asked. 'What will he do in the light of the briefing?'

'Nothing yet. There's nothing for him to react to because neither Griff nor Rogozin were named. But as soon as Lennox's story runs there will be. Our piece this morning calling for the FAI into Rogozin's murder hasn't attracted much attention, but with the story it becomes relevant. While she's at work, tell Jack Darke to call Jane Balfour in the police's Edinburgh press office and put two questions, one about progress in the Coats-Montell investigation, the other asking for a reaction to the *Saltire*'s call for an FAI into Rogozin. That'll go to Lowell; let's see what he volunteers.'

'Which will be what you've told him to volunteer, let's hope.'

'I haven't told him anything, June. I can't be seen as his puppet-master, especially not because we have a family connection through Alex's mother. I don't even know if Sauce has let him hear the Coats' tape yet.'

'What if he stonewalls it?' she countered. 'Gives Jack a po-faced "no comment" on the FAI question and "no progress" on the Torphichen Place investigation?'

'You tell me,' Skinner said. 'You're the editor.'

'We run the story anyway,' she declared, 'incriminating Montell in the murder of Rogozin and describing it as a quarrel among thieves, and tying them both to South Africa, and we say that they're both suspects in the Aisha Karman murder. Then we say that police refused to back the FAI call.'

'No,' he replied firmly. 'That pretty much nails me down as the source. Our rivals would go to town on that and Sauce would be caught up in it. We have to rely on Lowell, and be prepared for him to issue a general press statement if he does decide to give Darke a full and frank answer.'

'Do you think he would do that?'

'I think he will do that, because if I was Mario McGuire, it's what I would tell him to do.'

'Speaking of Mario McGuire,' Crampsey said, holding up a printout. 'What do you think of this? It's a release from the police communications department saying that Chief Constable Steele is taking an extended leave of absence on health grounds. All media enquiries to Peregrine Allsop, Director of Communications.'

'I think it's a good time to be slipping out a three-day-old story. Allsop's got something right, for once.'

'You knew?'

'Of course, I bloody knew! I chose not to tell you, that's all.'

'Will she be back?'

'No comment.'

Sixty-Eight

'What did you tell him, sir?' Haddock asked.

'I gave him the story his editor was hoping for,' ACC Lowell Payne replied. 'I told him that diligent enquiries by our officers had uncovered evidence linking Griff Montell and Anatoly Rogozin to a twelve-year-old multi-million-pound robbery in South Africa, and also evidence incriminating Montell and Terry Coats in the murder of Rogozin and in another crime under investigation in Manchester. Of course, he asked me what that evidence was, but I said that he'd have to wait for that until the FAI takes place into Rogozin's death. The Crown Office will announce that this afternoon. That last thing I said was that he had an hour to get the story out on the internet before Jane Balfour issues a general press release. Against that background, he's not going to give a bugger that there's been no progress in discovering who killed Montell and Coats themselves.'

'That's not quite true, sir,' the DI corrected him, with a smile that was a mix of smugness and relief. 'Just before you got here, I had a briefing from Arthur Dorward by video link from Gartcosh.'

'Was he as pleased with himself as you seem to be?' Payne asked.

'For now, although he did tell me that if I send him back to Terry Coats' flea-pit one more time, I'll be a victim myself.'

'I'll defend you from him the best I can,' the ACC promised. 'Run me through each search and the circumstances.'

'Yes sir, they were like this. The first search was focused on Coats himself and his activities in the house. Through that we established that Montell had been there, but nothing more than that. On the second visit we knew that Montell had taken Rogozin there from the airport, so we looked for evidence of his presence there and of his murder. We got results on both counts, and they closed that part of the investigation. It was only then that Sir Robert received the recording from Coats that told us Montell had been hiding out there after he missed his flight to Johannesburg. That's why I asked Arthur to take his people in there for a third time.'

'So,' Payne said. 'What did he find that's made you both so happy?

'With the brief they had the third time,' the DI explained, 'they went further and looked in the garage. They hadn't gone in there before, and that's where they scored. It was roomy: there was plenty of space for Coats' estate car and more. In there they found traces of blood, from two men. In addition, they recovered brain tissue, and a bullet embedded in the wall with part of an eyeball. That's where Montell and Coats were killed, sir, no question about it. I've got officers out there now, doing door-to-door interviews with the neighbours, to see if anyone saw or heard anything around midnight.'

'Heard anything above the sound of fireworks and Jools Holland's bloody *Hootenanny*?' the ACC chuckled. 'Good luck with that one. But well done the pair of you, we really needed progress.'

Haddock's grin widened. 'And there's more,' he declared. 'In the garage they recovered a single fingerprint that didn't belong to either of the victims, or to Rogozin either. They ran a check, and it's been identified as belonging to a man named Raymond Bright. We might actually have a suspect. All we need to do now is find him.'

Sixty-Nine

The owner of the crime scene was less than pleased. 'When are you lot going to take your tape away and let me use my premises again?' he asked. 'You're costing me money.'

'If your warehouse had been a bit more secure, Mr Jessop,' Mann shot back, 'maybe none of it would have been necessary. My crime-scene investigators are still laughing at how easy it must have been to pick the padlock you had on it. One of them said that it would have held up a first-year student at burglary school for about a minute and a half.'

'We sell those things,' William Jessop protested. 'They're perfectly adequate.'

'Do you sell long-shafted screwdrivers too?' John Cotter asked. 'That's all it would take to get past it.'

'Okay,' the merchant grumbled. '*Mea culpa*. I'll know better next time.'

'Once DS Cotter and I have had a look at the scene,' the DCI told him, 'we can lift the restriction, and you can get a specialist cleaner in here. *Festina lente*,' she added.

'Who? I've never heard of them. I'll look for them in Yellow Pages.'

'Clearly not a fluent Latin speaker,' she chuckled as the proprietor walked away.

'Why? Did you just tell him to fuck off, boss?'

'Yes, but not to be in a rush about it. So, what are we looking at here, John?' she continued, as they walked towards the wall where the victim had died. The smooth white paint was disfigured by several holes where he had been nailed up, and by lines of dried blood leading down to a great dark red circle on the floor. 'A messy death, that's for sure. More than that; there was real feeling behind it, a punishment killing if ever I've seen one. What do we know?' she asked aloud. 'Forensically, it's a fucking nightmare. From a fingerprint viewpoint it looks as if the whole of Monklands has been through here, none of them with gloves on.' She consulted her omnipresent notebook. 'The victim's name was Walter Thomson, aged thirty-seven, known to the police. Several convictions and three spells inside, the last being two years in the Bar-L, out of a four-year sentence for a ram-raid in a jewellers in Paisley. Released on parole three years ago, three arrests since then but no convictions, no charges, even. Time of death, early on the morning of January the first, cause of death, probably exsanguination, according to Graham Scott.'

'When did the warehouse close for the holidays, boss?'

'The Friday before Christmas,' Mann replied. 'Twelve days before he was killed. Ligature marks on his wrists and ankles, plus the fact that he was severely dehydrated and Graham reckoned that he hadn't eaten for at least seventy-two hours before he died, indicates that he was left here for a while before his captors decided to deal with him.'

'Whatever their issue with him was,' Cotter observed, 'it must have been serious. I'm glad we weren't on the scene before he was removed. Seeing the photos and being at the autopsy was bad enough. Was he reported missing, did the local CID say?'

'No, because he wasn't missed. He lived with a twenty-two-year-old prostitute, Trudy George; he left her with enough of her earnings to buy drugs but no more, so she wasn't going to be making any nine-nine-nine calls. I need you to check her background, though. If she has any male relatives who decided that enough was enough, we need to be looking for them. You get on with that, and we'll let Mr Jessop get back to business. When you tell him, find out the make of that padlock. I want to be bloody sure that I never buy one.' She paused, smiling. 'It's nice to be back on the uncivilised side of Scotland, isn't it, John? Edinburgh's far too genteel for me.'

Seventy

'Raymond Bright?' Skinner repeated, gazing at the face on his computer screen. 'It means nothing to me, Sauce, and if he was an Edinburgh criminal it probably would.' Outside, the rain was turning to sleet, and he found himself looking forward to the following week's InterMedia board meeting in Girona with even more enthusiasm than usual. He had persuaded Sarah to come with him, the clincher being the use of the company's new Gulfstream jet.

'No, gaffer,' Haddock said. 'He's Glasgow. He's fifty-one years old; he has two convictions in his teens for assault, then did five years in his early twenties for an attempted murder in Easterhouse, a few years after the ice cream wars. There are no convictions on his record after that until thirteen years ago when he was sentenced to eighteen years for drug offences, again in the East End of Glasgow. He had several failed applications for parole, until he was finally released four months ago.'

'How does he relate to Terry Coats?'

'That's the thing. He doesn't; not that I can see. All of Bright's convictions were for offences in the same area. He was known to be active in the drugs trade, not at the top of the tree

328

but quite high up, again always in the East End. When he was active Terry Coats was stationed in Ayrshire, in uniform at first, latterly in CID. He was never part of any specialist units that might have brought him into contact with Bright, and Bright's record has nothing in it that connects through to Ayrshire. Terry did work in North Lanarkshire, but not until Bright was inside.'

'Has he been lifted yet?'

'I've asked Lottie Mann if she can do that. Bright operates in her area, and technically she's still attached to the Torphichen Place investigation. She's caught up in a new investigation of her own, a crucifixion in Airdrie . . .'

'You're kidding me,' Skinner exclaimed. 'Is she looking for a Billy Connolly fan?'

'What?' Haddock stared at him, bemused.

'It was a famous comedy sketch: the live version was recorded in Airdrie.' His protégé continued to stare. 'Never mind,' he sighed, 'before your time. Come to think of it, it was almost before mine. Have you been in touch with Mary Chambers?' he asked, changing the subject.

'No, gaffer, I haven't. Should I? Are you saying she might have known something about Spring and Griff's other lives?'

'No, I'm not. Am I suggesting you should be asking her that? Am I suggesting that if I was in charge of your investigation I would be looking at her financial affairs, to see if there's anything inexplicable there? Am I suggesting that if you don't, the fiscal might ask whether you were turning a blind eye because she used to be your station commander? You tell me?'

'Point taken, boss. Am I thinking that maybe I should call her up for a sympathetic chat and let her tell me anything she needs to? Yes, I am and, yes, I will.'

'You do that, and fairly soon, because we have a *Saltire* reporter flying out there this evening to interview her. If there is anything, emm,' he hesitated for a second, 'unfortunate, it would be good to have a hint of it before we run a nice cosy sympathetic feature and make an editorial arse of ourselves.'

'Jesus, gaffer,' Haddock laughed, 'you're good at walking on both sides of the street at the same time.'

Seventy-One

'This used to be bandit country, John,' Lottie Mann said, as they approached the address they had been given by the probation service. 'It looks all right now, but you can bet your life that some of those bandits are still there. A new generation maybe, but the same principles apply. It's a sort of parallel universe, the counter-cultures in cities, the world you can see, the one that runs the schools and empties the bins, and the one that you can't, the one that meets other needs, life-threatening cravings that it creates and then satisfies, whether the customers can afford it or not. I fucking hate people like Raymond Bright. Every time I lock one of them up, a happier woman goes home than the one who woke up that morning.' She pressed the bell in the centre of the bright-blue-painted front door of the terraced house.

And waited. In vain.

'How do we get round the back?' Cotter asked.

'Through that door there, son.' The gruff voice came from their left, from the house next door. Its owner was in his sixties, grey-haired and in want of a shave. 'But there's nae point. Him and Phoebe are away.'

'Do you know where they are, Mr . . . ?'

'Grimm, son, Joe Grimm. Aye, they're away at their place in Tenerife. They left last Friday, so they'll be back the morra. Raymond was looking forward tae it. He hasnae seen it for a while, but youse'll know that.'

'Do you know who they're flying with, Joe?' Mann asked. 'There can't have been too many options at this time of year.'

'Ryanair, out of Prestwick. Raymond was lookin' forward tae seein' the Elvis Presley bar again. That's if it's still there.'

'Thanks.' She paused. 'You realise, don't you?, that if for any reason they don't get on the return flight, you'll be the first person we talk to.'

'Nae worries,' he assured her, 'but ye never talked to me the day, right?'

'Right.'

The detectives turned and walked back to their car. 'I'll get on to the airline,' Cotter said, 'just to make sure he wasn't sending us in the wrong direction.'

'He wasn't,' the DCI assured him. 'I don't imagine he likes having Bright as a next-door neighbour. Do we know who Phoebe is?'

'She's his sister. Bright's never been married, and neither has she.'

'We'll be waiting for them, then . . . the morra.' She smiled in anticipation. 'Nice and quiet; I'll make sure we have two big plain-clothes lads just past passport control. We'll stay out of sight until they're in custody, then we'll have them driven straight through to Edinburgh.'

'Both of them?'

'Of course. There were two people involved, remember. Two cars drove into Torphichen Place, one drove away, with the driver of Coats' car as a passenger. We'll take Phoebe as well, until she proves it wasn't her.'

She was fastening her seatbelt when her phone buzzed, signalling an incoming email. She took it out and read it; as she did, her eyes widened. 'This is the full background report on Walter Thomson that I asked for,' she told Cotter. 'As fry went, he was pretty small, so he didn't rate a criminal-intelligence file, but what a gem just fell out of his past!'

Seventy-Two

Skinner gazed at the screen of his iPhone as the image of his youngest daughter was replaced by the name of an incoming caller. 'Mary Chambers,' he murmured. 'Now, why am I not surprised by that?'

'How are you holding up?' he asked, as he accepted her call.

'I'm still in shock, but now I'm just a wee bit concerned. Bob, am I somehow a suspect in this awful business?'

'Why are you asking me?' he replied. 'You know I'm long retired.'

'I also know you're mentoring Sauce Haddock, and others. Griff told Spring; he wasn't happy about anyone being given special treatment ahead of him. I just had a call from Sauce, and I suspect you knew about it before it was made.'

'Maybe,' he conceded. 'Mary, you were one of the best officers I ever worked with in CID. You know that certain questions have to be asked, even when they know the answers. No, you are not a suspect and I doubt that Sauce came close to suggesting that you were. I'll ask you straight out . . . which he probably didn't . . . did you ever suspect that Spring had access to funds that she hadn't told you about?'

'No. She said that she and Griff had an investment through

an offshore trust fund that would mature when they were forty-five. She said it was an inheritance from an uncle that had always been managed for them by an agent. She was always flush with cash, yes, but she told me that her design business was flourishing. She showed me her accounts and they bore that out. Okay, I know now they were phoney, but I had no reason to doubt her, or to suspect anything.'

'What about Griff?'

'You mean did I know that he had a gun in his safe and a medium-sized fortune in cash and gold? No, I didn't. You knew him as well as I did. You'll remember the explosion when Spring came out and he found out about us, but once he had got over that he was never anything but pleasant towards me. Okay,' she added, 'he was never going to be like a brother, but he didn't freeze me out either. We didn't talk much but he did let the odd thing slip, mostly about his frustration at being promoted into uniform. He said he only accepted it because he thought it would be short term. He got it into his head that Mario McGuire had manipulated him out of CID.'

'He could have got back into CID any time he liked,' Skinner told her. 'All he had to do was accept a move to Inverness.'

'He never told me that!'

'He never told anybody that.'

'The reporter you're sending out,' Chambers said, suddenly. 'Will she be asking me this kind of question?'

'No,' he replied. 'Lennox will be asking you about yourself rather than about them. The feature will be sympathetic, as I know she promised.'

'Can she be stopped?'

'I suppose she can, if you don't want to go through with it.'

'It's not that,' she confessed. 'I want to go home. I'll talk to her, no problem, but I would rather do it in Edinburgh. This place is a nightmare for me just now. There are press photographers in the street outside. Louis Pollock has promised to keep them in order, but I feel like a prisoner in my own home.'

'Will Pollock let you come back?'

'He'll have to arrest me to stop me. If he needs me as a witness I'll return, but I have no evidence to offer him.'

'Then go for it. I'll ask June Crampsey to tell Lennox to cancel her flight . . . unless . . .' He stopped as a possibility occurred to him. 'Maybe she still could go out there, but to interview Spring instead. I wonder how Pollock would react to that? You book your flight, Mary: your meeting with Lennox Webster will still happen, but maybe not for a day or two.'

'Jesus, Bob,' she said. 'You're turning into a journalist.'

'If I am,' he said to his empty office after the call had ended, 'there will be nobody with better sources.'

He unlocked his desk drawer and removed a small green notebook with a gold House of Commons crest on the cover. It had been a gift from Aileen de Marco, his former wife, and it contained a list of telephone numbers, landline and mobile, that were too sensitive to be included in his handphone directory.

He turned to the third page and called an entry that was prefixed 'DAD'.

'Just when I thought my day couldn't get any worse,' Dame Amanda Dennis sighed, 'I get a call from my favourite trouble magnet. What have you got for me?'

'Nothing,' he told the head of the Security Service. 'You don't pay me for my consultancy services, so I want something in kind. It's well below your pay grade so it shouldn't be a problem. There's a name that's been run past me. I know nothing about him, but I'd like to know everything.'

'Is he a threat to national security?'

'I doubt it very much, but if I'm wrong I'm sure you'll let me know. You got a pen handy? It's quite a long name.'

Seventy-Three

'Sauce, I'm busy here,' Skinner complained, frowning at the face on his screen. 'I've got our IT manager coming to make a presentation any minute now.'

'Sorry, gaffer,' Haddock said. 'I just thought I should let you know that I spoke to Mary Chambers. Your reporter can do the cosy piece you talked about. She's in shock. I tried to make it as gentle as I could. I hope I succeeded.'

'You may have fallen a bit short. She called me, for reassurance as much as anything else. Don't worry about having upset her, 'cos you didn't. She understood you had to ask her, given that Rogozin's murder happened here, and Spring could have had advance knowledge.'

'I'm working on that. We still don't know why Griff had that prepaid phone, but I've asked Jackie to get hold of Spring's mobile records. If he used it to call her in advance of sending the email that lured Rogozin to Scotland and to his death, and I can prove it, she'd be implicated.'

'Forget it,' Skinner said. 'You'd need to extradite her, and I think you'd find that the South Africans won't be letting her go anywhere until they've done with her, which will probably be at least twenty years from now. Also this; he had an untraceable phone, so the chances are she had too. It's not worth it, Sauce.'

'There's justice, gaffer.'

'For whom? What's it worth to the Scottish taxpayer to prove that she knew in advance that her brother was going to kill their co-conspirator in a crime on another continent? To do that, you'd need to keep your investigation open until she was available for a very expensive criminal trial which might not take place for years. As long as that was a possibility,' he pointed out, 'the Crown wouldn't be able to hold the FAI into Rogozin's murder, and the Aisha Karman file in Manchester might have to stay open too. There's justice, Sauce, but there's pragmatism too. If I were you, I'd tell Jackie to stop looking.' As Haddock digested his advice, he carried on. 'Oh, by the way, the reporter didn't go; Mary's decided to come home as soon as she can get a flight. They'll meet here.'

'I can understand that,' the DI said. 'She sounded very low when we spoke, depressed even.' On screen, he smiled. 'It's my turn to change the subject. I checked out that Billy Connolly sketch; very funny but I doubt that he'd get away with it now. I also had some interesting feedback from Lottie. It's her investigation but she thought I should know. The crucifixion victim, his name was . . .'

'Barabbas?'

'No, he must have escaped. His name was Walter Thomson; he seems to have been a man of no great distinction, and Lottie still has no idea what got him executed Roman-style, but his last arresting officer was Detective Inspector Terry Coats.'

Skinner stared at the young detective's Facetime image. 'What was his name again?' he asked.

'Walter Thomson.'

'Fuck,' he whispered.

'No, Walter Thomson.'

'Don't piss about, Sauce, and don't go anywhere either. I'm coming to see you.'

'What about the IT manager?'

'Sod her, she can wait. This is much more important.' He ended the call, and reached for his overcoat, which hung on a hook behind his desk. He was halfway into it when his mobile sounded on his desk. 'Dame Amanda,' he exclaimed, as he took the call, 'I didn't expect you to call me in person.'

Seventy-Four

'This isn't an airport, Lottie,' John Cotter remarked, 'it's a ghost town.'

'I know,' she agreed. 'It makes me sad. This used to be Scotland's only transatlantic airport. More than a few emigrants to Canada left from here, in aircraft with propellers on the wings that had to refuel before they reached Toronto. Nowadays, just look at it.'

'Why is it still open?'

'Ask the First Minister. Maybe it'll come into its own again when Brexit finally happens, I don't know.'

'What was old Joe, the neighbour, saying about Elvis?' the DS asked.

'My Dan would tell you that.' She felt a familiar frisson as she used the possessive. 'He's an Elvis buff. Legend has it that The King only set foot on British soil once, and it was here, when he was flying home after doing his national service in Germany. They've traded on it ever since.'

'Is it true?'

'There is another story, but I don't know that it's ever been verified. The one thing I know for sure is that Raymond Bright and his sister are on the flight that's coming in right now, so let's get moving.'

They walked into the baggage hall, showing their accreditation to the lone Customs official on duty, then made their way through the baggage hall, emerging at the police desk behind the Border Force check point. As Mann had requested, two large men in plain clothes were waiting there. One of them was middle-aged, the other much younger. She knew the former; he had worked on the same team as her ex-husband, before his fall from grace. For a second, she wondered how he would react, for Scott, her disgraced ex-husband, still had friends on the force, but he greeted her effusively.

'Lottie, how ye doing? Sorry, that should be, ma'am.' He touched his forelock.

'Only in front of strangers, Mac,' she laughed. 'I thought you were still in a black tunic.'

'I am, but I grab any excuse to wear a suit. I hear you're with Desperate Dan these days. That was a long time coming, but we all knew he was fond of you.'

'I wish you'd told me,' she said. 'It was a complete surprise to me when it happened.'

'This guy Bright we're here for. What's he done?'

'He's wanted for questioning about the New Year murder in Edinburgh.'

Mac's face darkened. 'Terry Coats?'

'That one, yes. Him and a serving inspector.'

'Indeed?' the veteran growled. 'In that case the van might hit a few bumps on the road on the way through there. I liked Terry; a bit of a spiv, but an okay guy. He didn't deserve what he got from that chief constable. On yis go now,' he said, as the first passengers began to appear at the end of a long corridor, 'get out of sight and let us collect him for you. At least we know he's not goin' to be armed, getting off a flight.'

'If there was any chance of that,' she said, 'you would be too.'

To their right was a double door, no more than four yards along a corridor. Mann and Cotter stepped back into it and waited. The flow of passengers was slow but steady; almost invariably they were couples, a few with children, but mostly middle-aged or elderly. Some were tanned, others showed various skin tones from pale pink to bright red. Nearly all were dressed for the weather conditions they had left rather than those that awaited them outside. The only exceptions were two Asian families, whose women and children were covered from head to toe.

The detectives waited in their alcove, impatient at first, then tense as the human tide crept past them. 'Are you certain they were on the plane, boss?' Cotter muttered. 'I didn't see any air bridges when we got here. They'll have walked across the tarmac. Is it possible that they've slipped out of the queue and found another way out?'

'Anything's . . .' Mann began until she was silenced by a glance and an imperceptible nod from the senior constable. As they looked on, two figures stepped into their eyeline, without noticing them. Phoebe Bright looked ten years older than the passport photo they had sourced. Raymond, her brother, was twelve years older than his last arrest photograph, but aside from greying hair around the temple, he was little changed: around six feet tall, heavily built with a thick jaw that gave him a simian look.

Mac and his colleague stepped across, blocking the passageway. 'Mr Bright, Miss Bright,' the senior man said.

'Would you come with us, please? Our colleagues would like a word with you.'

Glancing to his left, Raymond Bright noticed Mann and Cotter for the first time. His small eyes flared with anger. With unexpected speed, he dropped his cabin bag, head-butted Mac, spun on his heel and headed for the waiting detectives. Cotter moved towards him; he was much smaller and was swept aside easily, but in the time he had gained for her, the DCI had drawn an extendible baton. She went low with her first stroke, back hand, smashing an exposed kneecap below Bright's cargo shorts, then high on the follow-through, catching him on the side of the head and sending him crashing in a heap at her feet.

'That was not clever,' she told him, very quietly, as the DS snapped cufflinks around his wrists. 'In fact, you'll have a ninety-mile drive to reflect on just how stupid it was, given that the officer you just nutted will be one of your escorts.'

Seventy-Five

'Sorry, Sauce,' Skinner said as he stepped into the office, 'I had an unexpected call, one that I had to deal with.' To Haddock's surprise he was not alone. 'The good news is,' he continued, 'it's given ACC Payne the time to get here from the Secret Bunker.' The nickname that the lower ranks had bestowed on the police service national headquarters had found its way into the public domain. 'What I've got to tell you, you'd have to report to him anyway, so this speeds things up.'

'So what is it?' the DI asked, with the faintest sign of impatience, 'and how does it relate to Walter Thomson, the dead man in Airdrie?'

From inside his overcoat, as he removed it, Skinner produced a green folder, and laid it on the meeting table. 'Come and sit along here,' he said, 'and I'll explain.' He waited until Payne and Haddock were in place, facing him, then carried on. 'Lowell,' he began, glancing at the ACC, 'you'll remember my predecessor as Chief Constable of Strathclyde.'

Payne nodded. 'Only too well,' he confirmed. 'Antonia Field, parachuted in from south of the border. Everyone in Scotland knew that she saw the job as a stepping stone on the way to being Commissioner of the Metropolitan Police.

Nobody could stand her, but equally, nobody would have wished her fate on her either.'

'That's right. The only way that I'd have ever gone after the job as chief of the national force would have been to stop her getting it.' Skinner turned to Haddock. 'Sauce, how much do you know about the circumstances behind Terry Coats' resignation from Strathclyde, before it was wound up?'

'I know he was outed by a blog, Brass Rubbings, that focused on police corruption and general misbehaviour. It claimed that he had protected a criminal from prosecution because he was a source of useful information that had led to him putting various people away. It got wider press coverage and Chief Constable Field decided to throw Coats under the bus. She offered him a transfer that she knew he wouldn't accept, a uniform job in Oban. Noele was CID then, in North Lanarkshire like him, but she wasn't offered a move. He quit, as she knew he would, and he was bitter about it until the day he died.'

'That's correct,' Skinner agreed, 'but you left out one crucial consequence of the Brass Rubbings report. Its author, Austin Brass, was ruthless, or reckless, or stupid enough, depending on how you looked at him, to name Coats' informant. As a result, the man was found murdered, chopped up and fitted into a suitcase. The crime was never solved and the connection to the blog story was hushed up.' He opened the green folder and pushed it across the table.

'When I took over from Toni Field,' he continued, 'I found this file in a secure cabinet in my new office. It tells the whole story, but a casual read doesn't make Field look too good because it includes the fact that Coats was exonerated by an investigation by the professional standards department, yet she went ahead with axing him anyway, to preserve her own reputation. What it also includes is the name of the victim. He was called Alan Mason, a small-time criminal from Airdrie, in North Lanarkshire, and he was twenty-two years old. No one was ever charged with his murder but there was one outstanding suspect, a man who had done time as a result of information given by Mason to Terry Coats. His name? Walter Thomson.'

Lowell Payne whistled. 'Bloody hell, Bob,' he gasped. 'We have Coats and this man connected to Mason's death and murdered within hours of each other.'

'That's right. And,' he added, 'you have a suspect for Coats under arrest.' He smiled at Haddock. 'Join the dots, Sauce. Join the fucking dots.'

'I will, gaffer,' the DI replied. 'But can I ask you, how come you've still got the file?'

'I've got it because I kept it, lad. Nobody else seemed to want it, but I had a feeling that one day someone would. So . . . there you are.'

Seventy-Six

'You did us all a favour, Lottie,' Haddock said, 'when you cracked Bright so hard with that baton that the doctor wouldn't let us interview him until this morning. We've got more to put to him now.'

'Maybe that wasn't me,' she pointed out. 'Letting Big Mac ride with him in the van was a risky decision.'

'Big Mac?' Skinner repeated.

'Aye. His name's McDonald and he's big, so what else were they ever going to call him? I didn't have much choice though. I couldn't let Phoebe go in the van without a female escort, so she had to come with John and me.'

'Whatever,' Haddock continued, 'it let us execute the search warrant on their house. There's no way back from that. Tarvil,' he called out to the sergeant, 'go get him, please.' He turned to Mann. 'You and me in there, Lottie, yes?' She nodded assent. 'John, you, Tarvil, and Sir Robert can watch on video. Is his lawyer here?'

Singh stopped in the doorway. 'He said he didn't want one, Sauce.'

'Fuck that!' the DI exclaimed. 'He's been cautioned, so he's entitled to a solicitor present. He's having one, like it or not.

I'm not having him claiming later on that it was denied. Bugger! I want to get on with it; now we've got a delay. Can we whistle one up here?' He looked at Skinner. 'Gaffer, is Alex busy today?'

'It's Saturday, Sauce,' he reminded his protégé. 'But even if it wasn't, no way would she sit alongside a guy accused of murdering her boyfriend. The Law Society would shit itself collectively at the thought. Her associate, Johanna DaCosta, on the other hand, she might be available. Want me to check it out?'

'Please do. It'll be a legal-aid case, but we can top up today's fee if necessary.'

Skinner whistled. 'Wow! She can book her Caribbean holiday right now.'

Seventy-Seven

'Are you sure you don't mind?' the young solicitor advocate asked. 'Things might have come to light about him but even so you and he . . .'

'Johanna,' Alex Skinner exclaimed, 'he was a friend, at least I thought he was, and he was a good shag, but that's it. We were not romantically inclined, ever. My father is right that the Law Society might argue that we were close enough for it to cloud my judgement when to comes to acting for Bright, but you didn't know him and you're an associate of my firm, not my employee. You earn your own fees from your own work. There's no reason why you shouldn't accept Bright's instruction. That's if he gives it to you. Dad told me that he waived his right to legal advice; it may be that you'll get to Fettes and he'll still refuse to engage you. If he does, Sauce will ask you to sign a statement that you offered your services but the prisoner refused. That's all he really wants; he doesn't give a stuff whether Bright has a lawyer beside him.'

'If you say so, Alex,' DaCosta decided. 'I'll take it on. The police statement I read this morning said that two people had been arrested. What about the other one?'

'That was Bright's sister. They thought she might have been his accomplice, but she's been released on simple police bail. I see no other distractions, on you go.'

Seventy-Eight

'Aye, fine,' Raymond Bright grunted. 'As long as youse are payin' her.' He looked up towards the camera in a corner of the interview room, and tapped the side of his head, gingerly touching a purple lump. 'I hope youse all see this.'

'For the record, Ms DaCosta,' Lottie Mann said, 'your client had to be restrained at the airport. He's been cautioned in respect of an assault on a police officer and, be sure, he will be charged with that in addition to anything that happens after this interview. But I don't imagine that a three-month sentence on top of thirty years will be much of a bother to him.'

'Let's carry on,' Haddock declared. 'We've been delayed long enough. Mr Bright—'

'Haud on,' the prisoner exclaimed. 'What about oor Phoebe? Where's she?'

'She's at home,' the DI advised him. 'She was detained because we thought she might have been your accomplice. When we discovered that she has an eye condition that means she couldn't possibly have driven the second vehicle, she was released on bail. That doesn't mean she's off the hook though. If we find out that she was aware of your plan to murder Mr Coats and Inspector Montell, she may still face charges.'

'Can they do that?' Bright asked his solicitor. 'Let her oot and then haul her back in again?'

'They have that power,' Johanna DaCosta confirmed.

'Okay, let's get straight to the point,' Haddock continued. 'While we were following concussion protocol yesterday, it gave us time to search your home, in accordance with a warrant granted by a sheriff. We removed certain items of your clothing for scientific testing. This revealed traces of blood, which on first examination matched Inspector Montell's. DNA analysis is still being done, but I'm going to hazard a guess that'll confirm it was his. In addition to that we found these.' He paused to reach down and take a plastic evidence bag from the floor. 'As you can see, these are three distinctive gold coins, called Krugerrands. On each of them we've found fingerprints; they were partials but there are enough points of similarity for us to match them with those of Terry Coats. That means we can tie you to both murder victims, Mr Bright. In addition to that, we've got video footage of a man getting out of Mr Coats' car, just before twelve-thirty a.m. on January the first, after it had been parked in Torphichen Place in Edinburgh, outside the police station where Inspector Montell worked. The driver was wearing clothes similar to those we took from your house. He also wore a black balaclava. Not unlike this one.' He reached down once more and produced another evidence bag. 'It was also recovered from your house; to be precise, from a garden waste recycling bin, where it was wrapped around these.' He went to the floor for a third time and came up with a heavy revolver. 'This, or something similar,' he said, 'was used as far back as the Boer War, and in dozens if not hundreds since then. It's a Webley Mark Six, point four five five calibre, the same as the bullet that was recovered from Terry Coats' garage.

It's in good enough shape that we were able to match it to this gun.' He reached down for the last time. 'Finally there's this, a nine-millimetre Luger pistol, possibly from a later war. Ballistic tests have determined that it's the weapon used to kill Terry Coats.' He leaned back in his chair. 'In the face of all that, Mr Bright, do you have anything to say? If you want, I'll give you time for a private word with Ms DaCosta before you answer.'

'No thanks,' he grunted. 'I'm saying nuthin' until youse can explain to me why I'd want tae kill two fellas I've never met, one of them a polis and the other one ex-filth.'

'Okay,' Haddock replied, amiably. 'There's someone else here who can do that. Sir Robert,' he called out, 'would you like to join us now?'

Bright stared, frowning, at the door of the interview room until it opened and a tall middle-aged man with close-cropped steel-grey hair stepped through it, carrying a green folder. He picked up a chair from a corner of the room and set it down between the two detectives.

'For the recording,' Mann declared, 'Sir Robert Skinner has entered the room.'

'Skinner,' the prisoner repeated; for the first time, he seemed nervous. 'You were the big polis were ye, no? But ye're no' a polis any mair. What are you doin' here? Can they dae that?' he asked DaCosta.

'They can,' Skinner replied on her behalf, showing her a police warrant card in his name, with the designation 'Special Constable'.

'Yes, Mr Bright,' she agreed, 'they can.'

'You were asking about motive,' the newcomer said. He laid his folder on the desk, took out a photograph and slid it across. 'He's your motive. His name was Alan Mason. He was nineteen when that was taken.' He paused and displayed a second glossy print. Bright recoiled as he looked at it. DaCosta winced.

'He was twenty-two when this was taken, just before the autopsy that followed his murder. He was killed, after he'd been named online as a police source of criminal intelligence, having passed information to then Detective Inspector Terry Coats . . . information that put several people in prison.'

'If he wis a grass,' Bright blustered, 'fair enough.'

Skinner laughed. 'Give it up, Raymond,' he chuckled. You know what I'm going to say next. We've got your DNA, and naturally, his is on the database too. Alan Mason was your son, Mr Bright. There's no point in denying it. Grass or no grass, he was your boy, and you blamed Terry Coats for him being murdered. And you killed him,' he continued, 'for a very simple and traditional reason, revenge. The only thing I don't get is why, when Alan's birth was registered, he was given your middle name, rather than your surname. Okay, there's no record of you and his mother being married, but if you didn't want to lumber him with being Raymond Bright's son, why not just give him her name? She was Abigail Richardson, according to his birth certificate.'

'That's what she wanted, okay,' Bright snapped, banging his fists on the table. 'Aye, okay,' he shouted. 'Clever bastards all of you. Terry fuckin' Coats got my son killed and Terry fuckin' Coats paid for it.'

'Unfortunately,' Haddock said, 'so did another man, one who had nothing to do with it.'

'The other fella . . .' Bright's eyes narrowed. 'If Ah'd known he was there, Ah might no' have gone that night; Ah might've put it off for a bit. There was somethin' about that guy, and Ah'm no just talking about him bein' a polis. The way he looked at me, I knew that if he'd had the gun I'd have been fuckin' dead in a second. He made a mistake though. He told me he was a cop. Funny thing, though, he said that if we saw sense and fucked off, there would be no more said about it. Ah told him it was too late for that. He said we wouldn't fuckin' dare. Ah dared all right. We turned up the telly in the hoose, took them into the garage, then when the bells started, well, Ah gave the guy nae chance, shot him right through the back o' the heid. He never knew a thing. Coats did though. Ah let him realise what was coming, although the job was done before the bells wis finished.'

'Why did you leave the bodies outside Inspector Montell's station?' Haddock asked.

Bright's eyebrows rose. 'Was it? I knew there was a big polis station in the middle o' the town, so we went there. That wis the only reason. An' that's the whole story.'

'Not quite,' Skinner said. 'Who shot Coats? He was killed with a different weapon, and why would you carry two? No, he was shot by your accomplice. If it wasn't your sister, who was it? Tell us and it might get you a few years off your life-sentence tariff.'

'That Ah'll never do,' Bright declared. 'Ma boy might have been a grass, but Ah'm no'. Go on, charge us an' let's get this over wi'.'

'Not so fast,' Mann intervened. 'We haven't got to Walter Thomson yet.'

'Thomson?' Bright snorted. 'Why should you lot care about fuckin' Thomson? He wisnae a polis.'

Seventy-Nine

'He didn't deny it when I put Thomson's murder to him,' Lottie Mann insisted.

'No, he didn't,' Skinner agreed, reaching for the mug that sat on a coaster on Haddock's table. 'He laughed at you and said, "No comment".'

'He knew who Walter Thomson was,' she argued. 'He knew he'd been murdered.'

He countered. 'Thomson did his time in Shotts Prison; Bright spent part of his sentence there too and they coincided. They met, for sure. Thomson's death was reported in the Scottish press. You can buy the *Daily Record* in Tenerife, so you can't hold his knowledge of the crime against him.'

'Logistically, it's feasible,' the DCI persisted. 'Thomson's time of death is uncertain because of the time that elapsed before he was found, plus the temperature in the unheated warehouse and the way he was killed. There's evidence that he was bound, though, before he was nailed up. Bright and his accomplice could have picked him up before they killed Coats and Montell and left him there to be finished off later, when that was done. We've got opportunity. If we find his DNA and fingerprints at the scene, haven't we got him?' she challenged.

'You'll have a case, no denying that.' Skinner smiled. 'But if I'm the defence counsel, I'm going to ask if you've looked at Bright's background. He's got a day job. He's a self-employed builder. So it's quite natural that his DNA, his fingerprints, and maybe even a sample of his urine on a toilet bowl in the gents should be found at a builder's merchants. Then if I really want to make you squirm in the witness box, Lottie, I'm going to produce a receipt for goods purchased there a few days before it closed for the holidays.'

Haddock intervened. 'Come on, gaffer! He did it, for fuck's sake. It's obvious he did it. Find the physical evidence of his presence, and I bet you we do, and the most cautious, arse-covering fiscal in Scotland would go to court with that.'

He shrugged. 'You're right, Sauce. He'd probably get a conviction too. It's just . . .' He paused as the door behind him opened, turning to look over his shoulder.

'DS Singh said I'd find you here,' Johanna DaCosta murmured. Her gaze settled on Lottie Mann. 'My client wants to see you,' she told her. 'He's decided that he wants to make a statement confessing to the murder of Walter Thomson. He knows he's going to get the maximum tariff for Montell and Coats, so he's thinking that it'll be more or less a freebie.' She smiled, and her cheeks turned pale pink. 'He's asked me to represent him in the High Court,' she added shyly.

Skinner grinned at her. 'It'll be good experience for you, Johanna, but I'll tell you: the clouds could part, a dove could fly down from heaven and land on your client's shoulder, but he still won't be getting out before he's eighty-five.'

Eighty

'Gaffer, Bob, what the fuck do you want that for?' Haddock hissed. Mann, Cotter and DaCosta had gone, leaving them alone in the DI's office.

'You don't need to know. You just need to trust me; both of you.'

'What authority have you got?'

'Which one would you like? My Special Constable warrant or my Thames House card. Just ask her for me. I'm not asking you to do anything furtive; I need her consent. I doubt that anything will come of it. Even if I'm wrong about that, it won't affect her personally. It will either eliminate a possibility or it will . . . Look, if she insists I will explain why I want it, but I'd rather she didn't. It'll help me answer a question that's bugging me; you know what I'm like with them.'

'Bob, she's pregnant. Will that have any effect on whatever you're up to?'

'None. Congratulations though, you're a dark horse. Sauce,' he sighed. 'If she won't, I'll understand. If she will . . .'

Eighty-One

'So it's happy endings all round,' Sarah said. 'Sauce has cracked his first big solo case, Noele McClair has a nice promotion, Maggie Steele has decided that there is happiness in the world, and best of all Alex seems to have found herself again.'

'Happy isn't the word I'd choose,' Bob replied. 'Satisfactory on those four counts, yes, but Terry Coats and Griff Montell are still dead and so are seven other people. Then there's the collateral damage.'

'Seven? How do you work that out?'

He counted them off, a finger at a time. 'Anatoly Rogozin, the co-conspirator in the robbery, Fannie DeWalt, the cop Griff shot, the two security guards who died there, Aisha Karman, the unlucky flight hostess, Alan Mason, the boy that was hung out to dry by Brass Rubbings, and Walter Thomson, who almost certainly killed him.'

'And the collateral?'

'Spring Montell, who is probably as sociopathic as her twin, and Mary Chambers, who's back in Scotland looking at the wreckage of what she thought was a happy retirement.'

'I suppose,' she conceded. 'The Montell twins must have

had huge strength of will. To pull off such a big robbery, to dispose of the proceeds in the way they did, and then to live normal lives. I wonder what their end game was?'

'Spring told the South African prosecutor that they intended to disappear when they were forty-five; to sell the airline at a huge profit, buy new identities, go off to a bolt hole, and never be seen again.'

'That sounds . . .'

'Almost incestuous? Yeah, don't fucking go there. Enough's enough.' He winced. 'The final irony,' he sighed, 'was that it all went wrong for them through Griff being an innocent bystander . . . No! Definitely not innocent, but he was just in the wrong place at the wrong time.'

'And now it's all over?'

'They think it is. Some people are on the pitch,' he chuckled, quoting an iconic piece of football commentary.

'So why do I suspect that it might not be?' Sarah asked.

'It isn't. There are people still at liberty with blood on their hands. Raymond Bright confessed to the murders of Coats and Montell, and of Walter Thomson, but he didn't act alone. He had a partner in crime, the person who drove him away, in a Renault with false plates, after he dumped the bodies outside the police station. The plates were found in a rubbish bin in Polwarth, but the car never did turn up. The team's first thought was that it might have been his sister out to avenge her nephew, but she's half blind. She can't see well enough to ride a bike, let alone drive a getaway car, and she certainly couldn't put a bullet through the middle of someone's forehead from far enough away not to leave any scorch marks around the wound.'

'No,' she agreed. 'That was a very neat job.' She touched her forehead just above her nose. 'Very professional, special forces style. Do you think that it might have been Bright, with another gun?'

'No chance. Why would he need another? He'd just spread Griff's brains all over the garage. No, there was somebody else, and my gut tells me that it wasn't just an underworld pal who owed Bright a favour. This was a personal crime, retribution. It was natural to suspect Phoebe Bright, the principle was correct. Okay, it wasn't her, but you know, she wasn't poor wee Alan's only family member.'

Eighty-Two

'He wants what?' Cheeky Davis exclaimed.

'A sample of your DNA,' her partner repeated.

'Why the hell would he want that? Does he think I'm a fucking criminal just because I'm Goldie McCullough's niece?'

'Not for a second, love. I can promise you that. He said he needs it to help him answer a question. He wouldn't tell me what it is, but he said that he would tell you, if you really want to know. Look, my darling, the only thing I can tell you for sure is that if he wants this it must be to help him uncover a truth, because that's what he's all about. Look at how easily he's slipped into his media work. It's an extension of what he did in his other career. He's a truth seeker.'

'Sometimes we might not like the truth, Sauce,' she whispered.

'But that doesn't make it go away.'

'Okay,' she said. 'I'll do it for you, because you're one of those people too, and that's part of why I love you. On one condition though; whatever it is my DNA helps him discover, I don't want to know. Ever.'

Eighty-Three

'So how was the Ice Hotel really?' Skinner asked.

Cameron McCullough smiled. 'Truth? It really was fucking freezing, like I said. But we were all so full of schnapps that we barely knew it.'

His two guests laughed.

'I'm glad you guys decided to come tonight,' he continued. 'You know you've always had an open invitation, Bob, both you and Harold. No better night to take me up on it than a mid-week postponement against the champions. Too bad about the result, but at least my team put up a decent show.' He swivelled his chair until it faced the window that overlooked the football pitch. 'This room's the chairman's hideaway,' he said. 'It's just like one of your interview rooms, mirrored glass that nobody can see through. I could watch the whole game from here, but I need to let the customers see me, wearing the scarf and all. Usually I'd be putting myself about in the boardroom as well, at the post-match reception. What is it about football and meat pies?' he asked. 'I've had God knows who in that room next door, the Chairman of Barcelona, three international team managers, the President of UEFA and they've all wolfed down the pies.'

Haddock held up the remnants of his. 'They are pretty damn good, though.'

McCullough winked at him. 'Even without the sauce?'

'You know, Cameron, I really hate that stuff,' he confessed. 'I can think of nothing more disgusting than a fish supper smothered in HP.'

'You'll get on well with your future stepmother-in-law. She's very much a vinegar person. It was a nice suggestion that I should ask her along tonight. Mia's teeth were a bit clenched when I told her, but having Ignacio here as your driver mollified her. They can't stand each other, Mia and Inez. I shouldn't say this to you, Harold, but my daughter Inez is an irredeemable twat. She was a breech birth and from that time on she never stopped being awkward. Cheeky's gran and I brought her up, you know; she barely saw her mother until she was eight. I'm not surprised Cheeky didn't come tonight. They've barely spoken since that time Inez got her into trouble.'

'It wasn't that,' Haddock told him. 'I didn't tell Cheeky that Inez was coming. Her problem is she's off her food at the moment; the very sight of those pies would have been too much for her.' He smiled, diffidently. 'I might as well tell you now; the secret won't keep much longer. You're going to be a great-grandpa.'

His host stared at him, wide-eyed, then exploded in a huge guffaw. 'That's amazing! Harold, Sauce, that is terrific, I couldn't be happier for both of you, and aye and sure, for me. I don't know how Mia's going to handle being the youngest great-granny in Scotland.' He reached across and placed a hand on Haddock's sleeve. 'Anything you need, son, anything you want. There's nothing I wouldn't do for that girl.'

'Other than telling her she had a brother for twenty-two years of her life?'

'What the fuck do you mean, man?' McCullough stared at Skinner, stunned by his words.

'Yes, gaffer, what are you saying?'

The other two men ignored him, as their eyes locked together, unblinking. As Haddock looked at them, McCullough seemed to shed one persona, letting another emerge.

The pair had met face to face on perhaps a dozen occasions, but never before had Skinner been offered even a glimpse of the man who had worn such a fearsome reputation in his home city. 'You know, Cameron,' he replied. 'You know exactly what I mean. Sauce doesn't, though. He's still a relative innocent, not quite the finished article. To use an old cliché, I may have taught him everything he knows, but I hadn't taught him everything I know, not until now. His last lesson is this: never stop asking questions until you are absolutely one thousand per cent certain that there are no more left unanswered. You have to chase evil, you have to chase the truth of it, right down to the roots.'

'Bob?' Haddock whispered.

'Alan Mason,' Skinner said, his gaze never leaving McCullough. 'The boy that Terry Coats died for was Cheeky's half-brother.'

'What?'

'You heard me. His mother wouldn't let him have his father's name . . . that doesn't even appear on Alan's birth certificate . . . but she wouldn't let him have hers either. The reason? She was so afraid of her own father, of what he might do if he found out, that she didn't even put her own name on his birth certificate. What has Cheeky told you about her father, Sauce?'

'She said that he ran off as soon as her mother found out she was pregnant,' Haddock replied. 'She never knew who he was. Inez wouldn't even tell her his name; she never has.'

'Okay,' Skinner said, 'this is what I know. There was a missing person reported in Dundee twenty-eight years ago, seven months before Cheeky was born. He was a seventeen-year-old boy; his name was Samuel Trott and the report was filed by his aunt. It's very unusual for boys that age to vanish without trace, but the Tayside cops don't seem to have looked too hard for him. Indeed, he's still missing. You can ask Inez about him if you want. He was a year ahead of her at Morgan Academy. I have a notion that Inez remembered him when she registered her son's birth. When she did that, she called herself Abigail Richardson.' He looked at McCullough. 'Tell him who Abigail was, Cameron.'

'He doesn't have to,' Haddock said. 'I know. Granny Abby, that's what Cheeky calls her, whenever she talks about her.'

Skinner nodded. 'The DNA sample you got from Cheeky last week, Sauce, that's the proof. There's a close match between hers and Alan Mason's profile; that was kept on file after his cremation.' He paused, turning to his young friend. 'Get out of here now and leave us to talk. That's all you have to know, and Cheeky never needs to. Go and find Inez and don't let her out of your sight.'

Without argument, Haddock left the room.

'You're a bastard of the first order, Bob Skinner,' McCullough growled as the door closed. His eyes were still volcanic.

'That's been said before, Cameron. You might need to come up with a better description in a few minutes, after I've finished.'

'Have you not done enough, man?'

'Fuck no, I've barely started. First off, how did you get here tonight?' he asked.

'Mia drove us.'

'Not Vito Tremacoldi? I was looking forward to meeting him.'

McCullough reached out to the table at his side and poured himself another two fingers of Lagavulin. 'No,' he said, 'I let him go back to Italy. I was giving him a few months' trial in the job, but he never settled here. The language was a problem too.'

'Really?' Skinner exclaimed. 'I thought mercenaries needed a decent command of English.' He smiled, took a photograph from his jacket and tossed it on to the table. It showed the upper body of a man in camouflage colours, with a shaved head and very blue, very cold, eyes. 'Don't bullshit me, Cameron. I had Tremacoldi checked out by people with resources way beyond yours. I know everything about the man, including the details of certain deniable jobs that he's done for intelligence services, Britain's included. So I'm finding it just a wee bit strange that you hired him around the time Raymond Bright got out of jail, and that you let him go a few days after Terry Coats and Walter Thomson were both taken care of.'

'Go on then,' McCullough snapped, 'spell it out.'

'When did Inez run off?'

'Two years after young Cameron was born,' he replied. 'Sammy Trott's in Australia, by the way,' he added. 'He's a flooring contractor in Melbourne, well off too. His parents were dead, and he lived with an aunt he couldn't stand, so I flew him out there and got him a job with one of my suppliers. He doesn't know he has a child; he was told that Inez was having an abortion. I did the lad a favour, Bob, I really did. I liked him and my daughter was trouble from the day she was born. I mean that literally, too.' His eyes narrowed; Skinner read pain in their depths. 'Her birth wrecked Abby downstairs. She could never have any more kids. She died when Cameron was fifteen. She had surgery on her waterworks and developed sepsis; that was another gift from Inez.'

'You really hate your daughter, don't you?'

'Vehemently. But I love hers. When Inez did her runner, aged eighteen, when Cameron was two, I didn't chase after her. But I did find out early on that she'd met a Weegie bloke at one of the clubs I had then and gone off with him. I found out also that he'd been dealing drugs there. I had him punished for that, severely, but I left the pair of them to get on with it.'

'When did she come back?' Skinner asked.

'When her son was four. She didn't want to be stuck with him, so she left him with Bright and his sister. If she had brought him with her, I'd have acknowledged him, but she didn't. After she came home, I kept her on the periphery of young Cameron's life; effectively Abby and I were the lassie's parents. I never met my grandson, ever, but that was the choice that Inez made.'

'It wasn't Bright's choice?'

'Bob, I could have squashed Raymond Bright, had him sent a lot further away than Australia, but he wasn't worth the investment. Inez went off with him to Glasgow and her fucking vinegar chips. I'd had enough, so I left her to get on with it. I took her back when she finally ran away from him, to get off the drugs, and I made fucking sure that he was taken off the street by your lot not long after that. The boy stayed with his aunt, but I kept them fed and clothed. He grew up a toerag though; he was in bad company, in and out of court, and eventually . . . You know what happened to him.'

His face contorted with what seemed to Skinner to be genuine pain. 'Now,' he exclaimed, 'you're going to ask me if I feel guilty about just leaving the kid to it. Yes, of course I fucking do, and when I heard that Bright was finally up for release, I made sure he felt guilty too.'

'And Inez?'

'Who knows what Inez feels? Who knows what's in that woman's head?'

'She drives a Renault, doesn't she?'

'Yes, a Megane. A company car registered to the radio station. Why do you ask?'

'Like the one with false plates that picked up Bright in Torphichen Place.'

McCullough's eyes found his once again. 'That was a Megane? Oh Jesus,' he gasped. 'You're saying that she . . .'

'Yes, I am, but the police won't trace the car now. They haven't been able to place it in Airdrie either, outside the warehouse where Walter Thomson was crucified. They've tried,' he added, 'but the false plates were dumped in Edinburgh, having been stolen off a car there. Now why would anyone have done that, before,' he emphasised the last word, 'going on to commit another murder? And yet,' he continued, 'that's a crime of which Bright's insisting he's guilty. And everybody's happy to believe him; Lowell Payne the ACC, Lottie Mann, and Sauce too; they're all happy because it's a nice neat finish, guilty pleas all round. Even the Lord Advocate's happy, because it will save her the cost of a trial.'

He reached out, topped up McCullough's malt and refilled his own glass with a Spanish red that he knew must have cost two hundred euros a bottle.

'They're all so fucking delighted,' he continued, 'that they're not looking at you at all. They're not asking about the missing time between you and Tremacoldi leaving Black Shield Lodge and checking into the Glasgow Airport car park for your private jet to Big Bozo's bloody stag do. A two-hour journey that took a shade over three hours.'

He raised his glass and took a sip, savouring the quality of the Pesquera Reserva, wondering why one vintage could be so superior to another. 'And you know what, Cameron?' he said, 'I'm not asking either.'

'You going to tell me why not?'

'Sure. It's because I have no wish to lob a missile into young Sauce's career, or to darken the happiest time of your granddaughter's life. I'm sure it was you, Cameron; it had to be. Your Inez might be a determined woman, but Bright is not the most subtle guy in the world. Plus,' he laughed, 'I question whether, even together, they were capable of nailing a big man to a warehouse wall. Yes, they might have had it in them to burn his balls off with a blow torch, or Inez might, but would either of them know how to bleed someone out through the femoral artery? Maybe not. Tremacoldi would though; he'd have been capable of all of it.'

He drank a little more wine, then replenished it.

'Here's what I'm saying. You never acknowledged Alan as your grandson, but nonetheless he was; he was your blood. When he died in the way he did, I see you consumed by guilt, and determined that those who were behind his killing should pay. That included the cop who used him. It might have included Austin Brass too, the blogger who named him as a grass, but he had enemies all over the place and one of them got to him first.'

His gaze seemed to drill into McCullough. 'You weren't going to do it yourself, though,' he continued. 'No, you waited for Alan's father to finish his prison sentence so that you could use him to get even. Cameron, I believe that everything Raymond Bright did was at your prompting. There will be nothing on paper, no orders given, just hints and indications, but nonetheless, I reckon you set it in motion, everything. Apart, that is,' he added, 'from the death of Griff Montell. That was a major complication, one that you couldn't influence; I doubt that you'd have approved that. God, I hope not!

'As for Walter Thomson,' he continued, 'the world knew he killed Alan Mason. It couldn't be proved, but that didn't bother you and Raymond Bright. I believe that Bright picked up Thomson at the weekend before Hogmanay, after the warehouse had closed for the holidays, that he abducted him and left him there, tied up and helpless, waiting for whatever was going to happen to him. And I'm suggesting that turned out to be your man Vito Tremacoldi, your mercenary, with you parked out of sight all the while, maybe listening to the screams but knowing that on Hogmanay, that night of all nights, the polis would be elsewhere, keeping drunks in order, and knowing too that you wouldn't be leaving any trace of yourself on the premises, and that Vito wouldn't either, because he's a professional.'

McCullough raised his eyebrows and stared at him, with a trace of mockery in his eyes. 'And here was me believing,' he chuckled, 'that cops' greatest weakness is that they have no imagination.'

'I'm not a cop any longer,' Skinner replied. 'I was always a bit more than that anyway. None of that is imagination; it's a logical conclusion. It fits you too, Cameron. I have you sussed as a guy who'd always wait outside while the bad stuff was being done. It's part of the reason why you've been Teflon all these years: you had that fearsome reputation, and secretly you liked it, I'll bet, but inside you were just a wee bit Chicken Little, afraid that the sky would fall on you. The manner of Thomson's death fits that to a T.'

'You believe that and you're just going to let it lie? You? The mighty, incorruptible Bob Skinner?'

'Yes, I am, as much as I fucking hate it. But,' he added, 'only because it's unproveable, and because Bright's already confessed to killing Thomson, being done beyond redemption for Coats and Montell. It would fit my scenario if he's been incentivised by whatever you're going to pay his sister.'

He turned his attention back to his glass.

'I could, of course,' he murmured, 'tell the whole story to my editor at the *Saltire* and let her use her judgement on whether to run it or not. She's a brave woman, June, so she would . . . and I doubt that a defamation action would follow. Man, you've spent decades building your reputation, but it would be gone in the time it took your bankers and business associates to read the *Saltire* article.'

'So fuck off and do it!' McCullough shouted, anger fuelling his bravado.

'I'm prepared to,' Skinner said, 'but before we get there we have one more thing to discuss.' He paused. 'Cameron, it would be nice to think that your granddaughter might never get to hear of her brother, of how he was treated and what happened to him, but I fear it's inevitable that she will. There's one person who would tell her, if ever she feels guilty enough or, more likely, vindictive enough . . . and that I can well imagine. It's probably a miracle she hasn't done it already.'

'You're talking about Inez.'

'Exactly. So you see, Cheeky has to be told, and I reckon that if you want your relationship to survive, you should be the one to do the telling, rather than Sauce, or me, or my newspaper, if that's how this plays out. Are we agreed on that?'

'Yes,' McCullough said, quietly. 'Yes, we are. I'll tell her about her dad too; I might as well get it all over with. She'll explode, but she'll get over it eventually. She's as pragmatic as me in her own way.' He glowered at Skinner. 'Now are we done?'

'No, not quite,' he replied, 'because this goes along with it: it absolutely sticks in my throat that your daughter should walk away from three murders. In fact, I can't allow it.'

'Jesus, are you asking me to kill her?' he exclaimed.

'Don't be daft, man,' Skinner laughed, 'I'm not a barbarian. Just listen, will you: the only thing I don't believe about this business is that you knew that Bright would use an accomplice, even less that you knew who it would be. You proved that to me a few minutes ago, by the way you reacted when I told you about the car.'

McCullough sat silent, waiting.

'What I haven't told you yet,' he continued, 'is that forensics recovered a viable DNA sample from the second firearm that was found at Bright's house, the Luger that killed Terry Coats. There's no match for it yet, but that's only because my friend Arthur Dorward hasn't compared it with the profile of Alan Mason and found that there's a maternal match. Whether I tell him to do that, or whether we run the *Saltire* story instead, that's down to you. So, Cameron, this is my question. Does Inez pay the price for your continuing good name, such as it is and will be? Does she go to jail for the murder of Terry Coats, and for Montell and Thomson?'

'Is this blackmail, Bob?' McCullough asked.

Skinner gazed at him, contemplating his feelings about the man. He knew that he was more than a legitimate businessman, but was he capable of such savagery? He was convinced that he had procured Coats' murder and, unknowingly, Montell's, but his vision of how Walter Thomson had died was no more than a theory, and he was much less sure of it than he had let McCullough believe.

'Hell, no,' he replied, quietly. 'It's only this. Most of your life's been a closed book, Cameron. Just this once, I need you to open it, and get your hands dirty, because it's the right thing to do. Well? Do I call Dorward?'

Grandpa McCullough drained his malt and nodded.